CHARRED-DONNAY

Blood, Wine, Magic: Book 2

JUSTIN GODEY

Pinot Noir - Blood, Wine, Magic: Book 1 by Justin Godey

Written and Published by Justin Godey

http://www.justingodey.com/

Thank you to my family for inspiring me and supporting me when I decided to try my hand at writing.

Thank you to Sarah and Thane Knutson for asking me the simple but important question, "Why don't you write a book?"

Thank you to Erika Boudreaux for fact-checking my knowledge of the wine industry.

Thank you to Sativa January for continuing to bring a literary perspective to my work.

Thank you to Elizabeth Hooper for continuing to be my mentor and guide on this journey.

And thank you for taking the time to read my book, I hope that you enjoy it.

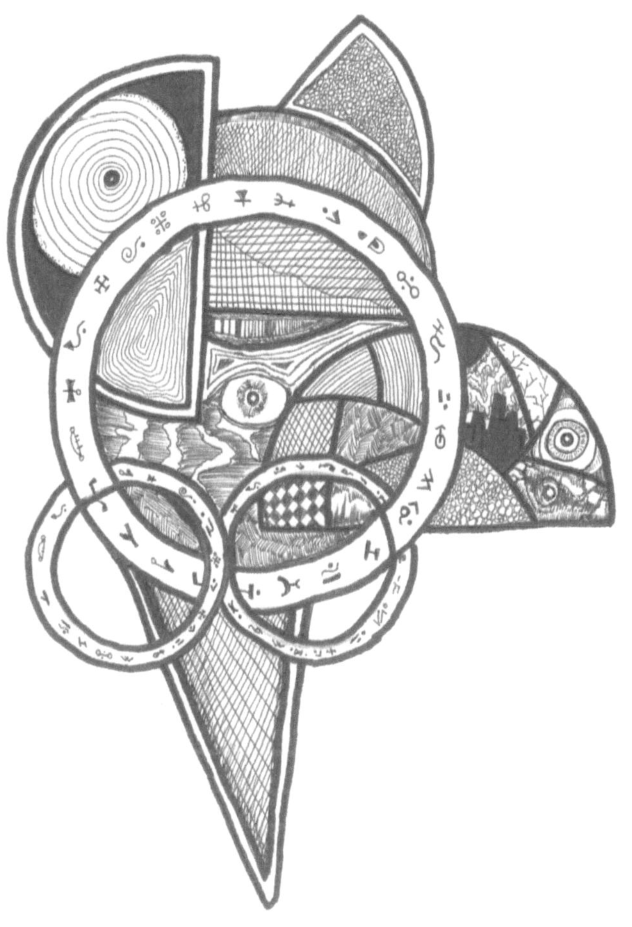

"Two roads diverged in a yellow wood, And sorry I could not travel both And be one traveler, long I stood And looked down one as far as I could To where it bent in the undergrowth..." - Robert Frost

"Listen. Time is malleable. It stretches. It contracts. Imagine the first time you find your way in a new city. Each road, each avenue, your progress seems slow and crawling. You focus your attention on every detail of every turn, stop sign, and landmark. Just the second time you make the same trip, it seems faster. The third time. Even faster. Before long, it becomes rote, and the familiar route is flying by at the speed of your consideration.

It doesn't take any longer according to a clock, at least. The clock is a social convention like direction or gender. When we fall into a routine, and nothing new or different threatens our perceptions, days can pass when we aren't paying attention. Immune to the social conventions of clocks and calendars, time passes at the rate we perceive it. When under duress, seconds can be dragged out to eternities.

Time is, therefore, not only malleable; it is shapeable. Our individual perception of it gives it length, width, and depth. You control time, not the other way around."

- Source unknown

Prologue

GRANITE JUTS from the earth like an ancient spire worn down by millennia of wind and rain. Lichen spreads across the rocks like hard, flaky green armor. From this perch, I look down at the valley below. The earth is mottled green and yellow. Vast verdant swaths of vineyards are broken up by the dry, brittle yellow grass of late summer. The sun bakes into my skin like the world is a giant oven but the air is dry and a light breeze blows across my face making the temperature bearable. I look down at one swath of grape leaves, a fiery array of vibrant reds, yellows, and rusty browns. It is beautiful and picturesque.

"That vineyard is beautiful, all the reds and yellows; it looks like fire," I say.

"Yeah, that's GRBaV Grapevine Red Blotch Disease, maybe Leafroll. Either way, it's caused by a virus. Very contagious. It spreads like wildfire. They will have to pull up that whole vineyard and burn it to the roots," Jeff says matter-of-factly.

"Oh," I say, "I did not know that."

"Yeah, it's weird because you always see the red leaves in posters, ads, and stuff. It looks pretty, but it is a tragedy for the vineyard. The whole thing has to be torn up and replanted. Someone is going to lose a lot of money on that."

"Huh, you learn something new every day."

I climb down from the rocky outcropping. This is one of my favorite places in Napa to hike. You can get some fantastic views from up here. I love finding my way to places where I can stand on solid ground and look down on flying birds. It makes me feel free.

Jeff sits down on a log. With a grunt, he takes a giant gulp of water from his water bottle. He's dripping sweat and a little red in the face. I notice with alarm a familiar plant with broad, spiky leaves sticking up beside him.

"You should move to your right a couple of feet. There's some stinging nettle by your elbow there," I tell him.

He grunts and slides over in the direction I indicated.

"You confuse me sometimes, Miles."

"Oh?"

"Well, you don't know what leafroll is, but you can identify a stinging nettle at twenty feet."

"There was a lot where I grew up. I once ran through a field of it. I didn't know until I was halfway across. Nettles go through clothes. I got thousands of stings on everything below my belly button."

"Everything?" Jeff asks, raising an eyebrow.

"Everything," I say, wincing at the memory. "Anyway, after an experience like that, you tend to notice these things."

I look around and see a cascade of red, yellow, and green leaves hanging down the side of a tree. Each leaf has an oily sheen and sparkles slightly in the sun.

"Like there is a nasty-looking batch of poison oak."

He glances back at it and nods.

"Yes, yes it is," he says.

"I fell into a whole briar patch full of that whitethorn and poison oak. A great combo, the whitethorn put little scratches all over me, and the poison oak oil got all over my skin and into the scratches. My whole body swelled up like a balloon. My eyes swole shut. I couldn't see for a week."

"Ugh. How old were you?"

I shrug. "I don't know, maybe nine or ten. But something like that sticks with you."

He nods in response.

We sit in silence for a while. The sound of the wind blowing through the trees is calming. White clouds billow in the sky above, casting huge dark shadows that roam across the valley floor like great stalking wraiths. The screech of a hawk breaks the quiet. Or an eagle. Or I don't know some other bird. I think it is a hawk, but I don't know birds as well as plants. I have a very different relationship with birds than I do with plants. A bird has never given me a rash that lasted for three weeks.

Suddenly, Jeff breaks the silence. "We should get going. It's gonna take us an hour to get back to the cars and I need to get cleaned up. We've got reservations at Rochard."

"You and Emily?" I ask. I'm authentically curious. Then, I worry that my question could be perceived as jealous. I hope it isn't perceived that way. I'm not jealous. Since Emily and I almost dated, it's become clear that it wouldn't have worked out between us.

While I am not jealous, worrying that it might be perceived that way makes me anxious. That anxiety I worry might be perceived as jealousy, which makes me more anxious. It is a vicious cycle.

"Yeah," he says, pushing himself off of his log. If he thinks I'm being weird, he doesn't show it in any way.

He turns toward the path and goes to take a shortcut to start back down the hill. I begin to follow him and then some bit of pattern recognition in my brain stops me.

"Jeff wait…" I start to say but I am too late. He has already stepped into the patch of green spiky-leafed plants.

"Shit!" Jeff yells and jumps back.

"…there's more stinging nettle," I say, deflated.

"Yeah, I figured that out the hard way," he mutters. "Let's get out of here."

"Okay," I say, shaking my head.

We trudge back down into the valley with Jeff shaking his leg wildly and muttering profanity.

Chapter One

I FIND myself in my apartment. It is eleven thirty PM. I should be sleeping, but I can't. I'm sitting on my rumpled sheets and blankets. I'm staring at a book that I'm not reading. It's a pulpy sci-fi that Emily recommended to me. She works in a bookstore, so I always expect she will recommend literature, but she prefers pulpy sci-fi. I want to have read it. That way, I can say I did and reference it in conversation. But the truth is I don't want to read.

I sit and try to fill the silent void in my head with thoughts.

Time. When I was young, my father told me we only had so many words in this life. That when we had said them all, there would be nothing left to say, and we would be gone.

I realize now that this was one of his tactics to persuade me to cease my constant talking. Like many things, I suspect he shared a passing thought for that specific purpose, but it made an impression on me.

How do we measure our lives?

Do we measure our lives by the number of heartbeats? Do we measure it as grains of sand through an hourglass? The ticking of a clock? The rising and setting of the sun?

There was a time before time. There were no clocks or watches. Everyone did not have a device in their pocket that was cleverly linked to a network of atomic clocks counting down the instants in perfect synchronicity.

We now have devices that break our lives down into hours, minutes, and seconds. Does having each moment of our day planned, scheduled, and organized change our perception of time? Are the best parts of life missed between the inevitable pulses of Network Time Protocol? Are we so hypnotized by this incremental measurement that life passes us by in our attempt to cling to each second?

My phone rings, dragging me out of my pontification. It's a number I don't recognize. It is an East Bay phone number, Oakland or Berkeley. Probably a telemarketer. I'm not sleeping. I have nothing better to do. So of course, I answer.

"You spell 'em, I uh tell 'em..arket Hi, my name is Miles, and I'm calling from the National Union of Organizational Representation Association. I am contacting you today because I have an excellent resource for you and your business. Do you have a moment to hear more about this exciting opportunity?"

I rarely mess with telemarketers, but sometimes I can't help myself.

"I think I have the wrong number," a deep but uncertain masculine voice says on the other end of the line. They sound tired and suddenly defeated.

"Sorry! This is Miles Ward, Apotropaist at Large…and in Charge!" I say. There is a long silence on the line; the deep, uncertain voice speaks.

"You are the guy who deals with black magic and all that?"

"That's me."

"I'd probably lead with that."

"Hello, Miles Ward speaking. I deal with black magic and all that."

The line is once again silent for a long time. I should probably not answer the phone after nine o'clock.

There is a long sigh.

"Right, I'm Paul. Paul Donovan. I am going to be honest. That was a little weird, but I need help," he says, his voice sounding strained. "I'm…I'm running out of options. Who knows, maybe weird problems need weird people to solve them."

"Sorry about that," I say abashedly. "I get so many telemarketing calls these days I assumed an unknown number at this time of night…."

"Yeah sure I get it. I need help."

"What can I do for you this evening, actually, almost midnight?"

"There are people in my house."

"I'm sorry, what? That's not my area of expertise."

"I mean ghosts. Ghosts are in my house. They are Mexican."

Oh boy.

"Okay, so you think your house is haunted by…Mexican spirits? That is very specific and frankly…"

"Right. Um. It's not. I mean, I see how it might sound racist or something, but it isn't like that, really."

"Okay. So why do you think they are ghosts, and why do you think they are Mexican?"

"Because I hear disembodied voices singing in Spanish at all hours of the night."

"They might be Spanish ghosts. Or Cuban?"

"They are singing Himno Nacional Mexicano."

"Oh. That is unusual. Maybe you should start at the beginning."

"Right. Yeah. Okay. Um, I guess it was like a month ago. I started hearing this singing; it would wake me up in the middle of the night. I couldn't quite make it out then. It was faint. By the time I got out of bed and put on a bathrobe and slippers, it would have faded. At first, I assumed it was a neighbor playing loud music or watching TV. But it got louder each night. It wasn't like a big disruption at first, but it started getting more frequent and louder. Eventually, it was so disruptive that I went and asked some neighbors about it. Nobody knew what I was talking about," he pauses briefly like he's waiting for something.

"Go on," I say.

"*Mexicanos al grito de guerra el acero aprestad y el bridón*!" He sings. His pronunciation is good. "To be clear, I don't know Spanish, but I know every word of that song now. It wakes me up every night. I've called the police. I've hired a private eye. I had a priest come to exorcise my house. I've even called exterminators. I mean, I don't think it's singing rats in my bedroom, but I was getting desperate. I've tried recording it, but nothing. I feel like I'm losing my mind, but I know I am not. Anyway, a guy I know says he works with a guy who recommended I call you. That you deal with weird stuff like this all the time."

"I do deal with weird stuff a lot, and this seems to fall into that category."

"That's reassuring, I guess…"

"So good news, it's not a haunting!"

"How do you know?"

"Because in my life dealing with 'weird stuff,' I have not encountered evidence of a single haunting. I have no reason to believe that the spirits of the dead return to harass the living."

"Then what is going on?"

"I don't know, but if I were to guess, I'd say someone is hexing you. Some mystical gaslighting."

"So, can you help me? Preferably tonight?"

"Can I? I don't know. I can try to figure out the problem, and maybe I can help with it. I've had bad luck lately with overcommitting how much I can help before I know what's happening."

"I know it's late, but can you help tonight? I have a big day tomorrow and…I can't sleep; every time I do, I hear that song."

"Have you tried sleeping in a hotel or not in your house?"

"I can't hear the voices, but I still do. You know?"

"No, I am sorry, I don't. What do you mean?"

"Like. Um. Like when you get a song stuck in your head. You aren't listening to it anymore, but it's kind of always there. It's like I can't get the song out of my head, and I find myself humming it to myself at night. I get some sleep, but barely, and it's not good sleep."

"I see."

"It's still exhausting, and I can't afford to live in a hotel room. Besides, it's not like I sleep well in a hotel bed, song or no song. Especially sitting around thinking about it. All the time. It's always there. You know?"

"I understand," I say, but I don't.

"I'll pay you to triple your normal rate. Anything! Just help! Please!"

Sometimes, the magic words are ancient phrases uttered over a bubbling cauldron. Tonight the magic words are 'triple your normal rate.' Being a contractor in a niche market doesn't exactly afford me a stable income.

"You are in luck. I am far too caffeinated to sleep. But before I say yes, I do have a few more questions. First, you say you have a big day tomorrow. What's going on?"

"I have a presentation before the county planning commission."

My interest is piqued.

"Can I ask what the presentation is about?"

"It's a third-party environmental impact study on the use of new water reclamation techniques being proposed to be put in place for vineyards. That's what I do; I'm an environmental engineer."

"What's the finding?"

"The techniques are great! It will change the landscape of water use in agriculture."

I rub my right temple with my hand and sigh.

"And what's the economic impact on the wineries if they are required to adopt these techniques?"

"I'm an engineer, not an economist. I don't know."

"But it would cost them?"

"I see what you're getting at. Yeah, I guess there would be a cost."

"How long have you been on this study?"

"About six months."

"And the late-night singing started a month ago?"

"Around there, I don't know; I didn't keep a journal at first."

"At first, but you do now?"

"Yeah, for the last…" he pauses, and I can hear paper in the background, "Eleven days."

"And Himno Nacional Mexicano, does that have any special meaning to you? It is awfully specific."

"No, I've never heard it before this all started. As I said, I don't even speak Spanish; I've heard it so many times now… I had to look the lyrics up online even to know the song's title."

"Last question. Do you live alone?"

"Yeah, I have a little townhouse on the northeast side of town."

"Give me your address; I'll need to grab some things. I'll be over in a bit."

He gives me the address, and we hang up. I look the location up on my phone. It's in a condo complex near the river on the northeast side of town. I've run by it many times, but I've never been inside it. I remember it because all the buildings have these odd round windows that look almost nautical. It's distinctive.

An internet search reveals that the place has an interesting but not supernatural history. Japan Air originally built it to house flight attendants who trained at the Napa Airport. Apparently, there was a time when Japan Air used the Napa Airport to train all of their flight attendants for US-bound flights. When Japan Air pulled the program out of Napa, the housing space was sold off and converted into condos.

I grab a bag of salt and a bottle of Goldschlager from my

cupboard. I toss them and a few more items from my desk into my handy-dandy courier bag. I crack my knuckles and walk toward the door.

"It's almost midnight, and I am heading out to meet a guy that hears voices in his head. What could go wrong?" I ask back into my empty apartment. Part of me expects Hank to chide me and tell me that at least I'll be around my people. But the apartment stays silent. I sigh and walk out to my car. I miss Hank's rubber face.

It doesn't take long to get across town at this hour. The joke has long been that Napa closes at eight and doesn't open again until ten the next morning. These days, there are a few nightlife options, but they are targeted chiefly at tourists. Even those are pretty much wrapped up by midnight. The streets are empty, and I get to the condo only about fifteen minutes after Paul and I get off the phone.

It is weird being called in the middle of the night with something like this. A part of me is carrying some trepidation. But another part of me is looking forward to something to do instead of sitting around my apartment and feeling lonely. At least this one isn't putting more magical wards up on yet another winery.

I meet Paul in front of his condo. His voice was deep and had some gravitas on the phone; the man before me almost doesn't seem to match. He's tall but rail thin. Balding but not gracefully. He seems to be clinging to the hair he has left by growing the back out long and keeping it in a ponytail while his pate is shiny and clean. He's wearing sweatpants and a t-shirt with a corduroy jacket over it, complete with patches on the elbows. It's a look.

"Hi, I'm Miles," I greet him.

"Paul," he says, holding his hand out to shake.

I shake his hand.

"I am going to look around if that is okay with you. See if I can't figure out what's going on."

"Yes, please."

I take the small crystal from my bag, hold it to my eye, and examine Paul's aura. He scrunches his face in an expression of judgment but doesn't say anything.

His aura looks normal, maybe a little chaotic or jumbled, but it's got all the swirling, changing energy I expect from a healthy person. But then I notice something; it's not much. It looks like a shadow cast onto his aura, a faint darkening. I watch it more carefully. It takes me a few seconds, but I pick up that it has a clear and defined shape; Ovoid but pulsing slightly. It gets a little bigger and smaller in a rhythm—an almost heartbeat-like pattern. I've never seen something like this before. But I have a theory.

It is easy to have a theory about an aura. This is because the lens through which you perceive an aura is your own perception.

That's confusing.

One's mind shapes what is seen in an aura. One person might look at an aura and see a lot of green. They associate green with envy, so they might intuit that the person is envious of someone else. Another person might associate envy with orange, so when they look at the same aura, they might describe it as orange. It can be hard to compare impressions of an aura because the viewer shapes the view.

So I know what I think the thing I am seeing means is probably indicative of what it means, at least to me. This is why aura reading isn't an exact science. It isn't a science at all; it isn't even an art.

My impression, whatever this is, it is like an egg. An egg that is pulsing because it is almost ready to hatch.

"I want to look around the house. Have you had anyone doing work on the unit recently? Repairs? Remodel? Repainting?"

"No."

"Any signs or indications that anyone has broken in?"

"Um. No. I don't think so."

"Okay, let's start upstairs."

He ushers me into the little townhouse. Immediately across the entryway from the front door is a stairway to the second floor. The first floor is one open floor plan. The living room, dining room, and kitchen area are all together. There is an island counter topped with a composite-stone slab separating the dining area from the kitchen and a large freestanding bookshelf separating the living and dining rooms.

It's a nice place with nice furniture. I get the sense that he is normally a tidy person but that lately, he's let things slip. There are empty take-out containers everywhere. The dining table is covered in papers and pencils, some of which have overflowed onto the floor. The couch has dirty clothes and blankets strewn on top of it. I can see in the kitchen that the sink is filled with dirty dishes. With the amount of takeout he seems to consume, I wonder how he manages to dirty dishes. Maybe other people don't eat their takeout directly from the carton.

Paul leads me up the wooden staircase. There is a short hallway with three doors off of it. He shows me each door. To the right is his bedroom. There is a king bed, a couple of dressers and a chair. It's even worse than downstairs, with clothes, towels, and used tissues carpeting the floor.

The door on the left leads into a smaller room that is probably sold as a second bedroom, but it's too small to function as such. He has it set up as an office. A whiteboard on the wall is covered in inscrutable but entirely non-magical scribblings. There is a desk, an office chair, two bookcases, and a filing cabinet. The room has a cramped feeling, made worse by the same level of clutter as the rest of the house.

The door at the end of the hall leads to the bathroom. It isn't huge, but it has a large linen closet in it. It has no windows but a very powerful vent fan instead. There is a fancy toilet; I'd guess it's imported from Japan. The toilet has seat warmers, multiple flush settings, and an array of buttons to control some other features. I think it includes a built-in bidet. One corner of the bathroom is dominated by a large shower stall. Unlike the other rooms of the house, this one is clean and tidy. The toilet is clean, and the floor is swept. I glance at the toothbrush holder and notice two toothbrushes: one red and one blue.

"Two toothbrushes in the toothbrush holder, messy house, clean bathroom, the office space is too cramped for a guest. Do you have a regular companion?"

"Huh?" He says, looking affronted.

"A boyfriend, a girlfriend, a partner? Do you have someone that stays over regularly?"

"Regular companion sounds like I'm hiring prostitutes, which I'm not, and no, I don't have a significant other," Paul says.

Significant other, yeah, that sounds better than 'regular companion.'

"Sorry, I wasn't trying to imply anything. I didn't want to make any assumptions."

"I get it now."

"But two toothbrushes?" I say I was proud of my detective work, and I'm feeling a little crestfallen that it has fallen short.

"Red for the morning, blue for the evening," he says in a matter-of-fact tone that makes it seem like this should be obvious. Confused, I shrug.

"All right, Colombo, what's next?" He asks.

"Why Colombo? Why not Sherlock or Magnum?"

"Colombo was the goofy-looking one that asked a lot of stupid questions, right?"

"Right," I say and hang my head a little. "Anyway, I want to climb onto your roof."

"Why?"

"Because so far, I am not seeing any signs of magic on the inside, and so I want to look on the outside."

He leads me into the bedroom and motions me to a window.

"Shouldn't you check the ground level first?"

"No. I've got a hunch that what I am looking for will be up

high," I say. I gingerly tiptoe my way across the room, working hard to avoid the soiled tissues. I open the window and stick my head out to look around.

The pitch of the roof is steep. I look down at my Chucks. I lift my foot and glance at the sole. It is worn almost smooth. I sigh and start unlacing my shoes while we talk.

"Why do you think up high?" He asks, watching me with a look that might be horror or might be amusement.

"Because," I say as I lift myself up onto the window sill and lower my bare feet onto the shingled roof below. "Eggs come from birds, and birds fly. Symbolic context is important in magic."

Based on his slack-jawed expression, I think I didn't clear anything up for him.

Slowly and carefully, I shift my weight from my arms on the sill to my feet on the roof.

Paul is right up at the window now, his hands on the sill very close to mine. It occurs to me now that I've made some enemies and untrustworthy friends in the past month. I know nothing about Paul other than he called me in the middle of the night for help. Now, I am barefoot and hanging out his bedroom window in the middle of the night. I'm suddenly feeling very vulnerable.

He could easily pluck my fingers away, and I'd probably fall and break my neck. There is a fence directly below the roofline that separates the townhome from the river trail. If I slipped, I'd fall directly onto that chain-link fence. I'd break some bones and then slump onto the river trail. From there, my dead or unconscious body could easily be rolled into the river. My bloated corpse could wash up anywhere between here and the San Francisco Bay.

But Paul doesn't try to murder me.

A second later, I am scurrying across the roof on all fours to a place where the pitch isn't as steep. I take my phone out and use its light to examine the roof. It only takes a few minutes before I start to find them. Sigils drawn in permanent marker all around the exterior walls of the building. I bear crawl and pause to take pictures of each of them.

The roofline itself is not regular, and it has very odd lines. The whole complex has a vaguely nautical and steam-punk feel. Weird little circular windows. Large jutting stove pipes. Fake walls whose only purpose seems to be to make the roofline more irregular and interesting to look at.

Conveniently, the irregularities also work well to hide sigils and magical symbols. The sigils describe to the universe how to shape and channel the magical energies of the spell. Despite the relatively chaotic roofline, the sigils have been placed very methodically. It doesn't take me long to pick up a pattern. I crawl around the roof, taking snapshots of the sigils as I go.

The placement of the little drawings is so predictable that I am flummoxed when I come to a place where I expect a sigil and don't find one. The spot is directly below a window. I scratch my head and stand up, and peek in said window.

I feel my face flush, and my stomach churns with embarrassment when I realize that there is no sigil because this is the adjoining townhome. I am not peeking into one of Paul's windows; I am peeking into someone else's bedroom window. A bedroom window where a couple is sleeping right in front of me.

Feeling ashamed and stupid, I quietly crouch back down, make my way back to Paul's bedroom and lift myself in. I sit on Paul's cluttered bedroom floor and put my socks and shoes back on. I try not to think about what I might be sitting on.

"Did you find anything?" Paul asks impatiently.

I nod.

"Yeah, give me a minute," I say. I'm feeling a little shaky still. Clinging to the roof was a little bit of work. Add to that the adrenaline rush of realizing that I was an inadvertent peeping tom. It takes me a minute to be ready to speak.

I finish tying my shoes.

"Okay," I say, and I guide us out of his bedroom and

downstairs to his cluttered dining room. "There is a hex on your building; it is definitely something meant to influence your mind. I will need a little time to figure that out. I'm pretty sure I can get rid of it by the morning and even engineer something that should prevent this from happening again."

"You are going to stay up all night working on this?"

"Well I mean, I can. Or I can wait till morning. It is whatever you want to do. Either way, I think you should sleep in a hotel and get some rest. Whatever rest you can because I don't think you will get it here."

"Um," Paul starts to object, but I cut him off. Sometimes, you have to remove choices from people's vocabulary.

"So go get your stuff. All your stuff, your clothes for your presentation, your materials, absolutely everything you need for tomorrow. You will then book a hotel. You go get a good night's rest. Do your presentation tomorrow. This should all be over when you get home."

"You seem confident."

"Well yes, I am. But I'd also bet that once this presentation is over, there is no more need to harass you. I think this is all about making you flub that presentation."

"Why? It's only presenting some findings to the planning commission. It's not like I have any decision-making power."

"Findings that ultimately will cost a bunch of rich people money. It's my experience that motivation in these cases is fifty-fifty. Jealousy or money. Sometimes both. Magic does not lend itself to impulse crime. It's complicated; it's slow; it's dirty. It takes planning. Unlike with a firearm, you can't make a split-second decision and then regret it later. Using magic to do something like this brings with it a lot of time to consider. Your perpetrators are usually determined, premeditated, and committed. That also means that whatever the motive is, it's big. If the motive is money, it is a lot of money. Petty squabbles don't warrant this kind of detail."

"Okay," Paul says. He excuses himself to his room.

This spell-work it's solid. Well planned but simplistic. This isn't the inexplicable complexity of Hizarin's work. I've only encountered two members of the ancient order of assassin sorcerers. Circe and her partner Morgan Le Fey. Their spells were of a level of complexity and power that I'd previously thought were the province of legend alone.

This hex is less complex but still professional work. It is composed of all medieval European sigils. But no signs of Enochian, so probably not an amateur. I think this is a small-time contractor. If I wanted to find the caster, I could probably loiter around Tienda Magia, our local magic shop, for a while and figure it out. But I don't actually care about the spell caster. This isn't about them.

A few minutes later, Paul comes back with two small bags. One is a duffle that must have clothing and toiletries in it. The other is a large laptop case. I assume it has his work in it.

"I called and made a reservation at a hotel up the street."

"Good," I say.

We walk outside his house.

"Oh, one more thing," I say.

"Yeah?"

"I think I should do a little spell break on you."

"Huh?"

"I think that this whole thing has been planting a little…I don't know, like a psychic time bomb? An egg that's going to hatch during your presentation."

His eyes go wide in horror.

"Something is going to hatch inside of me?"

"Not literally. I mean, I don't think literally. I think it's more like…an idea? A compulsion?"

"An idea is going to hatch in me?"

"Yeah, so I do recognize some of the sigils placed around your house. They remind me of 'love' spells I've seen in the past," I say, using my fingers to air quote the word love. "Causing the victim to have little whispers in their head about how great the person they are supposed to fall in love with is.

It builds up and builds up, and then at some trigger, like drinking a special potion or something, the spell activates. This flood of thoughts and emotions come in, and the person becomes overwrought with…well, not actual love, more like lust or infatuation. It doesn't usually last long, at least not the first time."

"I'm going to fall in love with someone?"

"No, no, it's just a similar construction. This feels like that, but I think it's more like a hate spell. I think it is going to trigger a spontaneous ugly racist rant."

"I don't understand."

"So the song you heard, the Mexican National Anthem. It wasn't making sense to me. Nothing seems to have any particular relation to Mexico. The building you live in was built to house Japanese flight attendants. Your findings are going to impact wealthy winery owners, some of whom might be Mexican, but probably most, if not all, are Anglo-Americans. It wasn't adding up. But then, when I saw the sigils like a 'love' spell, I thought, well, what if it's a 'hate' spell?"

"I don't understand. Why?"

"Imagine if you are in the middle of your presentation, and before you get to the good bits, the juicy bits, you break down and go on some hate-filled tear in the middle of the planning commission? You can't even finish your presentation. It won't look like coercion or anything. It will look like you were unreliable, bigoted, and unstable. Even if they hear testimony from you, everyone is going to consciously or unconsciously dismiss it. If they decide to get another study done, it won't be by you. You'd clearly have some weird biases, and it will take six more months."

"The commission will be done by then."

"Exactly," I say, but I didn't actually know that.

"It will be delayed at least or possibly mothballed completely. Your name will be ruined. Any of your findings discredited."

He sits staring at me. He sighs.

"I'm tired. I'm desperate. That theory sounds shit-house-rat looney, but at this point, I don't know what choice I have. What's involved in this 'spell break'?"

"It isn't invasive. It might seem weird. I am going to draw a circle around you and do some chanting. Maybe draw some stuff on your forehead, and then you stand here in the dark in your front yard for a while."

"Out here? What if my neighbors see us? Why can't we do it in the house?"

"Because the spell is in there. Out here, if we break it, it will be gone. I think it will start affecting you again if you are in the house. You go stay in a hotel, and I clean the spell in your house up. And that's it."

Paul spends a minute glowering at me in deep thought. Finally, he breaks his contemplative silence. He looks dissatisfied but resigned.

"Okay fine. Let's do it."

It only takes me a few minutes to carefully salt and chalk a circle around him on the concrete walkway to his house. A little chanting, a little pig's blood, and we wait. I watch his aura with the gazing crystal. Cut off from the Ley in my circle. It will take a while for the spell to fade.

It isn't fading fast enough. I wish I had a little more of Jeffs magic eating bacteria. That would speed the process up.

I wonder.

"Hey, do you have any wine in your house?"

"Yeah, I have a few bottles in the kitchen."

"Cool, I'll be right back," I say.

I run into his house and hunt around in the kitchen. He has three bottles of wine. I grab them all. I find a bottle opener in one of his kitchen drawers. I bring them all back outside and open them. They have a whiff of the familiar smell of wine going bad from magic. It's faint. I might not even notice if I weren't looking for it. It isn't as pronounced as it was at JMBaptiste, but this spell is nowhere near as powerful as that one was. I dump the wine out in the circle around Paul's feet.

"What the hell are you doing?"

"It's weird, I know, but trust me, okay?"

"I mean, at this point, why the hell not."

I step back to examine my work. It's the middle of the night. There is a bald, middle-aged environmental scientist standing outside his home in a puddle of wine inside a circle of salt. He's got an overnight bag in one hand, a laptop in the other, and a sigil that means 'out' written on his forehead in charcoal.

This is what I call a job well done.

It takes an awkward shivering hour or so before the spell fades completely from his aura, but it works.

"All done with that. You should be able to sleep song-free. Have a good night. I'll lock up when I'm done."

He stares at me bleary-eyed.

"Okay, good night then. If this works, I'll pay you triple. If it doesn't, I'm definitely giving you a zero-star review."

"Fair enough. Wait, am I on review sites?"

He nods drunkenly and starts to walk toward the parking lot, leaving red wine prints as he goes.

"Oh hey, one more thing," I call after him.

"Yeah?"

"You mind if I help myself to your coffee pot?"

He doesn't actually answer but sort of shrugs and walks off with a blank look on his face.

I go back into his house, make myself a pot of coffee, and set to work. It's easy; I erase the sigils off his roof without waking or spying on his neighbor. My trick for erasing permanent marker is writing over it with a dry-erase marker and then wiping the whole thing clean. The solvents that make it so you can wipe away dry-erase ink also break up permanent ink.

I then put a series of runes around his condo that will protect him from such an attempt in the future. A couple of drops of blood to activate them, a quick note to tell him what I did, and the job is complete.

I lock the door on my way out.

It's late morning, and the sun is high in the sky as I get to my car. I start driving back across town. It's now closer to noon than midnight when I started this little adventure, and the streets are busy.

I'm sitting at an intersection when my dashboard lights up. 'Incoming Call' it says. A loud chime echoes through the cabin of my car. I'm still not used to the hands-free setup in my new car. I didn't have one in my old Jeep. I had to use a headset.

I jab at the button on the steering wheel a couple of times. Nothing seems to happen. I wait for a second, but there is no further ringing. Either I have answered and am now sitting in awkward silence, or I just hung up on whoever was calling. I clear my throat.

"Um, er. Uh. Hello? Miles Ward speaking. A ward a day keeps the warlock away?"

Chapter Two

"UM," a faint but familiar voice on the other end says, "Miles? Are you there?"

"Yeah, I'm here!" I say, wildly slapping buttons on my dashboard, trying to turn the volume up and regain some sense of control of my technology.

"Oh!" The voice booms over the sound system. Now I recognize it as Emily's voice. "Is this a bad time?"

"No, I'm not used to the phone in the new car. What's up?" I ask, fiddling to get the volume under control.

"Okay," she says. I now sense something in her voice. Nervousness? Trepidation? Fear? It's hard to tell, but she is speaking quietly, and her voice is muffled, like she isn't speaking directly into the phone.

"What's going on?"

"It's. I don't know; this whole Redbrook thing is getting to me."

"The Redbrook thing?" I ask. I am confused. To my knowledge, Emily has never interacted with Lorelei Redbrook. It was only a couple of weeks ago that I confronted The Lamia in her seedy dive bar, The Lantern. It was a crazy night that involved me getting immolated, shot at and chased. I lived, but Lorelei Redbrook did not.

The night didn't go so well for Emily either. Emily was held hostage by a sorcerer-assassin who called herself Morgan LeFey. However, that didn't have anything to do with Lorelei Redbrook.

"Yes. I mean, how is she alive? You saw her burned to death, right?" Emily asks.

"Circe used Redbrooks' own magic against her. She burned to a crisp," I say, recalling the moment. Redbrook's soul had been bound to mine in a blood pact. The other sorcerer-assassin, Circe, used that to kill Redbrook. She tried to kill me in the process. If not for my Simulacrum Hank, may he rest in peace, I would have been turned into a smoldering lump of cinder myself.

"Miles," Emily says. She sounds sad. Exhausted. Maybe a little annoyed.

"What do you mean she is alive?" I ask, the full import of Emily's statement now sinking in.

"You haven't heard? Yeah, she's alive and well…maybe not well according to what I read, but alive."

I fall silent for a long moment. There is a low droning in my ears. My vision narrows down to a thin tunnel in front of me. Lorelei Redbrook is alive?

"How is this possible?" I say I only intended to think it, but it comes blurting out anyway.

"I don't know. I was hoping you could tell me."

I sit quietly, thinking through ways she might possibly have survived.

"I don't know. I guess maybe she has a simulacrum. Or something like it. But I saw her. She was reduced to a putrid pile of ash," I speculate.

Thinking about it brings the memory flooding back. The smell that's the part I remember most clearly. There is no good way of describing it. Like burning flesh and fetid stagnant water left in a sealed black bucket in the sun for a couple of days.

"Those kids," Emily says.

"Kids?" I ask.

"I mean all those kids she takes in…I mean, now that I know what she is, what she must do. I," she says, but she doesn't finish the sentence. She falls silent.

I don't know what to say exactly, so I sit on the phone in silence.

I am shocked out of my silence by a loud blaring sound behind me. I jump, but thankfully my seatbelt keeps me from flailing around too much. I realize that I have been sitting at a stoplight, and the light has turned green. In my distracted state, I didn't notice.

I pull into a shopping plaza and park in front of a Taekwondo studio. There are kids kicking a dummy that is just a head and torso. It makes me think of Hank.

"Why do we train kids to beat up paraplegics?" I mutter to myself.

"Huh?" Emily responds. I had half forgotten she was still on the phone.

"Oh, nothing, sorry, I pulled off the road, and there's this martial arts place with kids hitting a dummy that's just a head and torso. I was wondering what the point of that is. It's sort of the least threatening part of the human anatomy."

"Um. I don't know."

"Just talking to myself."

"Can you come over?"

"Yeah, I guess. I don't have anywhere to be. I didn't sleep last night. I am going to grab some coffee on the way. Do you want anything?"

"Sure, a coffee would be nice."

I realize that I've known Emily for years. I crushed on her until it became clear that we weren't going to work, and now she's dating my best friend, Jeff. Despite all that, I have no idea what her caffeinated beverage of choice is. For a guy that lives by the Code of the Caffeinated, this seems sacrilegious.

Code of the Caffeinated? It's a good thing Hank isn't around; he'd have a field day with that one.

"How do you like your coffee?" I ask.

"Anything is fine."

Well, that's not helpful.

"Okay, I'll be over in a few."

Soothsayers isn't exactly on my way, but the ritual of driving there and getting my usual is somehow soothing to my tired brain. It takes about half an hour before I get to Emily's, but at least I have coffee.

"Thanks!" Emily says as I hand her a large mocha. Her tone is artificially chipper, and she has a forced smile. She's exhausted.

"Of course, I grabbed you an extra scone as well."

"Oh, thank you," she says, taking the small crinkled white paper bag from my hand. She sets it on a table. She clearly has no intention of eating it. She motions me into her living room.

"You look like hell, Miles," she says. She's not wrong. I know it. I haven't really slept. It's been weeks, but I'm still scraped up and bruised from my last encounter with Redbrook. I'm hitting that point in the healing process where the cuts and black and blue bruises have faded to scabs surrounded by swaths of sickly yellow-blue skin. It honestly looks worse now than when the injuries were fresh. If I walked under a black light, I'd look like the living dead.

I haven't been in Emily's house since Morgan LeFey took Emily hostage in order to try to get to me. The high vaulted ceilings of Emily's dining and living room are still incongruous with the rest of the house. Emily has a mismatched set of chairs around her dining room table. A variety of colorful couches, tables, and chairs adorn her living room.

Shabby Chic, I think the look is called, and it was popular over a decade ago. I suspect, though, that for Emily, this is a pragmatic reuse approach and not an attempt to apply a particular style. I suspect this, but I don't know it. I feel like since we solidified as 'just friends,' I'm actually getting to know her as a person.

Emily sits down on a purple couch and motions me to a red and green patchwork armchair directly across from it. I can't help but examine the corner from which Morgan LeFey attacked me with magic. My head scans over to the corner where her partner, Circe, jumped out of the shadows to defend me.

Seeing my glances, Emily says, "I still get anxious when I sit in here alone after dark."

I nod. It makes sense. It was a pretty traumatic encounter for everyone. Probably most for Emily, whose only involvement was in making a date with me. I know from Jeff that she stays at his place most of the time now.

"So Redbrook is alive."

Emily nods and takes a sip of her mocha. It is tentative and small and feels like nothing but a polite gesture. Maybe she doesn't like coffee.

"So it seems., She's leveraging the shooting at The Lantern. It supports her whole narrative that Napa is going to hell. She's actually getting a lot of public support and sympathy now."

"Maybe I should have worked with the Knights of Saint George," I say, sighing.

The Knights of Saint George are a loose-knit militant group of monster hunters. They approached me about helping them dispatch Lorelei Redbrook, aka The Lamia. I refused because I didn't like their methods. I didn't think they would try it without me. In hindsight, that was arrogant and foolish. They showed up and shot her bar full of lead anyway. I happened to be in it at the time.

"What do you mean?"

"They approached me about helping them deal with Redbrook, but I didn't. If I had, maybe I could have mitigated the damage they did."

"Maybe," Emily says, "But that part isn't on you. I'm not saying I approve of all of your decision-making. But choosing not to help a militia shoot up a bar. That doesn't sound like the wrong move."

"I think the world would have been in a better place without Redbrook, but I mean, it isn't the end of the world. She's running for mayor. It's like a figurehead position at best."

"I'd call it more like a flagpole position," Emily says.

"What do you mean by that?"

"I mean, yeah, the position doesn't come with a lot of executive authority. But it's a flag, a semaphore advertising what we stand for. It's an invitation. A dog whistle to others like her that this is the kind of community we are."

I nod. I don't focus much on politics, national or local. They don't much interest me. But what she is saying makes sense. Redbrook more or less told me that this was her goal.

"Okay," I say, "And I don't mean to diminish the impact here. I've met her in person now, and she's the worst. Don't misunderstand me. But you seem pretty worked up about this in a way you weren't before. Like this is personal?"

She takes a deep breath and looks up at the ceiling. When she looks back down, a strand of her long brown hair falls over her wire-framed glasses. She pushes it up behind her ear.

"I never liked anything I'd read or heard about her. The way she talked about caring for kids was like they were only publicity tools. It always rankled me. But then, when you came to me with your questions about her. About the Lamia. When you told me, that's what she was. It started to sink in. It's more than just using them for her political gains. It's more than using them for labor. She's a literal child-eating monster."

I stay quiet and listen.

"I grew up in foster care, Miles. I don't think I ever told you that. And I was lucky. I spent most of that time with a great family. I had a foster brother who is still like a brother to me. I was supported and encouraged, and loved. But it wasn't always good. I bounced around a bit before that, and it was a varied experience."

"I didn't know."

"How could you? It's not something I talk about much. Anyway, when I realized exactly how bad it was, Miles. I was glad she was dead. And I feel awful guilt saying that about anyone, but I was glad."

"You shouldn't feel guilty," I say, trying to be comforting.

"I don't know. It was eating away at me. But she was dead, so it was over. And then suddenly she's not."

"Yeah, I am still confused by that."

Emily takes a breath and then starts to explain.

"They never found a body, and then last week, she started calling the newspapers. Posting on social media. She has this whole narrative about how this gang showed up to silence her and her message. Now she is alive and recuperating in an undisclosed location."

I sit, scratching the stubble on my chin and thinking out loud.

"How is she still alive? I mean, I guess I was the victim of the same spell, and I'm still alive. When I last saw her, she was reduced to a foul charred mess."

"Yes, how did you survive?"

"Simulacrum," I say. To most people, I'd probably have to explain this. The process of building an effigy of myself and using sympathetic magic to channel energy directed at me into it. How the mannequin I kept in my bedroom melted away in my stead. But Emily's knowledge of the arcane seems to be almost boundless, so I don't bother.

"Clever. Maybe she did something similar. Like a Homoculous," Emily says.

"That's the medieval alchemical thing where man makes life without a woman by putting his seed in cow dung?"

Emily makes an appropriately disgusted face.

"No," she begins. "Well yes. That's the origin of the word, the idea of making life without reproduction. But no, it's a process by which one makes a sort of animated puppet that they project their consciousness into. The process is pretty gruesome. They have to be made out of flesh stitched together and disguised."

"Like Frankensteins Monster?"

"I've read speculations that Shelly was inspired by a Homoculous for that story, yes."

I think about this for a minute. I reflect back on that night.

"I'm not familiar. I can see how a process like that could work, though. Something like that would take a lot of energy."

"And it couldn't just wander anywhere; it would need to stay within a control structure. Somewhere that it would have an ample supply of energy," Emily says.

"Like within a specific building? One with a bunch of spells woven into its construction? That might explain a bunch of the sigils and symbols I didn't recognize on The Lantern. Maybe she never left The Lantern because it wasn't her there at all. Maybe she ran the show from afar."

"It couldn't be too far, though," Emily clarifies.

"About the same as a Fetch?"

"Yeah."

"So," I say, "She'd still have to be in town."

"It's a hypothesis anyway."

"What do we do with it?" I ask.

"We've got to stop her, Miles. I mean. I know I said I didn't want to get involved in this stuff. I know what I said," she looks at me with pleading eyes. "I know."

I nod. We didn't date because she didn't want to get involved in the weird and dangerous chaos that seems to follow me around. Now she's dating Jeff, and that door has closed. That's okay. Emily is still my friend, and she is asking for my help. I also agree that Redbrook has to be stopped.

"I agree. But we are going to need a plan. And we are going to need help."

"Jeff, obviously," she says.

She's right; Jeff is the Blethspah Amah. The chosen one. Chosen for what? I have no idea. But he was anointed that by a dragon. I don't know anyone else who is in a dragon prophecy. Jeff also happens to have discovered a very handy concoction of magic-eating bacteria. I wouldn't have survived my encounter with Redbrook or Morgan LeFey without it.

"And Russ," I say.

"Who is Russ?" Emily asks. That's right. She's never met him.

"He's a Dreamwalker and kind of my mentor. Both he and Jeff helped me with Redbrook before. Russ is pretty weird and seems flaky, but he's actually pretty reliable."

"Okay," she says, but she sounds a little skeptical.

"We should all try to sit down and go over the problem. Figure out a plan."

"We need to act fast. The election is only a couple of weeks away."

"What? Really? That soon?"

She nods at me, her eyebrow quirked in a look of condescending concern. Apparently, I have no idea what is going on around me.

I sit in Emily's armchair and call Jeff and Russ.

Initially, I try to offer up my place to meet, but Jeff insists that he host. He describes my place with words like 'small' and 'cramped' and 'no one wants to sit on the floor, Miles.' Feeling a little insulted, I settled for his place.

We meet in Jeff's game room. It is the same space in which Jeff and I usually play our weekly poker game in. It's nicely decorated. There are vintage neon signs on the walls. A refurbished 1950s Wurlitzer that has been outfitted with a modern streaming audio system. Antique slot machines decorate one of the wood-paneled walls. A stiff burgundy carpet gives the room a mid-century Vegas feel without being too much.

At Emily's bequest, Jeff has rearranged the room with the table in the center and four chairs around it. She has piled newspaper articles, books, and even maps on the table. I am not certain what her use for all of it is, but these props seem to give her confidence. She stands at one end of the poker table like a five-foot-two General about to send her army off to war.

Jeff sits down next to her at the card table. I can tell that they want to hold hands, being in that mushy new relationship stage. But they are controlling themselves. Probably to keep it from being awkward. I appreciate the gesture, but it isn't necessary.

Russ arrives unabashedly late. He's wearing jeans and a Grateful Dead t-shirt. Based on how worn it is, I wouldn't be surprised if he owned the shirt before Garcia died. A long plait of thinning grey hair bounces on his back.

By the time he arrives, nobody else is surprised by his appearance or tardiness. I have explained that Russ is older, hippyish, and has a sort of obsession with the fluidity of the universe that extends over and consumes his concept of promptness.

Introductions are barely made before Emily begins.

"Russ, I don't know how much Miles has told you. But we are here to discuss how to deal with Lorelei Redbrook. If Redbrook's candidacy is met with anything but outright rejection, it is a message to every monster and boogeyman out there that we are here to serve them."

This feels a little on the melodramatic side, but I'm not going to say anything.

"Yeah, chica Miles mentioned something about that," Russ drawls.

I can see from Emily's expression that she's not fond of Russ's choice of language. Her brow furrows, and her mouth pinches tight like she just bit into a lime.

"Has he mentioned that she's a Lamia? The Lamia? A verifiable monster?"

"It has come up in a conversation or two, sista," Russ says. "I am up to speed on the life and death and undeath or undying or whatever of Ms. Lorelei Redbrook Lamia at large."

"Can we not with the chicas and sistas?" Emily says, glowering, "You can call me Emily or Ms. Dickensen."

"Woah woah like chill ch…Ms. Dickensen," Russ says, holding his hands up defensively.

"Your name is Emily Dickinson?" I ask.

"Not son sen with an e. Why?"

Jeff makes eye contact with me and shakes his head at me slightly. I think he is warning me away from this conversation.

"It's just that…you know?" I say, my mouth speaking before my brain can process Jeff's warning.

"Know what? What thing about my name could I have possibly gotten this far in my life working at a bookstore and not noticed?"

"Nothing, only that I didn't know your last name," I stammer out awkwardly.

"Yeah, I don't incorporate it into a random rhyme every time I answer the phone," she says.

"Okay," I say. "That was a little hurtful."

"Sorry," she says. "Sorry, it's a little bit of a sore spot. You'd think the quips would stop once you got out of high school, but they don't."

"Believe me, I know," I say.

She quirks an eyebrow at me curiously but moves back onto the topic.

"We need information," she says.

"What do you have in mind?" Jeff asks.

"I have a thought, but I don't think Miles is going to like it," Emily says.

"Oh?" I say.

Jeff raises an eyebrow at Emily.

"Dude, if it's not a cup of coffee, Miles ain't gonna like it," Russ chimes in.

Emily smirks at him. There's a passing crease of the eyebrows that quickly goes back to her previous and more intense expression.

"Miles. I think you should go work for Redbrook."

"What?" Jeff says, eyes widening.

"I have to say," I sigh, "I don't love the start of this plan. Please explain."

"Hear me out. When last you saw Redbrook, she thought you owed her."

"For Whitman's debt, yeah."

"Does Redbrook seem like the type who is going to forgive that?" Emily asks.

"Honestly, I hadn't thought of how that would play out now that it turns out she is not, in fact, dead. But no, I'm sure she's not going to let that lie."

"She might have you murdered like she was going to have Whitman murdered," Jeff says.

"That doesn't seem like her brand," I say, shaking my head from side to side.

"She's a bully first and foremost," Emily says. "And she's not too bright."

"I don't know. She's had some pretty intricate plans," I say.

"I've gone to her campaign events. If she's that bright, she sells the dumb thing well," Emily says. "And I realize that her folksy, down-home thing is a big part of her persona, but it's little things. She makes mistakes where it feels like she forgot her lines."

"What are you saying?" I ask.

"She's saying, dude, that Redbrook's the frontman, man. She's saying that there's like a mastermind. Someone behind the scenes pulling the strings is what she's saying."

Emily raises a surprised eyebrow at Russ and then nods. "Yeah, that is exactly what I am saying. I think she's powerful, but I don't think she's the one calling the shots."

"How does that help us?" Jeff asks, "That sounds even more dangerous."

"It means if we get close to her, we can manipulate her."

"Even if she's as dull as you are painting her to be, I can't call her up. If I volunteer to work for her, she will be suspicious for sure."

"Miles," Jeff says. "You aren't actually considering this? Do you remember all the crap you went through last time you dealt with her?"

"Yes," I say, "I remember. And yes, I am still considering Emily's plan."

"Why?" He asks.

I look from Emily to Jeff and back. The truth is that I can see in Emily's eyes that if we don't help her, she is going to do this on her own. She is going to be scared and alone, but she is going to plunge into this by herself. And it will eat her alive.

"I back my friends up, Jeff. You should know that."

"It's Miles Ward, the reluctant hero again," Jeff sighs, running his fingers through his thick dark hair.

"Come on, Jeff, you know it's not like that."

"Miles, the only person who doesn't see it is you. And it's not just all the apotropaist magic curse stuff. Do you remember that time we were downtown, and those tourists asked you for directions? You escorted them to the tasting room and spent the rest of the afternoon bitching about it. You try too hard, Miles."

"I don't do that," I start to say, but Russ and Emily are giving faint but knowing nods.

I cross my arms over my chest and slouch back into my chair.

"Whatever, Emily, I will do this for you because I help my friends," I say petulantly. Vocalizing that again puts me in a worse mood. I feel like a sulking child.

"Thank you," Emily mutters quietly. She is looking at her shoes. The whole tone has shifted.

Jeff sighs, his eyes downcast. He nods, "Fine. All right, if that's what you want to do. I'll do what I can."

Emily gives a reluctant half-smile to Jeff. He smiles back.

"You should do what you do best, babe, breed some acetobacter!" Emily says. Her tone is chipper but fake. The pet name comes out awkward and forced.

"What do you need from me, boss-lady?" Russ asks, seemingly unperturbed by the shift of tone in the room.

Russ's way of talking and some of his dated slang can be a little grating. What I like about Russ is that he doesn't seem to shy away from anything and seems genuinely happy to be anywhere he is and doing whatever it is he is doing. I admire that and wish I could be more in the moment.

"You back Miles up," Emily says. "I don't know much about Dreamwalking, but he says you are good at it, so…do that?"

Emily makes eye contact with me, and one side of her left eye scrunches up a little. I don't know what this facial expression means exactly. But it's clear to me, though, that Emily is wondering why I included Russ.

"Hey Russ, man," I interrupt.

"Yeah, Miles?"

"That night, The Lantern, Redbrook, all that. You found me in the Dreamtime. You said you followed me."

"Yeah, that's right, man."

"I know you aren't going to like this, but I think it is important. Can you find Circe?" I ask.

Russ bites his lower lip and shakes his head a little bit.

"Yeah, I can, but I don't think that's a good idea, man. She is not trustworthy, and she is like mucho dangereouso if you know what I am saying," Russ says.

"Peligroso," Emily snipes from the side.

"Yeah, I know," I say to both Russ and Emily, "But the only person that Redbrook seems to be worried by is Circe."

"Fine, man, I mean, I can try. I'm just sayin' I don't think it's a great idea, dude."

"Objection noted," I say, turning back to Emily. "So how do I get into Redbrook operation without it seeming like it was my idea?"

Emily's stray hair falls over her glasses again, and she

twirls it around her forefinger while she thinks. Finally, she pushes her hair back behind her ear.

"What if you made it confrontational? Like you were trying to get out in front of it and get her to back down before she threatens you?"

"That doesn't sound like me," I say.

"Doesn't it?" Emily asks. Jeff smirks. It's a smug look that rubs me the wrong way. He wants to laugh but doesn't think it will be well received. He's correct.

"You've walked into her place to confront her face-to-face before."

"Yeah, but I didn't know who she was then. What she was," I say weakly.

Emily shrugs. "I'm telling you that from where I am sitting, it doesn't seem out of character."

Jeff shrugs at me helplessly. I look to Russ.

Russ nods. "Dude," he says as if that single word somehow encapsulates a whole thought. I think he's agreeing with the others, but honestly, I'm not sure.

"Fine."

"See, any of the rest of us would have said no way," Emily says, half smiling at me, "QED."

"I'm not happy about it," I say, and I turn to walk out the door. "I'll text you."

I don't wait for a reply before closing the door. I need some time to think.

I sit in my car, and I ponder. I said I wasn't happy about this, but is that true? Is Jeff correct? If I am unhappy about it, why do I feel this weight lifted off my shoulders? I feel unburdened. Is the weight of inaction so heavy?

I guess that I feel like if anyone is going to go delving into the monster's lair, it should be me. Is it that I feel that I am more capable? Or is it that I feel that I'm more expendable? Is answering those questions going to make doing what I have to do next any easier? Probably not.

How do I get in touch with Lorelei Redbrook? Is it as easy

as searching for her on the Internet? Forty seconds on my phone reveals that, in fact, it is that easy. It's easy to talk and drive with the new car, so I call Redbrook up as I drive home.

"Redbrook Residence," a bored staccato voice answers. The voice sounds young, like a teenager. Probably female.

"Hello, I'm trying to find Lorelei Redbrook," I say as boldly as I can.

"May I ask who is calling?" The voice remains flat.

"Yes, please tell her that this is Miles Ward."

"One moment, please."

It is quite a bit more than a moment. By the time I hear Redbrook's voice on the line, I've been sitting in the parking lot in front of my apartment building for about four minutes.

"Miles!" Redbrook's falsetto shriek pierces my ears. "I thought I was going to have to hunt you down, but here you are calling me up."

"I thought you were dead. I just got the disappointing news."

"Miles, Miles, Miles," she clucks at me. "That is a rude way to talk to an old friend."

"We aren't friends."

"Oh, don't be like that."

"I figured at some point you'd come hassling me, so I figured I would take the bull by the horns and call you to hash this out."

"Hash. I like that. Yes, let's hash this out. But not right now. Right now, I am afraid I am entertaining. I would normally not be taking calls, but I heard it was you, and I thought, Miles Ward? Yes, I will talk to Miles Ward! Anyway, be a dear and come by my place tomorrow morning."

Her voice gets distant, as if she has moved the phone away from her mouth.

"Bella? Sweetheart, would you give Mr. Ward my address? I need to get back downstairs."

And suddenly, Bella, the teenager with the bored voice, is

back on the phone and giving me directions to Redbrook's 'Estate.' Her word, not mine.

Chapter Three

THE NEXT MORNING, I find myself driving west of town. I turn off a wide paved road running through the Browns Valley neighborhood. I turn up one street and onto another, winding my way back and forth up a green hillside. I see a large lone valley oak on the top of the hill, looking down on the valley like an ancient sentinel.

As the roads climb higher up the hill, they narrow, and the houses become larger, and more spread out. Soon, there are no houses to be seen, just gated drives.

Finally, I get to the turn to Redbrook's home and turn up the drive. The house and grounds are not visible from the road as a large imposing cast iron fence surrounds them. The fence has a matching gate, glazed black. On a pedestal by the gate, there is a keypad with a camera in it. The gate begins to open before I've even arrived at the pedestal. I roll my eyes to myself at this bit of melodrama.

A short drive leads up a slope through a small stand of well-kept olive trees to a rather large parking area in front of the house. Sitting on a hillock surrounded by olive trees and overlooking a vineyard, the Mediterranean-styled building doesn't quite qualify as a mansion. At least not a modern mansion, but it is big. I thought Jeff's house was large, but it is a shack by comparison. The bright white stucco arches and columns of the house seem incongruous with the iron fence that encircles the property.

I park my car, get out, and make my way up the terra cotta tiled walk to the front door. There is a low stone wall that borders the walk. The wall is set with tiles that have a series of reliefs depicting Greek myths. Specifically myths about monsters. More specifically, monsters brutally murdering and consuming people: The Hydra devouring a man. Polyphemus devouring a man. The Chimera devouring a man etc. There is a clear theme.

Integrated among the tiles are a series of magical glyphs and symbols that I recognize from dealing with the JMBaptiste winery job. They are all Greek, and they are all protective symbols. The work here looks nothing like the offensive sigils and spells woven into The Lantern. The Lantern was a giant magical trap designed to draw people in and make them gamble their lives away. This is a defensive bastion.

The front door is massive and a little gaudy. The large wooden double door is covered in gold gilt and carved with classical-looking faces in the corners. All female. None are immediately recognizable to me. I spend a moment scrutinizing. I think the top two are Gorgons. There's Echidna on the bottom. Right in the center of the door, Lamia. Subtle.

I ring the doorbell. I can hear the doorbell echoing inside. It plays a tune that I don't recognize. The notes are high chiming sounds. It reminds me of a church choir.

A haggard-looking teenager answers the door. He's wearing a red three-piece suit and a bright blue fez. The hat clashes angrily with the shock of bright orange hair sticking out from under it. Seeing the outfit, I can't help but think of a trained monkey dancing around a hurdy-gurdy.

He waves me in without a word and then leads me into a huge entryway with a vaulted ceiling. Two sweeping marble staircases arch upward. Hanging over our heads like a giant glass spider is an excessively large crystal chandelier.

The young man walks up the stairs slowly. There is something wrong with his gait. His movements fall into the uncanny valley, like a robot's movements or most computer-generated animation. Something is a little off, and I can't reconcile what it is. I know Redbrook has thralls, but I've never seen a Fetch that moved like this.

At the top of the stairs, he leads me down a short hallway. Paintings line the hall. Each is executed to look like a Greek fresco. Each depicts some act of horror and depravity being enacted by Maenads, the crazed female followers of Dionysus. The god of wine.

"This is some classy decor," I say to the youth in the blue fez, indicating a painting of Maenads defiling a young man while simultaneously eating his flesh. The youth doesn't respond in any noticeable way.

The hall ends in a large door made of glass and framed with gilt wood. The teen stands at the door and motions me through it, leading me back outside onto a large open balcony area.

The balcony is entirely tiled in the same horrific tile work from the front. It's subtle enough that most people probably register it as having a very Greek motif but not actually processing the monstrous content. On the walls adjacent to either side of the door are two large stone fountains with vines growing up and about them.

Sitting on a large daybed in the center of the balcony is none other than Lorelei Redbrook, with half a dozen girls sitting around her. They are all wearing sun dresses and have glassy looks to their eyes. Two are fanning Lorelei with huge fans made of peacock feathers. Two are massaging her feet, and one is feeding her grapes. The last one stands at the ready with a large carafe of wine.

I am certain that this is all a show for my benefit, though I am not certain what the intended effect of this show is.

Lorelei Redbrook herself does not look well. She looks human again, but her skin looks too loose and flaccid. She has strangely mottled discolorations all over. She's got a new wig. This one has a more golden tone than the stark white one she was wearing before. She is wrapped in a gaudy muumuu that features all the colors of the rainbow arranged in the most clashing pattern possible.

"Miles!" she greets me. "You are late."

I look at my watch. I crossed through the gate on time, but it took me a couple of minutes to climb my way up to this Caligula-like scene that she's prepared for me.

"Lorelei Redbrook," I say in my grumpiest tone.

She grins a toothy grin at me.

"Can we get this over with?" I say.

"Miles, Miles, Miles, you are always so crabby! Why can't we start with some pleasantries? Some socializing! We don't have to get straight down to business," she says. Her voice has returned to the nails-on-chalkboard falsetto that makes the back of my neck feel all prickly. There is a hot feeling in the back of my throat, and I can't tell if it's because I want to scream with rage or vomit from disgust.

"I'm only here to get this behind us," I say, motioning between her and myself. "If I had any other options, I'd be anywhere else. I know that. You know that. So let's skip the bullshit and get down to business."

"That is the wrong approach," she says. "Miles, we are going to be working together for a while. Probably the rest of your life."

She takes a dramatic pause to make sure that the threat sinks in properly.

She gazes off into the distance behind me. I turn and look at the rolling yellow hills crowned with valley oaks. Below us in a little valley is a swath of verdant grape vines. A hot gust of wind blows across my face, bringing with it the earthy, herbal smell of foliage roasting in the sun. With the architecture and view, it all looks very Mediterranean.

"It smells like home, right?" Redbrook says wistfully. She turns back to me with a serene smile on her face.

"Mmm," I grunt in non-commital response.

"You should try to enjoy this time," she says and motions to the girls around me. "What's mine is yours. Enjoy yourself."

"Gross," I say, but now I get what this show is all about. She wants to make me feel uncomfortable. She wants to size me up to test my boundaries. She wants to see what is going to entice me and what is going to disgust me.

She huffs and makes a cranky hand motion. The girls all get up and fall into a single-file line to march back into the building. The teenage boy in the inexplicable fez follows them in and closes the door behind them all.

"Down to business, it is," her voice shifts to low croaking tones. "You owe me a big debt, Miles. And you seem to have some misconceptions about our relationship. You owe me because I say you owe me. You owe me because I want you to owe me, and you have no recourse. If I decide you are no longer useful, I'll kill you. I'll kill your friends and your family. Not quickly."

She sneers and makes pointed eye contact.

"If I am feeling very cruel, I'll have them brought back from the dead so I can kill them again. Anyone you think you might go to for help, I own. Anyone you think might save you, I own. My reach is long, my roots are deep. And now I own you too."

"Okay," I say as flatly as I can. Her eyes dart away from mine, and she looks at the wall for a few words before making eye contact again. A slight quaver of uncertainty is in her voice as she continues. It's something, a tell, but I don't know her well enough to know what it means.

"Now get in line and stop acting like you are anything but my errand boy!" she raves, and little bits of noxious spittle hit my face.

"You've made your stance abundantly clear, so I'm here, but I'm not going to be happy about it," I say, wiping my face with my sleeve.

She smiles a terrible smile. All sharp teeth and tongue. It's not a smile of joy but of predatory intent.

"I wouldn't have it any other way."

"Now we've gotten that villainous monologue out of the way. What do you want from me?"

She sits up straight and goes back to her falsetto voice, adopting her folksy accent once more.

"Well, to start, it is pretty simple: I want you to help with the repairs of The Lantern. I want you to rebuild my wards the same way you did for the Syzmek building. You tore my old work down so easily, I was impressed. Now, I want you to build them back up. I want the best magical protections that can be mustered, and I think you are the person for the job."

She pauses and pokes a finger at me before continuing.

"If you do a good job there, we have more work for you. If I don't like the results, I've got plenty of less skilled labor I could be using you for," she says.

I try not to let my imagination come up with what she might mean. I'm certain, in this case, that ignorance is bliss.

"I don't do coercion and offensive spells. Everything you did with The Lantern was about assaulting people that came into The Lantern. I only do defenses. Exclusive magic," I say. "I don't know how to recreate what you had on there."

"I don't want you to recreate it. I want you to do what you do."

"Why?"

"Just be a good boy and do what you are told and stop asking questions."

"If I don't know what you are trying to keep out, it's hard to know what I should build."

"I want you to seal it up like you did the Syzmek building. I want the full Miles Ward protection. I don't want riff-raff like that Circe Baros phantoming in and out of my place of business anymore. So like I said, seal it up tighter than a banker's smile!" Redbrook says finally.

Is she slipping up and revealing a fear or weakness in

telling me she wants to keep Circe out? Or is that an intentional misdirection? I can't tell, but I log that away in my brain as a possible confirmation of her suspected fear of Circe.

"Fine. Is there a contractor I am working with or…?"

"Yes, come into The Lantern tomorrow morning, and you'll meet Alfonse. He is my construction manager for this little renovation. He will work with you."

Redbrook motions to a large, thick yellow envelope that sits on a little glass-topped table by the wall.

"I'm paying you upfront for this job. If you need more materials, let me know."

I look from the envelope to Redbrook and back. Part of me wants to walk out, but part of me is curious to look inside. All of me could use the money. I walk over and take the envelope and open it. It's filled with cash. Lots of cash. Neatly stacked and banded groups of hundred-dollar bills.

I flip through one of the stacks carefully. I put it back into the envelope and sit staring at it for a second. Part of my brain screams not to take the money. To put the envelope down and walk away. That voice in my head says that if I take it, I'm complicit, I'm an employee, I'm under her thumb. Another voice in my brain says that we are a contractor and that accepting payment for services rendered does not imply that we relinquish our agency. Another voice says that this much cash would pay a lot of rent and car payments. Finally, I decide that I have to take the cash because she would be suspicious if I didn't.

I shove the envelope into my courier bag and snap it shut. A little ripple of shame passes through me, but I rationalize it away quickly.

"Alfonse tomorrow, Lantern. Got it. Okay, can I go now?"

"Tsk. Tsk. Miles. If you must, but I would love you to stay. I can show you all the perks of working for the Dominium. Whatever your predilections, I can provide," she says in an overly suggestive tone.

"You already know my answer there."

"I could make you."

I actually don't think she can. I think she's bluffing. That she is trying to feel me out for where I am going to push back, I think that I worry her. But if this plan is going to work, I have to play along for now, and playing along means letting her think she's got control of this situation.

I shrug.

"Can I go now?" I ask but don't move.

She sits there, clucking for a minute.

"Fine, go," she says, putting on an overly dramatic tone of disappointment.

I turn to let myself out.

"And Miles?"

I stop and turn back around slowly and pointedly.

"Yeah, yeah, I know if I tell anyone anything or try to sabotage the project or fart when you haven't given me permission, you'll kill me. You'll kill my friends, my family, and Sarah, the girl I went to prom with, even though I haven't seen her in fourteen years. Then you'll resurrect my childhood dog so you can torture him in front of me, yada-yada. I got it. You need to read something other than comic books," I say.

"Good," she says, smiling to show me all her pointy filed-down teeth. I wonder once more how she hides her mouthful of sharp, predatory teeth when she speaks in public. Magic? Dentures? I guess that is not at the top of my list of worries. I turn and walk away without further comment.

Inside the upstairs hallway, the young women all peel off and walk back out to the balcony with Redbrook. The teenage boy silently escorts me once more to the front door.

I drive back downtown to Soothsayer. Hopefully, a nice hot coffee and a scone will help to wash the bad taste of working with Lorelei Redbrook out of my mouth.

Chapter Four

THE SUN IS bright and warm on my face. The grass is a vibrant green. So green it almost looks like it was painted on. Little yellow flowers dot the landscape. I can see the buds slowly swaying in the breeze.

So serene. So peaceful. I pause to gaze at the flowers. My eyes track up to the horizon, a perfect dark green line that separates the earth from the deep blue sky above. I turn around in a circle, and the green stretches on and on in every direction. I keep spinning, and I look up at a few lazy, billowy white clouds that drift above.

I feel at one with the world around me, and I raise my arms up toward the sky. As I do, I begin lifting up and up. Everything is buoyant and light. There is no strain on my limbs. The little aches and pains of daily life seem to float away as I do. Higher and higher, still drifting. The unbroken, endless green field below me. Soon, the little yellow flowers fade away, and I have no context to judge how high I am or how fast I am rising. The world is just two hemispheres of unbroken green and blue.

Then I panic. Just a little.

How high will I go?

Will I drift off into space?

Now, I am beginning to panic. I am going to float away into the void! At some point, the air will get cold and thin, and I'll be deprived of oxygen. I'll probably die of asphyxiation long before I get to freeze in the icy, bleak depths of space.

What the hell is going on?

I try to scream, but the air is too thin, and nothing comes out. I start thrashing my arms, trying to steer, trying to navigate my way back to earth. The instant my arms drop below my waist, I feel a sudden churning in my gut, followed by that sensation in my inner ear of suddenly changing direction.

Then the air is blowing across my face. It blows faster and harder as I gain speed, plummeting back toward the endless emerald field below me. My voiceless scream has gone, and now I am yelling incoherently and panicked. I can feel the tension and strain in my vocal cords. I can see the tiny dots of little yellow flowers growing and growing as I plummet, thrashing toward the earth.

Wait. This isn't real.

This isn't how the world works.

I'm dreaming! Russ told me to become aware of the dream, become lucid, break the dream, and…

I hit the ground, and the wind is knocked out of me in a rush.

"Fuck!" I scream.

I'm lying on the floor of my room. I must have rolled out of bed thrashing in my dream. The sudden impact on the hardwood floor snapped me awake. I am not getting the hang of this lucid dreaming thing.

I sit on the wooden floor, taking some deep breaths, trying to lower my heart rate and reassure myself that I am safe. That I didn't fall.

Well, I did fall, but only a couple of feet out of my bed. Not the miles and miles it seemed like in my dream. There is something at the back of my brain. A little primeval animal voice that howls in panic and terror. Until recently, I rarely remembered my dreams when I woke. Until recently, I've never awoken terrified like this. Over the past few months, my dreams have amplified. Something is changing. Am I being pursued? I think I've heard Russ mention something about that. Or is it a side effect of the Dreamwalking exercises I've been doing with Russ?

I look at the clock. It's four in the morning, a miserable time to wake up. Too late to get much more sleep but too early to get out and about. I pull on a T-shirt and sweatpants, and I go out to my office space. I make myself a small bucket of coffee and sigh as the nutty, sweet aroma fills my apartment.

Armed with Java, I sit down at my desk and open my laptop. I have an e-mail from Emily. It was only sent two hours ago and has a bunch of documents attached. I skim through them. She's managed to get some data on Lorelei Redbrook. Credit scores, real estate title transfers, newspaper articles. She's already managed to piece together bits and pieces from Redbrook's past. Social media posts and local newspaper interviews with Redbrook. Emily has inserted a number of annotations pointing out the vast discrepancies between Redbrook's personal statements and public records.

The takeaway is that Redbrook claims to have been born sixty-two years ago and raised in a foster home in Indiana. In interviews, she has listed a dozen different jobs and roles that she filled throughout her life. But if you take them all at face value, it amounts to about fifty years of employment history. I guess she could have started working at age twelve.

Redbrook claims that she gained enough money and experience to become an entrepreneur and start her own interior design business. However, there are no public records of her prior to forty years ago when she moved to Napa and bought The Lantern. She has no previous real estate in her name. There is no internal consistency to her claims. None of the math adds up. Her whole narrative is impossible.

Somehow, Emily did find a newspaper article from the sixties covering a woman in Pittsburgh named Phyllis Granger. Phyllis Granger ran a pub called the Magic Lantern. The pub was investigated by police when a gruesome murder was discovered in the alley behind it.

I sit staring at the grainy, blurry face in the newspaper article. Emily must have used a facial recognition search to find the article.

The newspaper was obviously photographed, put in microfiche, scanned, processed, and uploaded into a digital database. It is blurry, grainy, and pixelated from its transfer from media to media to media. Despite that, there is still no doubt in my mind that the woman in the picture is none other than Lorelei Redbrook.

Unfortunately, this is anecdotal confirmation of what I already knew. This information alone doesn't actually help in any way. But there is something about seeing the photograph that makes this very real. Very tangible.

This isn't her first town. She's probably traveled to hundreds of cities, had hundreds of names, maybe thousands, and killed everywhere she's gone. She's nothing less than a very sophisticated and very old serial killer.

And in one evening, Emily found evidence. Not a damning amount of evidence, but evidence nonetheless. Evidence that could be taken to the media. But that is what Lorelei wants to be found out, to be out in the open. Though, I suspect Redbrook wants to do it in a certain way.

I've only encountered Redbrook a couple of times before. In The Lantern weeks ago, she explained her goals to me. She wants to frame herself in a way that will be sympathetic to the populace. To allow her and her fiendish allies to throw off their facades and be celebrated for what they are. Evidence could be damning, or it could support her cause. Like so many things, it is about circumstance and context.

Circe said that Redbrook's goal to go public went against the wishes of the Hizarin. She said that this was why they tried to assassinate Redbrook. Is it this threat that is keeping Redbrook from going public? I can't shake the feeling that more is going on here.

I need to be careful. I'm too used to doing this alone, but I'm not. This is Emily's fight, and I'm just helping out. We need to be careful. Very careful in how we approach this. We are going to need more evidence, and we need the right kind of journalist if we are going to try to do something with this evidence.

And I know the journalist. I met her at MystiCon last year. Genevieve Gale. I don't want to end run the group. I am going to talk to them before I bring this to Genevieve. But I should probably lay down some groundwork, not dump this in her lap out of the blue.

So I dig around inside my desk. I have this old tin that once held a collection of coffee samples from around the world. I received it as a Christmas present shortly after I left college. My estranged stepmother sent it to me. She knew I liked coffee, and that was about the only common ground we had. Pun intended. I finished the coffee long ago, but I've kept the tin ever since.

Now, every time I get a business card, I toss it in the tin and put the tin back into the bottom drawer of my desk. I think I've gone back into the tin looking for a business card maybe twice in my life. Ironically, both times, I forgot whose card I was looking for halfway through the stack and never got around to figuring it out.

But there is a first time for everything.

It takes me about twenty minutes to shuffle through all the cards. Mechanics plumbers and an accordion instructor. I wonder why the hell I picked that up. Eventually, I find Genevieve's card. I write her a quick message reintroducing myself and asking how she's doing. I include some talking points about the more recent professional developments in my life.

At first, I include the bits about baby-eating monsters and vampire assassins. Then I decide that this might be counter-productive, and I delete those parts.

By the time I am finished, I look at the clock, and it's

about seven thirty and time to get showered and dressed to go to my new "job." I hold my fore and middle finger up on both hands to air quote the word job as I think it. It occurs to me that this is weird, and I look around self-consciously. But, of course, nobody is here to notice, not even Hank. Is it weird to miss a mannequin? Is it less weird if the mannequin got melted, saving your life from an immolating curse?

Chapter Five

I PULL up in front of The Lantern. It looks even worse than the last time I saw it. There is a crew there pulling bullet-riddled boards off the side of the large building.

It now has a skeletal look to it. The broken window panes on the first floor look like shattered glass teeth, and the two front bay windows on the second floor were shot out. Now they look like great empty eye sockets. The whole of the building makes me think of a giant skull leering menacingly over the landscape.

I turn to look in the direction that my imagined skeletal visage is glowering. I would never admit this, but I want to see something prophetic or symbolic here. It gazes down on rows of concrete bunkers. Storage units for rent. Beyond that is the sewage treatment plant. If there is symbolism here, I don't know what it is.

I park at the far side of the parking lot, away from the work trucks, the construction workers, and the growing piles of debris. I'd hate to blow out the tires of my brand-new car on a bunch of nails and broken glass.

I see a man with a clipboard under his arm standing in front of the building. He seems to be the only person who doesn't literally have their hands full, so I approach him.

“Hello!” I say as I walk up behind him.

He turns around. He appears to be a Latinx man about my age. He’s got a wiry look, someone who has done a lot of hard work throughout his life. However, he has a little paunch. I am guessing he is now enjoying a hard-earned supervisory role.

“I’m looking for Alphonse,” I say.

“You found him,” Alphonse says. He’s got a hint of an accent, but I can’t quite place from where.

“I’m Miles Ward. I am supposed to talk to you about the work I am doing for Lorelei Redbrook.”

A shadow of disgust and resentment passes his face when I say Redbrook's name. His body posture becomes slightly defensive, and his overall mood cools.

“Yeah. You’re supposed to put some chicken bones over the door or something?”

Working with this guy is going to be hard if he hates me. It doesn’t seem like he cares much for Redbrook, so I decide to take a gamble interacting with him.

“I’m getting the sense that you don’t much care for Redbrook. I’m no fan, either. I wouldn’t be working this job if I didn’t literally have to. I have no choice.”

He looks me up and down thoughtfully for a minute.

“What’s she got on you?” he asks.

It’s a good question with a lot of additional implications. I ponder. What she has on me is nothing other than that I know what she is, and I know exactly what she is capable of. But that alone doesn’t make a convincing blackmail. But there is a legitimate half-truth here.

“Gambling debt,” I say. “A big one.”

“Yeah, that sounds about right,” Alphonse says, looking out at his crew. “The bruja. She’s got something on all of us…”

He pauses wistfully for a moment.

“Or someone,” he says, all but whispering. I think this last bit was more intended for himself than for me.

I don't know what to say to that, but it breaks my heart and adds another item to the list of reasons why I hate Redbrook.

"Anyway, I just want to get this job done, pay my shit off, and move on."

He laughs. It isn't a humorous laugh. It's a laugh that sounds like it could break into sobs at any second.

"Friend," Alphonse says, "She doesn't let anybody pay their shit off. You're in this for life."

"I'm afraid that's probably true."

"Anyway, what do you need from me, Mr. Miles?" Alphonse says he's not exactly warm toward me, but I get the sense he's more relaxed. He was probably worried I was working willingly with Redbrook and didn't want to associate with me any more than he had to. I can't blame him.

"I'm going to need to look around, take some measurements and look at any blueprints or schematics you might be working with."

"Knock yourself out. Look around. Measure. I'll work on getting those documents for you, but it will probably be tomorrow before I can make that happen. Maybe the next day."

"Thanks," I say and give him the thumbs up. I'm in no rush to do any actual work. I want to keep the appearance of progress up. I turn to walk toward the building, but he interrupts me.

"Mr. Miles, you are going to have to wear one of these," he says as he fishes one of those construction worker helmets out of the back of a truck and tosses it to me.

"And watch out for Ms. Lorelei's lawyer. I saw him walking around earlier. He's a real piece of…" he pauses to reconsider his words, "he's a real creeper."

"Thanks for the advice," I say. "And thanks for the helmet. I'll talk to you in a bit."

"We call it a hard hat."

"Hard hat. Thanks for the hard hat," I say. I knew there was a different name for this thing.

I adjust the hard hat to fit my head and slap it on. Thusly armored, I march toward The Lantern.

I spend about an hour or so taking measurements and making notes. The dimensions of The Lantern have all been built to very exact sets of dimensions and relationships. The Pythagorean theorem can easily be found in the relationship of all the lines of the building. It is located perfectly on the cardinal points. The location it is built on is the intersection of a dozen major flows in the Ley. This will actually be the easiest place to ward I've ever worked on.

It's so perfect that it makes me wonder. Emily and I had theorized that maybe Redbrook protected herself with a homunculus, a sort of magical flesh puppet that acts in her stead. Emily said that it would take a lot of energy and be bound to a specific place. The dimensions, location, and everything else about the place would support that hypothesis.

I know the building was not originally built here. It was relocated when the highway went in, but I wonder if perhaps it was the highway that was relocated so that the building could be moved here. And if that is true, then this place was designed with some arcane intention or purpose long before Lorelei Redbrook came to it.

That is interesting. I may have to dig into the history of this building more thoroughly. That is a question and a task for another day, however.

"Miles!' a voice interrupts my train of thought. It's a voice that makes me feel like there is a cold hand on the back of my neck. My stomach goes wobbly.

Coming from behind me, echoing over my shoulder, is a voice I haven't heard in decades, but I still recognize it. It is the voice of John Hale. The false friend whose abuses and betrayal led me down this path as an apotropaist.

I turn around. He isn't wearing the leather jacket and motorcycle boots that he did back in our college days. He's dressed in Armani with shined leather shoes, a thousand-dollar tie, and a pocket square.

His wardrobe might be more expensive, but he still looks like a poser.

"Hale," I say. I attempt this in a nonchalant tone. I don't think it works. My voice sounds squeaky and hoarse to me.

Chapter Six

I AM DREAMING. That's what I tell myself. This is my chance to take control of the dream and find that door. The world feels frozen around me. It takes only an instant before I know that this isn't some nightmare, but that instant takes forever. It slowly sinks in, and I realize that I am not going to suddenly wake up.

No. This is real.

John Hale is standing in front of me dressed like a Wall Street lawyer and smiling like we are nothing but old friends who haven't seen each other in a few years.

Emotions fly through me, violently cascading in and out of my mind. Fear. Anger. Guilt. Terror. Hate. Sorrow. Rage.

I don't know what to do with all of the emotions. Part of me wants to run, part of me wants to attack, and part of me wants to fall into a ball and sob.

I am all for emotions, but not right now. Right now, emotions are going to betray me. I grab them, drag them down inside my gut, and lock them in a knot that will almost certainly become an ulcer someday.

"What, no hello for an old-school chum?" Hale says jovially, and there's a sly little twinkle in his eye.

"You might spend more money on your clothes, but you still look like a loser Hale," I say.

"And you still look like a lost and unloved ragamuffin."

"Go to hell," I say. "And ragamuffin? Chum? You know this is the twenty-first century, right?"

"That's no way to talk to your boss," Hale says, laughing.

"You aren't my boss."

He shrugs and looks me up and down.

"Lamia and I are business partners," he says. "By transitive logic, that makes me your boss."

"No, that makes you my client," I say. "I'm a contractor."

"I think you fail to understand the nature of your current engagement. But no matter not my place. I only came by to say hi to an old friend."

"Hi," I say. "Okay, well, we said hi, so now bye!"

"What, you don't want to catch up?" he says. At first, I think he's feigning shock, mocking me. But then I look into his eyes, and I wonder. I can't help but think he authentically wants to chat.

I am missing an opportunity here. I could be trying to finagle information out of Hale. Engaging is a risk; he might be able to get some information from me as well. I'll need to play this carefully. The less interest John Hale has in me and my life, the better. In college, he used and abused everyone around him. If not for luck, I'd be another of his magically lobotomized victims.

"Fine, let's catch up," I say, continuing to sound angry. I can't change tactics too quickly. "You're Lorelei's partner now? So what? Are you in the Dominium Dolores? Sounds about right, John Hale joining the Masters of Pain."

"That's right, Miles, I am counted among the ranks of the Dominium," Hale says haughtily. "If you get on board, I expect one day you might too."

"So how did that happen? You responded to a job posting? Seeking an arrogant douchebag to join an elite cabal of monsters? Do you get dental with that?"

"Oh, it's far more exclusive than that," he says, a look of hurt crossing his face. Again, I can't tell if it's authentic or if he is mocking me.

"What? You had to include your resume?" I say, "You list what you did to Shelly on that?"

"Oh, Shelly, sweet Shelly," he says, his face contorting briefly into a look I can't place. "I was talking to her about you yesterday, Miles. She did not, I am afraid, have much to say."

The way he delivers this, I can tell he's baiting me. He is guiding the conversation down this path intentionally. He wants to brag about Shelly. I resist an urge to hit him.

"You visit Shelly in Denver?" I ask. He must have connections. I was never able to visit her at the private facility she was in.

"Shelly isn't in Denver, Miles," he says. "She's here right here in Napa."

His tone is mirthful. Is he trying to get a rise out of me? Or does he think that I'll be happy about this?

"What?" I say incredulously.

"Yes, here at the State Hospital."

"What? How? That doesn't make any sense," I say. It really doesn't. Why would she be moved from a private facility in Colorado to a state facility in California?

"I don't know," he says, shrugging in a suggestive manner, his face puckered with feigned guilt. He bats his eyelashes theatrically.

The smug bastard had her transferred here…somehow. It cannot be a coincidence that she's here in the town where I live. I can think of no good or logical reason to do this that doesn't involve playing mind games with me. But mind games are Hale's specialty, so I shouldn't be surprised.

On the plus side, I know one thing that he doesn't know. I can get some of Jeff's acetobacter, and I can help Shelly.

"I've got what I need," I say, turning on my heels and starting back toward my car.

“Miles!” Hale calls out to my back, “We are going to be working together a lot. We should bury the hatchet.”

“Sounds like a plan to me,” I call back. “Right in the empty hole where your heart should be. I’ll bring the hatchet next time!”

He calls something else out to me, but I slam the plywood sheet that is currently the front door of The Lantern shut. It muffles his voice so that I can’t understand what he’s said, probably for the best. Now I can feel like I got the last word in, and he can feel like I calmly ignored him. I am anything but calm.

Alphonse is standing at the bottom of the front stoop of The Lantern. He shakes his head grimly as I slam the plywood door shut.

“I can see you met the lawyer,” he says.

“Unfortunately, not for the first time,” I say. “What an asshole.”

“Amen to that,” Alphonse says.

“Have a good one, Alphonse. Great to meet you. You seem like a good guy,” I take two steps, then pause to add, “You don’t deserve this.”

“Thanks, good to meet you too, Mr. Miles,” Alphonse says.

“I’ll probably be back tomorrow. See you then,” I say, putting the hard hat back into the truck.

I stride quickly across the lot to my car, hoping Hale doesn’t emerge from the building before I am gone. As I pull out of the parking lot and onto the street, Alphonse waves at me, and I wave back. I’ve already learned a lot.

Redbrook plays dirty with all her contractors, blackmailing or strong-arming them into working. I’m guessing she overpays for the first contract, as she did with me to get them in the door, and then drops to less desirable compensation later when she's got even more leverage.

I’ve learned that Redbrook is working with John Hale, my college nemesis. A man I never thought I would see again.

Hale has had Shelly moved to Napa somehow. All of this is too much to be a mere coincidence. Hale is here for a reason. He moved Shelly here for a reason. Probably in order to taunt me. Maybe he thinks he can use her as leverage? Or maybe he had her brought here as some twisted attempt at a reconciliation gift to me? Regardless, that's my first stop.

Chapter Seven

BACK ON THE ROAD, it occurs to me that it's not my first stop. It would be useless to go visit Shelly now. I realize that first, I need to see Jeff and get acetobacter. So I call him.

"Hey, Miles," Jeff answers after a couple of rings.

"Hi, Jeff," I say more brusquely than I intend.

"What can I do for you?"

"I need a big dose of your acetobacter formulae and stat."

"Magusficedula!"

"That's a mouthful. How about I call it your magic juice?"

"Magusficedula!"

"Magic Juice."

"Fine," he says, "but I won't have my current batch all ready until tomorrow."

In my car, I squirm with impatience. My encounter with Hale has left me feeling anxious, guilty, and overwhelmed. While at some level, I know that it wasn't my fault that Hale lobotomized Shelly, I've always felt responsible. Now I have one thing I can do that might have an actual effect, and logistics postpones me. It's frustrating, but it's not Jeff's fault.

"Okay. Please let me know as soon as I can get some."

"What's going on?"

I sigh. I don't want to get into this story. It's heavy, and it's dark, and it's a burden I've been holding this in for a long time. The longer you keep something bottled up, the harder it can be to open up about it.

"It's a long story. In summary, there is someone whom I could have helped or should have helped, and I was too young and dumb to see what was going on, and I didn't. I thought I would never be able to try to fix my mistake and that it was all beyond my abilities. That this person was beyond my reach. Well, now you have the capacity, and I just found out the person is here in Napa at the State Hospital. Now I can do something."

"Oh..." he pauses for a long while before continuing. "Sounds intense. I'll let you know as soon as I've got a good culture and enough bred to make the whole thing work. As I said, it should be all ready to go tomorrow."

"Thanks, Jeff," I say. "Seriously, you are a rock star. I can't imagine getting through the past couple of months without you."

"You're welcome."

"I'll talk to you later."

"Later."

I hang up and drive to the State Hospital anyway.

The Castle. That's one of the nicknames for the hospital. An immense gothic structure whose turrets and minarets loom over southern Napa. It was constructed in the 1870s as part of the moral treatment movement, a mental health reformation spearheaded by people like Dorothea Dix. The intention of the movement was to make mental health care more humane. By which, I think they mean less trepanning, forced hysterectomies and lobotomies. Ironically, times have changed, and the conditions of this facility are now often questioned.

The edifice is huge, ornate, and imposing. My friend Alistair is in private practice therapy now, but he used to work here and has told me many stories. Most of the staff wish that the place would burn down. Apparently, the aged facility is fraught with infrastructural problems. Hard to heat in the winter and impossible to cool in the summer. Bad plumbing, asbestos, lead paint, archaic electrical systems, and the list goes on. Many feel that simply being in the building is cruel and unusual punishment, an ironic juxtaposition to its intended humanistic origins. But the archaic building is a protected historical sight, and so love it or hate it, the State is stuck with it.

Despite what Alistair's husband Jon might tell you, I've never actually been here before.

Until now, I've never had a reason.

There are no voluntarily admitted patients here, so I wonder what kind of strings Hale had to pull to make this happen. As I learn more about the Dominium Dolores and their tactics, I shouldn't be surprised by anything.

It turns out you can't just show up to a mental hospital and expect to see a patient. There is a process. There is paperwork. After twenty minutes of talking to people, I walk back out to my car frustrated.

In order to visit, I'll have to fill out an online request form that gets reviewed by the care team and the individual's conservator. That process can take as long as two weeks. After over a decade, I have an opportunity to try to do something finally, and I am held up by red tape. While I understand that this is how the world works, it is still very frustrating.

I do what any normal person would do. I drive to my favorite coffee shop to drown my sorrows in java and pastries. Jesse isn't working today. Karen, the owner, is behind the counter. That is unusual.

"Good morning. What can I get for you?" she asks.

"No Jesse this morning?" I ask back.

"No, he had to take a personal day."

"Personal day?" I say with the implied question. This is change. I can deal with a lot of change but not change in my coffee routine!

"Personal," she says pointedly. I guess no matter how chummy I am with the barista; it isn't her place to give me details. Jesse is such a fixture in my routine. Having him not here is a little surprising.

"I'll have a double espresso and…I'll mix it up. I'll have that cran-rosemary-sconey-thingy," I say, pointing to a tasty-looking treat and butchering the English language.

She rings me up, and I pay.

"Name?" she asks. I'm a little hurt that she doesn't remember me, but I guess I don't interact with her too often.

"Miles."

"Miles. Got it," she says, then pauses. "Miles Ward?"

"That's right."

"Oh, I've been meaning to call you! Jesse gave me your card," she says, glancing behind me. There are no other customers in line, so she continues, "I wanted to see about procuring your services."

"Yeah, Jesse mentioned. Have you had problems? Anything specific?" I ask. I've never been hired to ward a coffee shop. Wineries, estates, mansions, corporate buildings, a haunted outhouse once, but never a coffee shop.

"No, no, I've been reading stuff about new crimes involving hexing or cursing people. Shadow thieves who can walk through doors that sort of thing."

"While I am happy to help, I will say that you can't believe everything you read on the internet. In my experience, people who get targeted are usually the rich, the famous, and existential douche-bags."

"That was pretty much how I felt, but then a couple of weeks back, I saw a woman literally vanish into a shadow. It was crazy, but I know what I saw."

"Really?" I ask flatly.

I am about to tell her that this isn't a thing that can be done and that magic doesn't work like that. But she interrupts me.

"Yeah, right down the street from here. This like six-foot-three woman in black leather steps into a shadow, and poof! Gone. I thought I was losing my mind, but then I saw the same woman a few days ago parking her motorcycle around the corner," Karen says.

Circe.

Now that I think about it, vanishing into shadows is a thing that can be done. Apparently, magic does work like that. My perceptions of the world are changing.

"Yeah," I say, thinking about the implications of this information. Circe's lack of discretion surprises me. "Wait. Did you say a couple of days ago?"

"Yeah," Karen says, nodding. I must look surprised because she raises an eyebrow quizzically. Apparently, Circe is back in town. That's news. Karen waits a moment for me to say something but then forges on.

"So anyway, I figure if there are people that can, like, walk through shadows or whatever, maybe I should get some magical barriers on my business. Probably my home, too. That's a thing, right? Magical barriers? I tried reading up a little on the internet."

"Yeah, that's a thing, and it's what I do for a living. Such as it is. I'm happy to help. However, I'll say I don't think this is the kind of place usually targeted by magic. The cost-benefit in robbing a coffee shop with magical rituals is pretty low."

"Thank you for being honest about that. Though I'll be honest, it's also kind of a marketing thing. This magic stuff is getting kind of…you know, trendy now? Having a magically protected shop, I think, will be a selling point for a certain kind of customer. A novelty to others. Besides, it fits in with our shop name, Soothsayer like a prophet kind of thing?"

"I have always wondered why Soothsayer. It's an odd name for a coffee shop."

"Well, it's a bakery, really. But I'm Karen Sooth. Soothsayer is a nickname. A long story, an ugly divorce—my friend's not mine, and my friends started calling me Karen Soothsayer."

I nod and quirk one eyebrow questioningly. I'm interested to hear her story if she wants to tell it.

"See," she begins, seeming eager to tell the story, "I had told her when she got engaged exactly how long I thought it would last. Eerily, a year and twenty-three days was spot on. Wedding certificate to the finalized divorce. I even threw in some hours and minutes, which my friend also claimed were exactly true, but I think that's just storytelling. So to make a long story short, it became a kind of a thing, and when I opened the shop, I went with the nickname. Soothsayers," she says.

You learn something new every day.

We talk about pricing and scope and all the other details for a few minutes. I agree to email her a proposal by the end of the week. I leave with a coffee, a scone, and another small job.

I'm sitting in my car, eating my scone, and deciding what to do next. I've already decided to drag my feet on The Lantern job. I'll try to draw that out and get as little done as possible while trying to learn as much as possible.

Having Hale involved is a complication, to be sure, but one I think I can work around. My thoughts are interrupted by my phone. It's an unknown and out-of-state number, but I answer it anyway.

"Miles Ward, don't be vexed by a hex, no spell too complex for me to perplex!" I answer.

Peals of laughter greet me.

"I'm sorry," an entirely pleasant voice gasps between guffaws. "I'm sorry. That's ridiculous."

"It's a work in progress," I say, feeling slightly hurt.

"Hi, Miles, it's Genevieve Genevieve Gale. You emailed me," she says, and now I recognize the voice.

"Genevieve, thanks for calling me," I say. "I am sorry about my most recent failed tagline."

"Oh, don't be. That was the most I've laughed in a week."

"Thanks?"

"It's funny that you e-mailed me. I am actually in San Jose doing a little legwork on a piece. When I got your email, I was already considering a little side trip to wine country," she says.

"Oh!" I say. She lives in Portland, I recall, so her being in the Bay Area is a bit of a coincidence. Sometimes coincidence is just coincidence, but I've been having too many lately not to feel suspicious. Of course, I guess I am always suspicious.

"Want to grab lunch on Saturday, and maybe you can show me around the valley, you know, insider's tour?"

"Yeah, that sounds great."

"There's this place I've heard amazing things about there, Luka's? Have you heard of it?"

I shake my head and laugh to myself. Luka's of course. My least favorite overly popular sandwich place in town.

"Yeah," I say, chuckling. "I've been there a couple of times."

"All right, I'll meet you there. Say twelve-thirty on Saturday?"

"We should either make it one o'clock or eleven o'clock. It gets pretty crazy from noon to one."

"All right, let's make it eleven, then give us a little more time to catch up."

"Eleven. Saturday. Luka's. Got it."

"It's a date. I gotta go, see you then! Chowsers!"

She hangs up the phone.

"Chowsers?" I say to myself. That's a weird expression.

In the car, I turn on the radio and flip through about thirty stations before I realize that I don't want music. I want to be alone with my thoughts. And there is a lot to think about.

The best thing I can do now is come up with a proposal for Karen over at Soothsayers. I spend the afternoon putting that together. It's pretty simple. This is a set of wards I've set up a thousand times before.

An exclusive boundary with The Hanging Sloth at each of the four cardinal points to guide magic out. The Bitten Donut faces the north wind to reinforce the boundary. The Piper Pipes at the Western Dawn let enough ambient magic in to be comfortable. And the King's Crown allows the whole thing to draw on the energy that passes through it to power itself.

I never share my stupid names for the sigils with anybody else. They all have their own names in the language of their origin. I find it easier to remember them based on what they look like to me.

The Hanging Sloth is a kind of upside-down omega symbol with a little whorl that looks like a head and a little curl that looks like a tail.

The Bitten Donut is like two concentric circles with a little notch on one side of the outer circle, and then some squiggles and dots inside that look like sprinkles to me.

The Piper Pipes at the Western Dawn is...Well, I don't know. It looks like a bunch of random lines and squiggles. But if I squint really hard and look sideways at it, it looks like a guy in a kilt with bagpipes exploding. You always put it facing the Western sky, so I added the Western Dawn in.

Finally, the King's Crown is one of the most useful sigils in my repertoire, a sort of zig-zag line with a line to the left of it and some circles in between. If you turn it sideways, it looks kind of like a child's drawing of a crown. The King's Crown allows a spell to continue funneling energy into itself to self-sustain.

Having completed a proposal for Soothsayers, I type up all my notes on The Lantern.

I sit at my desk and eat a bowl of tepid pot noodles for dinner, my mind buzzing and stressing over everything that's happened today. After an hour or so of mental spiraling and building anxiety, I conclude that I am not going to change anything tonight. I binge-watch mindless tv until I fall asleep.

Chapter Eight

THE HOUSE.

Again.

It's my house, but it's like nothing I've ever lived in before. I only know it is home because it feels familiar. It feels like home. There are elements that remind me of my apartment, a corner here, a painting there. There are elements that remind me of my parent's home: a book-cluttered office that I'm not allowed to go into, some kitschy dream catchers with fluorescent-dyed feathers hanging from them, a Tibetan prayer wheel over an unpainted wooden doorway. There are elements that remind me of every place I have ever lived. Really, every place I have ever been.

But it is none of those places not in design, construction, or decor. This is no place I have ever been before. Because nowhere that I have ever been was quite so damn creepy.

The bare wooden stairs creak ominously as I ascend to the second floor, and the sound echoes through the long empty halls and corridors. This house is massive, sprawling, endless, and labyrinthine.

Labyrinthine usually means maze-like, but a labyrinth isn't a maze. A labyrinth is one continuous winding path. There are no decisions, just convolution, and ultimately you will always get to the center. A labyrinth supplies no choices. A maze is more circuitous, with dead ends and paths best not traveled, but there are choices to be made.

This house is both, there are choices to be made, but ultimately, it seems like every path takes you to the same place, which is another set of choices that bring you to another same place and so on, like a series of magician's tricks. But each is as bare and bleak as the last, only somehow darker. I am steeped in a sense of foreboding like a teabag in a pot of murky boiling water.

Upstairs, down a hall through a door across a carpet through another door. I climb a ladder and crawl through a dusty attic. I descend some stairs and go through another hall. I open a door into a bedroom to a bathroom that has another door that leads into a bedroom to yet another hall to a door into a kitchen, and so on.

Each door I come to has a lock of sorts, a puzzle to be solved, a riddle to be answered, a trap to be disarmed.

Solve each puzzle, answer each riddle, and disarm each trap. I do this fluidly and without thinking. It doesn't feel like familiarity. It doesn't feel like I am doing it at all. It feels like my hands are being guided. Like I am a puppet. I am a vehicle for someone or something else to travel through this place.

And so I travel door to door, room to room, stairwell to stairwell, hallway to hallway in an endless slog of walking and puzzles and riddles and traps.

I would say that I am lost, but in order to be lost, you have to have the desire to be somewhere specific. You have to have an intended 'here' that you wish to be in so that you can be lost in the 'there' you are in. I don't have this. I feel that I am looking for something, but I don't know what. I am not certain that it is 'I' that is doing the looking.

This is a banal, pointless existence, but there is somehow something freeing in it as if a burden is lifted. Like all I can do, all that is expected of me, all that I must do is explore and solve puzzles and riddles and traps. Labyrinthine. No choices to be made.

What does it say about me that I find myself wondering if I've died and this is heaven?

"You aren't in Heaven, Miles," I hear Hank saying.

I turn, and I see that Hank is walking beside me. It's a weird thing for a mannequin to do.

"Hank, what are you doing here? Aren't you dead?"

"Miles, we are harder to kill than that you and I."

"I guess that's true. But what are you doing here?"

"What, a guy can't go for a walk with his friend?"

"We are friends, aren't we?"

"Together forever, amigo."

We fist bump, his knuckles are soft and pliable rubber, and I can feel them give beneath my bony digits.

"So what's next?"

"Well," Hank says, *"You are dreaming. So we could look for that door, right?"*

"We are dreaming!" I say. This hadn't occurred to me until now. "You're right."

"So where to boss?"

"Hmm, well, there are a lot of doors. But Russ said we should look for the one that we don't want to go through even though it's speaking to us," I say. "But the problem is I want to go through all of these doors. I want to explore everything."

"*What about that one?*" Hank says, pointing over my shoulder at something behind me.

"Oh, we can't go through that door," I say. I refuse to turn around to look at what Hank is pointing at. I don't need to. I know that door it's old and worn, and the paint is peeling off. Behind it, a black stairwell leads down down down.

Into the underworld.

"Pretty sure that is the one."

"Nope, not happening," I say. He is right. I know he is right. But that door terrifies me. It's the scariest thing there is. Just thinking about it makes my chest feel tight, my heart races and my vision narrows down to a tiny tunnel-like pinprick. "I am going to go open this one with a puzzle lock. That one looks good."

I walk toward a large wooden door with a brass puzzle where the lock should be. The puzzle is comprised of a bunch of gears that can be pulled in and out, some that can be swiveled side to side or up and down. There is a long crank sticking out one side. If you arrange all the gears on the face of the puzzle in the right places, the crank will open the lock. If they are wrong, the gears spin freely. It's insanely complicated. I start to fiddle with it. Suddenly, Hank grabs me by the arm.

"Hank! What the hell, man?" I say, trying to pull my arm away.

"For your own good, Miles, you gotta go through that door."

"No! I just want to solve puzzles!" I scream.

"Tough love buddy!" Hank says, and he throws his arms around me, putting me into a headlock.

I shove at him and struggle. Hank takes me to the ground. He's got me in a chokehold from behind. I can feel his rubbery arms tighten around my neck, wrenching it back. He's surprisingly strong for a mannequin.

I can feel a plastic knee pressed hard into my spine at my lower back. I'm twisted backward, so my arms can't get purchase on the ground. When did Hank learn Jujutsu?

"This is for the best, Miles," Hank whispers in my ear. *"This will all be over soon."*

I see little motes of light dancing across my vision. My chest surges like it's about to explode. I feel the pressure on my carotid artery, and I know I only have seconds before the lights go out. I struggle. I claw at Hank's arm, and little bits of rubber come away under my fingernails. He continues to hold my throat. I kick and thrash as the blackness envelops me…

And I wake up once more, sweating in my bed. The TV is still playing some old TV show from the 90s. I turn it off and look at the clock. It's four a.m. Again. Too late to get back to sleep too early to do much else. These dreams are becoming more frequent. They are becoming scarier. They are feeling more real. I tell myself it's too late to go back to sleep, but the truth is I am too scared to.

I sit on the edge of my bed. My dream has left me feeling shaky. I look at the empty spot in the corner where Hank used to stand. I miss him. Well, I miss the version of him that didn't choke me in my dreams.

It'll be another few weeks before the replacement mannequin made from a mold of my body arrives. It will take me another week or so to get it all ritually prepared as a full simulacrum. I wonder if I should name it Hank as well. Or is the memory of my first simulacrum better served by giving the next one a new name? I conclude that I will figure that out once I get the mannequin.

I'm still feeling tense and pent-up. I decide to go for an early morning run. I get dressed in running clothes and grab a headlamp. It's still dark outside, and I don't want to get myself run over by a car accidentally.

Chapter Nine

AFTER I'VE RUN, showered, shaved, and dressed, I sit down and review the proposal for Soothsayers. It's fine. Nothing special.

The plan requires no architectural or structural changes. It's mostly a prearranged set of decor. Each piece includes the proper mystic symbols and sigils to create a set of barriers that will prevent most magic from flowing over the boundary. It's like a cut-down prefab version of the defenses I helped with at MystiCon. Blood not included.

There will still be some measuring and adjusting to do to fit the context of the specific space, but in broad strokes, this could work for any space or building. I could even use it to ward a hotel room for an overnight stay. The advantage of a set of wards like these is that they don't require much blood to activate. Unless they are actively disrupted, by which I mean someone starts taking the decor down, they self-maintain.

Nobody wants to have to go around painting their store with blood on a regular basis. Actually, for a client like this, I wouldn't even mention the blood to them unless they asked. It'd freak them out for no good reason.

An idea is percolating in my brain, slowly darkening from the dirty water of thought into the deep rich coffee of inspiration. I could have a prefab set of wards. I could bundle this as a 'retail business' package. Actually, I could have a number of different packages, one for hotel rooms. One for retail businesses. One for residential use.

The proposal goes out, and then I jot down some notes about this prefab package idea. Karen seemed to think that there was a growing trend here. If more places like Soothsayers start looking for these kinds of protections, this could be an easy money maker for me.

"Miles Ward's patented Ward in a Box!" I say in my best cheesy advertiser voice. I wait for Hank's snarky retort and feel a little sad when it doesn't come.

It is mid-morning, and I don't know what to do with myself. I decide to head back to The Lantern. If Hale isn't there, I might get to do some snooping around.

Alphonse and his crew are there working. I park across the lot from the building and walk over to Alphonse.

"*Hola* Alphonse *que pasa*?" I say.

"Hola, Mr. Miles," he says. "Another day, another pitiful paycheck."

"Is Mr. Hale here today?" I ask. Alphonse's face broadens into a confused expression, so I clarify, "The creepy lawyer."

"Oh no, the *pendejo* isn't here today. He only comes by once a week or so."

"Great, I am going to go take some more measurements and stuff without him...distracting me."

"Have fun," Alphonse says. "But remember to grab a hard hat, okay? It's my ass if you get hurt and sue."

I laugh but grab a hard hat from the back of the truck he has indicated.

"Thanks," I say, slapping the white plastic dome onto my head into the building. I don't see how this helmet is going to keep me from getting injured, but it's not an argument worth having.

Most of the damage was cosmetic and done to the exterior of the building. The inside has a few bullet holes and some broken glass and bottles, but it isn't too bad. The Red Door itself still hangs intact at the back of the bar.

The Red Door. I remember the first time I came seeking out this door and the underground card room behind it. It was only a few weeks ago, but it seems like a lifetime. Then, it felt like an immense and impassable barrier lurking in the shadows at the back of the bar. Now, in daylight, with light flowing in through the plastic sheeting that now makes walls, it just looks like a door. Covered in pitted, faded, stained red velvet, there is nothing impressive or impassable about it. It looks run down, worn, and plain. It looks tacky.

I walk around the bar and go through the motions of measuring things. I pretend to type them into my phone, but what I write is a limerick that comes to my mind.

Lost in the lair of the Lamia,
Not in Greece or Mesopotamia.
It's just a shitty tavern
It should be a cavern.
But she is nothing but lame-ee-yah.

"Wow," I mutter to myself, "her lair isn't the only thing lame-ee-yah. Don't bring that to open mic night!"

I miss Hank. He was far better at roasting me than I am.

Eventually, I make my way through the ominous red door and up the black-on-black stairwell.

Upstairs, it's a bit more of a mess. I walk around, turning papers over and looking under tables. I poke around behind the bar. I don't know what I am expecting to find, but sometimes, if you look with a blank slate for a mind, you find something interesting. Finally, in one back corner, there is what looks like a thermostat on the wall.

It's a very old-fashioned thermostat with a knob on the front and a little orange hand that points to the temperature. It has a wild serif font, plastic faux oak, and maple veneer. Its design could only be described as 'boxy.' I'm not an expert on vintage heating systems, but I'd guess mid-century manufacture. It doesn't fit with the speakeasy-inspired decor, and it seems weird that this archaic thermostat would still be installed in a building that has been renovated so many times. I fiddle with it.

The knob on the thermostat doesn't move. In fact, nothing on the thermostat moves. I pull it, and the whole thing shifts a little. After a minute, I discover that when lifted and pulled at the same time, the thermostat swings aside. Behind it is a keypad recessed into the wall. It has all the digits 0-9 displayed, along with an * and a # key. There is a small LCD display at the top that currently reads 'Locked. Armed." A little brand logo at the bottom of the keypad reads 'Falcon Security.'

I take a quick photo of the keypad and then put the fake thermostat back over the top. I don't know the code, and there is no sense in guessing. Too many failed entries will probably set off an alarm, silent or otherwise. Maybe I can research more about Falcon Security and what kind of systems they provide.

Armed with the knowledge that there is a keypad on the wall here, I look around the wall more carefully and easily find the margins of a door. It is well concealed in the wall, and I'd never spot it if I weren't looking specifically for it.

I laugh out loud. I've wanted to stumble on a secret door all my life. Books and films would have you believe that secret doors are everywhere, but this is my first time encountering an actual secret door. I'm excited and very curious about what Redbrook has hidden behind the door.

"That's a weird coincidence, right?" I ask myself, reflecting on my dream last night of locked doors, riddles, and puzzles.

"There are no coincidences, dude, only connections in the strands of the, like, universe that you've failed to make yet," I respond to myself, trying to mimic Russ's new-age wisdom.

I spend another hour or so poking around The Lantern, but I don't find anything else of particular interest. I'm growing bored and a little hungry, so I decide to leave. By the time I do, Alphonse and his crew have gone maybe for their lunch break, though it's a little late for that. Maybe they pack it in early.

I get in my car and notice that I've missed a message from Jeff. His formulae is ready to be picked up. He has it in the fridge at work.

I drive Up-Valley toward Holtzhom Winery. I get stuck behind a small parade of limousines with inebriated people literally hanging out the windows and sunroofs. The people hanging from the limos are young and out of control. My guess is that this is a wedding party. I'm stuck behind them for miles, and they are not going very fast. They get up to a lot of champagne-spilling shenanigans: hurling clothes out windows, catcalling vineyard workers, and smashing half-full bottles of champagne against road signs.

I pull into the winery's small parking lot, relieved to be off the road with the mid-afternoon partiers. The parking lot is ringed in fan palms. Fan palms are about the only palms that will grow this far north. Fan palms are irritating because the only reason anyone plants them is to have palm trees. Unlike a date palm or a coconut palm, they don't produce anything useful or interesting. Their only goal in life is to rain fronds and seeds down on the world below them. These palms are no different, and there is a crunching as I walk across the asphalt to the winery. It's like I am treading on a carpet rice crisp cereal.

There is a woman behind a little concierge desk in the tasting room. The musky sweetness brought on by years of wine being spilled and mopped up greets me. I like the smell of wine must. Sweet and slightly funky. The smell here reminds me of that, only more subtle. I wonder if the employees even notice the odor anymore.

"Do you have a reservation?" she asks. She has a very uptight, all-business energy that puts me on edge.

"Um, no, I am here to see Jeff Reba. He's a friend of mine."

"Oh! Jeff's friend! He said you'd be stopping by," she says, her energy suddenly relaxing. This shouldn't surprise me. My friend Mike has told me plenty of stories about tourists that treat service industry people like crap.

"Jeff's great! He's through that door down the hall, and he's the second office on the left," she says, indicating a door.

The door is all stained oak panels and beveled wood with large handmade wrought iron hardware. It is oversized and clearly custom-made. It is one of a handful of such doors leading out of the tasting room. The tasting room itself has been designed and decorated with no expenses spared. The one door alone probably cost as much as my car.

"Thank you," I say and start toward the indicated door.

The tasting room side of the door is so luxurious looking. The other side of the door is a shocking dichotomy. A sterile, blank white hallway yawns before me. There are sterile, blank white office doors with little vinyl name plates shoved into metal brackets on them. With all the window dressing, landscaping, fancy cheeses, pomp, and circumstance of 'wine country living,' people often miss that the winemaking industry is fundamentally industrial food manufacturing. All the same rules and regulations apply to it.

Jeff's staff includes winery workers and the like but also compliance experts, sanitation staff, and people versed in the labeling requirements passed down by the TTB, the Alcohol Tobacco Tax, and Trade Bureau. As such, behind the scenes, the offices of a big operation like this are very office-like. The labs are sterile, and the actual winery is a large industrial space filled with giant stainless steel vats and high-tech equipment.

I get to Jeff's door and knock. He ushers me in. This isn't my first time in his office; I know what to expect. Two big windows with blinds permanently drawn. A table with a bunch of lab equipment on it. A large stainless steel refrigerator is in the corner. A single potted plant clinging narrowly to life on a little stand by the door. In contradiction to the neat and tidy state of his home, his desk is a cluttered mess.

"Hey," he says as I walk in. "How's The Lantern gig?"

"It's getting very weird," I say. "Someone from my past showed up. It turns out he works with Redbrook. Like, he's her lawyer or something? It has me a little shaken."

"Yeah, that is weird. A coincidence?" he asks.

I shake my head side to side.

"Any scenario that it is not a coincidence seems implausible. But so is any scenario in which it is a coincidence. So. I don't know. I guess my gut says it's not a coincidence," I say.

"Yeah," he nods, drumming his fingers on his desk, something I've started noticing he does when he's nervous.

"Oh! And the exciting part!" I exclaim, "There is a secret door!"

"Congratulations?" Jeff says, scrunching his face up in a bemused but confused expression.

"Anyway, I am going to need your magic juice for sure now. I have someone who needs help, another Fetch," I say.

"Acetobacter Magusficedula," he corrects me.

"Sure that," I say, distracted.

"Say it!" he says with a smile.

"No!" I say, grinning.

"Say it, Miles, say Acetobacter Magusficedula!"

"I don't think I can pronounce that!"

"Ass Eat…" he begins to say slowly.

"Woah, watch the potty talk now! Isn't it more like uh-see-tow?"

He laughs. "Uh-see-tow-bak-ter May-jus-fis-eh-doo-la," Jeff pronounces it slowly for me.

"Fine Acetobacter Magusficedula. Please."

"You have come to the right place, Batman."

I look at him, slightly confused. Why is he calling me Batman? He goes to his refrigerator and pulls out a large hip-pack. I recognize it; I have seen them at fairs and festivals. It's insulated and has ice packs that can be zipped into the sides like a little wearable cooler.

He sets it on the table in front of me and unzips it. He reaches in and takes out a spray bottle, and sets it down.

"The spray you are familiar with," he says.

"Yeah saved my life. Twice," I say, "Thank you again for that."

"You are welcome. But now I have more surprises."

He reaches into the cooler and pulls out a little plastic case, which he pops open. Inside are a half dozen little flechettes with syringes built into them.

"I've weaponized it," he says, pulling a pistol out of the cooler bag as well. "I ordered this online. It is **ridiculous** what you can get online, no questions asked. It's an air gun that will shoot these little flechettes. The kind that zoo keepers and animal control use for tranquilizers."

"I see I'm Batman because you are giving me my utility belt. That makes you Lucius Fox."

"Who?" he asks, scrunching his face at me.

"Morgan Freeman."

"Oh," he says, rubbing his chin in consideration, "Yeah, that sounds right. Okay, moving on."

He reaches into the bag and takes out a ball of bubble wrap.

"Magic Bubble Wrap? You shouldn't have!" I exclaim.

"Settle down, Mr. Funny-guy. It's delicate, so I wanted to keep it wrapped up."

He unwraps the object. It's a little glass ball filled with a liquid and some flakes of something at the bottom. It looks like an empty snow globe.

"This," he says, "Is my first prototype magic detector. Basically, you take it out of the cooler, shake it up well, and then set it down. It will measure the amount of magic built up in an area."

He sets it on the table and uses his hands to display it like a spokesmodel.

"The redder the liquid turns, the more acetone is forming in the mixture. If it turns red very fast, you know you are in a high concentration. The prototype has some problems. Obviously, it is delicate, but also it will naturally turn red over time as the Acetobacter Magusficedula slowly starts to colonize. Once it turns red, it doesn't go back. I am working on some other ideas to improve on this, but I thought I'd give you one of these."

He starts to wrap the ball back up and put it back into the cooler, along with the other things.

"Thanks, this will all be helpful," I say. I'm not sure it will be, but it can't hurt to be polite and supportive. "I was just expecting a spray bottle."

"You're welcome, and make sure to keep all this in the refrigerator when you aren't using it; it won't last forever," he says.

"Fridge. Check," I say, picking up the bag and strapping it to my waist. It's big and bulky and makes me look like I'm going to a music festival. It doesn't look intimidating or cool like Batman's utility belt. I guess every hero gets the utility belt they deserve.

"So what are the next steps for you?" he asks.

"I need to talk to Alistair about how I can expedite seeing someone at the State Hospital," I say. "And I was hoping you could reach out to Emily and Russ and arrange another meeting at your place. I am trying to be pretty low-touch. I'm worried that Redbrook is having me followed."

"Why do you think she's doing that? Have you seen suspicious people following you?"

"No, but it's what I would do. Sometimes, it's someone else that is suspicious. Sometimes it's me being suspicious."

"That's called paranoia."

"It's not paranoia when you're protecting friends."

"Fair," he says. "I'll give them a call."

"Thanks, Jeff," I say, tapping the bag gently. "This is some great work."

"No problem. Actually, figuring this stuff out has been the most fun I've had in a while," he says, smiling. I can't remember the last time he seemed so relaxed.

"All right, next stop. Alistair."

"Good luck," Jeff says. "I'll text you with a time to meet at my place."

We wave goodbye, and I walk back to my car, my oversized insulated fanny pack swaying back and forth on my hip. Suppose I added some board shorts, knee-high socks, sandals, maybe a Hawaiian shirt, and a broad-brimmed straw hat.

I could be Tourist-Man.

Beware evil-doers! I shall litter in your protected green spaces and stand in the middle of your roads taking selfies! I will pay your exorbitant prices, but I will not tip!

Chapter Ten

I SEE that Jon's car is in the driveway. I wonder if he and Alistair get into arguments about what car company makes the better hybrid. Alistair is my poker-night buddy Jon is his husband. A few weeks back, I left a magically lobotomized man on their doorstep in the middle of the night. I don't think Jon liked me too much before that; I'm sure that didn't improve his opinion.

I take a deep breath. On the one hand, Alistair warned me not to risk Jon's fury for a while. On the other hand, I want to help Shelly if I can. My own personal discomfort is a small price to pay.

I make my way up the front steps of their mint-colored suburban hideaway. Was it mint-colored last time I was here? I ring the doorbell and wait a moment. Jon answers the door. He says a few things in Spanish too fast and fluid for my general education requirement grasp of the language.

"Hi, Jon," I abashedly interrupt.

"Hi, Miles."

"Listen."

"No, Miles, I think it's you that needs to listen for a second. Okay?" he begins, and I stay quiet.

"I have heard your stories from Ali. Chaos follows you.

People don't go to a convention and then end up solving crimes where magicians fake their own death. People don't get hired to do security at a winery and then end up uncovering a secret plot to murder someone. People don't happen to go to a bar when a gang of domestic terrorists shoots the place up. They don't get chased across town and end up dropping catatonic people on their friend's doorsteps. These are not things that happen to normal people, Miles. Do you understand that?"

"I hear what you are saying, Jon, and yes, I understand that my life isn't most people's experience."

"Your life is no one's experience, Miles! It's not normal. And I married a normal man, okay? I married a man who is good with kids, kind and caring, and vulnerable. But I see the look in his eyes every time he retells me some story he heard from you at poker night."

He's pretty worked up, so I give him space.

"I know that sometimes he wishes he was still playing the card tables. I know he sometimes misses the late nights and the thrill. And I'd be okay with him going back to that...sometimes. But I do not need my normal, reliable, dependable partner to get dragged into your chaos. I don't need him dragged into the surreal mess that is your life, Miles. Do you hear me? Do you understand?" he says emphatically.

"Yeah, I hear you. I understand. I don't want to drag him into my business any more than you want him dragged in."

"And yet you are here."

"Yes. I am here. And yes, I am going to be honest with you, this is related to the chaos, as you put it," I say. I pause, thinking. Jon sits and waits for me patiently.

"Okay," I say. "Let me explain the situation and what I need. If that's a problem for you, I'll walk away. I'll let it go."

"Okay," he says, crossing his arms.

So I explain. My intention when I start is to give him the synopsis of Shelly. But once I begin talking, it's like a dam broke, and everything is flooding out.

"In college, I joined this group of people into like the occult and stuff. I was lost and lonely, and I struggled to find my people. You know? I guess, at first, it was fun. I had friends, and wc did things. But it turned out it was more of a cult than a social circle, and the leader, this guy John Hale, was doing bad things. I know you don't buy so much into the whole magic thing, but he was using it to take away peoples people's free will."

I pause and look at Jon for a second. He nods for me to go on.

"The same as that guy I left on your doorstep. It's a slow process, and it turns out he was doing it to every one of us, including me. I figured out what was going on and tried to stop him. But I wasn't so successful. Then Hale left, and pretty much everybody went back to normal and moved on. Except for this one girl, Shelly, she was never the same. It broke her. I always felt guilty about that, like I could have done something."

"Could you have?" Jon interrupts with an earnest tone.

"Honestly, no, probably not. But I don't know, have you ever seen something happen that you couldn't stop but wish you could?"

Jon nods again. I remember that he's a nurse. He's probably had that experience more times than I can possibly imagine.

"I worked for years to try to find a way to help her. That was, in many ways, what started me down my current career path. But I never could find a way, and I had honestly started to forget the whole thing when I got that job a few weeks back. JMBaptiste Winery was under a bizarre magical assault that was spoiling all their wine. Jeff and I discovered a bacteria that could eat magic."

Jon quirks an eyebrow into a dubious look.

"Yes, I know how it sounds. Anyway, it helped that guy I left on your doorstep. So now, finally, I have something that could maybe help Shelly. I got shot at, burned with magic, beat up, chased, and basically went through hell. I thought maybe it's all worth it if I can help Shelly and other people like her."

"That sounds all very noble and all of you, Miles," Jon begins. I can't tell if he's being sarcastic, "But what's this have to do with Ali?"

"Right, so a couple of days ago, Lorelei Redbrook, it turns out she's the literal Lamia ancient Greek baby-eating abomination, she coerced me into working for her. Well, more like I baited her into coercing me into working for her."

His eyebrow hasn't fallen from its skeptical position.

"It's complicated. I'm only doing it to help gather information to use against her. Anyway, it turns out that John Hale, the guy from my college, works with Redbrook. It turns out he has had Shelly moved to the State Hospital, and so now I have a chance to help her. The problem is that it could take weeks for me to get a visit approved. Long and short, I am only looking to see if Alistair can give me any insight on how I might accelerate that timeline. It's just one simple question. It doesn't require him to do anything or be in any danger whatsoever."

Jon sits there with his arms crossed for a moment.

I look down at my feet. I can't make eye contact with Jon. I worry that if I do, he will see the truth in my eyes. I do feel responsible. Responsibility, at least in this case, is an intellectual burden.

However, the truth, the real truth I don't want him to see in my eyes is not intellectual. The real truth is I feel like I should feel guilty. But where that emotion would sit in my chest and weigh me down, there is just another cold, empty space. I've spent the last decade doing anything I could to avoid thinking about Shelly. But now that Shelly is here and this is relevant again, I want to act now so that I can get back to avoiding thinking about that cold, empty space again.

"Well shit," he says. He sits silently for a moment, eyes cast up, biting his lower lip. He has given me space to think and talk, so I wait quietly.

"Listen, I actually know the answer to your question. If you ask Ali, he's going to be like, 'I have some connections,' and find a way to get involved. At the end of the day, what I am going to tell you is the best bet. If you can find out who the conservator is and contact them directly, they can probably get the process expedited."

"Okay, so how do I figure that out?"

"Well, that is where Ali's buddies from his state hospital days might come in, but you let me ask around, okay Miles? Then I will text you with the information," he says. "Let's just keep Ali out of this one."

"Okay, I guess that works."

"I just don't want to see that glint in his eye when you are telling him your story. This Shelly, what's her last name?" he asks.

"Sell. Michelle Sell," I say, and when I say it out loud, I think I understand why she went by Shelly.

"All right, Miles. Gimme your number, and I'll text you once I figure it out. Okay?"

"Okay. Thanks, Jon."

"De nada," he says. "Miles, you are a weirdo, but I think you have a good heart."

"I think you're normal and over-protective, but you've also got a good heart, Jon."

"Damn straight, I do."

We exchange phone numbers. He gives me a brief, casual hug, and we say our goodbyes. I get back into my car and drive away. I wasn't expecting to dump my life story on Jon like that, but I have to say it did feel good to get the whole thing off of my chest. I leave feeling like a weight has been lifted.

Chapter Eleven

THE DOOR to my apartment is just latching behind me when I get a single simple one-line text message from Jeff: 7:00 p.m. I look at my clock. It's four o'clock. I can't help but wonder where the day went. There is some light cleaning that I've been procrastinating on for a week, so I putter around doing that. I find myself fidgety and crawling out of my skin.

There are so many things that are making me anxious, and I want to address them all. I want something to change. I want Redbrook in my rearview mirror. I want to see Shelly and get that over with. I want to get back to my normal life of living hand-to-mouth, putting wards on wineries. Is that true, though? Do I actually want to do any of those things? If Hank were here, I think he'd make fun of me for my inner dialogue.

Finally, to kill time, I take my bicycle and ride downtown to Soothsayers. But they close at two. So does Roast! The only place that I know of that is still open is that big multi-national chain—the one whose name I don't even like to say. I do not want to invoke the demon sea god for which it was named.

I imagine marauding bands of cannibal mermaids rising up out of the river to devour hapless bystanders. I've never seen this happen, but I assume that is the behemoth cafe chain's end goal.

I'm exasperated. Under-caffeinated. Agitated. I remember that there is a beer garden that opened up here in town that also has a little cafe in the corner, and it's open late. So I bike over there to check it out.

Tin-Door is the name of the place. I can't help but wonder if that's supposed to be a pun or a double entendre. It is very nicely decorated. It has wooden paneling on the wall to hide the fact that it is just another bay in a long building of commercial space. It has shabby-chic lighting with old canning jars over LEDs and tables made of salvaged wood that's been sealed in resin and polished. You can see the old, weathered grain but won't get any splinters from it.

The decor is old and funky looking, but the place is kept spotlessly clean. It leaves me with an unsatisfying sense of dissonance. Part of my brain wants to see sawdust on the floors but not in my coffee.

I order a double espresso and one of their conchonitas, a tiny little morsel of pan dulce shaped like a button. I loiter by the register for a few minutes until my coffee is ready, then take my coffee and the bite of bread to a window-facing counter. I sip my espresso and nibble on my conchonita. It might be because it is a little late in the day, but I find the pan dulce tasty but dry. The coffee is fine, and I might come back here again for late afternoon emergency coffee, but it isn't going to replace Soothsayer anytime soon.

I'm about to slurp up the last of my coffee when I see a familiar figure outside. Circe. She's strutting down the street wearing a flowered sundress, big-lensed sunglasses, and a wide-brimmed hat. I wouldn't recognize her in that outfit if not for her very notable stature. The last I saw her, she was jumping into a shadow and vanishing from Emily's living room dressed like a kunoichi.

Karen at Soothsayers described seeing Circe recently, but I'm still surprised to see her here. I consider getting up and walking outside to talk to her since I do think I could use her help with Lorelei Redbrook.

I'm sliding my chair back when I notice that she is walking with someone, so I watch. There is a girl walking next to her, a teenager lanky and awkward-looking. The girl is probably tall for her age, but next to Circe, she looks tiny. She's got dark hair and dark skin. She's wearing a T-shirt with a logo for a band that I don't recognize and worn-out tennis shoes. The girl has a blue backpack on. I have a glimmer of recognition, but I can't place where I've seen her before.

The girl and Circe seem to be in a very involved conversation. The girl waves her hands emphatically as she talks, and Circe nods in response.

What is Circe doing in town? Why is she doing the Big Brothers Big Sisters thing? Is she babysitting? This must be connected to Redbrook and The Lantern. I can't imagine why she would be back in town otherwise. Maybe I can find out.

Once they turn the corner, I down the dregs of my espresso, pop the last mouthful of dry pan dulce in my mouth, and get my bike.

I know the downtown area pretty well. As much as I would like to get close enough to hear them talking, I don't think I can do that without getting spotted. But all I need is to keep the occasional line of sight in order to figure out where they are going.

I ride in the other direction from where they walk to a little footbridge over a creek. The whole area has been built out to function as an overflow in case the river floods. The footbridge rises in a high arch over the creek, giving me a better vantage of the street. I watch their progress moving up Main Street and then take off to follow.

I lag a good block and a half behind as they walk down to Soscol and turn left. I parallel them on a residential street until they come to a big hotel by the river.

As soon as they enter, I race my bike through the parking lot to an alleyway between buildings and loop around to the back entrance.

The rear of the hotel opens up onto a section of the River

Trail, a trail that winds its way along the river all the way through the city of Napa. There are a few breaks in the trail where roads, bridges, and the like interrupt it. But you can navigate on foot north-south through most of the city on this trail. Right behind the hotel is a relatively new flood wall to keep water from flooding the hotel if the river should jump its banks.

On the river side of the flood wall shadowed by balconies of thousand-dollar-a-night rooms are a cluster of tents and tarps hanging from the trees. A small encampment of homeless are cooking some meat on a dented black hibachi. A pile of sticks smolders under the grill.

I pause to lock my bike up in a rack filled with rented e-bikes. The rear gate of the hotel opens into a large patio where little fire pits give off fragrant cedar smoke. I wind my way between lounge chairs with people luxuriating and drinking wine. I make my way into the lobby and look around.

No Circe to be found. If I hadn't stopped to lock my bike up, I might have been able to catch her here. I curse under my breath. There is a young man sitting behind the concierge desk. He smiles a forced smile as I approach.

"Good afternoon, sir. How may I help you?" he asks with all the cheer of a broken brick.

"Yes, I'm looking for a friend of mine. She said she'd meet me here ten minutes ago. A tall woman: beautiful, with dark hair and dark eyes. You couldn't miss her."

"Yes, sir. She just came in," he says, nodding his head toward the elevator. "I'm sure if she's expecting you, she will be here shortly."

"Yes, I'm sure. Do you know what room she is in?" I ask, trying to sound casual.

"I'm certain that if I did know, it would be against policy for me to tell you. We respect our guests' privacy. Sir," he says with a strong emphasis on the Sir.

My ears feel hot all of a sudden. Way to make it weird, Miles.

"Of course, of course," I stammer out. "Well, I will wait out back. I'm sure she will be down soon."

"We have a bar with an excellent wine selection," he says, appraising me. "It's happy hour, and we have two-for-one well drinks if that's more to your taste. Or budget. Perhaps you could get a drink while you wait."

"Yeah, that sounds great."

I excuse myself to the bar, where I order soda water. I pay for the soda water, and I walk out to the back patio area. I sit on a chair by a small fire with a window view of the lobby. As I sit down, my phone vibrates. I take it out, keeping one eye on the lobby. It is Jon calling me.

"Miles Ward. If you're being pissed on, I'll piss you off," I answer. I do customize my catchphrases sometimes.

"You got that right. Hi Miles," Jon says.

"Hi Jon, what's up?"

"I got that name for you, the conservator?"

"That was quicker than I expected."

"What can I say? I got the game. Anyway, it's someone named John Hale."

"Shit. Well, that's not good," I say.

"Why's that?"

"Remember I told you about a guy in my college that made Shelly that way? Yeah, that was John Hale."

"Oh yes. Not good. What are you going to do?"

"I don't know, Jon. I need to think about this. Thanks for the info."

"Glad to help."

"Thanks again. I'll try to come and visit you and Alistair sometime soon. Chaos free."

"That'd be great. And Miles. Be careful."

"Yeah, that's probably not going to happen," I say, considering that I'm currently stalking a sorcerer-assassin. "I'll see you later."

"Okay. Later," Jon says. He sounds concerned.

We disconnect, and I sit and ponder. I shouldn't be

surprised. In hindsight, Hale all but told me he was Shelly's conservator. I guess I didn't want to accept it because it was so very wrong. I'm distracted now, and that is going to make tailing Circe dangerous. I should get out of here.

I wait another moment. Then I chug down my soda water and slip out the back to my bike.

I check the time and realize that now I don't have time to ride home and still get to Jeff's by seven. So I peddle my way there. It's a few miles, and I have to work to get across town. I'm about ten minutes late when I arrive at Jeff's dripping sweat.

The first thing I notice is that Emily's car is there already, but Russ's vehicle is nowhere to be seen. As I am locking my bike to Jeff's front porch railing, I realize I have no idea what Russ drives. In my mind, I had always envisioned Russ driving a VW Van or some funky old Volvo. I think he mentioned something about a suspended license. I recall that he walks a lot, but Jeff's house would be a very long walk from Russ's place.

I knock on the door, and Jeff answers after a minute. He waves me into his home with a dramatic flourish.

Emily and Russ are already sitting at a table eating chips and guacamole and drinking glasses of red wine when I come into the room. Jeff sits down and silently offers me a glass of wine. I shake my head no.

"Did you get chased here by Banshees?" Russ asks, "You're a sweaty mess, man."

"No, I biked here. I had to really pedal to make it on time."

"No way, dude, me too!"

"So, did you go talk to Redbrook?" Emily asks pointedly, talking over Russ.

I fill them in on the events of yesterday and today. I tell them about Redbrook, her house, her enthralled staff, The Lantern job, Hale Shelly, everything. For some reason, I decide to leave out Circe for now. I find myself wondering why I'm leaving her out at the same time that I'm doing it.

"For my part, I got Miles the Acetobacter Magusficedula he wanted already," Jeff says.

"Miles, I sent you most of what I found out. There is more, but it's pretty much all in the same vein. It looks like Lorelei Redbrook or whatever her real name is…" Emily says.

"Lamia, I'm pretty sure it's Lamia," I interrupt.

Emily squirms a little as I say that.

"I'm going to stick with Redbrook," Emily says. "It looks like Redbrook has a history of running bars and taverns. All of which are associated with gambling, prostitution, racketeering, etc. Each one has a different name but always light-themed. Lantern, Torch, Light, Lamp always seems to figure into the name for some reason."

"Odd," Jeff says, nodding encouragingly for Emily to continue.

"At some point, the place starts to get a bad reputation. People disappear and stuff like that. Then she vanishes only to show up a decade or so later with a new name and identity and starts to do it all over again."

"And how long has that been going on for?" Russ asks.

"As far back as I can find historical evidence to support it. Right now, the farthest back I can find evidence is in London, 1858. But the evidence is pretty flimsy that far back. I think it goes back even farther than that."

"Unsettling, but is this useful in any way?" I ask.

"Well, yes," Emily says. "It means that she's immortal but not unstoppable."

"What do you mean?" Jeff asks.

"Well, if she just couldn't be trapped or killed, why would she bother changing locations and identities? She'd have nothing to fear. No, she has fear. She wants attention, but she doesn't want too much attention," Emily says.

"That makes sense, but now she's changing her tactic," I

say. "She wants to come out in the open, she wants to be public."

"But she's not," Russ says.

"That's right," Emily says. "She wants to, but there is something she is waiting for in order to do so. Again, if there was nothing for her to fear, she wouldn't be bothering with this whole mayor campaign."

I nod and think that over. Jeff drums his fingers on the table.

"Okay, so we know there is a proverbial Achilles heel. We need to find it," Emily says.

"Russ, what do you have?" I ask.

"Oh yeah. Right dude. So. Here is the thing," Russ says, then he takes one of his infuriatingly long pauses.

"Yeah?" I say.

"Circe she like doesn't exist," Russ says.

"What are you talking about? Of course, she exists," I say.

"No man, like. Gosh, how do I put this? Okay, so like in the Dreamtime, right back behind what we see. Back behind, like you know, what we know, is the gestalt of the whole universe. Time and space, man, they are like illusions, so is self, so is, you know, like matter or whatever. You with me?" Russ says.

"Sure," I say. I'm not, but I feel like pointing this out will derail his already unstable train of thought. "And what does that have to do with Circe not existing?"

"Right, so like, I went out, and I started like, you know, asking the gestalt of the universe for this chick. Right, I went out, and I tracked, and I followed, and in theory, you can find anything in there…out there? Right? Cause you know it's like everything?" he says and then waits expectantly. I don't know what he's expecting, though.

"Okay," I say.

"Right, so if you ask for something and you can't find it in the gestalt of the universe, it like isn't there, right?" he says.

"You didn't find her anywhere?" I ask, "That doesn't make sense."

"Well, I didn't say nowhere but, like, not her, right? It's like people remember her, she's in thoughts and memories, and you know, even dreams and stuff. But I couldn't find her. You know? Just like. Her echoes in dreams? " Russ says.

"Okay," I say, "I guess I don't understand. What does that mean?"

Russ looks at me and gives me a big shrug.

"Hell, if I know, man, never seen anything like it. I cashed in a lot of chips and favors to get a lot of nothing here. I gotta be honest, it was not what I was expecting," he says.

"I mean, I know she does exist. I saw her today!" I say.

Everyone stares at me for a second.

"Kind of burying the lead there, Miles," Jeff says.

"I was sitting in a coffee shop," I say.

"That sounds right," Emily quips.

"And she walked by with this like a teenager. A teenage girl, they were talking like they were old pals," I say.

"But that doesn't sound right," Emily mutters again.

"Anyway, so I mean, I know she exists. I saw her press a stoplight button, and the light changed," I say.

"Is this relevant?" Jeff asks, "If she exists in the gestalt of the universe or just in our lives, is that a relevant point? Does it change our plans?"

"No, I guess it doesn't," I say. "It's pretty weird, though."

Jeff gives me a glowering look, eyebrows furrowed with the right eyebrow raised slightly. I read this look to say that he doubts Russ as a reliable source. Russ is odd, but in my short time knowing him, I've been given no reason to doubt his competence.

"I don't think you'll have to worry about it, though, Miles. I am pretty sure that she's going to find you," Russ says.

"Why's that?" I ask.

"Cause, well, she showed up at my house this morning and

said to stop looking for her. I told her you were looking for her, and she said she'd 'Take Care Of' you," he says.

"Well, that's ominous," Jeff says.

"Or hot," Emily says.

I glower at her, and she shrugs.

"So what's next?" Jeff asks.

"Next. Miles, keep working the inside and see if you can find anything useful. I'll keep doing research, and we will see what we find. We reach out if we find anything?" Emily says.

"Sure," Jeff says. His face is blank, almost expressionless, except for a slight downturn at the corners of his mouth. I don't think he's happy with this plan.

I nod.

Emily gives the thumbs up, and Russ nods. I grab a handful of corn chips from the bowl. The crunchy, salty taste is too satisfying after my evening spent biking around. I'm chipmunk-cheeked, crunching away at them, when I notice Jeff's glower and Emily's awkward look. They want us to leave now. I scarf down another handful of chips with guacamole and then wave my goodbyes and head for the door. Russ is close at my heels.

Russ pulls his bike out from behind a hedge in Jeff's yard. Apparently, Russ doesn't believe in locking his bike. I unlock mine, and we ride across town through darkened streets.

"Hey man, can I ask a question?" Russ breaks the silence.

"Sure."

"Like, why are you doing this man? Getting involved in all this Redbrook stuff?"

"Because it's the right thing to do?" I say. I'm not sure I convince myself.

"I mean, sure, man, but there's lots of bad shit in the world. Why this specifically?"

I think for a minute before responding.

"I don't know. Emily asked me, I guess."

"Nah, man," Russ says. "You feel like you gotta solve all the problems. It's like not my business, dude, but you should probably at least acknowledge that. Ask yourself why you know. Actualize yourself."

"Hmm," I grunt. Somehow, his saying this feels insulting, but I am not sure why.

"What about you, Russ? Why are you in?"

"Cause you asked, amigo," he says. "And I got a hero complex too, man, don't sweat it."

We ride another block in silence.

"How's the Dreamwalking coming, Miles?" Russ asks. I am getting the impression that he's not comfortable with silence.

"Not great. Sometimes, I remember to remember that I am dreaming, but usually, I forget. I see the door sometimes or think I know where it is, but I never make it."

"You gotta remember, man, it's only metaphorically a door. Really, it's a boundary built in your mind, one that you've spent a lifetime creating. The door is your ego's way of protecting your id from the truth of the oneness of the universe. Or is that backward? I forget. Anyway, you aren't gonna break that down overnight. The only thing holding you back from opening up your consciousness is you."

"You sound like a fortune cookie."

"Just 'cause it's printed on a piece of paper inside a nasty crunchy little cookie doesn't necessarily mean it isn't true, dude."

That would make a good fortune cookie quote.

We ride for a while more in silence. My mind is racing through a jumble of things. Dreamwalking, Lorelei Redbrook, Circe, her companion, life, the universe, and everything. Russ breaks the silence once more.

"Okay, amigo, I gotta turn off here to get home," he says. "Have a good one."

"You too, Russ. Have a good night. I'll talk to you soon," I say.

"Later, dude!" he says and turns off down a side street. The moment I can't see Russ anymore, I notice how dark it is.

The streets feel quiet and abandoned. Like the town is empty, and I'm going to turn a corner to see a shambling legion of the undead coming for me. Or something worse. I start to get up in my head. I think I see figures in the shadows and movement out of the corners of my eyes. Am I being followed? Am I being watched?

I pedal quickly the rest of the way home. I drag my bike upstairs and lock it. I get into my apartment and collapse into my office chair. My calendar is sitting on the desk in front of me.

It is empty, not because I don't have things to do, but because I never remember to actually write them on the calendar. Tomorrow is Saturday. I'm sure Lorelei Redbrook would love me to work all weekend, but I've got boundaries.

"Saturday. Saturday…" I mutter to myself, "There is something else going on Saturday. Oh Right! I am supposed to have lunch with Genevieve Gale."

Chapter Twelve

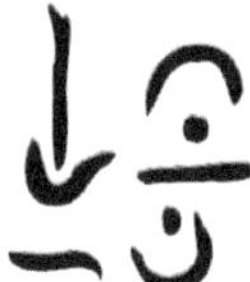

ONCE MORE I'M up early. Too early. I can't get back to sleep. I've had another dream where I am being stalked through a mysterious building full of puzzles and locks. The whole thing seems to get bigger and more elaborate each time. The sense of menace and foreboding grows.

My nightmares are persistent and seem to be getting worse.

Once the sun is finally up, I go out for a jog. Not my usual helter-skelter chased by zombies riding rabid hyenas run. A casual jog to get the blood flowing and clear the mind. Unconsciously, I find myself running a route near Soothsayer. It seems like as good a time as any to treat myself to a giant cappuccino. Misty, with sweat, I'm getting the stinky eyeball from the other patrons, but I ignore them.

Sometimes, it's nice to sit and stare out the window, sipping coffee and people-watching.

The tall paper cup is midline with light brown ambrosia. The foam has all dissolved into a milky haze on top. Is my cup half full or half empty? This motivational poster question has always perplexed me. Isn't it, by definition, both?

On the other side of the window, two men walk by. Something about them catches my eye. Both are wearing Knights of Saint George hats. I lower my eyes and look at the counter. It isn't likely they will look in the window, but I don't want to make eye contact with these guys and risk that they know me. Practically nobody in town knows me by sight, but for some reason, every one of these guys I bump into does. It's a little unnerving.

It's been a few weeks since the shooting at The Lantern. There is still a palpable sense of fear around town. It seems like there are fewer cars on the streets. Outside of the downtown area, many stores have temporarily closed. Locals seem to be living like prairie dogs, staying hidden and popping their heads out occasionally to scan the horizon.

But despite all that, tourist traffic seems to have barely slowed. Apparently, many people either haven't heard about the incident or simply don't care.

The Knights of Saint George are responsible for that shooting. I know it. I've slipped that tidbit to the police. But it doesn't seem like the KoSG fears any legal repercussions. I wonder why that is. I should probably ask my friend Chris about that at some point. Being a local police officer, Chris might have some insight.

Within seconds, the two men have passed by uneventfully. I take another sip of my coffee. People-watching has lost its appeal.

I take my coffee and check the time. I've only got an hour or so at this point before I am supposed to meet Genevieve for lunch. I down my coffee and run home to get cleaned up.

Lukas is a trendy sandwich shop located in what seems like an unlikely place. It is on one side of a little strip mall. There is plenty of parking in the lot itself. However, all the parking near Lukas is full, so I have to park near the supermarket on the other end of the lot.

People often wonder about the location of Lukas, the fancy sandwich shop in the strip mall.

I think when people imagine a popular place here in Napa, they envision something downtown. Something in the

Oxbow Market. Maybe something in Yountville or Oakville or one of the other quaint towns Up Valley. Something cute and old and modern all at the same time.

I think the strip mall placement is part of the appeal. It makes everyone that comes here think they've found an off-the-track local gem. Something that isn't aimed at tourists. Would a tourist trap be stuck between a big chain pharmacy and a pawn shop?

I can see the line has already stretched out the door and onto the sidewalk in front. I roll my eyes. I do not understand this place. I get out of my car and go park myself at the back of the line. Within five minutes, the line has doubled in length and is now blocking the entryway to the pawn shop next door, and I've only moved forward about three feet.

"Hi, Miles!" Genevieve says from behind me, breaking me out of my brooding stare in the pawnshop window.

I turn and look at her. She smiles at me, her face framed by long brown hair and her eyes hidden behind oversized sunglasses. Her outfit is what I can only describe as 'casual-tourist-dressy.' A bright blue sundress, a wide-brimmed hat, and sandals. It's the outfit that I've come to expect from women coming to Napa to go on a wine-tasting tour. She makes it look good.

I feel a little flush as I glance down at my own wardrobe. A black t-shirt that says 'Where the magic happens' and features Mickey as the Sorcerer's Apprentice performing a magic ritual complete with blood, candles, and demonic spirits rising from cracks in the floor. I've got on loose-fitting jeans, and my Chucks are untied. I am suddenly very aware that I threw on whatever was on the top of my dresser drawer.

"Hi, Genevieve," I say after a long awkward pause. "You look great."

"And you look…casual," she says, clearly amused.

"Yeah," I say. "Sorry, I…It's Saturday."

She smiles and nods, but there is a look of disappointment in her slightly downcast eyes.

"I'm sorry. I think I might have misunderstood something…was this a date? I mean, like a date-date?" I stammer out awkwardly.

"I was approaching it that way."

"Oh, um, I was not thinking of it like that; I kind of just wanted to talk shop," I stammer out miserably.

"Oh. Yeah okay. Keep it professional," she says, quirking a quizzical eyebrow once more at my attire.

"No, I mean. I don't mean I wouldn't want to go on a date; I didn't think you'd be interested. Ugh, I am making this awkward."

"I agree."

"How about this? I like your idea better. Can we start over and go with your idea?"

She sizes me up for a minute, then nods.

"Okay start over. But only because you're cute when you are foundering," she says. I feel my cheeks blush a little bit.

"There is a clothing store around the block. Give me a minute, and I'll get something better to wear."

"No, no. No need to do that. Besides, I think I prefer having this to lord over you a little more," she says, relaxing and smiling.

We stand in line and chat a bit. She lives in Portland, Oregon. She started her career writing pulpy sci-fi under a pen name. Now, when she's not writing non-fiction books about magical doomsday scenarios, she is a freelance journalist. She's written articles for a number of papers and online publications. I recognize more names than not. There is a break in our conversation, and we have just now broken the threshold of Lukas.

"This line is unbearable. Is the food worth it?" she asks.

"No. Honestly, I hate this place. It's so pretentious. And they didn't even bother to decorate."

"Then let's get out of here."

"Okay, where do you want to go?"

"Why don't you give me the Miles Ward tour? What's your favorite eats in town?"

"Tacos, Don Juan," I say. "It's a taco truck that parks over on Soscol most days. They have the best pastor."

"I love pastor! Tacos sound perfect."

"Are you okay leaving your car here? I can drive."

"It's a rental, so yeah, I don't care. I always pay for the loss-damage waiver, and I hate to see it go to waste. So do your worst, Napa!" she says. She has a jovial voice and seems to be authentically enjoying herself.

I walk with her to my car and quickly move a litter of empty coffee cups to the back seat.

"I might have a little coffee problem," I say apologetically.

"I've been known to overindulge in a latte or two," she says, winking.

"I think that we are going to be friends," I say as we climb into the car, and I start the engine.

The day passes in a blur. We have tacos. We get coffee.

I find that people visiting are often impressed when you have the hookup for free wine tastings. I want to impress Genevieve, so I take her on a tour of places where I know people.

We go to JMBaptiste Winery, where Charles gets us free wine. We get coffee. We go to Holzhom Winery, where Jeff gets us free wine. We go to whatever place my poker buddy Mike is working, and he begrudgingly gives us free wine. We get coffee. We go out to dinner at my favorite barbecue place, Smokeys. Then I get coffee, but Genevieve says if she has any more, she'll never sleep again.

I find myself talking a lot and oversharing. A voice in my head keeps telling me I am talking too much, but my mouth doesn't seem to hear it. Genevieve is funny and smart and a very good listener. I find that halfway through the day, I've told her pretty much everything about what's been going on. I hold back the stuff about the dragon Goldsmith and the prophecy of Jeff being the Bletshpah Amah. Otherwise, I tell her about Lorelei Redbrook, Circe, Hale, Shelly, everything.

Some part of my brain is whispering that I could be getting played here. That I'm telling her a lot, and I don't know her that well. But the rest of my brain is having too much fun to care. Before I know it, it's getting dark, and Genevieve and I are sitting in my car in a parking lot.

"You know what would make the perfect end to this day?" Genevieve asks.

"I'm not sure I could eat ice cream after all that barbecue."

She laughs.

"Rebobs."

"Rebobs? How the heck do you know about Rebobs?"

Rebobs are a local urban myth. The legend, as I was told, goes that in the 1950s, a scientist lived out at the end of Partrick Road. There, he had a secret laboratory in the basement of his home. He used it to perform experiments. Evil diabolical experiments. Tesla coils and bubbling vats and human cadavers kind of experiments. One of the products of his unwholesome research was the Rebobs!

Winged monkey creatures with terrible fangs and clawed hands. The story goes that the Rebobs escaped and murdered the scientist. Gobbling up his remains before flying off into the night.

Now, allegedly, Rebobs live in an old cemetery at the top of Partrick. There, they hunt their favorite prey, young people who drive up and park in the desolate place to make out.

"I like to read up on places I am going to visit. It came up in an internet search about myths and legends around Napa."

"Me too! I always research the local folklore of an area I am going to."

"Great minds think alike."

"Well, they are fake," I say.

"You think my great mind is fake?"

"No…I uh…"

"I'm teasing you. Rebobs are fake. I got it. But the cemetery is real," she says.

"Yes, but it's private, and they have it all fenced in. You can't even see it these days."

"Come on, Miles," she says with a little glint in her eye.

"What the heck."

"What the heck!" she laughs.

I start driving west.

Chapter Thirteen

WE CROSS town and head out Browns Valley Road until it turns north, and we continue west on Partrick. It is a quaint country lane for a little bit. As it climbs the hill, the road gets more narrow. There are an ever-increasing number of potholes. Soon, it's barely wide enough for a single car and bumpier than an antique rollercoaster. We pass fences and empty pastures where, during the day, cows and sheep graze.

In my headlights, a lone gate is revealed, and there are four snarling, growling dogs warning us away. I imagine the people that live out here hate the Rebob legend for drawing curious tourists and would-be cryptozoologists.

We go over the hill, and the road descends into a little hollow; trees loom over us, silent gnarled sentinels. It seems more like we are going through a tunnel than a wood. The road, if it can even be called that at this point, winds back and forth along the side of the hill. We drive in silence until we reach the end of Partrick Road.

The road ends abruptly, where it widens to branch off into gates leading into three different parcels of private property. I park to the side of the wide dirt turn-around, and we get out.

I motion to where, illuminated by the headlights, a section of chain link fence stands with barbed wire spooled along the top. There is a chain link gate built into the fence, locked with a chain and padlock. An angry-looking red plastic sign informs us to Keep Out! It makes me imagine a clandestine government facility more than an old family cemetery.

"Beyond this gate lies the hoary and ancient sepulcher, madam," I say in my best Vincent Price impersonation while dramatically bowing toward the gate.

Genevieve gets a sly look on her face and struts up to the gate. She pulls something out of her handbag and begins fiddling with the lock.

"What the heck are you doing?" I hiss at her.

"I'm picking the lock so we can get a peek!" she says in a fake whisper.

"What if we get caught?"

"We say the gate was open. I flash my credentials at them, and we make some stuff up. You are being overly paranoid. Nobody is going to come out here right now. If they do, nobody will care."

The lock pops off, and she opens the gate with a loud metallic screech that makes me cringe and look over my shoulder. But she's right; we are in the middle of nowhere. She returns her lock picks to her handbag and comes out with a large flashlight. The kind that is two and a half feet long and takes a half dozen D-cell batteries.

"That's a lot of flashlight."

"I'm a woman who asks questions for a living. Always need to have a backup plan," she says grimly, slapping the flashlight into her hand like a keystone cop's billy club. The light jumps and splashes around as she does, making me feel a little disoriented.

She seems to mostly write articles about fringe stuff. Exposés on UFO hoaxes, ghost sightings, and magic. Some of it is real, but most of it is bogus. People get pretty bent out of shape when you threaten their beliefs with reality. A lot of people into fringe stuff start out pretty fanatical. Thinking about it, I'm sure she's had to deal with some ugly crap in her line of work.

I don't know what to say about her burglary skills. That was a bit of a surprise. I shrug. My curiosity getting the better of me, I follow her in silence. I've been up to this gate before but never seen the Partrick Cemetery itself. We walk a short distance up a weed-enshrouded dirt drive to get to the cemetery.

The graveyard is smaller than I expected, a little family plot nestled in the trees. The stones are old and worn. It looks like it is maintained, but not regularly. Genevieve wanders around, looking at all the headstones while I stand quietly near the gate, straining my ears for the sound of an approaching car.

"Relax!" she says. "Come check this out."

I walk over to a gravestone. It's old and worn and can no longer be read. It has a row of scratches on it, like claw marks.

"It's why they fenced it off. People started coming up here and defacing stuff and playing pranks and getting a little out of control," I say.

"I read that this was like make-out point," she leans close and whispers. I can feel her breath on my neck, and it makes me feel warm in the cheeks.

"So I have been told."

"So there's tradition to uphold here?" she says. I realize she's flirting with me. I am very observant.

"That would be nice. I'm. I'm a slow mover, you know?"

I feel like I keep unintentionally giving Genevieve the wrong signals. She's smart, funny, and pretty. I am interested in her and frankly surprised that she's interested in me. However, I am feeling very exposed and vulnerable in this place.

I pause and look around at the darkened cemetery. Genevieve, standing there, the awkward feeling in my stomach. It all feels familiar, like I've done this before. Like I've been standing in this very spot talking to Genevieve before.

Not that I've been in a situation similar to this before, but that I've been in this exact moment before.

"Yeah?" she says.

I shake my head. "Sorry, *deja vu*."

Her brow creases a little. I am unsure if it is concern or confusion at my sudden statement. I try to recover from being derailed and move on from this odd feeling.

"Anyway, I feel like in our culture, men are always expected to go right for it. But every time I've done that, I end up wishing I hadn't. I like you, but I feel like…I don't know that if I jump right in on the first date, I'm going to over-invest myself and get hurt. So it's not a lack of interest."

"It sounds like you've been hurt before…" she says. She is going to continue, but we are interrupted by a loud squawking sound.

At first, I think it's a crow or something. Genevieve swings her flashlight dramatically up toward the sound, and there, crouched on a tree branch, is a creature the likes of which I have never seen outside of drawings or movies. The size of a small child with a roughly simian body, bat wings, and enormous claws. I've seen dozens of renditions of this creature when I was asking around town about the Rebobs. Some are hand-drawn, and others are carefully collaged together from digital pictures. All of them have done it justice. With only a glance, I know exactly what this creature is. Or at least what it is supposed to be but cannot possibly be.

From another tree on the other side of the plot comes another squawk, and then another from a different direction, then another. Genevieve swings the light in a circle around the clearing, and we are surrounded on all sides by a half dozen of them.

"I thought you said they weren't real," Genevieve says.

"They aren't," I grunt back. "Run for the car. I'll try to distract them."

"I appreciate the vote of confidence, Galahad, but how

about you run to the car, and I'll cover you. You have the keys after all, genius!" she says back.

Her sentence is punctuated with another series of cries or howls from the creatures as they dive from the trees. I turn to run and make it a half dozen steps before one lands on my head and starts batting at my ears. Another grabs my feet and trips me as a third hits me square in the back. I fall to the ground thrashing.

I can hear Genevieve grunting and a dull thud sound like someone hitting a water bed with a baseball bat. That is followed by the sound of a small body crashing into the brush. I manage to twist my head briefly to observe.

It's hard to see. Some light filters through the trees from my car's headlights. The brighter light is Genevieve's flashlight. Her light is careening around wildly as she's using the huge flashlight as a club. I see her strike another Rebob and send it flying like a rag doll.

Then I contort as the Rebobs on top of me raise its claws above my face and…begin to slap me mercilessly. I tense, waiting for the cutting pain, blood, and blindness from those razor-sharp claws hacking into my face.

It takes me a minute to realize that the claws aren't actually cutting me. It's like I am getting slapped over and over again about the head and shoulders with bundles of wet spaghetti. The one at my feet is desperately trying to slap me in the groin, but my hands have instinctively covered that area up. I fall to the ground, curl up fetal, and pull my arms over the back of my head as they stand in a circle around me, howling and slapping.

"You little bastards!" I hear Genevieve cursing and then a loud thud as one of the Rebobs attacking me gets batted away by a blow from her flashlight. I sit up just in time to see another go sprawling across the ground and melt into the shadows at the base of a headstone.

Something about it looks familiar, but my brain is too fogged with adrenaline to think it through.

The last Rebob looks at Genevieve and her enormous flashlight. Then, with a loud screech, it takes to the sky and flies off into the darkness like a bat. I sit up. Genevieve is standing over me. Her dress is torn, and her hair is tousled. She has a little bit of blood flowing from what looks like a bite mark on her arm. She puts the flashlight over her shoulder like a baseball bat and reaches one hand down to me to help me up.

"Your knight in shining armor is here to save you," she says, grinning.

"Did you stage that to impress me?" I say, "If so, it worked."

"I actually thought you staged it to impress me. I was going to say you know how to show a girl a good time."

"No, I'm serious. What the hell was that? I had nothing to do with it."

She looks pensive for a moment.

"I wanted to come out here and see Rebobs, and we came out here, and there were Rebobs. If you didn't arrange that somehow, then I can see how it might look like I did. But I didn't. I promise you I didn't," she says. I don't know Genevieve that well, but after spending the day with her, I believe her.

"Well, that means either someone is following us and trying to mess with us, or we happened to stumble onto something."

"The latter seems unlikely," Genevieve says.

"What do you mean?"

"Well, I don't know if you noticed, but you were basically getting a tickle-fest where the little fuckers were trying to bite me. So either Rebobs are naturally misogynistic, or you were being distracted, and I was being targeted."

I nod and think for a moment before responding.

"They are some sort of construct. They melted away when you hit them."

"Yeah, it was like they were made of water and sort of

turned back to water when they got smashed," she says. "Except there are no wet spots where they fell."

She shines her light across the places where the Rebobs vanished.

"Not water shadow. It's like they were made out of shadow," I say.

"I've never seen anything like that before."

"I have."

"Oh?"

"Yeah. Remember I told you about Circe the Hizarin? It looked like when she shadow-jumps."

"You mean you are being stalked by a jealous Hizarin?" she says. The only light is lighting the ground, so I can't see her expression. I can't tell from her tone if she's amused or concerned.

I shrug.

"It's a theory, but I hope not."

We sit there silent for a minute. Genevieve breaks the silence. "We should probably go."

"Yeah," I say, taking her hand and letting her help me up. She doesn't let go and keeps holding my hand as we walk back to the car, following the circle of light cast by her flashlight club.

Chapter Fourteen

I DRIVE BACK down Partrick Road. Genevieve and I ride mostly in silence. I'm still trying to reconcile the last five minutes with my own perceptions of reality. We come to a wide space on the road at the top of a hill. There are two cars with fogged-up windows parked by the fence there. One is a large, dark-colored older sedan. It makes me think of a teenager out on a date in their parents' old car. The other is a tiny little two-seater sports car, the make, and model unfamiliar to me. It looks brand new and expensive.

"Apparently, it's still make-out point," Genevieve says. I nod and grunt an affirmation.

On a clear day, you can see the San Francisco skyline from here. But the marine layer has already rolled in, and it's almost pitch black. We wind our way down the hill past this little lover's point and make our way back to town. I drive Genevieve back to her car, which is still sitting in the empty lot in front of Lukas.

"I'll follow you back to your hotel," I tell her as she gets out of my car.

"You don't have to do that."

"I'd like to. I'm a little shaken up after…whatever that was."

"Okay," she says and gets into her car. She doesn't seem shaken up at all. I follow her to her hotel. There is a moment when she turns onto Soscol that I think she might be going to the same riverfront hotel that I followed Circe to. That would be too much coincidence for me. However, she continues driving into the downtown and to one of the newer hotels on First Street. She pulls into the valet while I find a spot on a nearby side street.

We meet on the curb in front of her hotel. A cool, brisk fog hangs over the street.

"Do you want to grab a drink at the hotel bar?" she asks.

"I think I should get to bed. But what are you doing tomorrow?" I ask.

"Well, I need to get to the airport by two, but I could meet you for breakfast."

"I'd like that."

"Me too. How about here in the hotel restaurant? They have a brunch buffet that sounded edible," she says.

"Sounds like a date!"

"Good! Dress for it this time," she says with a wink. We stand there silent for a minute.

"Okay, I should go. I'll see you tomorrow," I say and start to turn.

"Miles," she interrupts me, "I had a great time. I mean it! This was the most fun I've had in a long time."

I smile, and she leans forward.

"Is this okay?" She whispers.

I nod, and she gives me a kiss on the cheek. My cheeks are warm, and I'm blushing a little.

"Thanks," she whispers.

"Thank you," I say as I jay-walk across the street, waving over my shoulder. I get to the far corner and turn to watch her turn and walk into the hotel.

In the car, my mind is racing. Being attacked by Rebobs was probably the most bizarre thing that's ever happened in my life. That is saying a lot.

Logically, everything about it makes me suspicious of Genevieve. She seems to get me a little too much. She seems unperturbed by being attacked by clawed flying monkeys. Either she was expecting it, or she is unshakeable.

It can't be a coincidence that she wanted to hunt Rebobs, and we happen to find Rebobs. Everything I've ever seen or heard tells me they are urban legends. All of it is very suspicious and weird.

My gut says I can trust Genevieve that she is actually unshakable. That she's the smart, pretty, funny lady that she seems to be and that something else is going on. Then my brain tells me that my gut is wrong a lot. But then my gut tells me that my brain is wrong a lot. Every part of me is technically correct. Useless ambivalence.

Ultimately, I decide to stay the course, keep my eyes open, and try to gather more information. I really like her, and I'd hate to throw that away because I'm overly suspicious. The adrenaline and excitement are wearing off, and the drive home is uncomfortable. I am grungy from rolling around on the ground and getting slapped by flying monkeys. A humiliation I am not sure I will ever live down.

At home, after my shower, I sit in bed. The intention is to do some reading, but I fall asleep before long and have a long and well-earned rest. The kind of rest one has when one's body and mind are both totally exhausted. I have no nightmares, and I wake up refreshed.

Rather, I wake up refreshed and annoyed at the sound of a large truck backing up outside my window.

My gummy eyes blink as I try to get my clock into clear view. It's eight in the morning. This is the latest I've slept in a long time. I'm supposed to meet Genevieve in half an hour, so I leap out of bed to start getting ready. I decide to look out the window to see what all the racket is about.

There is a large moving truck backing into our tiny little parking lot. A crew of three guys are guiding the truck up to the stairs. I watch for a minute as they park the truck, open the back, and start to discuss an unloading strategy.

This is not a new scene. Someone moves in or out of our apartment complex at least once or twice a month. The racket made by the truck is the only thing alarming about this situation.

I am about to turn away from the window when I see someone walk down the stairs and begin to talk to the movers. Normally, I wouldn't think much of this except that there is something familiar about this person.

She's a lanky, gangly teenage girl. She couldn't be more than fifteen. She's got her hair up into two pigtails and is wearing a long black kilt with chains on it, a red t-shirt with the sleeves torn off, and combat boots. It takes me a minute for the recognition to click, but it's the girl that Circe was walking with the other day. I can feel the small hairs rise on the back of my neck.

I hastily get dressed and, keep an eye out the window and watch the girl directing the movers toward the building. I walk window to window, watching them through the blinds, and discover that she is moving into Mrs. Saguaro's apartment.

Mrs. Saguaro was a nice old lady who lived in the next-door apartment and used to bring me bowls of *aji de gallina,* a dish she always made too much of when she had her family visiting. She moved out a couple of months ago. I was out of town at the time and never got to say goodbye or get another bowl of that delicious stew. Her apartment has had a 'For Rent' sign on the window since then.

I get myself all cleaned up and dressed. Then I keep watching out the window so that I can time bumping into the girl on the open walkway in front of my apartment.

"Oh hey!" I say as my apartment door slams behind me. "You must be the new neighbor."

"Hi," she says, looking a little defensive.

"I'm Miles. I live in the next apartment," I say. "Where are your parents? I'd love to bring them a housewarming gift."

I see her eyes narrow and her nose crinkle. I was more focused on trying to get information than actually thinking about what I was saying. That came out pretty creepy. I consider trying to apologize, but everything that comes to my mind makes it worse. Nothing says 'I am a creep' like saying 'I'm really not a creep.' There is a long and uncomfortable silence. Then, after a moment, her mouth falls into an ugly sneer. I can see her hands clench into fists slightly. I've put her in a bad mood.

"My parents live in fucking Ohio, and I'm twenty-three. I have a degree and a job, and now my own apartment. Jackass," she says petulantly.

"Oh!" I say, always ready to make a good first impression. "Sorry about that. You don't look a day over twenty-two."

"You look like a fucking creeper," she says.

"Well, aren't you refreshingly blunt?" I reply.

"Fuck yourself," she says, turning to walk away and flipping me off over her shoulder.

"And a good day to you!" I call after her. She vanishes down the stairs. I groan to myself.

"Real smooth, Miles," I mutter to myself.

Is she so prickly because I came off creepy? I certainly couldn't blame her. But I suspect that I caught her off guard introducing myself and that she threw up her prickly exterior to get some distance. I'm not going to let on that I know she is somehow working with Circe. At least for now, I think it will be easier if she thinks I'm ignorant.

When I get to the bottom of the stairs, she is directing the movers on where to put what furniture. I notice that she has quite a bit of furniture and it is all nice. This isn't the Ikea box unpacking that I expect from the first-time renter that she claims to be. She pointedly ignores me as I walk past her to my car. I get in and drive to meet Genevieve for breakfast.

When I arrive, Genevieve is already seated and sipping coffee. There is an extra mug, presumably for me. She waves me toward her table and starts pouring me coffee from a large carafe.

"Good morning," I say as I sit down at the table with her.

"Good morning! How did you sleep?"

"Well, I didn't wake up till eight, which is unusual for me. How did you sleep?"

"Fine for a hotel. I never sleep well in hotels. Which sucks because I end up staying in them quite a bit."

"Did anything weird happen this morning?" I say, "Because there was something weird at my apartment building this morning."

"No, I didn't notice anything. Why, what happened?"

"I mentioned that I saw that Hizarin, Circe, the other day walking with a girl. Well, the girl is my new neighbor! Which is too coincidental to be a coincidence."

"That's an oxymoron, but I understand what you mean."

"That's weird, right?" I ask for confirmation.

"Yes, that's weird. What do you make of it?"

"Well, if I were to guess, I'd guess that Circe is keeping tabs on me, spying on me. If we accept that as the case, then the theory that Circe summoned the Rebobs starts to hold some water."

She nods. "To what end?"

"What do you get when you cross an elephant and a rhino?" I ask, shrugging helplessly.

"I don't know what do you get if you cross an elephant and a rhino?"

"Hellifiknow."

She smirks at me. I can't tell if it's because she thinks I am cute and funny or it's because she wants to let me off the hook for my elementary school joke.

"But you are heading out today, so I'll deal with all that later. Right now, let's have a nice brunch," I say.

"Still technically too early for brunch, in my opinion, but yes, let's," she says.

So we get breakfast and spend the morning chatting,

trying to avoid the weirdness of the past day and focus more on getting to know each other better. It's pleasant, and I forget about all of the madness of my world for a few hours.

"Miles," Genevieve says, "I hope it's not prying too much, if I ask. How did you become a consulting apotropaist? I mean, that is unusual."

"Oh," I say. I tend to avoid talking about this mostly because I don't know that my story establishes credibility. In a world where people are obsessed with credentials and certifications, I think it is better to be mysterious than honest.

"Well, it's something I started in college. After I got out of college, I didn't have a lot of good job prospects. There was a lot of demand for people with basic computer literacy, so I worked in a call center doing tech support. The whole apotropaism thing was kind of like a side gig."

"You don't seem like the sort for sitting on the phone all day."

"Yeah, I hated it. I jumped from job to job and moved into network administration. Basically, the same thing but not on the phone."

"Here in Napa?"

"No, not initially, but then I got hired by a big corporate winery and moved here for the job. It didn't last long, and I got hired at a small family winery doing all their tech stuff. That was a weird job. I ended up helping out in the actual winery, moving barrels and doing pump-overs as much as I did the things I was actually hired for. Anyway, then there was this whole thing where the owners thought their house might be haunted. I offered up my services. It wasn't haunted, but their teenage kids were messing around in 'the dark arts.' I educated them and put some wards on their house."

"And?" Genevieve asks with a raised eyebrow.

"And they told some other people who contracted me on the side. They told some other people, and pretty soon, I had enough work as an apotropaist to keep me busy. I left the tech support stuff behind and made a full-time go of this."

"Do you regret the move?"

"Well, the pay is feast or famine. You know, I get a job here or there, and I have to make that pay the bills for months sometimes before I get another job. But still, it's better than tech support. It has its bad days, but at least it isn't dull."

"Oh!" Genevieve says, looking at her phone, "I lost track of time! I need to get going if I am going to get to my flight."

"Oh," I say. I can hear the disappointment in my own voice. "We should hang out again."

Is she trying to dodge out now? Did I say something that she didn't like?

"Yeah," she says, looking distractedly at her phone. "That'd be great."

We stand up, and she opens her arms out, inviting a hug, and I give her an awkward hug. Or at least I feel awkward about it. As I am about to pull away, she says, "Can I kiss you?"

"Um yeah," I say. I feel a warm rush to my head and am slightly dizzy. I'm confused, excited, terrified. In my head, my voice sounds very hesitant and unsure, which isn't what I am hoping to communicate.

She leans forward and kisses me on the mouth. There's no tongue, but it's still warm and intimate, and I feel like I can't breathe as I kiss her back.

"Bye, Miles!" she says as she disengages suddenly and flits away, leaving me standing speechless at the breakfast table. I feel like a heavy weight has fallen across my chest, and I am too weak to push it off. The truth is I am far more comfortable squaring off with a murderous warlock than I am with dating.

Chapter Fifteen

BACK AT MY APARTMENT, sitting at my desk, my mind is a whirl of thoughts. Happy, excited thoughts about Genevieve and how well that seemed to go. My excitement hangs in the balance with my generally suspicious nature and the fact that yesterday's Rebobs were improbably weird.

I'm unsure what to make of Circe's sidekick moving in next door. Behind all that, I'm concerned about what horrors I am going to have to deal with working with Lorelei Redbrook.

Eventually, the thinking is too much, and I need to distract myself. I try to read some more. I fail at that, and before long, I find myself sitting on the foot of my bed and playing video games on my game console.

Playing games for me is like hitting the pause button on life. It's a distraction so complete that I can lose hours. I can rarely tell you what happened in the game or what the game is about. It is frankly a joyless waste of time, but it is better than sitting in my apartment with nothing but my spiraling thoughts.

I get sucked in and miss lunch, and I'm starting to notice that my stomach is rumbling when there is a knock at my door.

I pause my game and go to the door. I open it without looking through the peephole, which is probably a habit I should get out of. Growing up, we never had a peephole or even kept our doors locked. We lived out in the woods 'off the grid,' and there was never a reason to lock the doors. People didn't come to your door. They'd get down the path and holler that they were there. By the time I was a teenager, my dad and I were always moving and never had anything worth stealing, so looking out the peephole was never a habit I got into.

Standing at the door is the girl that I have now categorized in my mind as Circe's sidekick. She's holding a fancy-looking bag that probably has a bottle of wine or maybe some distilled spirit in it.

"I wanted to say sorry," she says. "I was kind of a bitch this morning, and you were being neighborly."

"Oh, um, okay, apology accepted," I say. "I'm sorry if I came off creepy and condescending. I was trying to be neighborly and failing. I'm prone to put my foot in my mouth."

I'm honestly not entirely surprised by this change of attitude. It fits into the narrative I've been building about why she's here. Spying is much easier if you're on good terms with the person you are spying on. I suspect she had a plan for how that first exchange would go. I derailed that by uncomfortably introducing myself before she'd even moved in. She panicked.

In that regard, she does not seem like Circe, who always seems in control. I catalog this under useful observations about the girl.

"It's just these fucking movers? They didn't even get anything out of the truck before they broke shit. And yeah, they have insurance, but money doesn't buy memories, you know?"

"Yeah, that's a pain. I'm sorry that you have to put up with that," I say, trying to sound sympathetic. I've never been able to afford movers, and I always have had to move by myself. So usually, it's me, a car, a bike, and a duffle full of clothes. If it weren't for assemble-yourself furniture, I would still be sleeping on the floor.

"I'm Miles," I say and hold out my hand.

"Magdalena. My pronouns are she/her," she says and holds her fist out knuckles first. So I bump them.

"Good to meet you, Magdalena. Um, he/him. I mean, I use he/him, not that I'm trying to correct your pronouns," I stammer out. Oh boy, am I suave?

She laughs.

"Good to meet you, Miles."

"The pronoun thing is not how I was raised. It's a learning curve."

"I get it, you're old. But at least you are trying," she says, then continues before I can make the conversation more awkward. "As I mentioned before, I'm from Ohio. I recently got out of college and got a job here as social media coordinator for a winery. I don't know anybody in town, and I'm kinda freaking out. I can get a bit prickly."

She is suddenly very sympathetic. I think we've all had those moments when we were young and first getting out in the world. Honestly, I'd be eating her story up if I didn't suspect that it is, at least partly, bullshit.

"Yeah, that is hard. If you need anything, let me know. I know the town pretty well, and I can direct you where you need to go," I say, trying to sound chipper and helpful.

"Awesome. Mike, was it? Sorry, I know you just told me, but I'm absolute shit with names," she says. I don't believe that this was a mistake.

"Miles, Miles Ward. I am a consulting apotropaist by trade," I say. This is bait, and I am watching for her response.

She laughs.

"What's an apotropaist?" she says. I don't think I would notice if I weren't expecting it, but the question sounds rehearsed, like she is expecting to ask this question before I even tell her my profession.

"I make magic wards and protectives to interfere with or stop dark magic," I say as matter-of-factly as I can.

She laughs again.

"Dark magic, huh?" she says, sounding skeptical "Cool."

Again, it feels rehearsed to me, but in a way that if I were completely unaware, I don't think I would notice. Or maybe that's paranoid apophenia.

I take the bag from her.

"Thank you, but normally I think I'd be getting you a welcome-to-the-neighborhood gift."

"That's a sorry-for-being-a-total-dick gift," she says.

"I appreciate that, but not necessary," I say. "Anyway, welcome to the building. I hope you have an easy time settling in. Let me know if I can do anything for you. Now, if you don't mind, I have some post-apocalyptic mutants that aren't going to kill themselves."

She looks at me questioningly.

"I was in the middle of playing a video game."

"Oh sure, cool. Have fun. I'm sure I will see you around," Magdalena says.

"See you around," I say, waving.

I close the door and look into the bag. It's a bottle of wine, a Cab-Franc from a winery that I've never heard of. Coombsville appellation. Five years in the bottle. Not a cheap bottle of wine, but also probably not bank-breaking.

The wine goes in the cabinet where I keep all the wine that gets gifted to me. I pour myself a lunchtime bowl of cereal with milk and go back to binging video games.

It is late in the afternoon, and my doorbell is ringing once more.

Two unexpected visitors in one day; that is a record.

I pause my game and hop up from my bed. I smell myself and make a quick stop to throw on more deodorant before I answer the door. This time I think of looking through the peephole. I see Jeff standing outside.

"Come on in," I say, opening the door.

"No, I can't stay. I just had a quick question for you," Jeff says.

"Oh. Okay, what's up?"

"This might be weird, but like, what is the most powerful magical artifact you've encountered?" Jeff asks.

He's right. It is a weird thing to ask.

"Huh?"

"You know a magical tool or object? What's the most powerful thing?"

"Um, I don't know. Your Acetobacter Magi-whatever stuff is pretty impressive. Maybe that sword at Goldsmiths? Probably something at Goldsmiths."

"The stuff at Goldsmiths," he says flatly.

"Yeah, why are you interested? Is this some experiment with the anti-magic juice?"

"Yeah exactly."

"Well, I mean, you've got the Dragon's Favor. I'm sure Goldsmith would give you something for that. Who knows, maybe it's magic itself? That might be the most powerful magic I've encountered," I say, shrugging helplessly.

"The Dragon's Favor. Right. That's crazy that Goldsmith is a dragon."

"Yeah," I say. "Are you okay? You seem a little off."

"I'm fine. I've been working a lot. Crushing grapes. Fermenting stuff."

"Okay," I say, but I don't mean it. Something seems weird. "Are you getting enough sleep?"

"I've been pretty busy with work and, you know, everything else."

"You sure you don't want to come in? I could make you a cup of coffee?"

"No, actually, I should go. I have to get back to work."

"Oh," I say, "Okay."

Jeff gives a stilted wave and turns to walk away.

"Bye then," I say after him.

"Bye, see you later, Miles," Jeff says as he turns to go down the stairs.

From my doorway, I watch over the walkway railing as he takes the stairs down to the parking lot two at a time. He walks briskly across the parking lot, turns onto the street, and vanishes behind a hedge.

"Well, that was weird," I say out loud. I pause and wait for Hank's inevitable snarky comment, but it never comes.

The rest of my day is uninterrupted as I waste it playing video games.

Chapter Sixteen

IN MANY WAYS, not working on a contract while making it seem like you are working on a contract is harder than simply doing the work. I'm biding my time trying to make it seem like there is progress while I am mostly spinning my wheels.

I show my face at the Lantern construction site frequently but don't do anything. I send lots of emails asking for information and details that I don't actually need. I draw up lots of plans, then delete them and start over. I press ignore on a lot of calls from Lorelei Redbrook.

Fortunately, I am not the only one on this Lantern reconstruction that is doing this. Alphonse and his crew are in no rush to complete quickly either, so it's very easy to plod along. I spend my free time playing video games, going for bike rides, and texting with Genevieve.

On Wednesday, I get a call from the State Hospital informing me that I've been approved to visit with Shelly next week.

On Thursday, I get a call from Karen at Soothsayer that she would like me to go ahead with my proposal. I spend the rest of the week and the weekend implementing that. I make sure that all of my work is self-contained so I can start creating the small business package I envisioned. The work is smooth, and no more Rebobs show up to confound me.

Life is almost feeling normal. It's Monday, just over a week after Genevieve went back to Portland. I walk downstairs from my apartment at about seven thirty in the morning. My plan is to go get my morning coffee at Soothsayer and check in on the wards there. I climb into my car and yelp when I realize there is someone in the seat next to me.

Circe.

"Jesus Circe. You have got to stop doing that!"

She pouts.

"You don't wike surprises?" she asks in a weird, infantilized voice.

"No, I also don't like that voice. It's creepy," I say.

"Fine," she says, settling into her more normal husky tone.

"What do you want, Circe? You going to throw more Rebobs at me?" I ask. I'm going to need to reveal something if I want to get something.

"Rebobs?" she asks, looking genuinely confused, although I know from experience that she could stone-faced lie to her own mother about the circumstances of her birth and leave her mom questioning herself.

"Flying monkeys? Attacking me up on Partrick Road? Ring a bell? When they got squished, they got all shadowy the way you do when you do that shadow-jump thingy?" I fumble through an explanation.

Circe gets a dark look on her face. She looks genuinely put out.

"Not me. But I know who. I'll take care of it," she says.

"Morgan," I say, unsure why I didn't think of that before. "She's pissed at me for injecting her, and she's getting revenge."

"Morgan, yes. But that Morgan is dead," she says.

"Huh?" I ask, "Wait, did I kill her?"

"In a manner of speaking, yes, but no, not really. You need to understand how the Hizarin work."

“Isn’t telling me that against some kind of rules?”

“Yes,” she says, “But rules like men are meant to be tortured until they break.”

Well, that’s an upsetting and nonsensical twist on a common expression.

“Uh-huh.”

“You see how one becomes a member of the Hizarin is by apprenticing to a current member of the Hizarin. And then, when the apprentice thinks they are capable, they assassinate their master and take their place in the Hizarin. They take their name, their titles, wealth, etc. They take their life not only in the murder sense but in the sense of assuming their whole identity and persona.”

“Like the Dread Pirate Roberts.”

Circe looks at me with an expression I take to be confusion or maybe disgust.

"Morgan had an apprentice. When you took away all of Morgan’s magic, you made her apprentice’s job very, very easy. Maybe too easy.”

“Too easy?”

Circe's partner in assassination, Morgan LeFey attacked me and my friends a while back. Circe helped defend us against her for reasons I am still unclear on. I ended up injecting Morgan with a dose of magic-eating bacteria. I’m pretty sure that is what Circe is referring to. Apparently, she’s been replaced by a teenager.

“Well, honestly, I don’t think Morgan’s apprentice was anywhere close to ready to take her master's place, but here she is. Flying monkeys are a perfect example. Childish.”

“Oh,” I say, and I think for a minute. Circe sees that I am thinking and waits for me to catch up. I’m trying to figure out why Magdalena would send Rebobs after me.

“So.” I ask as a way of redirection, “Do you have an apprentice?”

“I’ve had dozens of apprentices. They all made their move before they were ready. Poor dears,” she says as if she were talking about children who had stomach aches from eating too much candy instead of sorcerers whom she murdered.

"So the new Morgan wants me dead?"

"No, I don't think so. You're still breathing. She isn't her master's equal by any stretch, but I don't think she'd have a problem with you."

Gee, Thanks.

"Well, I mean, I took care of the old one just fine," I say.

"They might be master and apprentice, but they have very different approaches to their work. The old Morgan was very Machiavellian. Her replacement more…direct," Circe says, and she quickly puts her forefinger to my head with her thumb cocked up like the hammer of a gun. She drops the thumb and says, "Pow."

"Oh," I say. I'd already picked up from Circe that the Hizarin weren't above using conventional tactics for assassinations.

"You're pretty good at dodging spells, I'll give you that, but it wouldn't help much if this Morgan wants you dead," Circe says. "I think she's toying with you."

"Why?" I ask.

Circe shrugs.

"Probably because she can," Circe says. "Kids. Am I right? Don't worry. I'll have a talk with her."

"Why don't I find that terribly comforting?"

Circe shrugs again.

"I'd be happy to comfort you, Miles, if that's what you need," she says once more, putting on the vamp routine, but honestly, she doesn't have her usual level of commitment to the bit.

"I'm good," I say. "But enough about her, Circe. Why are you here?"

"Oh. I heard you were looking for me. Your friend has been asking a lot of questions, poking his nose in a lot of places. So I figured I would save you the trouble and come see what you need."

"Redbrook," I say. "She didn't die."

"I know," Circe says. She has a kind of smug tone to her voice.

When I last encountered Circe, she claimed that she had killed Redbrook. She claimed she did so to prevent the Dominium Dolores from publicizing themselves and bringing monsters and sorcerers into the limelight. But since I now know the first part isn't true, I have to question the second part as well.

"Weren't you supposed to have killed her?"

"Yes," she says. "That's actually why I am here in town. I'm looking for a partner."

She's once more shifted into making it sound suggestive.

"Don't you have Morgan?"

"Yes, I suppose I meant we are looking for a partner, Morgan and I."

So, while she is working with this new Morgan, she doesn't see her as an equal or a part of her team. She also doesn't seem to have gotten along particularly well with the previous Morgan LeFey.

"Well, I was hoping you might have some insight into how to stop her," I say. "I'll help you, but we do it my way, no killing."

"Presumptuous. And no. If and that is a big if I accept your help, we do it my way," she says, her tone shifting to one of absolute authority.

"Why should I trust your way? We did that last time, and it seems like it came closer to killing me than her."

"Nonsense, besides, you owe me. Remember? I helped you deal with the Lamia, and you owed me a favor."

"No, I don't! You never came through with your part, Circe! Redbrook is still alive and kicking. I don't think I owe you anything."

She shrugs and starts to open the door. She's bluffing; I know she is. If she were going to leave, I think she'd make her usual exit of vanishing when I blink instead of this slow, dramatic exit from the car. Part of me thinks I should let her walk away. But that leaves me running out of time with no idea of what to do next.

Shit.

"Fine, but why all the theatrics?" I ask.

"Because Miles, it's more fun this way," she says wickedly as she closes the door again.

Great, that's reassuring.

"Okay, but we are even. Once we are done with Redbrook, we are done. None of this 'you owe me' bullshit. You leave Napa, and you don't come back." I say, moving my hand between us to indicate that we are through.

She shrugs and sticks her lower lip out into a contrived pout.

"We'll see," she says and winks at me.

I turn forward, depress the brake, and push the button to start my car.

"I have places to be," I say, and I turn to face her, but the passenger seat is empty.

"I am getting pretty sick of that," I mutter to myself. I'm eager to talk to Russ about this exchange with Circe, so I start driving in that direction.

Russ doesn't have a normal voicemail but an old-fashioned answering machine with a tape and everything hooked up to his phone. I leave him a quick message, but I don't expect he will get it before I get there; he seems to only check his messages once a week.

Again, I have to park a block away and walk to his house because there is no street parking available. I make my way up his walk, weaving between garden gnomes and ducking dream catchers. I knock on his door. The doorbell is still broken. I'd ask him how long it has been broken, but I am worried the answer might be that it's been broken longer than I've been alive.

A few minutes later, Russ answers the door in a bathrobe. He's sweaty.

"Hi, Miles. Is this an emergency?" Russ says, a little out of breath.

"Um. Not as such, I had a question."

"Come back in an hour. I'm having some private time with the old lady, if you know what I mean," he says and winks at me.

"Eww man, why'd you answer the door?"

"You know what, dude, make it two hours."

"Nevermind. I don't need to know anything. I'll see you later!" I say and hurry back to my car, nursing a valuable lesson in not dropping in unannounced.

I drive down to Grape Reads. Emily is just opening up the shop when I arrive.

"Hey, Em," I say as I walk in through the door.

"Hi, My!" she says in a sarcastic retort.

"You prefer Emily?" I ask.

"Do you prefer Miles?" she asks, winking at me. Ever since we decided not to date, she's been a lot more snarky with me. But it also feels more open and friendly. It's different, but actually, I think that it probably worked out for the best.

"Fair enough. How are you this morning, Emily?"

"Another day, another dungeon."

"Huh?" I ask.

"Obscure book reference. Never mind. You make any headway on the whole Redbrook thing?"

"Slow and steady wins the race, right?"

"So that is a 'no.'"

I sigh, and we stand there for an awkward moment.

"Oh, guess who showed up in my car this morning?" I say, breaking the silence.

"Was it a dead body?' she asks. "Former President Jimmy Carter? No? A werewolf, was it a werewolf?"

"None of the above."

"Was it an ancient vampire assassin that belongs to a mysterious and eldritch order of monks?" she asks.

"How did you guess?"

"Who else randomly shows up in your car when you aren't expecting it?"

"Fair point."

"What did the illustrious temptress have to say?"

"Not tempted, but apparently, the Hizarin have apprentices who only get into the order by assassinating their teacher. And by weakening Morgan, I set her up to be assassinated by her apprentice, and so now there is a new Morgan. Their names, it seems, are actually titles. The replacement looks like a sixteen-year-old girl, says she's twenty-three, but I suspect she might be a touch older than even that," I say.

"Wow. That's something," Emily says. She slides behind the front counter and starts writing something down.

"Oh, and this new Morgan is now my next-door neighbor."

"Busy week."

"Yeah, that's not half of it. Anyway, Circe has agreed to help deal with Lorelei Redbrook, but she insists we do it 'her way,' which has me a little nervous."

"Her way?" Emily asks, "See, that sounds reckless."

"Yeah," I say. I'd like to have a witty quip at Circe's expense, but that was the best I could come up with. We sit in silence for a while as my brain fails to find humor.

Emily sort of grunts to break the silence.

"What does she want you to do next?" she says.

I sigh and shrug.

"I don't know. She agreed to help. Well, I think she did. Now that I think about it, she was kind of vague. Then she vanished. I guess I should keep on keeping on and wait to see when Circe shows up again. I am not sure what her game is exactly. She says she wants to help, but she's got the new Morgan spying on me and apparently attacking my date?" I say, which feels a little awkward for me to say to Emily, considering. But this friend thing isn't going to work if I get awkward, so I plow forward.

"Oooh. A date?"

“Yeah, it sort of just happened. A journalist I met a while back. Genevieve Gale.” I say.

“Oooh! Genevieve Gale! You mentioned that you’d met her at a conference or something. Solved a fake murder?”

“Yeah.”

Emily makes a little squee sound that I did not see coming.

“She’s epic! I’m so jealous! I want to date Genevieve Gale!” Emily says. I think she's trying to be funny, but I feel myself blushing a little.

“Does Jeff know?”

She shrugs. “We haven’t gotten around to discussing our free passes yet,” she says with a quirky smile.

We both laugh.

“I’m happy for you, Miles. That’s great. She sounds like the kind of adventurous person who might be able to tolerate living in the nebula of chaos that is your life,” she says. It sounds friendly, but there is something to her tone I can’t place. Is it sadness? Regret?

“You wanted to get away from the chaos,” I say, “But you’re still right here in it.”

She bites her lower lip and then shrugs.

“So, where did you go on your date?” she asks, making a concerted effort to change the topic. I’m not going to press the issue.

“Tacos, got coffee, went wine tasting, got more coffee, went out to dinner, got some more coffee.”

“Is coffee a metaphor for something?” she asks slyly.

“No, it’s just coffee.”

“Well, it sounds like you had fun,” she says, “and a lot of coffee."

“Then she wanted to go up Partrick Road, and we got attacked by Rebobs.”

Emily laughs until she snorts. She looks at my face and bites the laugh back. It takes her a little bit to get control.

“You got attacked by Rebobs? Is that a metaphor?” she finally says when she can catch her breath.

"Yeah. We went into the old Partrick Cemetery. They flew out of the trees and attacked us. Thankfully, Genevieve made the all-stars in flying monkey bashing."

"Oh, you're serious?" she says. "Rebobs aren't a real thing."

"I don't think they were really Rebobs like in the story. I think they were some sort of…construct?"

"What do you mean? How's that possible? It doesn't make any magical sense. The amount of energy it would take to do something like that…unless, I guess, you actually ritually fused wings to a monkey. But how would you get them to attack? I guess you could enthrall them, but…" she is sort of babbling. Her eyes are downcast. I can see she's lost in her head, figuring out how one could create such a thing.

I agree with her; magically speaking, it is improbable. The logistics to make it work are mind-boggling. It would take months, and I can't imagine a way to get a reliable result. Obviously, neither can Emily.

"I have a theory, but I want to run a few things by Russ first to test the validity of my hypothesis and figure out how to test it."

Emily nods, still lost in thought.

"Anyway, I came by to say hi and kill some time while I wait for Russ to finish his…um business."

Emily is completely lost in thought now. She nods again.

"I have something I want to check. Do you mind?" she suddenly looks up from her reverie.

"Um. I guess not."

"Cool, can you stick around?" she asks.

"Actually, I should probably get running if that's okay. I'll try to come back later. If that works for you?"

"Yeah, that's great," she says, still very distracted. She turns and walks away toward the back room. This is a little weird. I've never seen Emily like that before; she completely checked out the minute she started trying to figure out the Rebob thing.

I turn to walk out the door at the same time that Ren is walking in.

"Hi, Ren," I say to them.

"Hi, Miles."

"Emily just stepped into the back room to look something up, I think."

"Oh," Ren says, looking confused. "Okay. I guess I'll cover the register then."

Ren looks slightly annoyed as they put their backpack down behind the counter.

"All right, good to see you. Talk to you later, Ren!"

"Bye!" Ren says, clear annoyance in their voice, "I'll clock in and stand here by myself, I guess."

I bustle out the door, leaving Ren looking huffy behind the counter. I get the sense this isn't the first time they've been stiffed and left covering for Emily. I begin to wonder if Emily has been blowing off work and spending time in the back room doing research.

Another stop at Soothsayers. I wander downtown with a cup of coffee and look in all the shop windows. It feels like there is a constant turnover as shops open fail to make enough to afford the outrageous rental prices and close. After a few cycles of that, they all seem to turn into wine bars and tasting rooms.

Finally, with another hour of loitering under my belt, I decide I've given Russ enough time.

Now Russ answers the door, fully dressed and looking very satisfied with himself. I try not to let my imagination get carried away.

"Come on in, man, come on in," he says.

I follow him into his house, and we sit down in his study.

"The best thing about having both the kids out of the house? Nooners, man."

"Too much information, Russ," I say. "I have a question about dream walking stuff."

"Shoot, man."

"So in the dream lucid dreaming, you can build things, right?"

"Yeah, man, easy peasy. The first lesson you know once you awaken is building your own *reva fortikaĵo. Your* dream fortress. It's like a place you can store all your dream stuff while you are awake. It also, like, um, protects you. Sort of."

"I see. Can you make creatures?"

"Yeah, yeah, man, lesson two. The *Cicerone,* it's a dream guide. First, you make it a…well, a body for lack of a better term, and then you invite a *volo* to it. A dream essence like, an um…like a familiar spirit. My *Cicerone* is named *Virĉevalo,* and in my dreams, he looks like a huge mastiff-man."

"Like a dog person?"

"No, like a huge mastiff. Comma. Man."

"Oh, Okay. So it is also possible to make a gate into the dream a passage between reality and the dream?"

"Oh, oh, okay, man, like I see where you are going with this amigo, and I mean, yeah, in theory, you could open a gate to let your *Cicerone* out, but…"

"But what?"

"But, like, there's a lot of problems with that. See. Um. How do I put this…It doesn't belong here. It doesn't have a place here. In order to give it a place, you'd have to displace something else. Like to bring it out, you have to swap it with something living of equal…*pezo,*" he says.

"*Pezo*?" I ask.

"It means like weight? But it's kind of like…I don't know. Um. Well, yeah, it's like weight but not in terms of mass weight but like…gravity. Yeah, it's spiritual gravity, man."

"So if I made a flying attack monkey in the dream, I'd have to send something into the dream in order to summon the dream monkey? What would that look like?"

"I don't know, I mean. That sounds like a lot of *pezo* to me," he says. "Probably like a squirrel or an actual monkey or maybe a small child?"

"I see. Is it possible to not bind a *volo* to your construct but to, I don't know, like make it a puppet? Like a homunculus but from dream stuff instead of like stitching together flesh?"

"A homunculus?" He says, pausing to ponder. I am about to explain in more detail when he erupts, "Oh! Homunculus got it a meat puppet."

He runs his fingers through his wispy beard and stares at the ceiling for a moment before continuing.

"Um. Well, I would have said no a few weeks ago, but actually that Phantasmagoricon discusses doing exactly that. It sounds like hard. Like super hard," Russ says.

The Phantasmagoricon, I've photographed the entire thing. I keep meaning to read it, but the handwritten journal on Dreamwalking is so sprawling, so confusing, and so poorly written that I haven't been able to bring myself to read it.

"But not impossible."

"Nothing is impossible...y'know, theoretically," he says. "But it sounds like you got something more than theory on your mind."

"Yeah. I got attacked by Rebobs last week."

Russ laughs. This seems to be a common trend.

"Rebobs are an urban legend, man."

"Yeah, that's what I thought, too, but it happened. The thing was, when they got smacked into the ground, they kind of...I don't know, like melted into shadows. It reminded me of something. It took me a while to figure out what, but it's exactly what it looks like when Circe shadow-jumps. That got me thinking. What if the reason you couldn't find Circe is she doesn't actually exist...she's a dream construct that gets put out into the real world?" I conclude.

Russ ponders this in silence for a minute. He scratches his chin, paces over to an electric piano in the corner, and plays a little tune. I sit and watch silently.

"I mean, man," he says, "That is a solid theory. But theory is just like, you know, theory?"

"That's what I thought. There are so many things about

her that don't make a lot of sense, but what if that's because the Circe we interact with is a…dream puppet?"

"I'm not saying it's a bad theory," he says. "But it isn't science without experiment…"

Russ takes one of his interminably long mid-word dramatic pauses. I restrain myself from clawing at my face with impatience.

"…tation."

"Agreed, but what kind of experiment could we do?"

"The first thing that comes to my mind, man, dream trap," he says and gives me a double thumbs up.

"Dream trap?"

"Yeah, Um. It's like. How do I put this? You sympathetically link a place in the dream with a place in reality with, like, you know, like, um. What's the word? You know it's like a thing that represents a thing but isn't the thing, but it can be used in place of the thing?"

"Um…" I squint at him. "Like a symbol?"

"Dude! That's it, like symbolically associate them, and then once they are ritually linked, you create an inclusive circle in reality, and you build a *sonĝkaptisto* like a dream trap in the linked place in the Dreamtime. It's like Bob's your uncle, man. Not super hard. I have it set up like that with my *reva fortikaĵo*."

"I don't understand half of what you said, but whatever. So there is a trap in the real world and a trap in the Dreamtime, and you link the two, so jumping back and forth takes you from one trap to the other?" I ask.

"Yeah, man. So she gets trapped in the circle in the real world cause a dream construct would have to follow the flow of the Ley and so couldn't leave an inclusive circle. And then, once trapped, she's gonna obviously try to shift into the dream. Shadow-jump. Is that what we are calling it?"

"That is what I've been calling it, yeah."

"Cool, so, then she shadow-jumps, and then she's in the

dream. She'll get trapped, right? Her dream construct will be trapped and her *Pneuma* within it," he says triumphantly.

"Which, of course, only works if what she is actually doing is jumping into and out of the Dreamtime."

"That's why it's called an experiment, dude."

"If I understand correctly, for this to work, we would have to know when and where she was going to appear. She seems to come and go whenever she likes."

"We don't need to know the when, man. We need to know the where. We can set it up for basically, you know, whenever."

"Okay. I suppose that is true."

"What happens if she is not this dream construct we are hypothesizing?" I ask.

"Um, well, she wouldn't get trapped in your circle, man, so she could walk right out. If, for some reason, she jumped into the dreaming right like inside the circle, then she'd be trapped in the dreaming, but she could probably just, you know, jump back and walk out."

"So if she gets trapped, she's a magical construct."

"That's right, my dude."

"So we have to figure out somewhere that she's likely to show up."

"Yeah, man, like when she visits, where does she show up?" he asks. "Like in your bedroom or…"

I ignore his innuendo. I think for a moment before responding.

"No, she never appears in my apartment. In fact, she has never shown interest in going into my house," I say, ashamed of myself that I hadn't noticed that before. She always keeps me so uncomfortable with her cheap come-ons and constant sexual innuendo that I never think about inviting her to my place.

"You have like a lot of wards on your place, right?"

"Yeah, like doomsday-preppers-call-me-paranoid quantities."

"I am gonna bet, dude, that a construct could not cross

that barrier. Everything you got that shunts the magic out, it'd shunt the construct out too."

"Okay, she's approached me at my old Jeep. Once outside my apartment. Once on the street. Again in my old Jeep," I say, counting on my fingers. "The time on the street was near my Jeep. She appeared in The Lantern, which is warded but not in the same way as my apartment Jeep not present. At Emily's and...in my new car,"

"So she likes scaring you in your car, dude. That is what I am hearing."

"Yeah, that's what I am realizing too. Actually, this might not be a bad idea. If we link a point in the dreaming with a point in the real world, can the point in the real world move?"

"Course, man, time, and space are like fluid. The oneness of the universe doesn't know the difference," he says. I have no idea what he means, but he seems certain, so I am going to work with it.

"Okay, so we ward up my car. You do your dream mojo. We do your ritual to link them, and...the next time Circe jumps into my car, she's stuck...maybe. But how do we check the trap? If she is that skilled a dreamer, she might be able to break your cage."

"That is a good point, man," Russ nods to himself for a moment. "Okay, I got it. I will leave my *Cicerone* to watch the cage. If Circe appears, he will stay hidden, and next time I am in the Dreamtime, I ask him."

"I guess that sounds workable. Just tell me what I need to do."

Russ has me pull my car into his garage for us to work on it. We spend the afternoon putting hidden modifications around my car, warding it to keep Ley energy in and linking the car to a space in the Dreamtime.

I do not understand the later process at all, and it seems like mumbo jumbo, but Russ has earned my trust at this point. His wife Cathy seems awfully supportive of us, considering we spend the entire day making a huge mess of their garage. She even comes to offer us some green tea and biscuits at one point. Cathy seems almost the antithesis of Russ; she's well-spoken, polite, poignant, cogent, and doesn't say 'dude' or 'man' once.

It's late evening when we finish all the work. By the time we are done, we each have bandaids on our arms and hands. Neither of us, it turns out, is particularly skilled at mechanic work. Luckily, it made getting blood to activate all the rituals a whole lot easier. Exhausted and never wanting to look at my car again, I thank Russ and Cathy and head home.

Chapter Seventeen

I AM BACK in the house. The giant labyrinthine snarl of corridors and rooms and doors. On each door, there is a lock, an intricate puzzle or riddle or mechanism. I walk from door to door to door. I solve each puzzle in turn. Time does not exist in this place. I spend an eternity finding the solution to a puzzle, but I pass through each door only seconds later.

I have a feeling of elation after each door opens, but I don't remember the previous puzzle by the time I get to the next. In fact, I could be solving the same problem over and over again, simply not remembering. Or caring. Door to door to door, I search and explore and solve. This is one of my favorite dreams.

Oh. I'm dreaming. That's good. I remembered. What's the next step?

I have to break out of the dream, become lucid and control it. Okay. I'm supposed to go door to door, solving puzzles. I won't.

So I sit down in the middle of the room I am in. A large puzzle door ahead of me. A minute passes. Another. A third minute. Okay. I guess that did it, right? What's the next step? Break out of the dream and control it, and then.

Find The Door.

Shit.

I am in a house. Is it a house? A castle? I'm in some kind of structure filled with doors; it's pretty much all doors and locks. How do I find The Door among all the others? If I do and I open the door, how do I know that isn't the dream also and that I never actually broke out? Well, this is infuriating.

So what's next?

"Oh, come on, do something!" Hank says.

Hank is behind me, looking down over my shoulder. He looks like he did back before I met Lorelei Redbrook. Before he melted.

"What?" I ask.

"Just do something seriously, like literally anything. Find something that doesn't work," Hank says.

"Oh. Um. Okay," I say, and I stand up. Something isn't right.

I walk forward, and I come to a door, then another door, and another, passing through each like before.

"That place, the place you are running from, that place you won't look at. That's where you need to go," Hank says.

"I don't know what place you are talking about."

That's not true. I do know the place he is talking about. It's a black empty spot behind my eyes, a place I am not supposed to go to. A place I am not supposed to even think about. And I don't want to go there. He's asking too much. I can't go to that place. But then I hear Hank's voice whispering deep inside my brain.

"You can do this. There is nothing to fear there," he whispers over and over again.

Eventually, I listen to his voice. Eventually, I believe it. I turn slowly as if each second were a lifetime and each lifetime filled with more seconds in an infinite fractal spiral.

And there behind me is a door. It's barely a door. It's not much more than a piece of plywood and some hinges. There's a large hasp on it and a lock hanging from the hasp.

The lock is huge. On the lock is a dial with numbers zero

through nine on it. I try my puzzle-solving magic and twirl the code numbers around. But it doesn't open. I fiddle and play with it for a while, and I do not manage to open it.

I'm stumped. I step back and look at the door more closely. I see there is a carved wooden gargoyle head on the lintel above the door. The carving and the lintel weren't there a second ago. I blink. The door is no longer plywood. It's big and sheathed in red velvet.

And it isn't a Gargoyle carved into the lintel. It is Lorelei Redbrook.

"No. It's not Lorelei Redbrook," Hank says from behind me.

"That is definitely Redbrook."

"Redbrook is an identity, a mask, Miles. Take off the mask."

"Lamia?"

"Now you're getting somewhere," Hank says.

"You think that is the password?"

"She's that arrogant. Couldn't hurt to try."

"Well, actually, it might…" I say.

I look back at the dial. There are only numbers, no letters.

"Okay, but there are no letters," I say.

Hank stares at me, brow furrowed, one eyebrow quirked up. His expression clearly communicates that he thinks I am an idiot.

The dial looks like an old-fashioned rotary phone dial. Oh, maybe the numbers match with letters like on phone keys! I reach into my pocket for my phone. But I don't have one.

"I guess I can figure this out…let's see, I think it skips the one and starts on the two. There are three letters on each key. Except there are four on the nine key. Zero is for the operator, so…" I say, counting on my fingers and drawing up an image of a phone pad in my head.

Hank taps a foot and crosses his arms impatiently.

"Five…Two…Six…Four…and two," I finally manage.

I rotate the dial till my finger is pointing at the five and release. It makes a clicking-clunking clatter as it trips it's way back to its original position with a ding. It wasn't making the ding before.

I dial two. Ding!

I dial six. Ding!

I dial four. Ding!

I reach my finger toward the two to finish the combination…

And I wake up lying in my bed. My alarm clock is going off. Was I Dreamwalking, or was I dreaming? I don't know.

I sit up suddenly. Epiphany!

"Holy smokes!" I say, "I think I know the code to Redbrook's secret door."

Chapter Eighteen

I DON'T KNOW how I know that this is the code to Redbrook's secret door in The Lantern. I also don't know why I just said 'Holy Smokes!' like some cartoon prospector. I know it, and I said that.

I can't help but wonder if someone is helping me, feeding me this information in my dreams. Somehow. I know that Russ was babbling on about the gestalt of the universe and the collective unconscious.

If I accept his perspective, which I am not certain I do, I don't see how, out of all the motes of thought in the universe, I'd manage to pull that one by accident. As certain as I am that this is the code, I am certain that someone or something is pulling my strings on this one, feeding me information. One doesn't get other people's passwords in their dreams by happenstance.

Just because I think it was fed to me doesn't mean I am not going to use it. I think it's good to know when someone is jerking your chain, even if it's getting jerked in a direction that you want to go.

I check my calendar on my phone. Today is a busy day. I add one more item to the agenda. This morning, I am going to The Lantern to see if I can sneak into that secret room, and this afternoon, I have an appointment to visit Shelly at the state hospital.

I shower and get dressed. I make myself a cup of coffee. It's not good, but I drink it anyway because it's coffee, and I love coffee. Even bad coffee. I brush my hair and teeth and generally try to pretend to be a normal, functional human being.

I then go out for my morning ritual of good coffee and a scone at Soothsayers. Satisfied with my caffeination level, I head to The Lantern.

At The Lantern, Alphonse and his crew are getting going. Most of them are still sitting around and drinking coffee and staring at the building. Its exterior is even more skeletal now. All the siding has been removed from the first floor. Wires and pipes hang between exposed beams like veins and sinew, and plastic tarps flap in the breeze like flayed bits of flesh. I hate this place.

I wave to Alphonse, and he waves back. I make a questioning face and wave my hand around. Non-verbally asking, 'Is that jackass lawyer here?'

Thankfully, Alphonse is better at charades than I am. He seems to know what I am asking without issue. He shakes his head from side to side, slowly indicating 'no' and giving me the thumbs up. I give him the thumbs up back.

I get a hard hat from the back of Alphonse's truck and head into the building. It is different now. All the furniture has been removed. There is no flooring; I am walking on the exposed subflooring. It's totally empty. It does not look like the same place at all.

I take a moment to examine the project. I'm stunned by the amount of work being done. I see that they are reinforcing the framing with steel beams.

Wondering what that is all about, I make my way upstairs. The upstairs now holds all of the furniture from downstairs stacked in it and covered in tarps. It's cramped and crowded, and navigating my way through is a little treacherous. A ten-foot stack of chairs almost topples onto me, but I catch the keystone chair just in time.

Grunting, I strain to move a card table with boxes of glassware on it to clear the wall where the secret door is hidden. I remove the fake thermostat and type in the code 52642. I stare at it for a second and then press the '#' key.

There is a click, and the panel swings open. I pause and look over my shoulder. I'm alone in the room. I'm a little trepidious to enter suddenly. This all seems too convenient.

"In for a penny, in for a pound, Miles," I whisper to myself.

I take a deep breath and then slide inside and close the door behind me.

The lights automatically flick on when I come in. I can't help but wonder for a minute how they have power. I can't imagine they didn't turn the power off to this building for construction purposes. Maybe they have a separate circuit for the upstairs. I should ask Alphonse about that on my way out.

Inside is an office. There is a large, expensive-looking wooden desk. An enormous throne-like office chair and some bookshelves. Sitting on the desk is a row of monitors and a keyboard. A steel file cabinet with a prominent and industrial-looking lock on it is in the corner by the door.

I slip into the chair behind the desk. The CPU is in a cabinet on one side of the desk. I note a large backup battery behind it. Maybe this whole room is on a backup battery.

I touch the mouse, and the four monitors all spring to life. The computer is asking for a PIN. It can't hurt. I enter 52642 again, and the computer unlocks. Apparently, being hundreds or maybe thousands of years old doesn't make one savvy about computer security.

There is a lot going on on this computer. I click through some files and find spreadsheets for The Lantern's finances. I find files that I think are tracking personal debts, but there are no names or any words at all, for that matter. They are filled with columns of clients referred to by number, dates, and dollar amounts. Without context, it has almost no meaning other than to reflect that there are some people who owe her a lot of money.

There is an app called MonitorPro. I open it up, and it shows me live feeds of security cameras all over the building. Most of them are currently offline, but they all have labels. I notice that there were even hidden cameras in the bathrooms. Sketchy.

I start to feel antsy about how long I've been sitting in here. I don't need to be found here mucking with Redbrook's secret office computer. So I take a memory stick out of my courier bag and stick it into the CPU. I start copying the entire drive over.

While that is copying, I get up and check out the filing cabinet. It is heavy. Too heavy to move. It's too heavy for me to even shift or slide at all. A small label on one corner reveals that this is in part because it is fireproof. The lock is serious, not the flimsy little lock you get on your standard office cabinet that basically anyone could force with a pocket knife. This would require a cutting torch or the key to get into this cabinet.

I check on the computer. The copying isn't going nearly as fast as I would like. I rifle through all of the desk drawers. I pull them out and flip them over, but no key, no secret compartments, no hidden notes, and no smoking guns.

I rifle through everything else I can think of. Under the mug full of pens on the corner of the desk. Under the rug. I even check to see if there's anything taped to the underside of the chair or desk. Nothing but some old dried gum under the desk.

Eww.

Finally exasperated, I sit back in the oversized office chair and lean back. I sigh and take in the room. I realize now that I had tunnel vision when I walked into this room. I was so focused on the computer and the filing cabinets that I did not look up.

The top of the wall in this room is circled with taxidermy animal heads. Normally, taxidermists put creatures into fierce or intimidating poses. Probably to make them seem like the trophies of some brave hunter who faced a fearsome beast. These animals' faces are all contorted into looks of panic or pain.

It is both strange and hideous. Directly across from the chair I am sitting in, a wild boar's head is contorted so that it looks like it is yelping in terror. The glass eyes bugged out of its head. I sit staring at the bizarre oddment. Its mouth craned open, and its plastic tongue curled upward like it's screaming in agony.

Who puts something like that directly across from their desk? Every time she'd look up, this was the sight that would greet her. I glanced at it once, and I never want to look at it again!

But that gives me an idea. Something so hideous I don't want to look at it. Let alone touch it.

I walk over to the boar's head and stand on my tippy-toes, craning my arm up so I can just get my fingers inside its mouth. Some atavistic part of my brain screams at me to stop to remove my hand to flee. I bite my lower lip and ignore the rising fight-or-flight response. Fishing around the plastic tongue, then underneath the tongue, I find a key.

Part of me is surprised.

Part of me is not.

Fear is the primary tool in Lorelei Redbrooks' toolbox. She assumes she inspires enough of it that no one would be stupid enough to dare break into her office. That no one would ever try to get into her private files. Besides, who would willingly put their hand into the mouth of that horrifying decoration?

She's obviously underestimated the stupidity of Miles Ward.

I take the key over to the filing cabinet and discover that it fits. I pop the lock and open the top drawer.

A brief scan through, and it seems like it's printed copies

of all of the files on her computer. Apparently, she doesn't completely trust technology. Each of the drawers contains records with no names or locations, just identifying numbers, dates, and dollar amounts. Leafing through, I find occasional obtuse notes scrawled in the margins. They are in a language that I now recognize as Ancient Greek.

The farther down in the drawers I go, the older the documents get. In the bottom two drawers, none of the documents are printed. Some of the newer ones are typed with an honest-to-goodness typewriter. While the oldest files are all handwritten ledger sheets. There are far too many documents to go through one by one, but a quick random sampling doesn't give any indication of where a key or ledger book to match names to numbers might be.

I take a few quick pictures of some of the documents. I start with both the newest and the oldest to get an idea of the range of dates I am looking at. The oldest in this cabinet date back to 1948.

I leave the cabinet open and check on my file transfer. I still have a few minutes to go. I sit in her giant office chair and think. I could erase her computer and destroy all her files. That might set her back a bit.

If I destroy these files, she might not be able to collect from at least some of the people that owe her. However, she will almost certainly know it was me that did it. I don't know what kind of consequences that will bring. Ultimately, I have no intention of helping her, and joining was a ruse to find out more information, which it looks like I have.

Destroying these files might slow her down, but she probably has backups somewhere else. I would have backups somewhere else. However, I remember Emily's assessment that she's not the brains of the operation.

Fortune favors the bold, they say.

In my experience, this is usually said by the few ignoring the mountains of human casualties who have boldly charged to their deaths for the fortunes of others.

The files are all copied onto my memory stick, which I stash in my bag. I restart the system into its BIOS mode and do a full secure wipe of the drive, copying random garbage over the drive many, many times. This should make it harder to use advanced techniques to restore data. That will take a while, but I can leave it going when I depart.

How to destroy the contents of the filing cabinet? I could burn it all, but that could go very poorly. We have enough problems with fire as it is. It's not safe to start a fire, not even in a fireproof safe.

I look around the edges of the room. It is, as I suspected, pretty heavily warded against magic. I examine the wards, and they are intricate and put there by someone who was borderline suicidal.

The wards are designed to violently amplify and redirect magic within the room back to the origin. Setting these wards up would have been like rigging a bomb to a bomb detector so that the bomb goes off when the detector gets a whiff of high explosives. The slightest miscalibration and…Boom!

But it is warded with inclusive wards; magic flows in and pools here to power the ward and probably a surplus. She might even have some crystals hidden here to store the extra energy. I don't have time to verify this, but it's a reasonable guess.

There is an ample supply of magic and a sealed room. Jeff's magic juice will have plenty to eat and, in time, start creating a lot of acetone. Acetone will act as a solvent on the ink on the pages. If I spray the pages all down with the spray, it will generate acetone that will destroy all of the pages. This could work.

"A completely daft plan," I say to myself. I try to pretend it is Hank's voice.

"But it could work."

"Probably not."

"But it could," I say. "It's better than nothing."

"I am going to do this, aren't I?"

"Yup," I say. "Pinnochio didn't listen to his conscience. Why should I?"

"In that case, Pinnochio was a dummy."

"Puppet but close enough."

"Didn't he end up getting turned into a jackass and get eaten by a whale?"

"Yeah, but that's nothing new…and I am talking to myself. I miss Hank."

The biggest problem with my plan is I have to visit Shelly in a couple of hours. If I use up all my magic-eating juice, I won't have any to try to help her. But if I don't use it all here, it might not be as effective.

I will have to try to balance it out. I put half the liquid into my hidden flask and spray the remainder into all the drawers of the filing cabinet. Leaving the drawers open so that it is exposed to the maximum amount of air and magical energy. I soak the pages down as best I can. Once I've sprayed as much as I feel like I can afford to, I leave the secret office and seal the door shut. I put the fake thermostat back and head back outside.

I glance at my watch and realize that I've spent far more time in Redbrook's secret office than I thought. I'm late. I need to rush to the hospital to see Shelly.

When Redbrook finds out what I did, she is going to be very upset with me. There are going to be consequences. In the moment, I thought it was worth it, but now that it is literally in my rearview mirror, I am having second thoughts. I can feel my heart pounding in my chest. I struggle to keep my breathing regular. I'm fighting down the panic of regret. Or is it the exhilaration of impulsiveness?

I'd like to change clothes and take a quick shower before heading to Napa State Hospital, but I don't have time.

Chapter Nineteen

AT THE STOPLIGHT in front of the state hospital, two fire trucks go roaring by. I look in my rearview mirror, and I can see a plume of black smoke curling up on the horizon. I do some quick math in my head, and if I were a gambling man, I'd bet that is The Lantern.

A sinking churning sensation begins to form in my bowels, followed closely by a sudden need to throw up. Reign it in Miles. This is no time to panic. I'm sure that it's not The Lantern. It's a coincidence. Stay focused on the moment. I feel emotions tightening my chest and squeezing at my throat. Panic. Terror. Is it? Or is it excitement? It doesn't matter right now; I need to keep it in check. I need to pay attention to the task at hand.

There is no way that the hospital staff is going to let me put a magic circle around Shelly. There is definitely no way they will let me put blood on it and douse her with some weird and suspicious liquid. But if I am going to help her, that is exactly what I have to do. Then, I'll have to let her sit in the circle for at least a few minutes. So I have a plan. A delicate plan. A plan that depends very much on circumstances going my way and a lack of interference.

I'm a little worried about this plan.

At the front desk, I tell a bored-looking receptionist who I am and why I am there. Then I get to sit in a chair waiting for an interminably long time.

"I just heard The Lantern caught fire," some staff members are talking in a hallway nearby. I can hear them, but I cannot see them. There is nothing else to do, so I eavesdrop.

"Isn't that the place that got shot up?" another person asks.

"Yeah, someone must have it out for Lorelei Redbrook," the first voice says.

"She's right. This town is going to shit," the second voice says.

"Someone needs to fix it up. It seems like she at least has a plan," a third voice chimes in.

"No way she's awful. I wouldn't be surprised if she set fire to her own place for the insurance money," the first voice says.

"Bull crap, she's speaking the truth, and there are people who don't want you to hear it," the third voice says.

"Seriously? You buy that?" the first voice says. "I read a piece about her this morning, child labor, weird inconsistencies in her background allegations of all sorts of criminal stuff? It was pretty convincing."

"Whatever, I'm voting for her," the second voice says. "This town needs to get cleaned up."

"Send me the link to that article, and I'll check it out. But I agree something has to change. This town is going to shit," the third voice chimes in.

"Well, I have to do my rounds," the first voice says, sounding huffy.

The unseen trio then disbands and goes their separate ways. One walks by me, a thirty-something man in scrubs. I look at my phone, pretending I wasn't listening to his conversation.

Shit. I think to myself. It sounds like it was The Lantern the fire trucks were racing to. I didn't do that, though. Did I? If I did, then it was an accident. Wasn't it? I know that acetone is flammable, but there was no ignition source. I wasn't trying to burn it down. That was an unintended consequence. For some reason, I can't quite convince myself that it is completely true.

After a while, an orderly and a doctor of some sort show up to escort me to see Shelly. The orderly is quiet and taciturn. The doctor gives me a rundown of protocol and procedure. He talks about her diagnosis, but I can barely hear what he is saying over the pounding of blood rushing in my ears.

I get that Shelly is non-responsive and that I should talk but not expect anything from her. He says I'm not to touch the patient and that I will be supervised by the orderly at all times. He says a lot more, but I'm not paying much attention. The Lantern burned down. That might be my fault.

We stop so I can sign some more disclaimers and waivers, and god knows what other forms. I do so as if in a trance. Then the doctor leaves, and I follow the orderly in silence. The brick halls are long and tall and wide. Each footstep echoes ominously as we walk through them, up an immense staircase that splits and spirals off, only to rejoin again on the second floor. He guides us to a small, cramped room, its brick walls painted white.

There is a table in the middle of the room bolted to the floor. The table is surrounded by four small flimsy plastic chairs. It's a small room with no real decor to speak of. I assume this is because they don't want anything that could be used as a weapon.

Shelly is sitting in a chair on the opposite side of the table. She's staring blankly. The face staring at me is a lot older than I remember. She is thinner physically, and she has less presence in the room. She takes up less space. I sit down, and the orderly parks himself next to the door. He's watching pretty closely; this isn't going to be easy.

"Hi, Shelly," I say. She doesn't respond. She doesn't even blink.

"It's been a while. I heard that you had been moved here,

and I had to come and visit," I say. She still doesn't respond. She seems to blink but only a couple of times a minute, and it doesn't seem to have any relation to my words.

I begin to carry on telling her about everything I've done in the almost twenty years since I've seen her. I have this planned out, and it is banal, dull, detailed, and uninspired. I haven't exactly rehearsed it, but I have gone over all of my key talking points in my head dozens of times in the last week. Jobs I've had, troublesome coworkers, women I've asked out, women I've been stood up by, food I've had, places I've traveled. You name it. If it is something I have done as an adult that no one wants to hear about, I talk about it at length.

After ten minutes or so, I can tell out of the corner of my eye that the orderly has checked out. He starts glancing at his phone, and after another couple of minutes of my droning, he's completely drawn in by the phone. Phase one is complete.

I casually slide a stack of business cards out of my pocket without ceasing my prattling on about a trip I took to Des Moines. I'm making this trip up. I've never been to Des Moines, but it seems like the perfect setting for a boring story about a conference I attended.

I watch the orderly out of the corner of my eye. He doesn't seem to notice. I begin flipping the cards under the table into a rough circle around Shelly. Thankfully, a magic circle doesn't need to be perfect, and it doesn't need to be contiguous. If I wanted to describe a specific effect or make something that would last, the locations would be important. But if I want to build up a little pool in the Ley, it's not as crucial.

On the back of each business card, I drew a sigil with a permanent marker. The tough part here is tossing them under a table without the orderly noticing and getting them to land in roughly the right places. I mostly get it right, but a few go too far afield or land with the wrong side up. Thankfully, I brought backups for all.

After ten minutes of re-throwing and carefully sliding

stuff around with my foot, I have a workable circle arranged. I roll my sleeve up and take the bandaid off where I had to cut my arm yesterday working with Russ. With a little scratching, I pick the scab away. I hate this part. I pause to murmur my incantation, and I let a couple of drops fall off my arm under the table and land on one of my business cards. Trying to look as casual as possible, I slide my sleeve back down. I grimace as I can feel blood smear and stick beneath my sleeve.

I pause and stretch my arms, taking the opportunity to look over my shoulder at the orderly. Judging by his intense facial expression, I am guessing he is now ensconced in some heated text or social media war. I'm sure he's not supposed to do this during work, but in his defense, my stories are really boring.

I check the time. I've only got an hour total to visit with Shelly, and I've used up well over half of that now.

The orderly notices my silence and looks up from his phone.

"Where was I? Right, so then, I moved to the East Bay, and I got some temp work with an accounting firm. The first thing they wanted me to do was reorganize their filing system based on date and alphabetical order of names..." I pick my story back up, and I can see the orderly's eyes glaze right over and go back to his phone.

A couple of years ago, I was in Arizona. A rancher insisted that his cattle were plagued by chupacabra, and he wanted me to set up defenses to keep dark creatures out. I spent a week and a half carving runes on fence posts. One day, while I was in town, I went into a western wear store. There I saw this belt. It was very ornately carved and had a huge buckle on it.

The buckle was big and chunky. Secretly, it was a flask held onto the actual buckle by a magnet. You wouldn't know it was a flask looking at it; You'd think someone had a thing for big trophy buckles. It amused the hell out of me at the time, and I bought the belt. I wore it for the rest of the trip, and then it got stuck in the back of my closet and forgotten. This is the secret flask I stowed half of the acetobacter in.

What better way to smuggle a concoction of magic-eating acetobacter into a secure facility than a tacky belt buckle? Well, at least it worked. I click the flask off of my belt, continuing my dull narrative. Then, I carefully pour the liquid into a pool at Shelly's feet. Once it is empty, I click the flask back into place. I continue prattling on for another ten minutes. The smell of vinegar begins to rise. Then, when I get the first hint of acetone, I finish up my story.

"Well, it was great seeing you, Shelly. I hope you feel better," I say sadly as I stand up.

The orderly begins to push himself off the wall. I move quickly, blocking his view of the floor with my body and forcing him to open the door for me. I see him sniff the air and look around, slightly confused.

"Thank you," I say to him. "I know it seems silly, but it was good to see her. I always wondered where she went."

He nods at me and motions me out the door, where he escorts me down the huge staircase and down a long, tall, wide hallway to the exit. I sign myself out and depart to my car. The whole way, I half expect the hospital police to come chasing after me.

But they don't.

I try to imagine the confused conversations that will occur when the staff discovers the little slips of paper and the pool of stinking liquid on the floor around her. I hope that it was all sufficient to help break the spell that is subverting her mind. If it did, it might still take her years to get back to some semblance of normal. Hopefully, it's a start.

Chapter Twenty

IN THE PARKING LOT, a tall figure dressed once again in black leather is leaning against my car like a jungle cat basking in the sun.

"Hi," I say brusquely.

"Hey there, hot stuff," Circe says, stretching her long frame back across the roof of the car. She's tall enough to make this look casual.

"I'm kind of in a rush Circe. Hop in. I'll drive, and we can talk," I say.

"Are you trying to trap me, Miles?"

"What do you mean?" I respond, but I am feeling caught in the act, and I think it shows.

"Well, I couldn't help but notice that you warded your car."

"Yeah, I keep getting attacked by weird stuff, Fetches, Rebobs, Lamia. I don't know what's next. Better safe than sorry. Besides, those wards wouldn't trap a normal person."

"I'm anything but normal, believe me, Ace," she says.

"Oh. Okay, I guess," I say. "How could you tell it was warded?"

She rolls her eyes at me and shrugs.

"You just have to look at its aura."

She doesn't seem to have a crystal or anything for gazing at auras on her. Her clothing doesn't even have pockets with enough space to fit such a thing in without a bulge. She sees me looking her up and down and raises an eyebrow.

"See something you like?"

"No, I was wondering where you kept a gazing crystal."

She laughs out loud.

"A gazing crystal? That's for kids. Are you telling me you can't see auras without a crystal?" she asks incredulously.

"Um. Yeah, I guess that is what I am telling you," I say sheepishly.

She laughs at me some more.

"Fine, you won't get in my car, so what do you want?"

"Well, I wanted to ask if that was you who burned down the Lamia's lair."

"Well, I wouldn't say burned it down." My sentence is punctuated by another fire truck siren screaming past, heading toward The Lantern.

"Then what would you call it when a building is so consumed in flames that there is nothing left but a pile of charcoal?"

"A fire sale?"

"Well, I am going to be honest. That very much changes my plans," she says. "Why did you do that?"

"It was an accident, an unintentional side effect. One that I have not yet lived long enough to regret. I am sure I will get there someday. I expect it by mid-afternoon. Tomorrow morning at the latest," I say, trying to sound nonchalant. It's a lie, though. I'm hella chalant. I regret most of my morning already.

"Now she's going to be on high alert. So what I need from you is going to be more involved. And more dangerous. So much more dangerous," she says. She seems almost smug.

"Can I ask you a question? Because I'm confused. Why does everybody keep assigning me tasks like I am their errand boy? I burned her...what did you call it? Her lair? I burned her lair down. Is that not enough for you?"

"You're not going to help me?" she says; her face is suddenly a blank, almost expressionless mask.

"Why do I feel like that is a threat?"

She shrugs, and then her smug smile returns as quickly as it faded. She continues as if my question has been answered, and we are back on track.

"Well, now we aren't going to be able to make our move on her when she visits The Lantern while it is weakened. Now we are going to have to make a move while she is at home and expecting it. This means I am going to need you to bring down her wards and other magical defenses and plant this," she says, holding out a large gem.

It's a purple crystal, probably amethyst. It's set in a metal bezel and is so large that I can barely palm the whole thing with my hand completely outstretched. The bezel has a series of runes on it that I do not recognize.

"What's this?" I ask.

"It is...a kind of magical trap, yes, let's call it that. I am going to need you to plant that under her bed or nest or whatever she sleeps in."

"How the hell am I supposed to get in her house, take down her wards and plant this in her bed?" I ask incredulously.

"Seduce her?" Circe says, grinning at me.

"Um, no,"

"Afraid your new girlfriend will be jealous?"

"Of my concerns, that is far and away the least of them," I say. Circe knows about Genevieve.

"Well," she says, suddenly getting very businesslike, "that's what I need you to do. That is the favor you owe me. Do it, and then we are done."

"I'm still not clear how I owe you a favor. That favor was in exchange for helping me deal with Redbrook. Considering our current conversation, it doesn't seem like you did that."

"Is Redbrook after your little winery manager anymore? No. Mission accomplished. You owe me."

"But she's after me now."

"Oh?"

I look at the gem. I consider what she is proposing, and I have no idea how I am going to pull that off. It sounds impossible. Redbrook has a small army of Fetches, and who knows what other magical security. I'm sure she keeps her Fetches well armed, too, and I don't even know what she herself is capable of. On the other hand, I have no idea what Circe will do if I say no.

"Fine," I say. I will try to delay this ask from Circe until I find another way to deal with Redbrook. "When do you need this done?"

"As soon as possible. I know it's no easy task, so take some time to plan, but if it isn't done in the next week or so…" she shrugs a helpless-looking shrug. "Then I'll have to go to plan C."

"What happened to plan B?"

"This is plan B, remember? Plan A was the bar. You burned down plan A."

"Oh. Right. Fine. Next week. Got it."

"Next week, Ace," she says as she sashays away, swaying her hips far more than necessary for ambulation. She gets beneath a tree, steps into the tree's shadow, and melts away, exactly like the Rebobs.

It isn't actual confirmation that she is a dream projection and not a real person, but it is definitely evidence in favor of the theory. She won't go inside of wards and seems to continuously check to make sure they aren't present.

In my car, I let the air-conditioned air blow in my face while I take a deep breath and think. Okay, so I have done something for Shelly. Hopefully, it is enough. I've burned down The Lantern, which was not exactly my plan. I have stolen all of Redbrook's files. Redbrook is going to be looking for retribution for sure, and now I have to make it into her house somehow and plant something Circe claims is a magical trap in her bed.

What's next?

An insurance policy. I need something to leverage over Redbrook to keep her off my back. She's not going to be happy about The Lantern. I need to make sure she doesn't come after me or Emily or Jeff.

Back home, I dash into my office. I take the memory stick out of my bag and copy the data to two other memory sticks. Then I pocket all three of them. I drive down to the post office. I wrap one of the memory sticks in bubble wrap. Wrap the paper around the bubble wrap and write in permanent marker, 'In the event of my untimely death' on it. It goes into a box. Then I mail it to Genevieve in Portland.

When I get back to my car, I glance at my phone and notice a text from Jeff. It reads, "911 tonight. SBTSBC"

SBTSBC? It takes me a minute to parse that. It's something Russ says. " SBTSBC Dude! Same Bat Time, Same Bat Channel." Jeff wants to meet tonight at his place at the usual time, which I think is seven o'clock. And it's an emergency.

One problem at a time. Right now, I want to know what Circe's game is. I don't trust her, and I don't think she's going to play fair at the end of our 'deal.'

I use the term very loosely. I reflect on the conversation we just had, and I am not sure how I walked away agreeing to anything. I'm flustered and frustrated, and I feel out of control of my interactions with Circe. I need an upper hand. I need control.

To that end, I need to figure out what she is exactly. Is she a vampire like I originally suspected? Is she a dream construct like I am now thinking? Is she both? Is she something else entirely that I don't have a taxonomy for?

It's not far from the post office to Grape Reads, so I walk the five blocks or so there.

"Hi, Ren," I say as I arrive.

Ren is standing behind the counter, looking through a

book. In the back, a couple of customers are quietly perusing books. The store is otherwise quiet and mostly empty.

"Hi, Miles," Ren says, barely looking up from their book.

"Is Emily around?"

"Nope, she took today off. She should be back tomorrow."

"Hey, Ren, are you up to speed on everything Emily and I have been doing?"

"There are no secrets working for Sergei."

I blink. Once again, a reference to the mysterious Sergei, the unseen bookstore owner. What weird kind of bookstore cult are they in?

"So yes?"

"Yeah, I'm pretty up to speed."

"So you know who Circe is?"

"Hizarin assassin, ten feet tall, bad taste in fashion. Still makes Emily insanely jealous for some reason."

I ignore the last bit. I'm trying to stay out of Emily's love life.

"What do you think Circe is?"

"What do you mean?"

"I mean, I thought Circe was a vampire, but now I am thinking there is more going on. I'm not even sure Circe is real. I think she's like...a dream projection?"

Ren stops and looks up. They put a finger to their pursed lips and think for a moment. Then they close their book, reach behind the counter, and pull out a few more stacks of books.

"Listen, Miles. I'd like you to do something for me," they say, spreading the books out across the counter.

"Okay."

"Organize these into stacks."

"Like...by title or author?"

"Whatever works for you, Miles," they say and lean back against a table behind the counter. They cross their arms and wait patiently.

I look over the books. There are twenty of them. I spend a

minute organizing them into stacks alphabetically by title. I have seven stacks when I am done. The deepest is the S pile, which is four books high.

"Okay," I say, "Done."

"You organized them alphabetically by title," they say, looking the stacks over. They then shuffle the piles around. Ren has quick hands like a Vegas card dealer.

"There, that is alphabetically by author's last name."

There is another set of uneven piles. Ren does more shuffling.

"There, this is alphabetically by author's first name."

"Here is by genre. Here, by cover dimensions. Spine color. Width. Page count."

Each new organizational method comes with it a quick shuffle into stacks. It is impressive how fast Ren works and how very familiar they must be with the books to do so.

"And finally," Ren says, "Here is by content."

Ren arranges all of the books individually on the table, each in their own stack of one.

"Organizing and creating stacks and labels are great tools to help us find things. Labels have their uses. But no matter what stacks we put the books in, no matter what labels we apply, the book doesn't change. It's still the same book. The stacks, the labels, the buckets, they are about us and actually have nothing to do with the book. The labels we use say volumes about us as the labeler but actually say very little about the labeled."

"I guess I see what you mean. But I'm not sure what this has to do with Circe."

"I'm saying maybe try finding out what the book is about. Not what shelf it goes on."

"Oh. I see. If I label her as a vampire, that's the metric by which I will measure her and possibly miss the details that are actually significant. The label is reductive. That is insightful."

"Don't sound so surprised! Anyhow, I'm always happy to help. But also, my point was more that people are people, and if you view them as something to categorize and order, you're sort of missing the point."

"I seem to do that a lot, miss the point, that is. It's a skill I'm working on. But seriously, thanks, Ren. I'll have to ponder how I do that, but it makes a lot of sense."

Ren puts the books back behind the counter and goes back to reading their book again.

"Have a good one, Miles," they say, clearly aware that I'm not going to be buying anything.

"You're a rockstar," I say as I turn toward the door.

"I know," they say matter-of-factly without looking up from their book.

I think Ren is right. Monster, Human, Vampire, Succubus, Werewolf, White, Black, Male, Female, Non-Binary, these are all just labels we apply to try to help us organize the universe. Labels are our attempts to categorize things. Labels exist outside and separate from the individual. There are as many nuanced variations on all these things as there are individuals. The labels are just a tool. And if a tool isn't helping you work, it should be put away.

Categorizing Circe isn't working. If I am going to navigate this situation that I've gotten myself into, I need more information. I need to take a new approach. But what Ren has proposed is getting to know Circe better. Understanding her. Is that really something I want to do?

Chapter Twenty-One

AT JEFF'S PLACE, I am a little early. Emily's car isn't there. I peek inside Jeff's hedge to see if Russ's bike is there, but it isn't. I knock on the door, and Jeff lets me in.

"What's up?" I ask as I walk past him into his front entry.

"Did you burn down The Lantern?" he asks.

"Why would you think it was me?"

"Because who else would it be?"

"Any of the hundreds of people she's blackmailing? The Knights of Saint George? I mean, they shot up the place. Teetotalers? Quakers?"

"What? Why would Quakers burn down The Lantern?"

"Honestly, I don't know much about their doctrine or politics, so I don't know, but I'm sure they must have had a good reason," I say in my best deadpan.

"Stop derailing with humor. You haven't answered my question."

"Technically?"

"No, not fucking technically, Miles, did you?"

"It wasn't my intention; it was an accident, and you know it might not have been me…"

"How did you accidentally burn down The Lantern?"

"Well, acetone is a solvent, right? There were these papers

there I wanted to destroy and a lot of magic, so I put your anti-magic juice everywhere…"

"And acetone is also volatile…" Jeff says.

"Yeah, which didn't occur to me until I saw the fire trucks."

"You didn't do something to ignite it?"

"I don't think so," I say. That's true. I've been wracking my brain to think if I did something that could have ignited the acetone. I can't think of anything.

Jeff sighs and rubs his temples.

"Miles. What the hell is going on? It's like everyone is going off the rails. You're burning down buildings, and Emily…well, I don't even know what to say about that."

"What are you talking about? What happened with Emily?"

"You haven't seen her tear on social media? The op-ed she submitted to the paper? She's really kicked the hornets' nest today!" he announces, looking a little bug-eyed.

"Is kicked the hornets nest an expression?"

"Goddamit, Miles, you know what I mean," Jeff grumps at me.

"Sorry. I don't do social media or read the paper," I say sheepishly.

"Oh well, then you should. She's everywhere with scathing stuff about Redbrook's mayoral campaign. She accuses her of child abuse, suspected extortion, basically everything except the actual baby-eating-monster part. She didn't hold anything back after all of her talk about not wanting to step in the line of danger. She pretty much painted a bullseye on her back."

"That doesn't sound like her."

"I know," he says. "You've become a firebug, and god knows what Russ is up to."

As if on cue, the doorbell rings.

Jeff turns to walk toward the door.

"Smoking pot and listening to Frank Zappa, that's what

Russ has been up to!" I call after Jeff, then I protest weakly, "And I'm not a firebug."

Without responding, Jeff continues down the hall. A moment later, Russ walks in with Emily only a few seconds behind him. We all sit down in Jeff's game room as usual. I notice that Emily sits at the far side of the table from Jeff, and they don't look at each other. There is some obvious tension between them.

"So. I spoke to Circe again," I say.

"And burned down the lantern," Jeff mutters. Emily gives a little sideways glower at this, but Russ doesn't seem to notice Jeff's quip and keeps talking.

"Oh, did you get her in the trap?" Russ says.

"Fire? Trap?" Emily says, confused.

"Yeah, Miles and I wanted to see if she is a dream construct, so we set like a trap for her," Russ says.

"A dream construct?" Jeff says.

"Yeah, I had this theory that this is how she comes and goes so quickly. It would explain why Russ couldn't find her. If she's not real at all but like a dream made manifest or something," I say.

"No way, that's crazy," Emily says.

"Well did it work? This trap?" Jeff asks.

"No, but kind of yes," I say.

"What does that mean?" Emily says testily.

"Woah, let him finish," Russ says. Emily casts a nasty face at him.

"No, she didn't get trapped in it because she refused to go into it. She wouldn't get near my car. I tried to invite her in, and she declined and then tried to make me feel uncomfortable. I think to distract me from the fact she wouldn't get in. So while it wasn't absolute confirmation, it was something," I say, "Oh, and did you know that Circe can read auras without a crystal or anything like that? I know there are people who can do that, but it is hard. I've tried, but it's never worked."

“It’s not that hard, anybody can do it with a little practice,” Emily says.

“Yeah, Emily taught me in like five minutes,” Jeff says.

Jeff looks at me with an odd facial expression. His brow is furrowed, and his mouth is tight. One eyebrow is quirked up a little higher than the other. He looks like he's having bowel troubles. I think this must be him reading my aura. If this is required to do so without a crystal, I'll keep doing what I am doing.

"Miles, what is going on with your aura? It looks like Swiss cheese." Jeff says. I have no idea what he is talking about. It is impossible to see your own aura, even with the aid of a crystal.

"What do you mean?" I ask.

"Yeah, Miles' aura is weird," Russ says, nodding sagely.

"You've got all those magical wards tattooed all over your body. It messes with the natural flow of Ley in and out. It makes black spots in your aura," Emily casually clarifies.

There is a moment of awkward silence. I feel sheepish, standing there with my mouth slightly ajar.

“So, what else did you do today, Miles?” Jeff asks in a leading tone, “Any other news of note?”

I sigh a long, heavy sigh.

“I might have burned down The Lantern.”

“What?” Emily says.

“Hah!” Russ says.

“By accident!”

I bring them all up to speed on the weeks and, more specifically, the days’ events. I don’t hold back any details except the fact that I sent the memory stick to Genevieve. I feel like the fewer people who know the specifics of that; the safer everyone will be.

“Well, you have had a busy day,” Emily says. She is in a really bad mood.

“Emily, you haven’t exactly had idle hands,” Jeff says.

"Oh, I was wondering why Emily had such a harsh vibe. What'd you do, chica?" Russ says.

"Again, don't call me chica. I've been writing what I've been finding. Revealing all the gory details on Lorelei Redbrook."

"You pretty much called Redbrook out," Jeff says. "I thought you didn't want to get into dangerous situations."

"No!" Emily snaps at him, her voice raised. "I didn't want a man dragging me into danger because he can't help stepping in front of every bullet and going around burning buildings down."

Emily doesn't stop looking at Jeff but stabs a finger at my chest. She's still about four feet away from me, so she doesn't actually touch me, but the message is clear.

"Accident," I mutter.

"If I jump into danger for myself, that is my business, and you..." she says loudly, continuing to glower at Jeff. "You don't get to tell me I can or can't or should or shouldn't. Redbrook has got to be stopped, if not physically, then politically. The stuff I have uncovered, the stuff she has done. Well, it's all out there now, but I imagine you cavemen couldn't read it if you wanted to."

Jeff starts to make a rebuttal, but Emily raises her voice over him and continues.

"So highlights! Did you know that one out of every three kids fostered by Redbrook ends up in the State Hospital? Did you know that a quarter of them are missing appendages from household 'accidents'? The rest live with her until they are emancipated, then they 'move away,' and I haven't been able to track them down. Not one."

"Not one?" Russ asks. He's lost his usual jovial expression.

"She's a fucking monster, and she's hurting kids, abandoned orphaned needy kids who need love and help. She works them, and she uses them, and they vanish, forgotten by society. While I don't have proof that she's **eating** them, I can't find anything to say she isn't!"

We all sit quietly in the wake of Emily's wrath. What Emily is revealing is horrifying.

"Um, well, I smoked a really killer joint today. I mean, stoned but not like nuts, mellow but not sleepy…perfect." Russ kisses his fingertips and then splays them forward and blows a kiss to the ceiling. Maybe some god is the intended target. I don't know. Everyone turns to stare at him incredulously.

I sit there staring, uncomfortable, and silent. Jeff is quiet, too, I assume, in the same discomfort.

Emily stands up and starts to leave.

"Emily," I say, shaking off my awkward paralysis. She turns and glares at me.

"What?"

"I think you are doing the right thing. Here, this should help your cause," I say and toss one of the memory sticks to her. She catches it.

"What is this?"

"It's a copy of everything on Redbrook's secret office computer. I didn't get to look at all of it. But I copied her hard drive before I erased it and then apparently burned her business down. Please believe that the last bit wasn't part of the plan."

"You know that you helped her, right? You know she is already leveraging that and the attack the other week as some conspiracy to silence her 'truth'? You know that right now, it's looking like she will win this election."

"Look, I am doing my best here," I say helplessly.

Her face and voice soften. A little.

"I know. And thanks for this," she says, holding up the memory stick. "But, Miles, you have to be more careful. Please think before you go charging in. You jump in front of every proverbial bullet like you think you're Superman. But you aren't. You're just a man."

"I know, but…I usually feel like I am the only one who thought to wear a bulletproof vest," I say. "I mean not literally.

I am trying to carry your metaphor because, well, I know I'm not Superman, but…"

"Yeah, I get it," she interrupts testily. "Thanks."

"The bulletproof vest thing might not be the worst investment, dude. You know with how things are going," Russ chimes in as Emily walks out the front door and slams it behind her. Russ, Jeff, and I sit there for an awkward moment.

"Yeah, I think I fucked that up," Jeff says.

"Being concerned isn't a fuck up," Russ says.

"The concern wasn't the problem. It was more my framing. We got into a bit of a fight. Well, more than a bit. She's all bent out of shape about something," Jeff says.

"What?" I ask.

Jeff shrugs dismissively.

"Well, if you want to talk about it, we'll listen," I say.

Jeff repeats his shrug. It's got a very dismissive vibe to it. If this was how he was communicating with Emily, I can see why she is in a bad mood.

"Yeah dude," Russ says.

"No, I'll deal with it. I think she needs some cool-down time. So do I," Jeff says.

"Was that what you called us here about? Or was there something else?" I ask.

"I called because it felt like everyone was going rogue and doing their own thing. I was hoping we could regroup and sort some stuff out. I guess I hoped this would make things right with Emily, but it looks like that failed," Jeff says.

"Well, we can still talk. I think Emily's approach is good. I think attacking her politically is the way to go. At least to stall and distract her while we figure out how to deal with her some other way," I say.

Jeff does nothing to hide his eye roll when I agree with Emily. I don't know what is going on between those two, but they are both in a mood.

"What about Circe?" Jeff asks.

"What, what about Circe?" I ask.

"What about her plan? Do you think she can take out Redbrook?" he asks.

"Can she? Maybe. She has a plan. I think instead of killing her, she wants to trap her. But I don't know that we can trust that Circe has the same goals as we do. She might want to trap Redbrook as part of some bigger plot. I don't know."

"So we need to depend on Circe as plan B then?" Russ says.

"Plan 2-C," I say.

"Huh?" Jeff asks.

"Circe has a plan A, B, and C, and apparently, I burned down plan A, which was also part of our plan A. So now we have two plan A's that got destroyed. Leaving us with plans 1-B and 1-C with Circe. But we only have a plan 2-C, so now we need plan 2-B."

"I have no idea what you just said," Jeff says.

"Yeah, what he said," Russ says, jabbing a thumb in Jeff's direction.

"So, um, there was a plan A," I start to try to clarify, then I realize the futility of the exercise. "Eh. You know what? Never mind."

We all three sit and ponder for a minute.

"Okay, dudes, what if, like, we trap her in the Dreamtime as we tried with Circe?" Russ asks.

"Well, I think that is Circe's plan," I say.

"We can't trust her, though," Jeff says.

"Like I said, we try to find a way to trap her ourselves," Russ says.

"That way, if Circe is actually on our side and her plan works great. If not, we've got another way to go," I say.

"Sounds good, dude," Russ says.

"I'm afraid the dream stuff is going to be all you, Russ," I say.

"What do you need from me?" Jeff asks.

"More of your magic..." I have to dig deep in the recesses

of my brain before I come up with his taxonomy of preference "of your Acetobacter Magusficedula."

"Not a problem."

"Russ, I'll meet with you tomorrow?" I say.

"Right on!" Russ says enthusiastically.

"No more burning stuff down, Miles," Jeff says as I start toward the door.

"No promises," I say. I am trying to be funny, but I don't think it comes off that way.

Once more, it is Russ and I standing on Jeff's porch.

"Do you need a ride?" I ask Russ.

"Thanks for the offer, man, but I've got my bike. I'll pedal home. It's cool to just enjoy the night air, you know, man?"

"It's a long way to your house from here," I point out.

"I'm cool, dude, I'm cool," Russ fetches his bike from behind the hedge.

The rest of my evening and well into the night is spent looking through Redbrook's files. There is a lot, and it has been intentionally obfuscated. It's a pretty huge waste of my time.

Chapter Twenty-Two

"MILES WARD, spell break for hire b-r-e-a-k," I answer the phone. I put my spoon back into my cereal bowl and then take a quick sip of coffee.

"Miles," I hear Lorelei Redbrook's voice on the other end, "Miles, Miles, Miles. You did not hold up to our agreement."

I knew this call was coming, but I still wasn't looking forward to it. I feel nauseous, and my head feels kind of light.

"What do you mean?" I ask, trying to sound innocent.

"You burned down my bar!" She yells at me in a voice both shrill and hoarse.

"No, I didn't."

"Miles, we have security cameras."

"Circumstantial."

"Now, you owe me even more."

I don't need the fear that's rising in my throat right now. I close my eyes and will it back down. I feel the hot panic cool as it sinks down into my stomach.

"Listen. You wanted The Lantern magically protected. I promise you that nothing magic is going to get in there now!" I say, my snark bubbling up to hide my terror.

"It has had some plus sides, but Miles, you owe me. You

owe me a lot. What am I going to do with you?" she says, sounding very pleased with herself.

"Here is the thing, Lorelei. Or should I call you Lamia? Here is the thing I copied all of your files. All of it. There is some juicy stuff in there. If you come after my friends, this stuff gets leaked. If you come after me, I've got a contingency set up there too. You are going to need to back off," I say. I have no idea if this is going to cow her or instigate her retaliation, but I am hoping for the former.

There is a long moment of silence on the phone. I sit there holding my breath, and finally, she breaks the silence.

"Playing hardball, now are we?" she says, then she pauses a moment before continuing, "Okay, Miles. I have to say I like this new, more assertive you. You have my files. I need my files. How do we come to terms here?"

I haven't thought this far ahead. I honestly wasn't expecting this reaction; I was expecting some veiled threats, some demands, some overt threats.

"We need to meet to discuss terms. At your place," I say.

"Tomorrow," she says.

"No. Monday. I have plans this weekend," I say. I don't have plans. Or rather, I do have plans now, but my plan is to spend the weekend planning.

"Monday," she drawls out. She does not sound pleased. "Fine. Monday."

I am surprised that she conceded to my terms. What the hell is in those files? I skimmed through, and there was a lot of suspicious stuff but nothing that would get her sudden and complete compliance.

"Like eleven thirty in the morning," I say, throwing out a time.

"Fine," Lorelei says and hangs up.

I put my phone down, grab my laptop, and begin looking through the files frantically while I finish my breakfast. I'm a few hours into this when Emily calls.

"Miles Ward apotropaist for hire. If you don't know what it means, look it up," I answer.

"That's the worst one yet," Emily says.

"Yeah, I know I am distracted. I was looking through Redbrook's files."

"Me too. That's actually why I am calling."

"Oh?"

"It's totally the smoking gun. It took a little going through e-mails and looking through her web history, but she posts on MonAnon.com."

"The monster hunter sight? Why?"

"Yes. But when I say posts, I mean she is a huge contributor. The attack on The Lantern? She orchestrated it. And attacks on others in Napa plus some attacks in other cities," Emily says. "She's the mastermind."

"Oh," I say, the implications of this slowly sinking in. "So she's using these monster hunters as her own personal hit squad. She used them to make herself look sympathetic, like she's the victim."

"And eliminate competition. There's more. So much more. Bribes, blackmail, extortion, human trafficking, child labor. This is huge," Emily says.

"Wow," I say. I didn't find any of that.

"Yeah wow. I don't know where to go with it," she says.

"The police?" I say.

"It's hard to say, but I'm pretty sure she's got some connected people in her pocket. I don't know whom we could trust. Besides, you acquired all this evidence illegally; it isn't admissible in court."

"Should we go Federal?"

"I don't know. I feel like that might end in stuff getting swept under the rug. I think we need to go public and force the authorities to step in. I feel like we need to go big with this and get the word out so that threatening us makes it look more guilty. I think we need a real journalist to help us cover this. Someone with connections," she says.

I am still thinking about all of this. My mind is racing. There is something Emily is fishing for, but I am not nibbling at the moment.

"Okay," I say vaguely.

"Genevieve Galc, I need you to take this to Genevieve to blow this story wide open. She's got the connections and know-how," Emily blurts out.

"Oh," I say. I am caught off guard by this request, which is illogical. This is the exact reason I reached out to Genevieve in the first place. However, our relationship has evolved so much that it has just slipped my mind.

"Here is the thing," I say. "These files are the only leverage we have. If we go public, Lorelei kills us and vanishes to start a new life, which seems like her MO. I want to take a second to re-emphasize the 'kills us' part."

"So you want to roll over and let her get away with all this?"

"No, no. I want to think this through and not do something rash."

"If this goes public, killing us makes her look more guilty."

"But what does she care if she's going to change identities? We need to think this through," I say.

"Well, there's a first. So now Mr. Burn-It-All-Down Miles Ward wants to think things through," Emily says. She sounds upset.

"Now that's not fair," I say. "Emily, what is going on? This doesn't seem like you."

"What do you mean 'what is going on'? There is a literal baby-eating fucking monster about to get elected mayor. A monster who wants to make our town a safe haven for baby-eating monsters. Isn't that upsetting enough?"

"Yes, of course, that's awful. And I'll talk to Genevieve. But you seem on edge. Is there something else going on?"

"Mind your own business, Miles," she says and hangs up.

I sigh and finish my breakfast.

Chapter Twenty-Three

I NEED to clear my head. I change into running clothes and step outside to go for a run. It's hot this morning unusually hot. It's not even 9 a.m., and it's already 90 degrees outside. Usually, at night, even in the summertime, the marine layer creeps in. The temperature drops down as a blanket of cold, wet air from the Pacific Ocean rolls in. It settles over the valley like a cold, damp blanket. But no cold, damp blanket this morning, and I start to question the wisdom of my run. On the open-air walkway in front of my apartment, I see a slightly familiar face.

Morgan LeFey. The new one. Magdalena. She's smoking a cigarette and blowing smoke rings when I step out onto the walkway. She still looks like she couldn't be older than fifteen, so I have a bit of a reaction when I see her smoking. Part of me wants to scold her, but she's told me she's twenty-three. Now, knowing who she is, I suspect she might be older than that, so I keep my mouth shut.

"Morning, Morgan," I say.

I am hoping to get a reaction, something that says she's inexperienced and easily shaken. I am once more in my life disappointed with the results of my efforts.

Morgan looks up at me with an expression of sardonic

condescension bordering on disgust. I imagine if someone chased her for hours across a sweltering desert beneath the blazing sun, then when they finally caught up to her, vomited at her feet and expired of heat stroke and exhaustion. This is the look she'd give them. It's a complicated look.

"Good morning. It's Magdalena," she says. This time she doesn't actually say 'dick wad' or anything classy like that, but it is clearly implied by her tone.

I decide to change tactics.

"Fine, Magdalena," I say with a shrug. "I know you were Morgan's apprentice. I know you are working with Circe and that, at least as far as the Hizarin are concerned, you're now Morgan LeFey."

I am putting all of my cards on the table. I've been thinking about this for a while. I don't know what Morgan or Magdalena or whatever her name actually is. I don't know what her goals are. I don't know how they relate or interact with Circe's plans. I don't know if she has anything to do with Redbrook. I don't need to be waiting for any more surprises. I am going to get this all out in the open.

"Huh. Circe said you weren't as dumb as you looked. That is a low bar, by the way," she says. "Fine, you figured me out. It's still Magdalena, though Morgan LeFey is just a title they call me at Hizarin staff meetings."

"You have staff meetings?"

"No."

"What are you doing here?" I ask.

"We are on the job."

"And you coincidentally just happen to move in next door to me?"

"You old people never understand that it's not all about you."

"I'm not old."

She shrugs.

"Seriously, why next door?"

"You're a wild card. Circe felt like I should keep an eye on you so you don't burn something down and fuck up our plans."

"Not succeeding there, are you?" I ask.

She shrugs. "Keeping you in check isn't my job. I don't care if Circe's got a thing for you or whatever. She can't tell me what to do."

"Oh. Well. That's something?"

"I told Circe we could solve the problem easiest by simply taking care of you," she says, making a motion as if to shoot me in the head. "But Circe thinks you're valuable. That we can't finish the contract without you."

Magdalena gives me an indifferent shrug.

"What's the contract?" I ask.

Magdalena raises an eyebrow at me. She doesn't actually say anything, but the facial expression does plenty of talking on its own. It's confidential, and only an idiot would ask an assassin who their target is. Therefore, clearly, it is no surprise to her that I asked. That the only answer I can hope for is a bullet to the head.

"I see. But if you can't do this without me, shouldn't I know?"

"Do what you're told," she says, blowing a smoke ring in my face. "And maybe you and your friends get out of this. Fuck this up…"

She shrugs at me again. She tosses her cigarette butt on the ground at my feet and pointedly stomps it out. Then she reaches down to pick it up slowly. Almost like she's miming, she stands back up, making eye contact with me. Her eyes are a deep, dark, piercing brown, and I can see a little spark of rage burning behind them. I realize in this instant that she is almost my height. Her awkward, gangly, slouching teenage frame gives the impression that she is younger and, therefore, shorter than she is. She holds the cigarette butt in one hand right near my face. I can smell the acrid odor of burnt tobacco.

I feel like I've been here before and had this exact same

interaction with her. The look on her face and how she holds the cigarette in her hand all feel familiar. *Deja vu*. That's been happening a lot lately.

Without breaking eye contact, she suddenly flicks it over her shoulder. The cigarette butt sails over the railing of the open walkway. My eyes track it as it sails down and lands in an open trashcan on the ground floor, some twenty feet horizontally and another eighteen feet down.

"Have you ever considered professional sports?" I ask.

I look back at her, and she's never stopped staring into my face. I could spend all day trying that trick and never get it. Her point is made: Magdalena doesn't miss.

"Do the job. Leave no trace," she says as she turns and walks into her apartment without looking back. I can't tell if this is an order to me, a threat, or a statement of her own work ethic. I have more than a sneaking suspicion that it is all three.

Magdalena scares me.

I go for my run, but I cut it short as the temperature is rapidly rising. I get home a sweaty, dripping mess and turn on my air conditioner. It's slated to get up to an unseasonable one hundred and ten today. I sit down at my desk and decide to call Genevieve.

"Miles!" she answers. She sounds happy to hear from me, which is a good feeling after my social interactions of the past few days.

"Genevieve! It's good to hear a friendly voice."

"I was actually planning on calling you today," she says. "I am glad you beat me to the punch!"

"I'm glad you have a moment."

"Listen, I had a great time the other weekend, and I'd love to come visit again."

"Yeah of course. I would love that. Anytime."

"I am glad you said that I can be in Napa in a couple of hours."

"Wait, what?"

"Yeah, I had to fly down for some follow-up in San Jose. I wrapped up yesterday, and I was just about to check out of my hotel. I was thinking I could swing up and visit. I scheduled my return flight for Monday...you know for if you were free."

I feel a little red in the cheeks. What is this sensation? Is this excitement?

"That's great. Yes, seriously, anytime. I am looking forward to it." I say I feel like I am fumbling over my words.

"Yeah, me too," she says, her tone sounding like she's going to get off the phone.

"Hey, can I ask you a couple of questions first?"

"Sure shoot."

"First question: did you get the package I sent you?"

"What? No. Though I have been making a bunch of these one or two-night trips lately. I might have missed it," she says. "Is it something exciting?"

"That depends on your definition. Also, would you mind if we talk a little shop when you are here?"

"Um. No, I guess that's fine. Why? What's going on?"

"Well, I think I told you about the whole Lorelei Redbrook situation. Well. It's gotten... complicated," I say, trying to be vague on the phone.

"I see."

"And I. We. Could use your professional expertise," I conclude.

"Okay," she says, though I get the sense she was maybe looking forward to some time away from work-related troubles.

"Great. I'll come up with some fun stuff for us to do, too. It'll be mostly fun and only a little work."

"All right. I am looking forward to it. I'll see you in a couple of hours!"

"Great. I'll be at my place waiting!"

We hang up. I try to get some work done. Or some planning. Or anything productive. But I am having a hard time focusing. I'm feeling giddy and excited about Genevieve's visit.

It doesn't take long before I give up and start playing video games to pass the time.

My phone rings, informing me that it is Chris Benson, my friend on the city police force.

"Miles Ward, if bad juju is coming to you, I'm here to get you through!" I say as I answer the phone.

"A little long but better than most. I'd put that on the short-list," Chris says.

"Wow, thanks."

I've never gotten a compliment on one of my failed attempts at a tagline before.

"I was wondering if you had half an hour or so to go for a walk?" Chris asks.

"Yeah, is now a good time? I've got a little bit of free time."

"Now is perfect."

"Usual place?"

"Usual place is perfect."

The usual place is the Oxbow Preserve. It is quite quick to get to and easy to have a private conversation while going for a stroll. I always feel like a Cold War spy when we meet there. The fact that he wants to meet at the preserve means that he wants to talk business.

"I can be there in like ten minutes."

"Great. I will see you there."

I throw on some shoes and a baseball cap to cover the fact that I haven't brushed my hair and lope down the stairs to my car.

The route from my apartment to the preserve takes me past Soothsayers. I figure I will stop in and grab a coffee to go. Once I am there, I decide to grab another for Chris in case he wants one. As an afterthought, I grab a couple of scones. Consequently, I roll into the parking lot of the Oxbow Preserve about ten minutes late. Ten minutes late with coffee and snacks is perfectly on time. Right?

Chris is sitting on the hood of his pickup truck when I pull up. He's wearing a pale blue polo shirt. It is a little too tight in the biceps. His khaki slacks are similarly stretched over his quads. He's drinking coffee from a little styrofoam cup and eating a donut.

"You're late," he says.

"I was getting you a latte and a scone…" I say weakly.

"I'm good," he says, holding up his half-eaten donut and laughing.

I shrug. It's not like I won't consume both lattes and scones.

"I haven't seen you in a while," I say.

"Busy, it's been busy. Very busy."

"Yeah, with everything that has happened the last couple of weeks."

"That's what I wanted to talk to you about, actually."

"Oh?" I say nervously. I hope that this isn't about The Lantern burning down. I don't want to lie to Chris about that. I also don't want to tell him the truth.

"Yeah, specifically that anonymous tip that you gave me, Knights of Saint George?"

I nod and wait for him to go on.

"I took it to my Captain, the hat and the tip. He basically shrugged it off. Said he'd deal with it. But it got brushed under the rug."

I nod again and fidget with my fingers. With what Emily has found in Redbrook's files, I guess I am not surprised.

"I've been seeing that symbol around more, not only in graffiti and stuff. Some of the other guys have bumper stickers with that logo."

I am also not surprised to hear that some police are involved. It makes a lot more sense as to how that whole affair happened without more response.

"I see that look on your face, Miles, but I wouldn't jump to judgment if I were you. I mean this job it's not easy. We all join because we want to help people. I mean, yes, there are people who join the force for the wrong reasons. There are people that start any profession for the wrong reasons. But most of us are here to help, and sometimes it doesn't seem like the world wants our help. It's a job that can put us at odds with the people we are supposed to serve. One where we are trained to respond one way then criticized for doing what we were trained to do."

I stay silent. I want him to be able to say his piece. Apparently, my facial expression is doing some talking because he seems a little more agitated as he continues.

"And that was before. Miles, things are getting weird out there. It feels like, suddenly, there is all this stuff happening that we weren't trained for. Stuff there are no laws for. No manual. Curses and hexes, and I mean even weirder stuff. When we first met Miles, I thought you were crazy, like pretty far down the crazy scale. In my line of work, we meet some very out-of-control people, you know? And now? Now I can't tell if you are the craziest person I know or the sanest."

I grimace.

"If I didn't have a Miles Ward to go to when I came across this stuff…someone to explain and fix the problem, I'd need something because without the clarity you bring? I don't think I could do this anymore. And then, well, a group like the Knights of Saint George would fill that gap."

I nod and sit silently for a minute, gathering my own thoughts. I wait to see if he has more to say. He seems to have said his piece.

"That makes sense. But there is more."

"More?"

"Some evidence is coming to light that some less than savory parties might be exerting control over some of the decision-makers in your department. Well, actually, in a lot of places. By less than savory parties, I mean Lorelei Redbrook and her compatriots."

"You are being cagey. Miles just come out with it."

"I think Redbrook is using methods from blackmail and bribery to actual mind control to manipulate a number of people in your department. People in the city operations. People in the county government. I also think she belongs to an organization with even broader reach."

Chris sighs uncomfortably.

"Also, the Knights of Saint George. I'm not sure if she and her friends founded them or are simply manipulating them. But there is evidence suggesting that she put them on to her own scent. That she is pulling their strings."

"You think Lorelei Redbrook had her own place of business blown up, burned down, and almost got herself killed on purpose?"

"Had her place shot up? Yes. Almost killed? No. She's kind of invulnerable."

"Invulnerable?"

"I'd like to explain it, but I don't totally understand it myself. She's some ancient monster. Maybe prehuman? But Ishe can't be harmed by bullets or any mortal weapon, for that matter. I have a friend who thinks she is doing it for publicity. That works very well for her narrative that Napa is going to shit. That it needs strong leadership, yada yada."

"What does that mean? Mortal weapon?"

"Honestly, I don't know. I think it means that there are things that can harm her, but nothing you or I could do would."

We sit for another minute in silence.

"I don't normally go in for conspiracy theories, but that makes sense," he says. "Too much sense."

I shrug.

"You say evidence. What kind of evidence?"

I sigh.

"Well…she may have had a secret office in the lantern, and I may have broken in there and copied a bunch of her files."

He puts his fist to his forehead and groans "And burned the building down?"

"I. Well, I don't know, not on purpose. The timing and

circumstances don't look good for me, I will admit. But timing and circumstances have not been on my side a lot of late."

Now it is Chris's turn to sigh a big sigh. He leans back on his truck and puts his hands over his face. We sit quietly. I can hear the vague gurgle of the river birds chirping and the distant thrum of traffic.

Finally, Chris breaks the silence.

"Okay, so she's already got her fingers in…well, it sounds like you are saying everything. She's blackmailing, bribing, and…mind-controlling people. Sowing fear, uncertainty, and doubt to spur the rest to action…what all to run for mayor?"

"Well, if she's to be believed, she wants the monsters and warlocks to run the show. She's tired of being in the shadows and wants to come out. And she wants Napa to be ground zero for it."

"Okay, but why here? Wouldn't a big city make more sense? New York? DC? Los Angeles?"

"No. Not really. There's a lot more going on. Those places are too big. There are too many players. This city is just the right size. Big enough to have some sway and small enough to be able to know everybody who does anything in this town. There's a lot of wealth per capita here. But I have a theory on why here and not say Carmel or some other small to midsized city with a lot of wealth."

"Yeah?" Chris says, his voice sounding suddenly tired.

"Well, the Lamia is a Greek myth originally. She's got a lot of Greek motifs in her home. Motifs with a lot of wine themes. I think that was the region she was from originally, and I think this reminds her of home."

He nods and takes that in for a minute.

"She is also not operating alone. I'm not even sure she's the brains behind it all. I think she's a sub-boss," I say.

"Sub-boss?"

"Sorry, I've been playing a lot of video games lately. I think she's nothing but middle management. I think there are people above her calling the shots."

"Okay, so what do we do?"

I think for a minute.

"I have a group of friends that are trying to deal with Redbrook specifically. We are taking a two-pronged approach. A political attack to derail the campaign for her. Slow her down while trying to figure out how to thwart her larger plans more holistically."

"How can I help?"

"I have thought about that. I have an idea. But it's dangerous."

"I am listening."

"What if you joined the Knights of Saint George? Make them see that they are being manipulated. Remove them from her toolbox. If they have members in the force, that could be a good in for you. I can show you a trick for telling if they are mind-controlled. There might even be a cure for it if people are."

"I'm in," Chris says without hesitation.

"You sure?"

"Yeah, if others on the force are being manipulated or controlled, I want to stop that."

"Okay," I say.

I give him a gazing crystal and spend the next twenty minutes showing him how to read auras and working with him to practice. I explain the principles behind enthralling people with magic and how to identify magical influence. I explain what it might look like if someone is too far gone.

Finally, Chris interrupts, "I need to get going. My shift starts in an hour."

I look at the time on my phone. I need to get going too! Genevieve will be at my apartment soon.

"Okay, good luck. I'll keep you in the loop. Welcome to the Not Redbrook For Mayor Club!" I say.

"Auxiliary only," Chris says.

"You don't want to pay union dues."

Chris laughs. "Let's keep in touch. I'll ask around and see what I can find out."

"Sounds good," I say, giving him the thumbs up. I chug down the last of the two coffees and start toward my car.

"Oh, and Miles?" Chris says before I get into my car.

"Yeah?"

"Let's try not to make a bigger mess than we've already got."

"If I were calling the shots…" I say.

He nods.

I get into my car and drive home.

Chapter Twenty-Four

BACK AT MY APARTMENT, I quickly get bored and fidgety. Anxiety, impatience, and stress are snapping and snarling in my mind like a hungry pack of Tasmanian devils. I pace. I pick up my video game controller but then decide I don't want to be gaming when Genevieve arrives. I put it down, walk to the window, and stare impatiently at the parking lot for a few minutes. I vacuum my floor. I shower and go to get dressed. I take out two identical sets of clothes. Then I realize Hank isn't here, so forlorn, I put one outfit back.

I pace some more.

It is less than an hour or so before she arrives, but it seems interminable. When I see her pulling up into the parking lot, I stand in the window and watch as she gets out of her car. She is wearing an off-white shirt. I don't know what the style of shirt it is. I guess it is a T-shirt, but it's not cut like any of my T-shirts. The neck is a little wider, showing off her collar bones, the sleeves are a little shorter, and it tapers in a little toward the waist. As casual as the outfit is, she looks stunning. She walks to her trunk. She fumbles with the keys while I tap my foot. She pops the trunk.

"Settle down, Miles!" I tell myself out loud. I move away

from the window and go to start a pot of coffee brewing. I get the grounds into the filter when the doorbell rings.

I all but run to the door and throw it open. There is a Genevieve suitcase in hand. I notice that she has a much smaller handbag than the last time I saw her. This little clutch is definitely not hiding that giant flashlight she used for Rebob bopping.

"Hi!" I say.

"Hi!" she says and leans forward and gives me a kiss on the lips that I am not expecting but reciprocate gladly. This new relationship is exciting, like a rollercoaster. But like a rollercoaster, I think it might be going a little too fast, and I worry it might not stay on the tracks.

I show her in, glancing curiously at her suitcase.

"Oh. I guess I should have asked. Can I stay with you?" she asks. "Please tell me if that's not okay, and I can get a hotel."

My face feels hot, and my shirt collar suddenly feels a little too tight. There is a strange flippy sensation in my gut, like the rollercoaster just did a loop-the-loop.

"Um, no, no, that would be great. I was caught a little off guard. I'll need to straighten up a bit," I stammer.

"Relax!" she says, pressing past me with a comfortable hip bump.

"Yeah. I am relaxed!" I say, not convincing anyone, especially not myself.

"All right," she says, sitting down in a chair on the client side of my desk. "Sock it to me. Let's get this work stuff over with and get on to the fun."

I sit down in my office chair across from her with a sigh.

"Okay," I say. Then I proceed to tell her everything. And I mean everything possibly oversharing. I even tell her all about almost going on a date with Emily, but Genevieve doesn't seem shaken by this at all. She jots notes down on a tablet as I talk.

"So," I conclude, "We have this information on Redbrook

that we want to get to the public. To attack her chances of getting elected, stall her plans, and maybe get some law enforcement involvement. But we also don't want to bring the whole monsters-among-us thing to light. At least not any more than we have to."

Genevieve nods.

"You are going to need to go big. It sounds like she's got leverage on too many people locally. Doing this is going to make you some powerful enemies. Enemies who are comfortable operating outside the boundaries of the law. Not only Redbrook and her little club. There are others. You could be getting yourself in pretty deep," Genevieve concludes.

"What do you mean?"

Genevieve sits back and crosses her legs.

"This story isn't new, Miles. It doesn't matter if they are powerful and entitled because they are immortal beings, entitled because they have access to powerful magic, or entitled because they are just wealthy. People with power don't like to lose it. And they don't like to see other powerful people lose it unless they are taking it from them. If you topple one house of cards, others in a similar situation will see you as a threat."

"I see."

"I've done some digging on the Dominium Deloris. Not much, but enough to learn that people that dig too deep…"

"Vanish?" I ask.

"No, they just kind of fade away. You can find them. In private care. Under conservatorship. In institutions. Living on the streets. Credibility and agency eliminated."

"I get it."

"Yes, but do your friends know?"

"Yeah, I think they do anyway. Are you okay with getting in this deep?"

She laughs. "I don't really start swimming till I'm in over my head. Don't worry about me."

"Oh," I say. I like Genevieve. I like that she doesn't seem to have any brakes on life. However, I worry a little about the spark I see in her eye when danger is even mentioned. That spark becomes veritable lightning when confronted with actual danger. When Rebobs attacked us, she seemed actually giddy.

"You always seem very, um, eager to swim the proverbial sharks," I say tentatively.

She laughs, "Or real sharks. Yeah, I don't know. I've always liked a little excitement in my life. My quiet, reserved parents always said my first sixteen years aged them thirty."

I nod.

"Okay. Can I meet up with your little gang of monster baiters?" she says, still laughing at herself.

"Really?" I say skeptically at her bad pun.

"Well, what else should I call you and your friends?" she giggles. "You aren't fighting or hunting them. You're trying to bait one out of local politics, right?"

"Yes," I say, rolling my eyes, "I can set up a little meeting. I don't know if Jeff and Emily will both show they seem to be having some sort of quarrel."

"If you have to choose, Emily sounds like she's the one with the clear plan. Honestly, Jeff sounds kind of like an ass," she says.

I shrug. Jeff is a good friend of mine. Sure, he's got his moments. He's got his blindspots like any of us. Though I agree with her, Jeff was acting like kind of an ass last night. I wonder what's going on with him.

"Here, let me send Emily a quick message," I say. This only takes a few seconds.

"Okay, so that's easy. The hard part is you have to get a gemstone into Redbrook's house for..." Genevieve briefly reviews the notes she took while I was giving her the background. "Circe, who is Hizarin and may or may not be...a dream?"

"Yeah, that's right," I say with no irony in my voice.

"Okay, how do we do that?" Genevieve asks.

"I am meeting Redbrook at her house on Monday. I think

that is my window. But I don't know how to get into her bedroom unnoticed. Hell, I don't even know where it is."

"I think it's cute how uncomfortable you get talking about getting into a lady's bedroom," Genevieve says.

"She's a Lamia. The Lamia? I'm not clear on that one. Anyway, she's an awful human-eating creature from the dawn of history, so yeah, I am a little terrified of what I'll find in her bedroom. Or even what she considers a bedroom."

"Poor taste in flirting, I retract my statement."

"It's fine. I'm a little high-strung right now."

"Okay. Well, I'll help you on Monday. You make a distraction. I'll get into her bedroom and plant the gem."

"I couldn't ask you to do that. It's dangerous," I say.

"You didn't ask me to do it. You didn't even imply you'd want me to do it. I volunteered completely of my own accord, and I know how dangerous it is. Danger is my middle name."

I smile a little at the cliche.

"No, seriously, my father thought he was hilarious. My middle name is Danger. Little did they know…" She takes her ID out of her clutch and shows it to me. 'Genevieve Marie-Danger Gale.'

"Marie-Danger?"

"My mother wanted to name me after my Gram Marie my dad wanted Danger, so they compromised."

"Huh," I say, realizing that she has successfully used her unusual middle name to distract me from the topic and concede to let her help by default. Part of me is trepidatious about it, but part of me is relieved to have the help.

"We can sort out those details. Right now, fun is not going to make itself!" Genevieve says, taking my hand and dragging me out my front door. "Show me the good stuff!"

We head downtown and walk up and down First Street. We get very expensive goose liver pate Banh Mi from a fancy restaurant. We taste wine at half a dozen different tasting rooms. I stay sober by not tasting too much and leaning hard on spitting.

I don't dislike wine. But it is also not something that brings me a great deal of joy. I can appreciate it in the right context. Taking a date on a tasting tour on a beautiful day that's the right context to appreciate it. Still, I find that after two or three pours, I can't tell the difference anyway. Genevieve is less reserved than I am. This makes her even more outgoing and energetic.

We go into a shop where she insists we buy matching hats. They are both woven straw hats, sort of a slightly wide-brimmed Panama style. Both with cloth hat-bands printed with a grape pattern. I think they are kind of tacky, but I don't say anything.

"We should go for a light hike somewhere, Miles!" Genevieve announces as we are leaving the store with our new hats, "Hats, this fabulous must be flaunted!"

"We could head to Skyline and hike up to Lake Marie. It's not long, but it's a bit of a climb."

"Lake Marie…Danger!" She says with a peal of laughter. I wonder if maybe she's overindulged.

"Hopefully not."

"Let's go! To the Miles-Mobile!" She exclaims and starts dragging me by the arm toward my car.

We drive to the southeastern side of town. On the far side of the State Hospital is Skyline Regional Park. Long ago, it was part of the hospital campus. However, the state turned it into a regional park when it closed the 'farm' portion of the hospital program. It has extensive hiking trails, camping spaces, a disc golf course, an archery range, and equestrian facilities.

I pay at the kiosk and pull into the parking lot.

We start the hike up to Lake Marie. It is only a couple of miles, but it is all uphill on the way there. About two-thirds of the way up the trail, we stop and sit on a bench in the shade of a large California Bay tree. It is getting warm, and my skin feels like it is slowly baking in the convection currents of the breeze. The pungent smell of bay and sun-baked grasses haunt my memories. I flashback to the bright summer days of childhood, free of school, galavanting through the hills. Those innocent and carefree days before everything changed.

"I've been thinking about your problem, Miles," Genevieve says, a thankful interruption to my thoughts.

"Redbrook?"

"Yes, but no, I mean the whole problem. There are a lot of question marks. Redbrook. Shelly. Hale, Circe, Morgan, all of that."

"And?"

"You're super smart. I watched you at MystiCon with that Solomon Grey guy. You figured his whole deal out in like a minute. You were like Sherlock Freaking Holmes!" she says, over boisterous. She uses her arms in an overly emphatic way to punctuate each phrase.

"Sherlock Holmes derives solutions primarily based on the knowledge that he uniquely and conveniently has. I only stated the obvious."

"In hindsight, obvious. Maybe. But no, Miles, it wasn't obvious. There is a mystery here, the same! Why aren't you solving it?"

I sit quietly in the shade of the tree. The balmy herbal smell wafts over me; the birds are chirping. Genevieve is the only other person I can see or hear. For the first time in days, I have a faint sense of calm, of peace, at least for the moment.

"That is different," I say finally.

"How so?" She snorts and pokes me in the left arm with a single finger.

"There are two kinds of 'mysteries' in my experience. There are things that happen that we don't understand, and there are things that are contrived. Stories."

"I think I know what you mean, but please indulge me and explain it."

"So Solomon Grey, if that is his real name…it's not, by the way, his real name is Matthew Smith," I say.

Genevieve laughs far too loud and far too long at this fact. She is clearly still buzzed. Maybe more than buzzed.

"Sorry," she says, making a concerted effort to regain her composure.

"Anyway," I continue. "His mystery was contrived. It was something he decided to do. So he came up with a story and then played it out. It was a story he wrote in advance, so it had discrete pieces to it and followed a narrative chain. He was using a pretty predictable stage magic trick to temporarily fake his own death in a grand and dramatic way to get attention."

"Yes, go on, tell me more about Matt Smith," Genevieve nods, grinning like she's about to have another giggling fit.

"Mysteries in the real world—I mean real mysteries, things that really happen—aren't like that. They are organic. They are the results of lots of people making a lot of snap decisions. Decisions that intersect and interact with each other. Few real thefts, for example, are the result of a heist, as you see in films. They aren't planned, at least not like that. They are simply things that happen."

I stop to take a breath. A man is hiking up the trail. He has a floppy, wide-brimmed hat, two walking poles, and one of those backpacks for carrying water. Either he is going a lot farther than we are, or he is wildly over-prepared. As he passes, I tip my straw hat to him. He nods in return. We wait in silence until he's turned the corner of the trail. I turn back to Genevieve.

"Someone is walking by a house. They notice there are no cars in the driveway, and the rear gate is open. They decide to walk around the house and see if there is anything they can grab. There's no plot. They don't engineer a distraction. They don't get a team of specialists together. For something like this, figuring out the 'who done it' is about getting evidence that the person was there or wasn't. There's no bigger scheme to figure out."

"Okay, so is all this stuff you are dealing with like that?

Matt Smith, noticing the door was open?" She says, grinning from ear to ear.

"Yes," I start to say, but then I interrupt myself, "Well, I mean no. There are definitely contrived plots. But it's like a combination of a series of different people's plots intersecting such that it makes it unpredictable. There is too much chaos."

"Who is the master of chaos?" Genevieve asks. She's looking at me pointedly.

"Um, I don't know that I agree, but based on your expression, I am guessing the answer is me?"

She nods.

"You are a hot mess, Miles Ward," she says, then quickly follows up, "Which is totally cute and irresistible, by the way. Take you out of the equation, and what do you have?" She asks. A couple of glasses of wine, and there is no filter on this woman.

I think about this for a minute. If I wasn't involved, what would have happened? Whitman would have died, probably. Circe would have left town, job complete. The Lantern would still be shot up. Redbrook wouldn't have been injured in the process. Would Redbrook still be winning the election? Is that how it would have played out? Would Circe be done and leave town?

"So what you are saying is that the reason I don't see plans clearly is because I'm muddying the waters for myself? That Redbrook does have a scheme with a story, like Solomon Grey. But that I keep messing up her plans."

"I'm saying you can't see the big picture because you are too busy defacing it. I did that in the Moma once. Step back and look at it. When you find it, you'll at least have answers."

I think this through. What would be happening if Jeff had never been tattooed as part of Circe's plan? If I hadn't been hired to the JMBaptiste and stopped Circe from killing Whitman? If I hadn't worked with Circe to take down Redbrook? And what did Genevieve do in the Moma?

I'm not the one causing the chaos. Circe and Morgan are.

I was just a tool. Circe is at war with Redbrook. Or at least she's been hired to war with Redbrook. Things Magdalena and Circe have said lead me to believe that Redbrook was always their target. There are multiple factions at work here.

"That's a lot to think about. Do you really think I am a hot mess?"

She shrugs and starts pulling me off the bench. "Enough talk, more walk!"

"Okay," I say, not sure if I should be hurt or flattered. Walking some of that wine off is probably a good idea.

Genevieve marches me up the trail like she's a drill sergeant and I'm a new recruit. The hike seems to be sweating the wine out of her, and she's far less goofy by the time we reach Lake Marie. I'm not sure that I'd categorize it as a lake. It looks more like a large pond to me. Created as a reservoir by building an earthen dam in a creek that flows down through the canyon, it's maybe a hundred yards at its longest. Filled with various water plants that I don't have names for. Its swampy surface looks un-swimmable. Despite that, there are signs warning us away from swimming in it. Genevieve doesn't suggest going for a quick skinny dip to spite the sign, for which I am both surprised and relieved.

On the way back down, Genevieve wants to take one of the other trails.

"Let's have a change of scenery and take this trail down," she says, pointing at a sign for the Skyline trail. Behind it, a narrow dirt path winds its way between poison oak-choked weeds up into the wilderness.

"Sure, but it's a little rougher a trail."

"Nothing wrong with rough every now and then," she says, winking at me as she starts up the trail.

I fall in behind her as we wind our way up the path. Genevieve seems comfortable outdoors, and I don't have to warn her away from poison oak or stinging nettle, or any of the other botanical hazards we come upon.

At the precipice of one of the hills whose name I don't

know, we stop to catch our breath and enjoy the view. Below us, rising above the trees in the valley, is The Castle. From the ground in front of the massive hospital building, it looks imposing and ominous. Like it was torn out of some gothic horror novel, looking down at it from on high, I can't help but think it looks like it is out of a fairy tale.

"Huh, it is kind of pretty from up here," I comment.

"What is that?" Genevieve asks.

"That's the Castle, the state hospital's main building."

She nods, and we watch in silence for a few more minutes before continuing down the trail.

A brief stop at my apartment ends with us staying in for the night and ordering a pizza. A day of travel, day drinking, and a hike seems to have taken its toll on Genevieve. So we stay in chat, read, and eat some pizza before turning in early.

Chapter Twenty-Five

"I'M COMING FOR YOU, Miles Ward," the voice echoes through the corridors. It reverberates back and forth through the hall and passage. Room to room. I cannot tell which direction it is coming from.

I quickly unlock a door to my right and step in. The door slams behind me, and the lock re-engages. No sooner is it locked than I can hear the door rattling on its hinges as someone shakes the handle from the other side.

"You can't lock me out," the voice says suddenly. It is right behind me, and I jump, turning in mid-air. I land staring at an empty room.

I take two deep breaths. I am startled once again by the door rattling behind me. I run to a narrow closet door in the corner of this small room and open it. There is a long hallway behind which I dash down.

"Running never helps. I am inevitable," the voice echoes through the hallway. I get to a door at the end. I slam through it and find myself back in the same small, unfurnished room that I just left.

I quickly unlock the door I first came through and lunge back out into the hallway beyond. It is empty.

"Am I in your mind, Miles?" the voice echoes through the

building. "Or are you in mine? Where does one end and the other begin? If I snuff you out in my mind, will you snuff yourself out in yours?"

I don't respond. I'm dreaming. But this is different. This is like when Russ shows up, but that's not Russ. There is someone else in my dream, and they seem more than a little bit hostile.

I run from corridor to corridor, room to room, but the voice is always there, taunting me. It isn't following me. This isn't the nameless fear that a Daunt brings. This is the very real terror of having a very real person stalking you. Stalking with intent to murder. Only this voice seems to be enjoying my confusion and fear.

Another Dreamwalker.

Dream. That's right, I'm dreaming, I remind myself. I can control this. I have to do what Russ said.

I continue running room to room, corridor to corridor. The voice seems distant but ever closer. Finally, I turn into a hallway and instinctively turn to the left. Don't go right. Don't look right. An instinct deep inside of me screams **avoid right**.

No. I have to turn right. I turn right, and there is a door. A familiar door.

The Door.

It's an old manufactured interior door. It's worn, and the wood has been stripped bare by the weather. The laminations are starting to peel, so the edges look like a dog-eared paperback. There is an old, tarnished brass doorknob. Above it, like a gaping maw, is an empty socket where a deadbolt would be. A faded red paisley bandana has been shoved into the open hole to keep the draft out. The bandana looks like a bloody tongue hanging out.

At the foot of the door, there is a worn, pitted, and moldy section of a once-burgundy carpet placed as a doormat on the old rotted wooden stoop. An unfamiliar brass contraption is bolted to the wall next to the door. An array of large chunky brass knobs and dials with a labyrinth of brass tubes wound around them. The lock is alien and foreign, but I know this door.

This door is so familiar yet so repugnant. This is the door that Russ said I should enter.

I dash to the door. The presence of the stalker closes in behind me, slowly savoring my blossoming fear.

I frantically flip dials and turn knobs. It comes to me in a flash. I move knobs and dials and switches until I've put in the right code. I don't know the significance of the series of digits, and I don't care. I know at this moment that it is correct. I turn the doorknob and lunge through the door. As I slam the door shut behind me, I can feel the talon-like hands of my unseen pursuer slice inches away from my neck.

I feel dizzy. Sick. A litany of pages turned uselessly, a story consumed and forgotten. A scintillating point in time whose significance is as great as the rising of a god and insignificant as the falling of a leaf in whose beauty the universe is reflected. Can a story tell itself? Are there stories at all? Just a jumble of words, all struggling and vying for meaning in the library of the infinite.

Orphaned, I starve in the stinking gutters of the ancient city. Why are you thinking this? My stomach cramps as I lay down in a nest of rat-infested blankets for the last time to dream of a silver skyline. Please stop. White lines of cocaine on a mirrored desk. Despair. Failure. Are you okay? Financial ruin, an open window. Freedom. Terror. Release. Why are you doing this to me? I sew till my fingers blister and bleed. Please make this stop. It is crowded and hot. Coughing fits. Waves of misery. How will I feed my family? Please. The bay of the dogs. The crisp black air in my lungs.

We are scared. We are the words lost in the sentence. The thrill and joy of a thousand names and faces as they look into each other's eyes. There, they see love and hate and pain and joy and misery reflected back upon themselves like two funhouse mirrors facing each other. Who are we? We are a sentence lost on the pages. Who are we? We are the pages lost in the word. Is this your story or my story, or our story?

We wake up, and we don't know who I am. I don't know where we are. There are a thousand voices in my head murmuring a susurrus of thoughts and words and ideas. I can only pick out a few, a confusing, maddening hodgepodge of ideas and emotions. I am we, but I don't remember which one of the we I am. I'm screaming. I am in my bed. Focus on that. Feel the sheets. The sweat-soaked pillow. What's my name? Where am I?

"Miles," a voice says. It's soft and comforting, and I am happy to hear it, "Miles, wake up!"

I am being ever so gently shaken awake.

That's right. I'm Miles. And the person talking to me is Genevieve.

My eyes snap open. I'm lying in bed. I'm soaked in sweat. Genevieve is next to me, one hand on my shoulder, trying to comfort me. She looks concerned.

"Miles, are you okay? You must have been having a terrible nightmare," she says.

"I think someone tried to kill me in my dreams."

"What?" she says, sounding confused and alarmed. "How does that work?"

"Redbrook. She's got a Dreamwalker on the payroll. I think they're trying to kill me."

"Can people be killed in their dreams? Why would they try to kill you? Don't you have dirt on her? All her files that she's expecting to get from you tomorrow?"

"Well, yeah, but I'm not going to give them to her. She probably suspects that at this point. Maybe they are trying to find out where it is, dig it out of my mind, or…I don't know. Something."

"Is that possible?" Genevieve asks.

I shrug helplessly. I have no idea.

"I am going to call Russ. He's kind of my dream mentor."

Chapter Twenty-Six

THE SMELL of old books is the first thing that greets us as we arrive at Grape Reads. I let Genevieve go first. The passage between bookshelves is too narrow to walk side by side. Ren is behind the counter. They're on the phone. Ren gives me a little hello wave when I come in and then points toward the door to the back room. I nod and lead Genevieve through the store.

"This place is cute," Genevieve says. "Oh look, my book is on the staff picks shelf."

"Yeah. I think Emily has a little author crush on you."

"Oh," Genevieve says. There is no inflection to it. I can't tell if that is interesting to her or if it's an awkward source of dread.

"Don't worry. I don't think she's going to be a gushing fan girl."

"It's the 'I want to wear your skin' fans that I'm more concerned about."

I look at her, alarmed.

"I'm just kidding. I've only had one of those, and he's in jail now."

"You're still kidding."

She turns waggles her eyebrows at me with a Mona-Lisa-smile and turns to push her way through the door.

Emily and Russ are inside. Emily is sitting on a bench with a laptop in front of her, looking anxious. Russ is thumbing through a book with his usual relaxed grin.

"They're here!" Emily says, jumping up and speed-shuffling across the room, releasing a long 'squee' sound. Oh right! Emily is absolutely a gushing fan girl.

Russ closes his book. I can see the cover as he does. It's a work on tantric magic.

"Great, dude!" Russ says, raising a hand to wave to us.

"Genevieve," I introduce her.

"I'm a huge fan!" Emily gushes. "I know you're doing non-fiction now, but your early work. So good."

"Thank you. Always good to meet a fan," Genevieve says. Again, the flat and unreadable inflection.

"No, Jeff?" I ask.

Emily gets a dark look on her face and shakes her head no.

"Jeff and I are…taking some space."

"Oh," I say.

At least I don't say, 'Well, that didn't last long,' 'What happened?' 'I should have started that pool,' or the dozen other inappropriate things that pop into my head. I don't know what to say. Everything that comes to mind seems like it will make things worse, so in a rare turn of events, I keep my mouth shut.

"Emily!" Genevieve cuts in on the awkward turn of the conversation. "I hear you are the brains of the operation, and I'd love to go over all these Redbrook files with you."

Emily perks up.

"Yeah, there's so much. Miles might have committed arson to get it and set Redbrook up to look very sympathetic, but at least he got us this smoking gun!" Emily says in another burst of enthusiasm. Genevieve walks over, and they start looking at Emily's laptop.

"Hey Russ," I say, "I had a dream last night that I wanted to talk to you about."

"Yeah, sure thing, Miles," he says, and we sit in a corner away from where Emily and Genevieve are pouring over the computer. Emily is talking very fast and very loud. She is, in my opinion, entirely too enthusiastic.

Russ and I hunker down for a much quieter conversation.

I explain last night's dream to him as best I can. The ending is a little difficult to describe, but I muddle my way through it. Russ sits silently, nodding as he listens. When I finish, he sits thinking for a moment, one hand twirling the whiskers on his chin.

"All right, my man, here is the thing," he says. "You made it too far too fast that took you like what? Two tries to make it in the door?"

"It was more like a half dozen."

"Fine, sure, sure, but usually it takes like hundreds of tries. A half dozen, that's unheard of."

"Really?"

"Yeah, like suspicious fast. Anyway, so normally after you came to me like frustrated 'cause you got to the door like twenty or thirty times or whatever, I'd give you this advice. But until you get good at finding the door and like getting your hands on it, this advice just confuses things. So anyway, you got to build yourself a context," he says.

"Context?"

"Or maybe like a filter."

"A filter?"

"Yeah, man! You are opening your mind to the gestalt of the whole universe, man, like every thought or idea or thing or dream that ever was and ever will be in all of existence. It's too much for the human mind to handle, right? You can't make sense of that! You need context to process it all in. A filter, dude. Dreaming is like the opposite of magic," he says, speaking faster than I've ever heard him before. He sounds a little manic.

"What do you mean the opposite of magic?"

"Well, with magic, you are opening up reality to let things from the outside in. With dreaming, you are opening up yourself to let things from outside in. I guess that's not really the opposite. But either way, it's all about letting things in. You're all guarded, always sealing stuff away. So the first time you open up, it's like all or nothing. You gotta let some stuff in, man, but like filter, let the right stuff in. You do that. You'll become an excellent Dreamwalker."

"Is that safe? Nothing can hurt me in my dreams. Can it?"

"Oh no, no, no. Dude, stuff can totally hurt you in your dreams."

"But you said Daunts could only do real damage if you physically confronted them."

"Yeah, that's right, Daunts, dude. But it sounds like you are dealing with a Dreamstalker. A person, they can definitely hurt you."

"Okay…"

"A Dreamstalker can like put thoughts in your head. Ideation, man. Crazy ideas. They can make your brain think your heart doesn't work, and then like, man, it doesn't, right?"

"So this person could kill me in my dreams?" I ask, alarmed.

"Yeah, man, Dreamwalking is not like guaranteed safe. I mean, it's pretty safe, but other people are the biggest threats. There's plenty of other bad stuff that can happen when you get off the ride and go exploring without preparation or a plan."

"Why didn't you tell me that sooner!" I say, raising my voice a little.

"Settle down, settle down. Once you build up a few like tools, you'll be good. You'll be good! You gotta build context like I said, a filter, man."

"A filter," I say, looking blankly. "How do I do that?"

"Okay, right, so you've got to build your *reva fortikaĵo* your dream fortress, right?"

"What?" I ask.

"Like, when I 'walk right when I become lucid and open my mind to the universe and all that, it's a grand adventure. I am Rusty Russ, the Russet Ranger. That was my Dungeons and Dragons character when I was a kid, man. Anyway, so I contextualize it by going on an adventure, you know, monsters and treasures and whatever. It doesn't have to be that. It can be whatever is comfortable and works for you. You make a story your mind can handle, so you aren't drinking from a proverbial firehose of thoughts and ideas."

"Okay, but how do I do that?"

"Right, man. So dig my *reva fortikaĵo* is a little hunting shack in the woods that Rusty Russ lives in. It's a familiar place that I've built up through decades of mental repetition and focus, man. I have built all the tools I will need in it, and it gives me a basic framework and a context from which to go out and assimilate the Dreamtime. It's like my little safe space between here and there that I can start filtering from."

"Okay," I say. I don't feel like he's answering my questions. I grind my teeth a little in frustration. "So how do I build this...*reva fortikaĵo*?"

"Right. So when you get to the door, imagine the space on the other side of it. Imagine it in detail. You have to, like, convince yourself it is there, and you go in, and you keep imagining it. You have to impose it on the universe, dude. Paint it like a picture and sculpt it like a block of clay so that when you go through, that's where you are. It takes years, man, but then you get to where you like can imagine it all, build it all as like a reflex, right? So it's always there."

"What you are saying sounds great, but it's like handing me a box of toothpicks and telling me to build an actual size model of the Eiffel Tower. I can't even say I don't know where to start. I don't even know where to start figuring out where to start."

"It's something you gotta feel, man. I don't know how to tell you. When most people finally get through the door, it's easy. The focus required in getting through sort of, I don't know, trains them," he says. "But I don't think you got through the door on your own, man. I think someone pulled you through or opened it and shoved you in or something. Nothing about what you described sounds normal."

I furrow my brow and glower at the floor. Who would do that and why?

"You gotta be careful, Miles. You could mush your brain opening your mind up like that with no filters and no preparation."

"I see," I say, but I don't really. I'm not sure that Russ is going to be able to clarify anything else to me at this point. "This is a lot to think about. Can we pick more of this up later?"

"Yeah man, yeah. But we shouldn't, like, wait too long, not if this Dreamstalker stuff is going to become a regular event."

We sit in silence for a minute. Then, my curiosity gets the better of me.

"*Reva fortikaĵo*. What are all these words you keep using? It sounds kind of like Latin, but they aren't."

"Oh yeah, no, man, it's Esperanto."

"Esperanto? Why Esperanto?"

"Oh, it's kind of like Dreamwalker tradition. I've heard as many stories about why as I have met Dreamwalkers. Most involve Ludwik Zamenhof being a Dreamwalker. Some say that he learned the language in a dream. Some say it's the true language of the dream. Some say he invented it so that Dreamwalkers had a way to talk about dreams. Some say one of the early Esperanto devotees was a Dreamwalker and used Esperanto to speak to his friends about it without being overheard. I personally think he had nothing to do with it. I think it's one of those things that happened over time, like emoji."

"Emoji?" I ask, "Actually… never mind."

"Sure. So, we use Esperanto. I don't know the real reason it started, but it is useful to delineate ideas specific to

Dreamwalking as separate from like real world stuff," he says then, almost as if it were an afterthought adds, "Man."

"We should probably go see what Genevieve and Emily are up to," I say, glancing toward where they are huddled over Emily's laptop.

"Oh hey dude, like quick reminder we were supposed to, like, you know, figure out how to trap the Lamia? You said you were gonna call, and you didn't?" Russ asks.

"Right! Sorry, there's been so much going on."

"You got a little romantic interest going on, man. I get it."

"I guess I'm also a little skeptical. If the trap didn't work on Circe, why would it work on Redbrook?"

"Yeah, man, well, I've been thinking about that…" Russ begins, but he doesn't finish his sentence as our conversation is interrupted when Genevieve calls us over.

"I have concerns," Genevieve says. Emily's arms are crossed, and she looks irritated.

"Yeah?"

"This is absolutely the smoking gun Emily says it is; there is a lot of evidence here and some easy avenues to verify some of it. Emily's done a lot of work to fill in blanks, name names, etc. It's quite thorough work," Genevieve says, looking at Emily. Emily seems torn on whether to stay peeved or be flattered.

"So…what's the problem?"

"The problem is it's going to be hard to bring all this to light and not start having some uncomfortable questions asked, particularly in regards to Lorelei Redbrook's, particularly unreasonable longevity. It's hard to present this information without bringing up a lot of questions that I don't know if we want to be asked," Genevieve says.

"So what do we do?"

"She wants to let Redbrook off the hook," Emily says.

"That's not true, not exactly," Genevieve says. "We cut some stuff out. We don't bring all the ugliest stuff to light. We can spin this to ruin her election chances, get the spotlight on this, and at the same time not raise a bunch of questions with impossible or very uncomfortable answers."

"That sounds reasonable," I say, looking at Emily. "What is your concern, Emily?"

"My concern is that Redbrook is a card-carrying human-eating monster that has destroyed thousands, if not tens or hundreds of thousands of lives across history. It might even be bigger than that! This is a slap on the wrist, and she gets to walk away and start her nightmare bullshit new again," Emily says.

We sit in silence for a moment.

"Emily, we've got this. It is a two-pronged plan. We ruin the election and send a clear message to her and hers. Meanwhile, we find another, more permanent way to stop her."

"You mean kill her."

"I don't know what I mean, Emily. We are still working on that. We don't need perfect right now. We need good enough," I say.

Genevieve looks at Emily and opens her arms into a posture that says, 'What do you say?'

Emily glowers for a minute, but her face softens.

"One step at a time. Yeah," Emily says. "We can do that. I guess."

"Let's get Kraken!" Genevieve says.

"Lamia!" I say.

"Wrong Greek monster, thank you," Genevieve says. "Let's get Lamia!"

Emily and Russ both roll their eyes at us.

"Russ and I will figure out how to deal with Redbrook's Dreamstalker."

Genevieve and Emily go back to working on the computer. I turn back to Russ.

"Is it possible to get information from someone's mind Dreamwalking?"

"I mean. Dude. Tough question. Yes. No. Sort of?" he says.

"That is all of the answers, Russ."

"It's like quantum physics, man. By observing the universe, you change it. So you can find people's thoughts in the Dreamtime, but you can never be sure if the thoughts were theirs or yours or someone else's. But there are more reliable ways of getting people to tell you things in dreams, sort of like dream confidence scams. Don't think of an elephant kind of stuff."

"What does that mean?"

"Whatever you do, dude, don't think of the first car you ever bought," Russ says.

I called it Diaper Car. A nineteen ninety-three Toyota Corolla. Tan colored. It had one hundred and three thousand miles on it when I bought it. I put another thirty thousand on it before the engine seized. It smelled like diapers, hence the name. I hated that car every mile I drove it, but it was the only thing I could afford.

"You totally thought of the car, didn't you?" Russ says, smiling.

I nod grimly. I think I see what he's getting at.

"You work on the Dreamwalking. I'll try to work on tracking this guy down. It's gonna be tough. I don't want to get too much attention while I do."

"Sounds good. We'll try to plant Circe's gem at Redbrook's tomorrow, and hopefully, whatever she has in mind helps as well."

"If you say so, man, I think trusting that broad is a mistake. Anyway, I'm going to head out. Man."

"Russ! Broad? Really?" I hiss at him.

I glance over to see if Emily and Genevieve heard that, but they are both engrossed in the screen they are staring at.

"Later, Miles, man! Later Aak-Eech!" Russ calls out to Emily and Genevieve.

"Don't call me chica backward either, Russ!" Emily calls back, but Russ is already gone.

"I am going to go get coffee. You two want anything?" I ask.

Genevieve and Emily are completely focused on Emily's laptop. They don't seem to respond to me, so I slip quietly out the door.

Chapter Twenty-Seven

AT SOOTHSAYERS, I get myself a large coffee to which I add far too much cream and sugar. It's almost closing time, and I don't know the person working the counter. I guess Jesse and Karen don't work on Sunday. So I sit by myself in a seat on the sidewalk and sip my coffee. My phone vibrates. I have a message from Jeff. Perplexingly, it simply reads 'Yes.' It takes me a minute to realize that it is a response to a message I sent days ago asking if he was around. A few more messages go back and forth like a ping-pong ball, and he invites me to stop by his place. I get a refill of my coffee, then drive to Jeff's.

Jeff looks unbathed and unkempt. He has a weird, hazy look in his eyes, like he might have been up all night.

"Hey, Jeff. You doing okay?"

"I was up all night working on something, but I think you will like it," he says. His eyes are wide and a little bloodshot, and there is a touch of mania in his voice.

"Oh?" I say. I am a little concerned.

"Yeah come on out back."

I follow him to the back of his house. There is a shed in the center of a little flower garden. We walk across the lawn and pick our way between flower beds. To the right of the door, there is a single window and another window on the left wall of the shed. It's a pretty standard-looking shed, but the sides have been shingled with redwood slats. Little redwood planter boxes are set below the windows. I think the shed is supposed to look like a rustic cottage, but with its modern hardware and windows, it looks confused.

"The shed was here when I bought the place," Jeff says as a way of some unclear explanation.

He unlocks a padlock, a deadbolt, and a doorknob lock. He clearly doesn't want anyone getting into his garden shed. As he opens the door, I see that the shed has been refurbished into a laboratory and workshop of sorts. The shed itself isn't big, so the whole space feels very cramped and crowded.

Jeff has a number of magic circles inscribed on plywood planks on one table. Inclusive, Exclusive, and Conclusive ones of a number of different sizes. He's got a clutter of high-tech-looking equipment. There are tables full of beakers, an electronic microscope of some kind, and a small refrigerator. I recognize a centrifuge and some alembics, but most of the rest of the apparatus is foreign to me. I had no idea he had all this here. He squeezes in between two benches.

"Wow. Your bat cave is impressive," I say.

I am basically standing in the doorway because there isn't enough room for me to fit in without standing intimately close to Jeff, and he hasn't bathed in a while.

"Thanks, it's my home lab. I originally set it up for enology, but I've added a few more tools since then."

"What have you got?"

"Okay, so remember I made you that little gizmo that could detect fields of magical energy?"

"Yes, I remember," I say. "I never used it, though."

"Yeah, honestly, it wasn't very practical," he says, "but I've made some improvements."

"Oh?" I ask.

He pulls out a semi-opaque plastic cylinder and holds it up, and shakes it. It has some fluid inside. He cracks it like a glow stick.

"I've come up with a set of compounds that will react to magical energy similar to the Acetobacter Magusficedula. It is actually derived from them, but it's more stable. The primary compound only activates with a catalyst, so when they mix, it starts reacting," he holds up the plastic cylinder.

I can see the fluid inside has started to turn a shade of light pink, with the slightest hint of a hue. Jeff tosses it into one of the circles on the table. I see there is fresh blood on it. He's been building up energy in the circle. The plastic stick gets inside the circle and suddenly flares up and glows a dull red. It looks like a red glow stick.

"It's a glow-stick."

He reaches into the circle and takes the glow stick out. It quickly fades and stops glowing.

"Woah," I say.

"Yeah, so these new sticks are stable until you crack them. Once activated, they last…I don't know, about an hour, maybe a little more or a little less. The brightness of the stick will change based on the amount of magical energy around them. You could use a series of them to map out an area of magic," he says. He sounds excited.

"That is actually useful and frankly incredible. How did you do this?"

"Well, I've been spending a lot of free time working on it."

"Is this why Emily is pissed at you?"

He glowers darkly for a minute. I seem to have touched a nerve.

"No. Well, yes, it is part of the reason she says I am getting fixated. But she's mostly pissed because I told her to stop the Redbrook investigation and that she was being stupid."

"Oh, that's brutal," I say. "Why would you say that?"

"Because it is stupid, and she's going to get herself hurt."

"Yeah, I am running more of a risk of that than she is, but you don't tell me to stop," I say.

"Well, we aren't dating," Jeff says.

"Have you stopped to look at it from her perspective? I

mean, I can see you aren't getting a lot of sleep, man. Could you be being a little…controlling?" I say.

"You sound like Emily."

I shrug.

"Just calling it like I see it. You should get some sleep. Seriously."

He looks at me. He looks haggard. He seems suddenly a little angry at me, but I can also see that somewhere in his brain, he knows I am right.

"The glow-stick thing is awesome. I'll totally buy those from you," I say, trying to change the topic to leave on a positive note.

"Oh! Yeah," he says, his tired brain seems easily distracted. He grabs a paper bag and tosses it to me. It is heavier than I expected. I look inside, and there are about two dozen sticks in there.

"The first one's free," Jeff says, giving me a wink. The previous thread of conversation seems to have been instantly forgotten.

"Seriously, I should pay you for the materials, at least."

"We can talk about that later. For now, if those will help you, consider it a gift," he says. "If you need more, I have a 3D printer to make the sticks, and I have plenty of the compound mixed up. I'll need like a day lead time."

"Thanks," I say, hefting the bag of magic glow sticks up. "Now get some sleep, man. Even the Blethspah Amah needs sleep."

"Yeah, you are probably right."

We say goodbye. He promises to get some more sleep, but I don't believe him. Something is going on with him, and I am a little worried.

Chapter Twenty-Eight

I STILL HAVE some time to kill.

Time to kill, it's a weird expression. Time is neither a living thing nor really a thing. If it were, why would we want to kill it? From one perspective, time is the enemy. Time slowly takes our lives away. We have a limited amount of it, and we don't know how much that is. I feel this perception of our impending mortality creates anxiety. Time is a constant reminder of our impending death and the unpredictable and ephemeral nature of life.

Killing time should be about opting out of it as a practice. Smashing our clocks and throwing out our phones. Living each moment on its own terms. Killing it would be letting go of it as a social convention. I think.

This isn't what we mean when we say we have time to kill, though. When we talk about killing time, we are talking about wasting it. Wasting is used as a synonym for killing sometimes, but in the sense that it is the pointless disposal of life. The idea behind killing time is the same. It is the pointless disposal of some amount of time.

But to truly kill time, we would have to accept that there are no pointless moments and that each moment has value and should be lived to its fullest. Time can no more be wasted or killed than quality love or any other abstract metaphysical concepts.

I'm not going to kill this time that I have; I'm going to live it.

I have some time to live, so I drive back downtown and park near Grape Reads. Walking around downtown used to be a great distraction for me, but lately, the sidewalks always feel crowded with tourists. The people-watching is always great, but I'm less of a crowd person every day. I like to keep track of who and what is around me. When there are too many people, I start to feel overwhelmed and out of control.

Out of curiosity, I take out one of Jeff's magic glow sticks, and I crack it, and shake it. As advertised, it starts to give off a faint, almost imperceptible pink glow. This must be a response to the ambient magic in the Ley around me.

On a quiet stretch of street, I take a roll of twine out of my bag, cut a foot or so off, and use it to tie the glow stick around my wrist. I note that it starts to glow brighter whenever it touches one of the warding tattoos on my forearm. I move it so it is tied to my belt loop and hanging on my right thigh. I'm briefly worried that this is going to look weird and get me undue attention.

I walk past a gaggle of tipsy young women dressed in short skirts and identical long knit vest coats, each with a giant puffy sequined hat and enormous novelty sunglasses. On the other side of the street is a gaggle of young men I can only describe as 'dude-bros' with Hawaiian shirts hanging open over muscle shirts or bare chests. One has a baseball hat on that says 'Cock' and has a silhouette of a rooster on it. They are lurching up the street arm in arm, laughing and crooning. They are all out of sync and tune with each other, so I have no idea what they are supposed to be singing.

My worries about my glowstick attracting attention melt away.

As I walk, I keep glancing at the glow stick. Its faint pink light waxes and wanes as I walk through slightly deeper or shallower swaths of Ley. I walk across town to Soothsayer, which is closed now. I put the stick next to the door and see it flare up to a perceptible but not intense glow in response to the wards set around it. The wards are constantly forcing magical energy out of the building like a pump pushing water out of a basement sump. This is a good way to test if they are working. I continue to walk around town, trying to gauge what the brightness might mean.

It is about time that I go back to meet Emily and Genevieve. I turn and start walking back toward Grape Reads. I see a throng of people on the sidewalk in front of me. Young. Well dressed. Inebriated. Boisterous. There are about twelve of them, give or take. It is hard to count as they are passing through another smaller group. The total number of people is more than the sidewalk can handle, and a couple of them step out into the road to make room.

My mind is trying to focus on all the people at once to track them. My focus is distracted and scattered. I can hear from behind me the roaring sound of a car approaching at an unreasonable speed. This is another problem that has increased in recent years. The downtown streets are narrow and filled with pedestrians, yet for some reason, people drive through it like it's a Nascar speedway.

I turn my head to see the car, a black SUV. It is probably going forty-five miles an hour and still accelerating. I turn back and see one of the drunken revelers staggering in the street. My brain is doing the calculations, and I start to call out, but it's too late.

I duck my head before I see the gut-churning result of the impact. I cringe from the squeal of braking tires. I look up and see the young man lying in a crumpled heap on the ground. Some part of my brain expects screams of horror, but mostly, people are silent.

"Oh my god," one voice breaks the silence.

I start to move to see if I can help, and despite his petrified friends being closer, I make it to his side before they do, just as the driver gets out of the car.

"Shit! He came out of nowhere! I am sorry! Is he okay? He'll be okay, right?" The driver is a young man. He's understandably panicking.

I kneel down next to the man who has been hit. I can see one arm is bent at an angle that arms are not supposed to bend at. Part of his skull has turned gelatinous from impact. I feel my stomach tighten, and I have an impulse to vomit. I bite back the bile and begin to pull my phone out to dial 911.

Suddenly, the glow-stick on my belt loop flares up. A blinding red light illuminates the whole street. I have to shield my eyes from the brightness. I can feel the warding tattoos on my forearms, shins, and chest get hot. I recognize the sensation. I am being protected from some magical force. I instinctively chant the ward activation under my breath, drawing energy into my wards and reinforcing them.

Then, the young man on the ground flutters his eyes and sits up.

"I'm fine!" he says. "I'm fine."

He's got blood on his clothes. Blood is matted in his hair. He's sitting in a pool of blood on the ground. But despite all that, he is, in fact, fine.

Magic.

I help him to his feet and look around. Two of his compatriots are vomiting into the trash can. The driver that hit him is leaning against his car, looking pale. I look up and down the street, and everyone looks pale, drained, and sick. I can see one person swooning and lying down on the street and many people leaning against walls and lampposts for support.

Whatever spell he had on him was probably designed to be triggered by blood. To drain the life energy from nearby things to restore him. Assuming that is the case, it's actually a very good thing that there were so many people here to distribute the drain. If there was only one person around, he would be trading a life for a life.

"That's a pretty dangerous protection spell you have there," I mutter to him. It's dangerous and complicated.

He shrugs.

"My dad paid some whack job to do that. I thought it was bullshit, but hey, money well spent, right?" he whispers to me and winks.

I turn away from him. His lack of awareness or empathy makes me sick. He reminds me of Eric Walsh, the psycho stalker that's tried to kill me a few times now. I text Genevieve to say that I am going to be a little late. I am going to have to wait to make a statement to the police.

I am about to call 911, but I can already hear police sirens incoming. I can see the police station from where I am standing, and there is a fire station on the other side of it, so I am not terribly surprised. Less than two minutes later, there are police and firefighters on the scene, and I can hear an ambulance coming in the distance.

It would be convenient if my friend Officer Chris Benson were one of the first responders. I could explain exactly what happened, and he would get it. But he isn't.

I get to sit around for half an hour while they talk to the driver and the drunk guy that got hit, and he gets checked out by the EMTs. They round up everyone who was an immediate witness and talk to them, and finally, a police officer approaches me.

"Mr. Ward," the officer says, "You witnessed the accident?"

I haven't yet identified myself in any way. I don't know the police officer I am talking to, but he seems to know me.

"Yes, Officer..." I start trying to get his name from his badge, but he beats me to it.

"Calder," he says.

"Officer Calder, yes, I was walking by when it happened," I say.

"Can you tell me what you witnessed?"

"Yeah, it's pretty cut and dry. The SUV there was going

very fast down First Street. I am not an expert at judging speed, but I'd guess forty-five miles an hour or more, definitely above the speed limit. The young man there stepped out into the street because there were a lot of people, and the car hit him," I say.

"Did you see him get hit?"

"Yes. Well, actually, no, I didn't see the impact. I could see it was going to happen, and I looked away. But I could hear it."

"Okay, and then what happened?"

"I ran over to help. I was getting my phone out to call 911, and he stood up."

"Some of the other witnesses said there was a blinding light. Did you see that?" he says.

"No, I didn't see that," I say. It's a lie, but I don't want to explain the magic glow stick.

"Okay. Thank you for your time, Mr. Ward."

"Gladly, Officer Calder," I say. "I have a dinner date to get to. Do you need me to stick around?"

"No, Mr. Ward, you are free to go. Thank you for your time," Officer Calder says.

"Thank you," I say and start to walk down the street.

I'm passing Officer Calder's patrol car when I notice there is a little sticker on the rear wheel well of the car. It's the now familiar logo of the Knights of Saint George.

When I get to Grape Reads, it is closed. I spent a great deal more time waiting to talk to Officer Calder than I thought. I knock and Emily comes and opens the store door for me. Over Emily's shoulder, I see Genevieve standing a dozen feet behind her, thumbing through a book.

"Sorry about that. You never know when you are going to witness vehicular homicide," I say.

"Oh my god!" Emily exclaims, one hand over her mouth.

Genevieve puts her book back on the shelf.

"Are you serious?" Genevieve asks.

"Yes and No," I say, which I realize is dramatic and

confusing. This describes the situation perfectly, so I continue, "The guy was dead or at least an inevitable breath away from it, but then some spell he had brought him back. Healed all his wounds, mended bones, put his brain back in his skull…"

"The amount of energy required to do something like that…" Emily says.

"Would drain everyone on the block, cause people to get sick, vomit in the gutters. Probably hundreds of people."

"Oh," Genevieve says, "Was that like a bit over an hour ago?"

"Um. Yeah," I say.

"Oh," says Emily. "Yeah, we both suddenly felt kind of dizzy."

"You think his spell reached this far? That doesn't seem right," I say.

"Something like that is basically a life for a life as far as energy transference goes, so if you wanted to make sure that it didn't kill someone else, you'd design it to draw from as many people as possible. However, the energy transference would be Gaussian in terms of loss over distance. The people closest would be the most drained, and the people farthest away would be the least. With a distance at which it wouldn't even be perceptible," Emily says.

"But to get that kind of range, it would take an insanely complicated spell and the blood sacrifice…" I start.

"Is his blood. To catalyze something with that kind of radius would require him to sacrifice willingly...well, his life," Emily says.

I'm always amazed at Emily's knowledge of the workings of magic. For someone who has, so far as I know, never cast a spell, she knows as much as anyone I've ever met.

"You're saying he wanted to get hit by the car?" Genevieve asks.

"No, I think it's more like when he realized he was going to get hit, he willed his death to power the spell," I say. "The distinction is nuanced, but the implication is a bit disturbing."

Emily nods.

"He also sort of gloated to me that the spell was a contract spell that his family paid a lot of money to have it cast on him," I say.

"So it begins. The meta-wave. Magic as a commodity. Soon we will see magic being technologized," she says. I glance down at the glow stick hanging from my belt.

"Is that a word?" I ask.

"It is," Emily says, ushering me into the bookshop. "Come on in while I get my purse."

I step inside Grape Reads. No sooner do I than the glow-stick on my belt begins to glow very brightly like an incandescent bulb.

"What the hell is that?" Emily asks.

"It's a magic detector that Jeff came up with. It lasts about an hour. Well, it actually seems more like a couple of hours now. It glows brighter the more magic it comes in contact with. Sergei has some pretty good-sized spells going on here, doesn't he?" I say.

"It's none of your business what **he** has going on with the bookstore," Emily says. She seems unsure if she should be annoyed or amused.

Genevieve snorts. I'm missing something.

"What am I missing?" I ask.

"You know Sergei is the name of an organization, right?" Genevieve says.

"We're a nationally distributed non-profit. We operate bookstores across the country and use the proceeds to fund literacy programs in underprivileged communities," Emily says.

She points at a small sticker in the window. It says 'SERGEI International' below an icon of a book with a sword as a bookmark. I have to lean close to read the fine print that encircles the edges of the sticker.

"Society for the Expansion of Radical Global Education and Instruction. Oh," I say. I'm feeling pretty dumb. The mystery of the great Sergei was right in the front window all along. "So it's a national bookstore chain?"

"We also have stores in Canada and just opened our first in Mexico."

"So barely International," Genevieve chimes in. Emily casts her a quick glower.

"Miles, for a smart guy, you can be dumb sometimes," Emily says.

"I'm famished," Genevieve says, quick to change the topic. "Where do we eat?"

"What are you feeling like, Genevieve?" I ask.

"I don't know what's good Emily?" She says, turning to Emily. Apparently, Emily has been invited to join us for dinner. Genevieve seems to notice a shift in my facial expression because she gives me an apologetic little shrug.

"It's fine," I murmur.

"Is there a problem?" Emily asks.

"No problem," I say.

"I forgot to tell Miles that we decided to all go out together," Genevieve says.

"It's fine. What do we want to eat?"

"Bowling Alley," Emily says.

"Oh yeah! Bowling Alley!" I say in agreement.

"Bowling Alley?" Genevieve says skeptically.

It's a little-known fact, but if you want shi-shi tacos in Napa, the bowling alley is the place. It doesn't make sense, but there it is. One of the great mysteries of the modern world. Emily explains this to Genevieve.

"We could go have a couple of tacos, grab a drink, and roll some rocks," Emily says.

"That sounds bizarre but fun, let's do it," Genevieve says.

"All right! Sounds like a plan," I say. I try to sound enthusiastic, but I'm not really. I'm still feeling sheepish about the whole Sergei thing. I'm also worried I am going to feel like a third wheel on my own date.

We pile into my car, and Genevieve and Emily decide to

sit in the back. I am left feeling like a chauffeur, but it's fine. Everything's fine. They seem to be getting along pretty well, probably because they are both smart, educated, and capable, and I'm…well, I guess I am nothing but the chauffeur.

We get to the bowling alley and go in through the cafe.

"Bowling alley tacos," Genevieve says in mild disbelief.

We order three of all the kinds of tacos and take them to a table in the lounge.

"You are right. This is amazing," Genevieve says, biting into a taco. "It's a great taco, but honestly, I think the low expectation set by it being in a bowling alley is what makes it amazing."

I shrug. I don't care if it's the setting; I really enjoy the tacos. They are a little shi-shi, especially for a bowling alley. They are small, well seasoned, and have a variety of flavor components that you don't normally find in tacos. Little bits of sweet pineapple on savory pork and a little chipotle crema on the fish. We ordered too many tacos, but we finish them all.

"All right, how about some bowling to work off those tacos!" Emily says vigorously as she jumps up, "I'll go get us a lane!"

She scampers off to the counter.

"She's fun," Genevieve says. "I can see why you'd date her."

"We never dated," I say flatly. "We had a date, but I was too busy getting shot at to show."

"I know," Genevieve says. "I'm kind of teasing you."

"Testing me?"

"Maybe a little," she says.

"She didn't want to date a guy who had multiple people try to murder him in one day."

"Yeah, she told me," Genevieve says.

"What about you?"

"What about me?"

"Is dating an inevitable murder victim a problem for you?"

"I think it's hot," she says and leans in to kiss me. Genevieve is a little bit of a thrill junkie.

"Lane 14," Emily interrupts. "Oh. Sorry to interrupt."

Emily seems legitimately embarrassed.

"Let's roll," Genevieve says, winking at me.

We bowl three games, which is definitely one game too many for me. We have a couple of drinks and joke around. Overall, we have a nice time. It's around midnight by the time we drop Emily off at her house. We sit in the car and watch until she gets into her door, and we see interior lights turn on before we pull away.

"It's okay if I stay at your place again tonight?" Genevieve asks.

"Yeah of course. You're always welcome."

"Great!" Genevieve says, "And tomorrow, we invade Lamia's home."

She's a little more excited about this than seems wise to me, but I am thankful for the backup. We drive back to my place. I'm exhausted, and my elbow and lower back are sore from bowling. I'm clearly not in practice or using proper form. I guess that's what happens when you bowl only once a decade.

Chapter Twenty-Nine

THERE IS a lock in my hands. It's old-fashioned. The kind that takes a skeleton key. It is large and chunky, and heavy. I think it's made of solid brass. It's about the size of a baseball but probably weighs ten pounds. I look into the keyhole, and the inside is deep and black. Too black. No light escapes the core of this bulky lock. As I stare into it, I think I can feel some part of me being sucked into the darkness. Some deep and basic element of what makes me into me is being lost into the stygian keyhole. I look up, and I realize the lock isn't attached to anything. It is just there in my hands as I walk down a path in a wood.

The path winds its way around some rocks and then does a handful of switchbacks down the side of a hill until we are in a wide, almost bowl-shaped depression. It's probably fifty yards across. I can see all the way because the trees here are all short and thin, and stunted.

I wonder if this was all logged and the trees are small because they are very new growth. When I get to the trail at the bottom. The loam and detritus from the trees are a carpeted layer over a silty layer of sand. They are stunted because they are growing in this sandy soil. This must be an old lake bed or something.

It's dusk, and there is a cool, crisp breeze in the air. It makes the hackles on the back of my neck stand on end. The cold wind is nothing compared to the soul-sucking chill coming from the keyhole of that lock. A lock with no door.

"That is odd," I find myself saying out loud.

Part of me wants to heft this lock. To throw it as far and hard as I can. To get it away from me. To get it away from whatever unnameable part of my essence it is trying to suck away. For some reason, I can't. I tell my arm to move to cock it back over my shoulder, but when I try to swing it forward to release and throw the lock, my arm refuses. I hold my arm out to the side and try to open my hand, but again, my body will not obey me. I can't let go of the lock.

I walk through the depression, kicking at the sandy granite soil. I walk up the other side, and at the top, there is a cabin. It is small and has no windows. Not in a way that the windows fell out, but it was clearly never built with them.

The cabin is made of wooden planks with rough-cut wooden shingles on the top. It has a flimsy plywood door opening outward, hanging from flimsy-looking metal hinges. The door doesn't match or fit with the rest of the cabin's otherwise sturdy construction. It looks like it was added on later. I see it has a hasp but no lock. I wonder if this is where the lock in my hand came from.

I trudge to the cabin. My feet feel leaden. I walk up the front stairs and look into the cabin's dark interior. It isn't large, maybe ten feet by fifteen feet. In the rear left corner, there is a wooden cot or bunk built in. It has a small wooden table next to it. I cannot make out the details of either in the gloom.

On the table, I can see there are some things, a book perhaps. I think that there is a half-melted candle. A pair of scissors or a knife sit next to the candle. Directly across from the doorframe, I see what is clearly a large bronze chamber pot. The pot is etched with symbols or writing of some kind, but they are illegible in the fading light.

My eyes continue scanning from left to right, finally falling on the right corner. There is something there, perhaps clothes hanging from a wall. Mottled in white, light gray, dark gray, and black. It's difficult to tell what the monochromatic shape is.

With my left hand, which is not encumbered with a giant lock, I pat my pockets looking for a flashlight. I note with dismay that I have nothing in my pockets. I don't have my courier bag. The only things I have are my clothes and this giant lock. I am about to step in to get a closer look at the clothes hanging in the corner when I see them move.

I start as I realize that what I mistook for clothes hanging on a rack is, in fact, a humanoid figure. It moves toward me in a disturbing manner. Anytime I blink or look away, or my eyes focus on something else, even for an instant, it is notably closer when I look back. It's not that it moves only when I am not looking at it. It's always moving, but the more I focus on it, the slower it moves.

I back down the stairs, trying to keep my eyes on it. You don't realize how much your eyes unconsciously blink, refocus, or glance around until there is something horrifying in front of you that seems to speed up when you lose focus on it. I lurch back and see the door hanging open. In the time it takes me to glance at the door, the figure closes in on me. It's only a few feet away now.

The figure has long, shaggy black hair that hangs down over its eyes. The figure is completely androgynous but clearly human. It is wearing a long white robe or gown. The kind that doesn't close in the back. The gown is splattered and soaked through with blood, which is what gave the mottled, almost camouflage-like impression from across the room.

The figure's legs, feet, and arms are bare. I can see the feet are calloused and scarred, like someone who spent their entire life walking barefoot back and forth across broken glass. Its eyes. I can barely make them out beneath the shaggy bangs, but they are black, deep soul-sucking. They are blackhole black and remind me of the inside of the lock.

My lips lock together into a tight grimace. I reach over and grab the door and slam it shut. Just as the door passes its face, I have a moment of recognition. The face glaring at me from beneath those shaggy black bangs is Shelly.

I throw the hasp on the door and raise the lock. I see that it is open, and I slide it through the hasp and slam the lock shut.

Clank.

It makes a loud, harsh, reverberating metallic noise that makes me jump. I slammed the lock too hard, and it begins to crumble in my hands. First, to big metal chunks, then the chunks break into smaller chunks, which break into tiny pea-sized bits, which then shatter when they touch my palms. My hands are filled with sand. The sand filters through my fingers to the ground in front of the cabin. Like grains through an hourglass, I find myself thinking time is slipping away before me.

Then it spreads from the lock to the door, which soon is also turning to ash and sand. The dissolution to sand spreads to the door frame, to the walls, the windows, and the floor, and soon the entire cabin is crumbling to ash and dust.

I turn to flee. The stairs turn to sand beneath my feet, and I fall to the earth. The wind gets knocked out of me as I strike the dirt with a dull thud. I look up, and the bloody apparition is floating above me, feet not touching the ground. I scream and jump to my feet, running wildly through the wood.

"It's a dream!" I scream at myself. But this affirmation doesn't help.

My panic is doubled when I remember Russ telling me that some things could harm a person in their dreams. Some primordial atavistic part of my brain knows that whatever this thing is, it can harm me. I am in peril.

I flee. I don't know where I am or where I am going, which is never a good sign. I dash down hills, through sandy marshes, up hills, and between thin white-barked trees that look themselves like ghosts in the gloom. Soon, I come to a path. I stop briefly and glance over my shoulder. The apparition is behind me, always behind me.

Over my shoulder, in the pale moonlight filtering down through the clouds, I can see blood dripping off the tips of the apparition's fingers. Off of its toes. Out of its nose and eyes. I dash down the path, which is little more than a three-foot-wide line of wood chips edged on both sides with chunks of granite. The mottled grey granite rocks look like they were broken from some great monolith.

The path winds its way through a copse of small pines and opens out into a clearing. In the middle of the clearing, the path splits again, with the right side heading toward what looks like a farmhouse with lights on in the windows. I feel it is inviting me to come and sit for a spell.

The other direction descends into a dark hollow, filled with and surrounded by aspen and birch trees. I am about to turn toward the farmhouse when something nudges at my brain.

The woods are lovely, dark, and deep. Robert Frost wrote, *And I have miles to go before I sleep.* Sleep. I'm sleeping. I'm dreaming. Right.

I have to become lucid.

"Two roads diverged in a yellow wood, and I took the one less traveled. Or something like that," I quote as I turn left.

The left path is where I don't want to go, but I am strangely drawn to the lovely, dark, deep trail. As I descend into the darkened vale before me, I glance over my shoulder. The apparition is all but on top of me. I have maybe a minute at my current rate of progress before it catches me. But again, I remind myself. I'm dreaming.

I sprint with all my might, pumping my arms and legs as high as I can. It is now dark. Very dark. I'm stumbling and staggering and tripping on rocks and sticks and other unidentifiable things. Then I hit something tall and flat and solid. I grope at it in the darkness.

A doorway.

I grope around for a knob or handle or latch, but I find

nothing. After a little more groping around, I find a lock hanging on the door. It feels a lot like the lock that was in my hands, the one that crumbled. However, it cannot be the same one that was destroyed. I glance back, and I can see the white of the apparitions, blood-stained clothes, and pale white skin in the darkness. The rest of its figure is camouflaged. I begin desperately yanking at the lock in the darkness. A strange pulsing at the nape of my neck tells me that the apparition is growing nearer and nearer.

Then, searing light blinds me. I pinch my eyes shut tight against the pain. It takes a few seconds, and the light seems to fade. I blink them open.

Standing behind me, between me and the apparition, is a figure I recognize. Circe. She's clad in white leather, and her hair is glowing white. She has a white-bladed sword in each hand, a Japanese Daisho. She looks like a biker angel.

"Go through the door. I'll take care of this," Circe says in her strange, unplaceable accent.

"Huh?" I say. I am confused. Why is Circe here?

She begins to move in toward the apparition. She makes a cut with both swords. The wakizashi in a downward sweeping motion, the katana in a horizontal slice.

The first aimed at the eyes, the second swung to hamstring her foe, striking with the second in the blind spot created by the first. The apparition is too clever and floats laterally and back to avoid both.

My brain doesn't keep up with events well. I feel like I am watching what is happening in one eye and a recording with a three-second delay in the other. It is disorienting.

The apparition's dodge brings it into the forward stab from another identical Circe that has appeared from the shadows. Blood sprays in a fountain from the wound. Regardless of how grave the wound is, it doesn't seem to slow the apparition.

It attempts to dodge around her and toward me. Another Circe sprouts from the first as the second vanishes, and a fourth drops from the shadows above. I cannot track as Circe splits and vanishes, jumps in and out of shadows in a ubiquitous and patternless series of coordinated attacks. I stand dumbfounded.

"GO!" she yells at me. "I can hold it off, but this is an apparition of death, of your own fear of mortality twisted against you. It cannot be destroyed, only delayed."

"Huh?" I ask stupidly. I have no idea what is going on.

"Idiot," four-and-a-half Circes say between clenched teeth. I think the half because that Circe begins the word but doesn't complete it as she vanishes into the shadows mid-word.

I turn back to the door. Right. I need a key. I can make a key, right?

I reach into my pocket and pull out a key. It's a skeleton key, both figuratively and literally. It is made of bone with a small human skull as the bow of the key. The blade is a spinal column with ribs broken to make the teeth of the key.

I shove it into the lock, wondering at the significance and symbolism here. I twist the key, and the lock comes free. I am about to throw the door open, and then I remember what happened the last time I did this.

I glance over, and Circe is still battling the apparition. If Circe is to be trusted…

"S*he is not.*"

…this is the specter of my fear of my own mortality. I need to make my *reva fortikaĵo* so that I have somewhere to enter and filter out the dream space into something I can manage.

My mind is blank. I have no idea what to make. I have no idea how to make it. I guess I am not that imaginative. Then I remember my favorite dream, the house of locks…when it wasn't filled with monsters trying to kill me. An endless array of puzzles to solve.

So I imagine that. It's easy. I've been there a thousand times in my dreams. Corridor after corridor of doors and rooms. Each with its own complicated, intricate puzzle to solve. Each room leads to more corridors of doors with more locks and more rooms, etc.

I imagine it as detailed as I can. As many rooms as I can. As many places and spaces as I can imagine or remember. It grows in my mind. I can see and feel the texture of the wood, the tiles on the floor, and the framed pictures on the walls. Once I have built and imagined as much in my mind as I can hold, the edges of the space are starting to fade in my memory. I grab the door, throw it open, and jump through.

And I land and wake up in my bed.

The sunlight is shining through the window in my eyes, and I can feel Genevieve's warm body pressed up against mine. I blink. I can hear a chime. Am I still dreaming? I sit up.

No, it's my doorbell. I slip out of bed as quickly and quietly as I can and pull on some pants. While I am hastily getting dressed, I check the time it's nine o'clock. We were up pretty late, so I guess I am not surprised we slept in. Still, this feels weirdly late for me to sleep in. I pull on a t-shirt as I dash to the door and open it once more without checking the peephole.

There is a delivery man there.

"Mr. Ward?" he says, holding up a tablet.

"Yeah," I say, bleary-eyed.

"We got a delivery for you kinda big. You want it inside or out?" he says.

I stare at him for a second, and then I realize. My new simulacrum is here. Hank will be reborn!

"Yeah, um, inside if you could. Thank you," I say as I sign the tablet with my finger.

"You got it, boss," he says and returns to the truck that is idling double parked in the parking lot. I hate when people call me boss.

It takes two men and a hand truck to wrangle the giant wooden crate up the stairs and into my apartment. By the time they have gotten it in, Genevieve is up and dressed. She thankfully has cash and tips them without hesitating even to ask me, which is good because they certainly earned it. There is no way I could have gotten the giant crate into my house.

I stand out on the walkway and thank them as they go down the stairs to their truck.

As I turn to go back inside, I see Magdalena watching me out her front window. I have that feeling of *deja vu* again.

"Creepy," I say as I walk back into my apartment.

Chapter Thirty

I HAVE A NEW SIMULACRUM BODY, but it will take weeks of rituals and preparation before it can fully serve its purpose.

This is too bad because today, I go to face Lorelei Redbrook and tell her that I am not giving her files back in an attempt to keep her distracted while Genevieve plants Circe's crystal device in Redbrook's bed.

This was Genevieve's plan. Not mine. Mine was much sloppier and involved a lot of me screaming, "Not in the face!" But even so, I could use Hank today.

"Good to have you back, buddy," I say.

"Just get me out of this box," I can hear Hank's voice, muffled from inside the box.

"Huh?" Genevieve says, looking confused at me.

I pry the box open and pull away the outer layer of foam packing material. There stands Hank naked as the day he was molded.

"And dare I ask why you have a naked mannequin of yourself in a crate? This isn't some kink thing, is it? Cause if it is...well...tell me more before I get too into this," she says, trying to cover some concern with humor.

I explain the simulacrum and how Hank works. She nods and listens carefully.

"It's still pretty weird, but okay, that makes sense. I guess," she says.

Genevieve helps me get the mannequin out of the crate. We stand him up in the corner. Hank is anatomically correct and based on a body cast. I start to feel a little awkward about him standing there in the buff.

"Let's get him dressed," I say.

"I'm not ashamed," Hank says.

"It's a little awkward," Genevieve says.

"It's a very average awkward. It was cold the day he had the cast made. Leave me alone."

I ignore Hank's jibes as we get him dressed.

I'd like to get some bonding rituals set up with this new Simulacrum before we head to Redbrook's. But we don't have time. We hastily get Hank dressed, and then I find matching clothes for myself. Some rituals have a magical effect, and some rituals are only psychological. I don't know that dressing him up like me will help magically, but I do find it comforting. We have breakfast and get ready for the day.

At about 10:30, I pour us two to-go mugs of coffee, and we get into the car to drive to Redbrook's.

"Let's go over the plan," Genevieve says.

"Okay. We park, you stay in the car, and I go in," I say.

"Then you spray your magic spray on the wards and stuff as you go and meet with Redbrook. Make sure to leave the door unlocked."

"And while I am doing that, you are going to sneak in and place that gem thing of Circe's in Redbrook's bed."

"And then..." Genevieve says.

"Then you sneak out, and I leave," I say.

"And that is where the plan starts to get too hazy for me. I'll sneak out fine. I'm like a ninja. How are you going to get out, Miles? Excuse yourself to the bathroom and jump out the window?"

I shrug. "It's worked on her before. But no. I'll just be charming."

Genevieve smiles at me and winks, "You might make it then."

I pull up to the giant black iron gate outside of Redbrook's estate. It silently opens before us. I slowly drive up and park in front of the enormous columned house. I take a deep breath and sigh it out.

"Wish me luck," I say.

Genevieve leans over and kisses me on the cheek. "Good luck."

"You too."

"I don't need luck; I've got skills," she laughs.

I get my spray bottle out and put it in my pocket. I slide a permanent marker into the other, and then I climb out of the car. I start up the granite staircase to the front door of Redbrook's ridiculously large house. The reliefs on the walls lear at me menacingly.

I am greeted at the top of the stairs by the glassy-eyed young man who escorted me around last time. He is still dressed in a ridiculous outfit, complete with the bright blue fez. Wordlessly, he motions me toward the door.

"After you," I say and wave my arm dramatically.

The youth stares at me blankly. We are in a stalemate, waiting to see who will go first. After a minute, it becomes obvious that he will stand here holding the door until his arms fall off.

This is going to complicate things having him behind me. I step through the door, and then, while he's still on the exterior of the door, I reach back and yank it out of his hands. I slam it closed before he can react. I slam the deadbolt in place. Immediately, I can hear him rattling the door handle from the other side.

I whip out my permanent marker and quickly jot an exclusive circle. It's sloppy, but considering I have about thirty seconds before he's gotten the keys out and is unlocking the deadbolt, it's not too bad. I brought a ziplock of blood in my bag for just such an occasion. I have enough time to splash a little on the circle before the door swings open. He charges in after me but gets caught in the circle.

As I suspected, it's a Fetch. The youth isn't acting under his own will and so freezes and then slumps to the ground. I quickly douse him down with the magic-eating spray and proceed to do so with the wards around the door. Leaving the door ajar, I make my way upstairs, stopping to deface every rune and glyph I see with my magic marker. A line here, a whorl there to change the meanings of runes that I recognize. I haphazardly reshape the ones I don't recognize. I spray everything down with Jeff's concoction as I go. This is splash-and-burn apotropaism.

I get to the top of the stairs and head for the veranda in the back. This is where I last saw Redbrook. It's a guess that this is where I will find her, but I get lucky. She's once more sitting in her ridiculous throne-like lounger. She stares off at the landscape, apparently lost in thought while being waited on hand and foot by a gaggle of enthralled youth.

"Miles. Miles. Miles," she says, "This is getting old."

"I'm not sure what you mean," I say, doing a terrible job of feigning nonchalance.

"You wreck everything you touch, don't you? Can you walk into a building without destroying things?" She asks.

"Well, there was this one time…"

"You have something I want, but I am entirely unclear on what it is that you want."

"I want you to leave me and my friends alone."

"That is what you need, but it isn't what you want. Come on, Miles. What do you **want**?"

"In life? I want a lot of things. From you? I want you to leave me and my friends alone."

"Your rigid ideals will be the end of you, you know."

"Maybe, but that's my problem. For now, I give you the drive. You leave me and my friends alone? Deal?"

"How do I know you are giving me the only copy, and you haven't copied it?"

"I have copied it. I've sent copies to a number of people as insurance policies. There is no way I'd give you the only copy. Then I'd have no leverage."

She sighs a long and irritated-sounding groan.

"Of course," she says, giving an immense and toothy leer.

"Deal?" I say.

"Fine."

I reach into my bag and toss her a memory stick. I'm lying. Of course, the only thing it has on it are the schematics I had started drawing up for the wards I was going to put on The Lantern. For the moment, she doesn't know that. Hopefully, Genevieve and I are long gone by the time she figures it out.

"So, are we done?" Redbrook asks, her voice almost a hiss with projected irritation.

I'm about to say yes, but I realize I've only been here for a few minutes. Hardly enough time for Genevieve to do her part. I have to stall more.

"No," I say.

"No?"

"No. None of this makes sense. You owe me some answers. Why me? Why now? Yes, I know you want to hire me, you want to use me as your poster boy or whatever, but I don't buy it. I'm a terrible poster boy. Nobody wants me on the cover of their book," I rant at her.

It's not untrue. I don't believe her. I rarely believe anyone when they tell me why they are doing something. I feel like everyone has what they say they are doing, and it isn't the same as what they are actually doing. In some cases, this is because people are great at deluding themselves, but sometimes it is an intentional ploy. With Redbrook, it certainly feels like a ploy.

"If I had any more to tell about this subject, why would I tell you? You are blackmailing me. I'm not the bad guy here."

"I'm not…." I start to say that I am not blackmailing her but pause and think it through. Oh. "Well, actually, I guess I am blackmailing you, but you are the bad guy here. You've done so much worse than that. I mean, blackmail is what you do while you eat your WheatieOs in the morning."

She looks horrified and affronted. "I'd never eat processed food."

"You pretty much run Mon-Anon.com! You had the Knights of Saint George attack your own business to garner sympathy."

She narrows her eyes, and I can see an ember of rage behind them. I can't shake the feeling that I might have shown too many cards.

"I see," she says. It's the final and matter-of-fact statement that feels menacing without being an actual threat. It's the same tone my father used when I was twelve and told him I was going to run away; right before he packed my bag for me and pushed me out the door as if I didn't dislike Redbrook enough already.

"No. I don't think you do." my stomach is churning, and my vision is narrowing from anxiety and fear. My head swims a little. "I have everything. I've figured out all your little codes and ciphers. You aren't as clever as you think. Every step you've taken, every bribe you've made, every person you've blackmailed, it's all laid out. I could shut you down so fast, so big, and so public that it will make your head spin."

"What's that to me? I can walk away, change my face, change my name. I've done it a thousand times. Mortals are of no concern to me," she announces. This is a lie. I know this is a lie. If we were of no concern to her, she wouldn't go through any of this. Why would she run a bar? Why would she run for mayor? Why would she do anything? I'd guess that mortals are her only concern.

"Yeah, but it will set your Dominium Deloris pals' plans back years, decades. What's their policy on failure?"

I'm taking a stab in the dark here. I know she belongs to the mysterious and illusive Dominium Deloris. Until recently, I considered them a myth, a shadow organization pulling strings from behind the scenes. The Illuminati if it was comprised of demons and cryptids. I'm gambling that they aren't going to brook failure from her well.

She stares at me, her face passive and calm. She has a tense, furrowed brow. She's angry but playing it cool. Not a twinge of worry or fear crosses her visage. But she doesn't say anything for a long, silent minute. That's her tell. And that's the solution. We don't have to deal with Redbrook. We have to make her a liability to her supernatural cabal. If she's setting the cause back, they will get rid of her.

She's still staring silently at me. I turn abruptly toward the door and start to walk out. I flip her off over my shoulder as I open the door. I am expecting her to say something. To stop my progress or order her entourage of Fetches to tear me to pieces.

But she doesn't.

"I'll send you my bill for The Lantern job," I call over my shoulder as the door slams behind me.

On my way down the stairs, I stop to draw crossed eyes and mustaches on the reliefs of monsters torturing and eating people as I go.

What can I say? I'm very mature.

Chapter Thirty-One

STANDING at the bottom of the stairs is a familiar face. Not a familiar face that I want to see, no. This is a familiar face with slicked-back hair and a tailored suit. Hale leans on the banister, clucking with his tongue. In one hand, a briefcase in the other, he holds up the large gemstone that Genevieve was supposed to have planted in Redbrook's bed.

"Here is the thing that I don't understand," Hale says as I get to the bottom of the stairs. He places his briefcase on the ground and starts tossing the gemstone back and forth from hand to hand.

"What's that, Hale?" I respond, eyes scanning the foyer for Genevieve. I can see no sign of her.

"You went through an awful lot of trouble to hide this," he says. "Confronting Lamia like that, having a friend sneak in behind you. Trapping Dane."

He indicates the blue-fez'd youth who is still lying unconscious on the floor of the foyer.

"No, no trouble," I say, and I start to try to walk past him. He holds an arm out, and I turn and step to the side.

He turns to face me so that now I am standing with the front door on my right. He's taller than me, not enough that I am looking up his nostrils, but I have to look upward to make eye contact. He's leveraging every centimeter to be more intimidating. I'm a couple of feet from the circle I drew in marker on the floor. Over Hale's shoulder, I can see an open door that leads into a long hallway.

"It's nothing but a rock, you know?"

"Huh?" I ask. I don't know what he's talking about.

"This gemstone," he holds up Circe's gemstone. "It's a rock. A fancy rock, it's got runes and stuff on it, yes. There is a little magic stored in it, but no more than a normal crystal would have. There is nothing special about it at all."

As soon as he says it, I know he's not lying. Somehow, this makes more sense. I curse inside my head. I'm not sure what Circe's game is, but I fell for it once again.

"Yeah, I know," I lie.

Hale laughs. I don't think he's buying my deception.

"Miles, you are really bad at this, you know that?" He asks.

I look down at my shoes and take a pointed breath. I'm not sure where this is going. Is he going to try to stop me? Will he let me walk out? Is he going to attack me?

I look up as he raises his hand. He's holding the gemstone out toward me. I reach up to take it from his hand, and we make eye contact. He's judging me, estimating me. Something in my brain says I can't flinch, that this is a staring contest that I need to win.

I'm holding the corner of the large gem, but it is still sitting in his hand. We are locked in some sort of contest of wills, but I don't know why. Maybe he's trying something magical on me. I can feel a faint warmth in the warding tattoos on my arms, legs, and torso. Is it real, though? Or is it psychosomatic? I can't tell. I see no indications that there would be a spell on me.

Our staring contest is interrupted when Hale makes a weird little sound in his throat and starts to twitch and spasm. I jump back, unsure what the hell is going on. His eyes roll back in his head as he jerks wildly, and his arms flap briefly at his sides before he slumps to the ground.

As he falls, I see standing behind him is Genevieve she's holding a device to his neck. I can hear a rapid pulsing click sound. Hale hits the ground, still spasming, and Genevieve follows him, still holding her stun gun to his neck.

I'm as surprised as Hale is, and it takes me a few seconds for my brain to shift gears from the staring contest to this. Genevieve holds the electric device to Hale until it stops clicking.

"Jesus!"

"Hardly," Genevieve says, standing back up. She winks at me. "He deserved it."

"You're not wrong. You just surprised me. Where the hell did that come from?" I ask.

"I told you I'm a woman who asks a lot of questions. You'd be surprised how many men don't like that," she says.

"I'm a huge fan."

"Good," she says with a coy smile, holding up the stun gun and then putting it into her tiny clutch. I have no idea how it fits in without causing the seams to burst.

"We should probably go."

We all but run out the front door and down the marble steps. Genevieve bounds across the wide driveway toward my car. I am right on her heels. We leap into the car, and I roar off down the windy drive. Genevieve laughs until she snorts a little bit.

"Sorry," she says. "That was nuts."

"Yeah, something was nuts," I say, looking askance at her, a touch of sarcastic judgment in my tone. She went to the stun gun awfully quick, and she seems awfully giddy about it.

"What did you want me to do? He was doing something to you. He had you…ensorcelled."

"Ensorcelled?"

"Besorcelled? Yeah, you were standing there staring at him like you were in a trance."

"No, I wasn't. We were staring each other down!" I say.

"For like seven minutes? I even asked if you two were going to kiss already, but neither responded."

"It was like fifteen seconds! Maybe."

"No, Miles, you were there for a long time. I wasn't timing, but it was several minutes. I went through like a dozen different scenarios. Do I hit him with a vase? Do I try to drag Miles away? Do I call the cops? Do I kick him? Finally, I decided to stun-gun him."

"Really?" I ask. I can't believe this is true.

"Really."

"Oh," I say dumbfounded. I don't know what to make of this.

"Circe set us up," I say.

"A Hizarin lied to you? Who'd have thought?" Genevieve says, grinning wryly.

"The rock. Not magical. Why would she do that?"

"Because she wanted to get you killed?"

"Maybe, but that doesn't add up. She could easily kill me if that's what she wanted."

"Because she wants Redbrook's eyes on you?" Genevieve asks.

I narrow my eyes.

"Yeah," I say, "That sounds more on brand. Use me as a decoy to make Redbrook worried about what I am up to. Keep her so focused on me that she doesn't see the real threat coming."

"How's that different from trying to get you killed?"

"I think my death wasn't the goal, it was a potential side effect."

"That must be comforting," Genevieve says quietly.

"Not so much."

"So what's next?"

"Next, I need to find Circe and get some answers," I say.

"How do you plan to do that?"

"Dreamwalking."

Chapter Thirty-Two

PREPARING A SIMULACRUM IS AN INTRICATE AND, if I am being honest, boring process. It mostly involves me sitting with a mirror and some markers and trying to emulate every tattoo on my body as closely as I can on Hank. Then there's makeup. Then, I take a little of my blood and put it in a vial in his chest cavity. It's a whole afternoon of detail work like that before the actual magic circles and incantations begin.

Genevieve offers to help, but it quickly becomes apparent that this is a one-person operation. Or maybe more accurately, there are some things I am not good at collaborating on. This is a very personal task for me.

It's mid-afternoon, and I am drawing The Hanging Sloth on Hank's right arm when Genevieve gets a call. She slips out the front door to take it while I continue scrawling on my mannequin.

She returns a few minutes later, looking grim.

"What's up?" I ask, putting my pen down.

"Nothing. Nothing important. Something's come up. Something back home. Are you okay if I skip out for a couple of days? You're pretty occupied here," she says, motioning at Hank. Her tone is clipped and awkward.

"Um, yeah. I guess. You sure you're okay?"

"Yeah, it's fine. Something I have to take care of. I should be able to come back in a couple of days."

"Oh," I say. Her sudden change of mood unsettles me slightly, but I don't know what to do about it. "If there is anything I can do…"

"Yup, I'll let you know. This is…it's a me thing. We…" she says, motioning between the two of us. "We are good I promise."

"Okay," I say.

Genevieve starts to pack her belongings into her bag. I get up to help her. The next few minutes are a whirlwind of packing, goodbyes, and a single kiss, and then I find myself standing alone and shirtless in my apartment.

"Women. Am I right?" Hank chides.

"Shut up," I say, picking up the permanent marker like a knife and stalking toward Hank. It's going to take me a couple of days to finish the bonding rituals with Hank, and I have some Dreamwalking to do. So it is probably a good thing that Genevieve had to suddenly and mysteriously leave town. Right?

Chapter Thirty-Three

"THE SLEEPER HAS AWAKENED."

I open my eyes. I'm lying on a hard wooden floor. I sit up and look around and see three doors, all sealed with intricate puzzle locks. I am in the house of locks and puzzles. I stand. This is a first for me. This is huge. I am Dreamwalking! I think.

I should wander around. Somehow, I know the way out of the sprawling labyrinthine house. I turn to my right and spin the knob on the door, press two of the buttons, and then the door clicks and swings open. In the next room, there are two more locked doors and a hatch in the floor. I quickly shift some dials until the symbols align in a pattern representing the cycles of the moon and turn a crank until the hatch opens. I hop into the hole beneath the hatch. After a few terrifying moments and one whirling sliding ride in pitch blackness, I am standing outside on the loamy earth.

I start to walk down a path into a dense thicket of trees. I'm feeling pretty giddy, and I consider skipping for a second. Then I feel self-conscious about the possibility of someone seeing me frolicking through the woods like a gleeful child in a fairy tale. A child right before they get eaten by a wolf.

Or a witch. Or a fox. Or bear...Or something.

"Hey, Miles!" A familiar voice says behind me and to my left. I turn quickly. There is Russ. Well, his face looks like Russ, and his voice sounds like Russ, but the rest of him looks like a Tolkien character.

He's wearing patchwork leather armor and leather boots that cinch up below his knee. He has a sword in a bejeweled scabbard and a quiver across his back. In one hand is an enormous and grotesquely innate bow. The bow stands out. It is thick. I don't know much about bows, but the whole thing seems too big and bulky actually to work. Its bulk is made of wood, a wood that has an interesting grain with whorls of different tones and textures to it.

The bow has been carved into an intricate dragon-like motif, with the grip being about the neck of the dragon. The bow's limbs are the dragon's outstretched body on the bottom and its arched wings on the top. It looks impressively ornamental but not remotely functional.

"Hey, Russ."

"Rusty Russel, the Russet Ranger of Russeoshire," he corrects.

"Right. What are you doing here?"

"We said we were going to meet up for a Dreamwalking lesson."

"Yes, yes, we did."

"Wow, you've been working on your *reva fortikaĵo* man."

I shrug. "Not really. I've tried, but nothing works out."

"If you say so," Russ shrugs. "Are you ready?"

"As I will ever be. I guess," I say.

"All right, follow me!" He says, and he takes off, jogging down the path we are on.

We run through the forest on the narrow dirt path. He dodges left around a tree, then right around a large rock.

"So you wanted to know how to dream track, right?" He asks.

"Yeah, that seems useful."

"Okay, man, tell me what you see here."

"This is all an illusion. Nothing here is real."

"That is **one** perspective, dude, but like from a different angle. Might I suggest that this is all an illusion, but...**everything** is real."

"Is this one of those 'loving everyone is the same as loving no one' things?"

"No. Yes. Maybe. But no, man, I mean, literally everything is here. Every thought ever thought. Every fantasy ever made. Every word ever spoken. Every breath ever taken. Every move ever made. All here...somewhere, dude."

"Yeah, you've mentioned that before the gestalt of the universe or whatever."

"Yeah man, exactly. But how do you find something in the middle of everything?"

"I don't know."

"Well, man, there are like two approaches, okay? So the first is if you, like, know something about someone, you look for that."

"How do you look for something inside...well, everything?"

"Man, how do you look for your keys when you lose them?"

"Well, I start by looking in the last place I remember seeing them."

"That's right, so what do you want to find?"

"Well, the secret to stopping Redbrook might be nice."

"There are secrets to be found for sure, dude, but man, we should probably, like, start off with some more low-hanging fruit. Y'know?"

"Sure. Okay," I say and pause for a moment to think. Russ stops jogging and waits for me while I ponder.

"The more familiar, the easier to find."

"A familiar secret?"

"No, man, I mean like trying to find a person or, well, your lost keys. Something you are familiar with but don't know where it is. Secrets are hard, man, because they are unfamiliar, and you have no idea where to start," Russ drawls at me.

"Okay fine. What if we find out what Circe is up to?"

"Tracking Circe is hard, man, she's a slippery one."

"Can we try anyway?"

Russ thinks for a moment and then shrugs.

"Sure, whatever floats your boat, man," Russ says.

"Okay."

"So the first step is you find the *vera vojo*."

"The true path."

"That's right, dude. The true path."

"And what's that?"

"Oh man, it's. Um. It's like this," he says, motioning around at everything. "This is all illusion. This path we are on is like a thought construct, right? Something I imagined and shared, your experience, and my experience, like most of reality, is subjective. It's more about what we expect to see, man, and what fits into our personal context. It's more about that than what is actually there. The *vera vojo* is…true."

"Yeah, that didn't clear up anything for me."

"Okay, so how about this? You want to imagine this road but then, like, forget all the stuff that you expect to see on it. Like there is this rock here," he points down at a pebble on the ground.

"Okay."

"Yeah, so that rock it's like something I expect to see, and you accept it could be there. So it's there, but it could easily not be there, so like…remove it."

I think I understand what he's getting at, and I sit and try to disbelieve a rock. I try to pretend it isn't there. I struggle to convince myself that it doesn't exist. We sit for a long time, me glowering at this small stone on the path. I strain my face contorted in concentration like a constipated aardvark while Russ watches patiently.

"No, man. No," Russ interrupts, "Like this."

Russ picks the rock up off of the ground and hurls it into

the sky. It goes upward at a roughly forty-five-degree trajectory and continues to sail into the sky at that angle until it fades from sight like an airplane vanishing into the horizon.

"So I just had to throw it?"

"No, man, no, you had to remove it from your context. Like, where is the rock now?"

"I don't know. Heading toward deep space?"

"No, man, it's gone because it was never here. If you sit there thinking about how it isn't here, all you are thinking about is it, so it is."

"What?" I ask. I am more than a little confused.

"Things in the Dreamtime, man. If you don't accept its presence, it goes away. It's all here because we suggest or think it is here like that rock. I suggested it was here, so it was, and you accepted that, so it is. Like, you can imagine accepting the rock is here. But you can also reject its presence, and it goes away. You can do this for people too, man, but like then they suggest they are there again, it gets more complicated," Russ explains, but little is clarified.

"So I pretend it isn't here, and it isn't?"

"Yeah, right, man. But you gotta like contextualize it? You dig?"

I notice a tree that stands on the side of the path a few yards away ceases to be.

"Woah!" I shout in confusion, "What happened to that tree?"

"What tree?" Russ asks.

"That tree!" I motion to where the tree was, and suddenly there is a tree again.

"Okay, progress, so I ignored the tree, and it went away, and then you reminded us it was there, so it came back. See, all you have to do is move on with your life, and the little stuff goes away. What's left once you've ignored all the little stuff is the vera vojo."

"Fine. It still doesn't make any sense, but fine," I say. I am getting to feel a little frustrated with this whole exercise.

"Okay, forget all you know, man, forget it all. Let the tides of the universe wash over you and let its salty brine invade your sense, okay, amigo?"

"Sure," I say because what else am I going to say to all that? I close my eyes, and I try to forget everything. Each tree does not exist. It is an illusion; I am dreaming. The ground; not there. The sun; not there. The rocks and shrubs and dirt; not there.

After what might only be five minutes or it might be five years, it is hard to tell if I open my eyes. I'm still standing on a narrow dirt path that winds its way through rolling hills and a deep pine forest. I can hear birds in the distance. Nothing has changed.

"Nothing has changed," I say out loud.

"Hmm," Russ says.

"Is there a different method?" I ask.

"*Cicerone,* a dream guide, could help, but summoning one of those is like real work."

"Okay, is it any easier than pretending a bunch of shit that is there isn't there?" I say I can hear the frustration in my own voice.

"Um. No?" He says, a little confused.

"Okay, well, what do we do?"

"Well, you need something to attract a spirit, a guide, and then you need to convince it to help you."

"I guess I was looking for more specifics."

"You need to have a new thought, one that's never been thought before."

"Oh, is that all?"

"Yeah, but like, don't tell me what it is. It's gotta be like, you know, your secret man. You can't ever share that thought with anyone, or it isn't yours anymore."

I sigh and close my eyes to help my imagination.

A thought that has never been thought before. The only way I can imagine doing this would be by getting very specific. There cannot possibly be an abstract thought that hasn't been thought of before probably countless times. It would have to be something that, while specific, is so implausible, so impossible that nobody would have considered it.

"Wait, didn't you say that this is the gestalt of the universe? That everything that has ever been thought or will be thought is here?"

"Yeah, dude, that's right. But some of them are things that only you ever thought they are yours uniquely in the whole gestalt of the universe. They are hidden away in secret pockets. There are not a lot of 'em, man, but you gotta find one. Some people probably don't have 'em at all. A thought that is yours and yours alone. That's your *Cicerone.* "

After a minute, I have it, but it's a hard thought, and it makes me sad. I keep it to myself; I lock it away from everyone.

"Even me?"

"Locked away from everyone, even you," I mutter aloud.

"That's right, man," Russ says, unaware that I wasn't talking to him.

"Okay. What now?" I say, opening my eyes.

"Check it out!" Russ says, pointing to a glowing light that is hovering right behind me.

"And this can lead us to Circe?" I ask.

"Well, I mean, eventually, yes, but you'll have to befriend it and train it all. It could take a long time," Russ has more to say, but he is interrupted by the little light zipping off down the path.

"It wants us to follow it!" I exclaim as I begin chasing the little light.

"Woah!" Russ says with surprise.

I start chasing the little light, and Russ falls in beside me.

"You don't see that every day!" Russ begins, but we don't say much more. The light is moving so fast that we have to basically sprint to keep up. Even so, we are slowly losing ground.

The light leads us at a breakneck pace through the forest,

then off the path through the underbrush and over a creek. Eventually, we come to a large open space between trees with a small cottage in the middle. We follow it up to the front door to the cottage, where it sits floating silently.

Just as I get to the door and reach for the door handle, the cottage turns to mist and evaporates. Suddenly, the ground opens up below me and pulls me in. The light blips out before my eyes, and I can hear Russ yell incoherently behind me.

The earth has sucked me in like a mire of quicksand. I am stuck up to my waist in the soil, which has contracted and hardened around me. I glance over at Russ, who has somehow dodged away from a similar pit, trying to swallow him. He has produced his longbow and has an arrow knocked on it. The shaft of the arrow is glowing with coruscating electricity. Russ is high in the air and is making a slow-motion descent to the ground, some fifteen feet away from where the ground tried to swallow him.

And good, too, for a shadowy figure is closing in on me. It is black and mostly formless; it has an outline reminiscent of a human, but the edges and details are all blurred. The thing is translucent. It has no discernible legs. Its lower torso seems to fade out of reality before it fully forms into its legs. However, the top is much clearer. The face, if it has one, is heavily cowled and discernible as a face only through the presence of two glowing baleful red eyes.

Russ fires his arrow at the creature, but the creature moves aside at incredible speed. Amorphous arms form from its black body and rise high in the air. As it does, a distant howling can be heard echoing between the trees. Pounding out of the underbrush comes a flock or pack of creatures.

They are sleek and grey with pointed noses and long, narrow bodies reminiscent of sharks or fish, but they have legs. Legs that end in huge claws. They have no eyes or nostrils that I can see, but they do have mouths. Huge mouths, mouths filled with teeth. Rows and rows of razor-sharp teeth. They are moving fast and in a coordinated fashion. Crossing each other's paths and spreading out. Whatever these things are, they have tactics.

"Daunts!" Russ clarifies as the creatures come into view.

I am struggling, mired up to my waist in the ground.

"But they aren't dangerous! Right?" I ask Russ. I can hear my own voice like it is someone else's. I'm screaming with a panicked timbre to my voice.

"Technically, yeah, but I don't think we should count on that. These ones are giving me the heebie-jeebies."

Russ springs into action. He fires a volley of arrows straight up into the sky. The speed with which he draws and fires is unbelievable. In a few seconds, he has fired dozens of arrows straight up into the air while he runs a semi-circle around the black form and its pack of monsters.

"Miles, do something!" He yells as he turns and fires a volley at the pack of monsters that are charging him. They leap and dodge out of the way of the arrows. However, the volley he fired into the air now rains down, and three of the creatures dodge directly into the rain of sharpened sticks returning to earth. The remaining four close in on him and surround him in a circle.

Russ raises a horn and blows it loudly. It is so loud it makes my head swim, and I have to press my hands to my ears. The horn echoes such that I can feel the earth around me vibrate, and I sink further as it sublimates.

The black figure is floating its way toward me. It isn't moving particularly fast, but its approach seems inexorable. It will be on me in a moment, and I have no idea what to do. I am stuck, slowly sinking into the earth.

Russ keeps firing arrows at an incredible speed. I wonder briefly at the number of arrows and how he seems to have an inexhaustible supply of them. Then I remember that we are dreaming and the rules don't really apply. I can see the beast behind him leap at his blind spot. The creature's maw opens wide, ready to consume Russ's head while I watch. I want to cry out, but I am too slow. Suddenly, out of the trees, a shape blurs and impacts the creature mid-air. The two forms fall to the ground in a snarling, flailing ball of teeth and claws.

The black wraith is almost to me. It pauses. It hesitates. It doesn't have eyes, only two red pools shrouded in black shadow, but I feel like if it did have eyes, it would be looking at something above and behind me.

A figure leaps over my head. Long, lithe, athletic legs landing in a crouch before me. It wields an immense broad sword being swung in a wide arc. I recognize the figure even before she turns to wink at me. Circe.

She is wearing armor made of form-fitting plates of metal. The metal is polished chrome with whorls and adornments in gold. Her sword is in a similar motif of chrome and gold. The whole ensemble is more than a little over the top. It's on brand for her.

She begins to attack the shadow. Her movements seem more like dance than combat. She is showy, graceful, and melodramatic. The shadow creature seems to fade, morph, and cease to exist in places she attacks. It coalesces back together in a way that defies physics or description. Wherever she attacks, it simply isn't.

"A little help here!" Russ yells, his bow has been discarded, and he's swinging a long dagger back and forth to defend himself from the remaining three creatures. The fourth is still rolling around on the ground in a vicious battle with a huge black mastiff.

The mastiff is jet black and the size of a pony. Blood and ichor splash like a lawn sprinkler as the two creatures claw and bite at each other.

Circe makes a notable and audible sigh. She jumps back and makes a hand gesture with her left hand holding the great broadsword in her right hand. Then she turns to run toward Russ. As she does, she also stays standing between me and the shadow, each form still holding the left hand up in the gesture. With each step, new Circes spawn off the previous one until there are a full dozen copies of her leaping and charging around the clearing. They attack in a coordinated effort, merging and splitting apart in a disorienting pattern. It is hard to watch and even harder to track exactly what is going on.

The shadow creature raises its arms and howls again. An ululating response can be heard from the wood. More of the grey Daunts will be joining us soon. The army of Circe quickly dispatches the beasts, but soon dozens more are crashing into the clearing.

A half dozen Circes fight the shadow creature, but its fluid form fades away from attacks, and new limbs flow dynamically out of its dark mass to retaliate. I am struggling to pull myself out of the mire that I am in with no luck. I don't know what to do.

I can't tell exactly what direction the fight is going at any given instant, it seems to be in the shadow creature or Circes' favor. Circe clones get struck and vanish. A new one spawns quickly from one of the others. Each of the grey beasts she slays is soon replaced as another leaps from the trees. The clearing is littered with grey bodies.

At this rate, I can see that Russ isn't going to make it. He's been bitten and clawed at blood pours from a number of wounds. His huge mastiff crouches back to back with him. Gaping lacerations on its sides and neck.

"Miles, do something!" Russ yells at me.

"Like what?" I ask.

"It's a dream. I don't know, come up with something."

I take a deep breath. I have no idea what I can do. It's a dream, right? So I should be able to do whatever I can imagine. But my mind is blank; I need some space to think.

"Miles, man!" Russ shouts.

The earth shudders and splits, rocks and dirt are hurled into the sky. They shower back down on us as walls rise from the earth. When I was a kid, I had a toy called a Jacobs Ladder with wooden slats connected by ribbon so that you hold it, and the slats seem like they flop down and fall forever as you grab the next one. The walls rise up and expand and grow in a manner that reminds me of the Jacobs Ladder. Each wall unfolds into a ceiling, another wall, or another level.

The four walls grow to eight. Those eight grow to sixteen to thirty-two and on and on. Each set of six encapsulates a creature. A cell for each Circe clone, one for the shadow creature, and one for each of the grey beasts. Russ and his mastiff are each trapped in their own cells of onyx black. The stone boxes stack on each other and grow out and wide. A spire of cubes rises up. A door forms. Soon, there is an enormous black tower standing before me.

The spire has hundreds, no thousands of rooms, and I am aware of each and every one of them. I don't know why. I don't know how. But suddenly, this tower is like an extension of my mind. I can feel Russ in a room. I can feel a tiny spark that is Russ's mastiff. Its canine form is only a construct or projection of the little spirit inside. I can feel Circe in one cell. But that's it. No shadow monster, no grey beasts, no Circe copies. I can feel them all, the energy that made them all flow, coalescing, returning to Circe's cell. There was no shadow creature. There were no grey beasts. They were all illusions projected by Circe.

A moment later, the tower ejects Russ violently onto the ground at my feet. He lies sprawled there in the mud. He's lying on his back, blinking up at me.

"What the hell was that dude?" Russ exclaims.

"I don't know! I didn't do anything! But this is my *reva fortikaĵo* thingy! I think."

"That's not a *reva fortikaĵo*...I mean, I've never seen or even heard of anything like that. That's crazy, man."

"That whole ambush was Circe," I say, changing the subject.

"Huh? No man, that was the Dreamstalker."

"That's right, and Circe was the Dreamstalker."

"How do you know?"

"I don't know. I do. It suddenly all makes sense; she's been telling me all along. The first thing she said to me was that she was my dream girl."

"I buy it. I said not to trust that chick. But to, like, what end? What's her goal?"

"I don't know. The obvious answer is to make me trust her. She shows up, and after a harrowing fight, she saves us by the skin of her teeth. It'd be a pretty convincing show."

Russ shrugs. "I guess."

He turns to look up at the huge black tower. He pushes his hat up to his brow, mouth agape in consideration and wonder.

"You see it don't you?" Russ says.

"That it's missing a giant baleful eye at the top?"

"No. No, man, it's the Syzmek building."

"No, it's not," I say, gazing up at the giant tower.

But after a moment's consideration, I realize I'm wrong. I mean, it is the Syzmek building if the Syzmek building were made out of giant slabs of onyx or obsidian and not steel and glass. I didn't see it before, but now that Russ mentions it, the similarities are too great to deny.

Chapter Thirty-Four

THIS HUGE BLACK TOWER, a building that I have some strange and inexplicable connection to it, looks like a copy of the Syzmek building but carved in onyx.

"Huh. I guess it is the Syzmek building," I say.

"That's weird, right?" Russ asks.

"Yeah, that's weird."

We sit staring at the huge black tower for a while longer. I feel attached to it; I am somehow aware of what is inside it. Each room is like an aching joint. Circe's presence is like an itching boil under the skin. There are other things in there, other little itches and discomforts, but they are dull, distant ignorable. Old wounds.

As certain as I am that I can feel this building in my bones, I am equally certain that this building is not mine. I am not its architect. Whoever or whatever built it has, for some reason, has connected it to me.

"*Donjon*," Russ breaks the silence.

"What?"

"This isn't a *reva fortikajo*. It's *The Donjon*. The word is French for like a castle or a keep, right, dude? But, like, it's also the origin of the word dungeon. But man like *The Donjon* capital T capital D? Like a proper noun you dig? Yeah, it's also like a thing or whatever, right, man? It's a place where one can be cursed to imprisonment for eternity. *The Donjon.* Such a bigger bummer than dying man."

Then, after a pregnant pause, Russ follows up, "Can she get out?"

"No, I think it'll stay locked up until she is released. The room she's in is itself in a room that is in a room, etcetera. Each has a more complicated puzzle to escape."

"What if she solves all the puzzles, man? She's pretty quick."

"I don't know. I have this sense that she isn't going anywhere."

"Okay, dude, well, we wanted to trap her, and she's trapped. So that's something. But you didn't put her in there? And you can, like, sense her in there, but you can't let her out?"

"I don't think so. I mean, I didn't do anything. I'm as confused as you are."

"Huh, well *The Donjon*. Perfect. So what are we going to do now, man?" Russ asks.

"I have no idea. Let's go see what she'll tell us."

I start into the massive tower, with Russ apprehensively following behind me. We enter the massive black stone portcullis at the entrance. There is a cyclopean spiral stone staircase that circles its way up the center, vanishing into the darkness above. A single, immense iron-clad door stands at each visible landing. There is enough light to see but no clear source for that light.

We start up the stairs. They seem to wind their way up forever, but in only a few steps, we arrive on a landing. It is as if the stairwell shortened itself for us. There stands a large wooden door bound with iron straps. It has an intricate puzzle lock comprised of a delicate sequence of flower petals that must be arranged in the right order. Clumsy red letters have been painted on the door. The letters read:

Circe.

I look back at Russ and shrug. I turn and knock.

"Circe?" I ask.

There is no response.

"You in there?"

"Let me out, Miles!" Circe's voice comes muffled through the heavy door.

"I can't," I say.

"Let me out, Miles!" She yells through the door. There is a faint thud. I think she hit the door, but its timbers are so thick and heavy that it doesn't even shake.

"You attacked Russ and me, and I want to know why. I think you've been messing with my dreams all along," I say.

"Let me out, and I will explain," Circe growls. She is somehow far less intimidating while locked in there.

"I told you I can't. I didn't do this."

"Then tell your bodyguard to let me OUT!"

"Woah, chica, I didn't do this," Russ says from behind me.

"Not you, imbecile. The spirit you had trap me here. Tell it to let me out."

"I don't know what you are talking about, Circe. Even if I did and I could let you out, I am not sure I would."

"I am going to die in here, Miles," her voice sounds suddenly more vulnerable, maybe even a little scared. However, I don't buy it for a second; it's too cliche.

"Again, this isn't a thing I am in control of."

"You know I have a normal mortal body. It's asleep, and if I don't wake up, it will sit there and dehydrate and starve to death. You will literally kill me if you leave me in here, Miles," she says. "You aren't a murderer."

"I don't feel like you are listening to me. I can't let you out. I didn't put you in here, and I don't know who did."

I can hear an incoherent scream from the other side of the door and more pounding, but the door is so sturdy that it sounds more like a finger tapping.

"You are an idiot, Miles!"

"Okay, well, I'll let you cool your heels in there for a while and come back," I say, but honestly, I have no idea what happens if I wake up. Does *The Donjon,* as Russ called it, go away? If I return, can I find this door again? I don't know.

"Bye!" I call out through the door.

I nod my head at Russ, indicating that I am going to leave. We turn back to the staircase, and I take a step to leave.

"Miles! What do you want? I can't be stuck in this cage. I hate being trapped, Miles. Please let me out, and I'll do anything you want, tell you anything you want."

"Answer some questions, and I will see what I can do, but again I don't know how to let you out."

"You ask your little guardian angel to let me out."

"There is no guardian angel Circe."

"Fine, I will answer your questions, then all you have to say is something like," she says, and then in a bored-sounding staccato, she incants, "Oh Guardian Angel, insert name here I beseech thee release the one I know as Circe from this prison which you hath wrought for her. With the cold breath of the north, I beseech you. With the hot wind of the south, I beseech you by the west and east winds or some other poetic shit I beech you. I have brought you this article of lameness as offering. Please free my beautiful and enticing comrade from her prison."

Her voice builds to a screaming crescendo. "It doesn't even have to be that formal just say something!"

I can hear the vague, muffled pounding on the door. I think she is having a temper tantrum.

"I don't think that is going to work, man," Russ says. "That's a little snarky for an invocation."

I hear Circe growl in response.

"Fine, sure whatever. Okay, first question. There was no Dreamstalker. That was you. You came to me and told me about the Daunts that Redbrook had in her employ. Her 'Hounds.' But those weren't what she was referring to. You told me about the Daunts. You summoned them. That was to ensure I would go to The Lantern. Ensure that I would help Whitman. Ensure that I would ask for your help."

"The great detective Miles Ward strikes again," Circe says sarcastically through the door. I think she's yelling, but I can barely hear her because her voice is so dampened.

"Why? Why go through all that trouble? Why me?"

"Because I couldn't finish the contract without you, Miles. You were crucial."

"The contract. So Redbrook was your target all along. The whole Whitman thing that was to…what? Get her trust? Get close to her?"

"Something like that, yes."

"But why me? Yes, I see how my presence helped you, but I can't see how you could have known that it would help you. I'm nobody."

"Bringing you in was part of the contract Miles. Using you as bait and distraction, that was the contract, Miles," she says, sounding exasperated.

"Getting me involved was part of the contract? But why would anybody want to drag me into this? Who would want to drag me into this?"

But before I finish the question, I know the answer. John Hale. It sounds exactly like him to hold a grudge against every person that ever said no. It sounds like him to do everything in his power to show he can manipulate and control those people anyway and at every turn. My involvement in this whole thing is some petty and juvenile grudge.

"The whole spell on Whitman, the whole JMBaptiste winery. Tattooing a friend of mine as part of it. That was all to draw me in?"

"The Lamia did contract me to kill Whitman horribly. A contract I normally would have refused. Small potatoes. But it was an in-road. So yes, we used the opportunity to drag you in."

"That is a very elaborate scheme you concocted to get my attention."

"Not me, Morgan, she was always the over-planner. I wanted to take a more direct approach."

My ears feel hot, and my neck feels cold and prickly. I feel manipulated, and I can't help but wonder how much farther all this goes.

"Okay, so next question. How did sending Rebobs after me fit into this?"

"I have no idea Morgan LeFey did that. She's young, foolish, impulsive."

"And by Morgan LeFey this time, you mean Magdalena. Just so you know, that gets confusing."

"That is the point of the tradition."

"Okay fine. Moving on. Question two: Who the hell are you?"

"That's like your thirteenth question."

"Whatever. Who are you?"

"I'm Circe, the oldest living member of the Hizarin."

"Okay, but that's not what I mean. I think the person I know that we know is only a projection. Is that true, and if so, who are you really?"

I can hear her laughing faintly through the door.

"You are the kind of guy who plays better, blindfolded Miles. For a bumbling shot in the dark, not bad. That's right, it's been my secret for a long time. I create constructs and project my consciousness into them to do things. It is handy having a body with no tissues or organs; that isn't bound by physical laws. That I can create or dismiss on a whim."

"Okay, who are you really? What's your story? Where's your real body?"

"Not telling you where my body is, that's very personal, Miles. Who am I? I don't know. Do any of us know who we are? I've lived a hundred lives and worn a thousand faces. They are all real to me. They are all who I really am."

"You're getting philosophical to avoid answering the question," I say.

"Fine. When I was young, I got a sickness, a sleeping sickness. I'd fall asleep for long periods, days at a time, sometimes. I was trapped in a prison of my own body, just like you've got me trapped here. I hate being trapped," she says, followed by a long silence.

"I hate being trapped, Miles!" She yells through the door for emphasis. It sounds like she is trying to claw her way through the door. Or maybe she is scrabbling at the puzzle lock.

Then silence. There is another long pause before she continues with a grunt. Her tone has returned to something more controlled and formal.

"So I'd dream I'd explore the world in my mind. As I got older, the bouts of sleeping got longer. But I dreamed and dreamed, and it was in my dreams that I found freedom. Eventually, I didn't wake up for weeks or months at a time. I had to be fed and cleaned by my family. I became an adult lying in a bed. Inert.

Finally, my family gave up on me. They decided I was a liability. My parents left my sleeping body in a cave to die. I was an inconvenience. I would have died, too, except for my sister. She didn't give up on me. She would sneak out wherever she could to that cave to take care of me. She found ways of keeping my body alive even though it should have perished."

"Ways like medicine?"

"This was before IVs and intubation, Miles. Ways. Magical ways. I learned how to control my dreams and how to make my dreams real. How to project my consciousness back into the world. I could make myself manifest outside of my body."

"So your sister still keeps your body alive?"

"No, Miles, my sister is long dead thanks for opening old wounds. No, I project myself and take care of my body myself. Hence, if I don't get out of here, I am going to DIE!"

"Wait, wait," Russ says, "You project your consciousness into a body to be a nurse to your own body?"

"Yes, why are we spending all this time talking about how I keep my frail, helpless body alive? This is going nowhere. Let me out!"

"The problem is I don't believe you, Circe. Your story is nice; it's tragic. It sounds like a fairy tale. I think you are making things up to get my sympathy."

"Well, I'm not."

"But you offer no evidence. It's self-contained and neither offers nor requires corroboration. No, Circe, I can tell a story when I hear it. You have lied to me so much that I can't ever believe anything you say."

"Miles, you can't leave me in here. I will die. I am not lying about that part."

"And I didn't trap you in there, Circe. I can't let you out because I don't know how. I am not lying about that part, either. Goodbye, Circe."

"Miles!"

As Russ and I turn to walk away once more, I can hear Circe screaming with rage through the door.

"Miles! Miles! When I get out of here, Miles…" her muffled voice can be heard fading away as we get some distance. Thankfully, I never get to hear what she has in mind for me if she escapes.

"Will this stay when we leave?" I ask Russ.

"Hell, if I know, man, I don't even know what this is."

"It's like a *reva fortikaĵo,* right?"

"Got me, amigo, but I'll tell you this man, this ain't like no *reva fortikaĵo* I've ever seen."

"But if it is, then it will stay?"

"Then yeah, man, that's the point once you build it, it stays till you destroy it, and that thing doesn't look like it's going anywhere. Though I am going to be honest, dude, this would take an experienced Dreamer a lifetime to build if it could be done at all. We've just seen bits and pieces, but I had no clue it was so big. Or even, like, how did you build something so big?"

"I didn't build it. It was already here."

"You keep saying that, but it doesn't make much sense, man."

I shrug.

Chapter Thirty-Five

I WAKE UP. My eyes are gummy, and I am not sure where I am at first. I have that half-sick, half-bewildered, completely drunk feeling that you get when you are awakened out of a deep sleep long before your body is ready to be alert. I sit bleary-eyed, trying to process. Why am I sitting up? Why do I feel so panicked?

There is a sound at my front door. Someone is knocking. Pounding. I get up and grab a robe and pull it onto my shoulders.

"What the mother of cheese," I mutter to myself as I stagger across my apartment to my door.

"Because that's an expression."

"Fromage off you moldering stilton," I mutter at Hank.

"Oooh, sick burn. Were you having dreams about dairy again?" Hank says sarcastically.

Alertness is coming to me like a slow trickle of coffee running rivulets through the folds and creases of my brain. There is a distant wailing sound.

"Miles!" A voice is yelling. There is more pounding on my door. I stagger to it in my robe and underwear.

Standing on the other side of the door is a young woman. Her clothes are torn and burned, and she has soot on her face.

I slap myself.

"I'm dreaming," I say.

"No, Miles, you aren't dreaming! Come on, wake the fuck up," the girl says.

I stare at her. Her eyes are wide, pupils large. She looks panicked. I recognize her now, Magdalena. But this isn't the Magdalena I have come to dread running into outside my front door. This Magdalena is disheveled, dirty, and not bringing all the bravado that I've come to expect from her.

"What, Magdalena?"

"I need your help."

I blink and look over her shoulder. The skyline behind her is shimmering with light. The wailing sound is sirens. I suddenly get more alert.

"What is going on?" I demand.

"Get dressed, get your things. There will be plenty of time to explain on the way."

"On the way where?"

"Just move it, Miles. We don't have a lot of time. You're the good guy, right? Damsels in distress, steal from the rich and give to the poor, slay the dragon, all that shit?"

"I've literally never done any of that."

"Whatever, I fucked up, and I need you to help me fix it."

"Fine, fine, hold on."

I run back into my house and get dressed. I don't have time to dress Hank, though this seems like a good time to have my Simulacrum at full ready. I grab a canned cold brew from my refrigerator and chug it while I retrieve my work bag and jacket. I grab another can of coffee for the road. Less than two minutes later, I get back to my front door. An impatient-looking Magdalena is there holding a ridiculously large duffle bag.

"You're driving," she says as she turns and rushes down the stairs. I follow her, fumbling for my car keys as I do. I unlock the car, and Magdalena leaps into the passenger seat with the grace of a stunt driver. I heave drunkenly on my door and climb inside with the grace of an unbalanced washing machine. I see the runes on my dash, the trap we put there for Circe. I notice it doesn't seem to phase Magdalena. I file that away for later.

"Where are we going?"

"East, do you know Hagen Road?"

"Yeah," I say as I start driving in that direction. "Okay, start telling me what's going on, or I am turning around…"

I look at the skyline to the east, and it looks like the sun is rising, but it's two-thirty in the morning, and it is definitely not the sun.

"…because it looks an awful lot to me like you having me drive into a wildfire," I conclude.

"I am. As I said, I fucked up pretty badly. I was doing this…thing, and I messed up the ritual. I had the wrong name or something. I guess I summoned a *Fotia Kakodaimon* by mistake."

"That's a…an evil, um, fire demon?" I stumble through my pittance of Greek padded out with some blind guessing.

"Yeah basically."

"Um. Okay. I have so many questions. But probably the most important. Why are you coming to me?"

"Honestly, I didn't know who else to go to. I can't find Circe anywhere. She kinda ghosted me. Actually, I only know a couple of people in town, and you are by far the most trustworthy of them. Also, you're Mr. Apotropaist, right? You're ready to scuffle with a fire demon," Magdalena says.

I don't know if I agree with her assessment.

I startle as she takes a large handgun out of her bag and starts cleaning and loading it. It's absolutely huge. In her awkward teen hands, it looks disproportionate and alien. I glance quickly into the open bag in her lap. It is filled with firearms and boxes of ammunition.

"I am not sure I am comfortable with all the ordinance. I am not really a shoot-em-up type. Besides, isn't all that ammo kind of a liability with…you know…a fire monster?"

She shrugs.

"Chill out. I didn't bring any high explosives," Magdalena says.

"Oh good, that puts my mind at ease."

She slaps a clip into the pistol. I glance over as it clicks in place, and I notice that she has her clips color-coded. She takes a holster out of her bag, shoves the gun into it, and clicks the holster onto her belt. I notice for the first time that she is wearing a harness that wraps around her hips and over her shoulders. It has a bunch of little tabs that are receivers for her clips and other gear.

"Are bullets even going to work on a fire monster?"

"Magic bullets," she says as if that is all the explanation she needs.

"Whatever, okay, how did you 'accidentally' summon this thing?" I ask as we pull onto Hagen Road. There are flashing lights ahead. A roadblock.

"Shit," Magdalena says. "Park, we are going to have to go on foot."

I pull off the road, and she hops out before my car has come to a complete stop. She's left the bag inside but somehow managed to clip three different firearms to her harness.

I put the car in park and turn off the engine.

"Magde…" I start to say, but she's already run off to the edge of my headlights. "SH…arp cheddar! Well. Gouda! I guess we are doing this."

I turn off the lights, grab my bag, and jump out of the car to follow her.

The air is thick with smoke, and the smell is making me want to wretch. It is hard to navigate. We are close enough to the fire now that there is light everywhere. There is so much smoke that it diffuses the light so that it doesn't seem to come from anywhere. It's just a dull glow in the air around us. My eyes are watering, and my nose and throat burn. I catch up to Magdalena. She's wearing a respirator now. It covers her mouth and eyes. With the burned, soot-stained clothes, harness full of guns, and mask, she looks like a post-apocalyptic marauder.

"Where the hell did you get the respirator from?" I hack out, "And did you bring one for me?"

"Yeah, stupid, it's back in the car," her muffled voice informs me from under the mask.

"Well, you could have said something," I choke and turn back to the car.

I run back, feeling sick the whole way. My eyes water, and my throat burns. I throw open the door to my car and rifle through Magdalena's duffle until I find another mask and put it on. It reduces visibility, but at least my eyes aren't watering as much. The burn in my throat quickly becomes a dull ache and the flavor of burning car tires.

I catch back up to Magdalena. She's crouched down, waiting for me.

"Okay," I say. My voice sounds weird to me, muffled as it is by the big rubber mask. "How'd you summon a fire demon of all things? I've never even heard of such a thing, you know, outside of books."

"Well. I was trying to find Circe. She's been missing, and you know we are a team. I was going to summon up like a tracking spirit to help me find her. I was going through my old mentors' books, and I found this spell to do just that, and I was like Fuck It! Let's do this, Maggie. But I think I got the wrong name or mispronounced it, or you know, Greek's not my thing, so I didn't get the tracking spirit I was planning to summon. Or maybe I did fuck; I don't know. But you know, to summon something big, you gotta sacrifice big. There's this ranch out here. They got a bunch of cows…now they gotta a bunch of cooked cows."

I am staring at her, mouth agape and eyes wide, but then I realize she can't see my look of horror through the mask.

"You aren't going to find Circe. She's trapped in the Dreamtime."

"And you know this because…you trapped her?"

"No, I have no idea how she got trapped, but I know she is. She's pretty pissed about it."

"Yeah, that'd piss her off."

"You are being awfully nonchalant considering the chaos and destruction you've caused here," I add after a moment.

"You're being awfully nonchalant about being an absolute tool. It doesn't matter how it happened. How do we stop it?"

I'm not sure I agree with her flippant viewpoint, but I do agree that stopping it should be our first priority. While we are screaming at each other through our masks, Magdalena leads me through some brush and trees to the top of a hill. Looking down into a little valley is an awesome sight.

By awesome, I mean the true definition: Inspiring great admiration or fear.

In this case fear.

The ranch below us is nestled in a small vale. A small creek runs through the center of the space. There are the blackened and still burning remains of what I can only assume was a barn. From that epicenter, fire is rolling like a wave to the north and west toward where the firetrucks were blockading the road. Magdalena has navigated us due west of the blaze and off of the wind's trajectory. Slightly off of the trajectory of the wind.

The fire is visibly gaining size and speed as it goes.

But that isn't the part that freezes me in place and burrows its way into tomorrow's nightmares. Lumbering out of the burning wreckage of that barn, turning its way toward the ranch house, is a figure. It is probably twenty feet tall and seems to be mostly made of fire. But it has a solid core, a skeleton of sorts composed of a dozen or so cow carcasses wreathed in flame. I've dealt with necromancers and sorcerers and all sorts of awful things in my life, but I have never seen anything like this. I stop transfixed. Every sphincter in my body contracts suddenly.

"Holy Scamorza…"

"Miles!" Magdalena sticks her masked visage directly in my face. "Miles! You have to help me put the Djinni back in the bottle, or it's gonna kill people. Lots of people. It's gonna kill lots of people in their beds; it's gonna kill firefighters, it's gonna kill cops, it's gonna kill baristas! Baristas make coffee, Miles! Snap out of it! We have maybe ten minutes tops maybe before it gets to a heavily populated area."

I shake my head. She's right now is not the time to panic and have a breakdown. I need to put the Post in Post Traumatic Stress. I close my eyes and tell the fear to leave. I feel my dread and trepidation flow out of me like water down a storm drain.

"Okay, so it's made of a lot of magical energy, but I can also see that the body is made of corporeal…stuff," I say, not wanting to get too detailed on what is actually made of. I don't want to dwell on the fact that, imagined or not, I can hear the screams of burning bovines in my ears. "That means if we cut it off from the Ley, it won't be able to animate the…stuff and lose its form. Right?"

"Yeah," Magdalena says, "that sounds right. I mean, there is also a whole banishing spell beseeching thing, but that looked complicated."

"Okay," I say. I close my eyes and imagine a plan. "Here is what we are going to do. You get its attention. Do you see that little pond over there?"

I point to where there is a small pond. It looks like it might be a small man-made reservoir for watering crops and animals. It's the perfect context for extinguishing a fire demon.

"I need you to draw it that way. I am going to try to build a circle to trap it and drain its mana."

"Got it. Tell me when it's go time," Magdalena says.

"Oh, it's go time."

I haven't finished the sentence before she is sprinting down the hill, leaping over bushes and sliding through the dust. She moves fast. Surprisingly fast. I start jogging at a much slower pace toward the pond. It is hard to see and harder to breathe in the respirator I am wearing, and I don't find navigating all that easy. I stumble and lurch and find myself scrabbling on all fours from time to time. I am amazed at how unencumbered she seems under the circumstances.

I'm still a hundred feet away from the pond when I hear the reports of gunfire coming from the direction of the lumbering mass of the demon. I glance in that direction. I can see it, but I can't see Magdalena in the smoke. The sound, too, is diffused, and the reports seem to be coming from everywhere around me.

I make it to the pond. It is roughly circular. That's good. The ground is a thick grey-blue clay. This pond has seen better days, and it looks like it's about four feet lower than it was intended to be.

Summer in California.

The pond doesn't have nearly as much water as I was hoping it would, but it will have to do. I pull out a pocket knife and quickly and hastily lay down a series of runes for an exclusive circle around the edge of the pond. It is easy to carve into the dry clay. I hope the demon doesn't mess them up when it crosses the boundary.

I look up briefly. The huge burning figure is lumbering in my direction, making much better time than I was hoping. I only have another minute before it arrives. I turn back to my bag, grab two vials of Jeff's Acetobacter formulae, and dump it into the pond water. I am hoping it should be able to breed quickly in there once it is trapped with the demons' reserves of magic.

I glance back up. Magdalena is running toward me, firing a small submachine pistol at the thing behind her back. Her arm, even though she isn't looking, seems locked unerringly on the creature's center mass as it lumbers forward.

It's so familiar. Did I see a movie where someone was running through a smokey field, shooting over their shoulder at a fire monster? I am having that sense of *deja vu* again. It occurs to me at this moment that almost every time I've had that sense of *deja vu,* Magdalena has been nearby. I need to figure that out, but this isn't the moment.

The fire demon is only a dozen yards away when Magdalena catches up to me.

"Now what?" She screams.

"Now we wait till it gets in the circle, activate it, run, and pray," I say.

"Are you a religious man Miles?"

"No, not particularly," I say.

"Then maybe let's not waste our breath."

I am about to say that it is just an expression, but the creature has arrived, and it is far more horrifying than I originally thought.

Bigger than a two-story building, the behemoth bears down on us. I can feel my exposed skin burning from the radiant heat, and my mask and clothes are so hot I am worried they will burst into flame on my skin.

The creature, if that's the right term, has a form that is vaguely humanoid but is mostly a mass of burning but apparently still living, bleating cows. It has no eyes, face, or other way of expressing itself, but it has an aura of hate. A palpable radiating anger and rage that washes over me like a tidal wave and threatens to smother me. Terror rises in my throat like bile, and I realize that I am screaming uncontrollably.

"We run now?" Magdalena asks.

I can only continue my terrified ululation in response.

"We run now," she says flatly and takes off.

I am about to follow her in a panic when some glimmer in the back of my brain reminds me that I need to activate my circle or this whole 'plan' isn't going to work. I shakily take my knife, slash at my arm, and drip the blood into one of the runes I carved into the clay. I can feel the familiar sensation of the magic circle taking shape. I nod to myself and turn to run.

The blood running down my arms activates my warding runes. I can feel the familiar sensation of magic washing over my body, and a little bit of my pain and anxiety drift away. I didn't plan that, but it's a good thing.

I can feel the heat increasing above me to an intensity I've never felt. This must be what it's like to burn alive. I glance up and see a makeshift fist of burning cattle flesh careening down toward me.

The world gets quiet. It gets calm. The heat isn't burning anymore it's warming.

"So this is how it ends?" I think to myself, and I find that I am calm, cool, and collected. The panic has gone, "We had a good run, didn't we?"

"*Yeah, we did,*" I can hear Hank say beside me.

"Hey, you're coming to help, buddy."

"*More like you are joining me on the other si…oh…nope, never mind! Heads up!*"

I get that feeling of *deja vu* again. Only this is the most intense sense I've ever gotten. Like I've lived here in this moment for eternity. I've seen that fist of burning cow flesh careen down toward me more times than I've taken breaths.

The overwhelming sense of *deja vu* is interrupted as I feel a hand grab me by the back of my shirt and physically lift me off the ground and hurl me. I've never wondered what it is like to be a baseball. Now, out of sympathy, I will never throw another one again.

I crash into the hard-packed clay dirt twenty feet away from the pond, my fall broken only by a dried pile of cow manure. The wind is knocked out of me, and I see little motes of light in my otherwise black vision.

After a second, I catch my breath and glance back to see Magdalena running toward me. The ends of her hair are literally on fire. She gets to me and drags me to my feet. We turn and face the demon, but it seems now trapped inside the circle.

I reach over and pat the smoldering ends of Magdalena's hair out.

"You came back for me," I say.

"We are partners on this hit. I don't leave a partner hanging in the wind," she says.

"Not a hit."

"We killed a goddamn fire demon, that's a hell of a hit."

"Well, thank you for saving me," I say.

"Thank you, you saved my bacon on this one. If this thing had gotten more out of control, the Hizarin would have my ass."

We stand in the fading light of the fire demon and watch as it begins to sizzle and crackle in the pond.

"We should probably chant the banishing spell, or the spirit will find a new sacrifice when your circle fails," Magdalena says. She holds up a little slip of paper. I squint at it through the smoke and firelight. She has hand-written some words there. She begins chanting, and I join in haltingly.

Finally, all of the demons' magic is consumed. Magdalena produces a knife from somewhere. She cuts the back of her arm and lets the blood drip onto the ground. The demon makes a terrible howling that sounds like the roar of a fire, if the fire were somehow in pain. Then, slowly, the demon expires, and charred cow corpses rain down into the water. It is absolutely nauseating to watch, and I have to turn away. I don't watch them fall, but I can hear the heavy, meaty splashes and thuds as the immense carcasses fall into the shallow water and hit the muddy clay beneath. The only thing I am thankful for is that I am wearing a respirator, which filters out not quite enough of the putrid smell.

I glance over at Magdalena. She has taken her mask off. She's smiling a faint smile, the firelight dancing in her eyes. I can't help but feel she likes watching things burn.

I can't trust Circe. I don't know what she is about, and everything she says seems to be a lie wrapped in a deception tied up in a scheme hidden behind a half-truth.

I feel like I can trust Magdalena. I can trust her the way I can trust an angry mongoose let loose in a preschool. I can't tell you exactly what destruction is going to be wrought. I can't tell how many tears will be shed in the end. But at least I know what kind of day it's going to be. She scares the hell out of me, but I think I can predict Magdalena. It's something I can work with, at least.

"Mind if I ask you a personal question?" I ask.

"Go for it. I got you out of bed to clean up my mess. I owe you that, at least."

"How old are you…exactly?"

"That's a dumb question. I told you already I'm 23."

"Really? I thought that was BS."

"No, seriously, I'm 23. Nothing I told you when we met was a lie. It just wasn't the whole truth."

"Are there a lot of 23-year-old members of the Hizarin?"

"Nope just me. Youngest member ever inducted. I'm a magical prodigy," she says, turning to me; she makes a goofy-looking V with her index and middle finger.

"Oh," I say. I want to ask why she looks like a teenager, but it feels awkward. I'm thinking of a tactic for approaching this without sounding like a jerk or a perv or something.

"You're wondering why I don't age."

"Yeah."

"We all know lots of magic, but we each have a specialty. Something we are naturally good at. I think different personalities are naturally better at certain kinds of magic."

"Some kind of time thing?"

"Yeah, Morgan's specialty was enthralling people. Circe's specialty is shape-changing. My specialty is temporal manipulation. Morgan 'apprenticed' me when I was like six. She saw I had a talent, and she wanted to manipulate it to her own benefit.

She started training me toward my talents. I was good at manipulating time, which is probably the hardest magic there is. I got better and better at it, and I don't know, got myself stuck outside of time. Everybody thinks it would be so great to be forever young, but fuck, dude, you have no idea how shitty it is to be permanently a teenager. Nobody takes you seriously. They talk down to you. It sucks."

I think back to my teenage years. At first, I think if you didn't have to deal with school and other teenagers, it wouldn't be so bad. Then I remember the mood swings and the inexplicable surges of emotions. The eternal bad judgment. Being stuck as a teenager for eternity would be hell.

"Yeah, that doesn't sound great. I am sorry."

"Not your fault, old man. I only have one person to blame on this front," she says and indicates herself with both of her thumbs. "And Morgan. I guess I blamed her. It made what I had to do easy."

I nod.

She pauses for a moment. I don't know what to say, so I let the silence fill the space.

"But it has benefits too well, the temporal manipulation, I mean. Being stuck in a teenage body forever, that sucks."

"Yeah, what do you mean by temporal manipulation?"

"Listen. Time is malleable. It stretches. It contracts. Imagine the first time you find your way in a new city. Each road, each avenue, your progress seems slow and crawling. You focus your attention on every detail of every turn, stop sign, and landmark. Just the second time you make the same trip, it seems faster. The third time. Even faster. Before long, it becomes rote, and the familiar route is flying by at the speed of your consideration.

It doesn't take any longer according to a clock, at least. The clock is a social convention like direction or gender. When we fall into a routine, and nothing new or different threatens our perceptions, days can pass when we aren't paying attention. Immune to the social conventions of clocks and calendars, time passes at the rate we perceive it. When under duress, seconds can be dragged out to eternities.

Time is, therefore, not only malleable; it is shapeable. Our individual perception of it gives it length, width, and depth. You control time, not the other way around.

We all do this unconsciously to allow ourselves to cope. Things we do, a lot of boring things, we contract time for ourselves to make them more tolerable. Enjoyable moments we stretch out.

I undertook a series of meditative practices to bring my own intentionality to this. To not only expand and contract time but to repeat it. You see me take a one-in-a-million shot? That's probably because I took the shot a million times. I practiced and practiced the same instant over until it was perfect."

Deja vu. I have that feeling again.

"Wait," I say, staring at her. "You can do that? You can rewind time?"

"It's more like changing my perception of time so as to perceive all possible outcomes and learn from them. I don't know it is easier to do than to explain."

"That doesn't sound easy at all."

"Prodigy," she says, pointing at herself again.

"So when you messed up and summoned the fire demon, why didn't you go back and fix it?" I ask.

"Oh yeah, it isn't quite like that. It's not exactly time travel. It's more like I don't know parallel experience. Also, I have to kind of know what moment I want to perfect before I do it. It takes focus, a state of mind, and control. It isn't really rewinding time. It's more like experiencing all the possible outcomes simultaneously. You know how they say failure is the best teacher? I experience every possible failure in an instant. More than a second or two is taxing. It's hard physically and emotionally."

"Emotionally?"

"You ever shoot a basketball from the free-throw line until you got a basket?"

"Sure."

"How many times did it take you?"

"I don't know, a dozen? I was never much of a sports guy," I am lying; I'm not sure I've ever made a free throw. I think I probably gave up out of frustration after six throws, but that was back in middle school, so I don't really remember.

"Yeah, imagine doing that like a million times in one instant. I don't mean figuratively, either. While others perceive it all in one instant, I live out the same second as many times in a row as it takes me to get it right. No pauses, no time to consider. If I take a break, get frustrated, space out, the second is lost, and I'm stuck with my failure."

I pause a second to consider what that must be like.

"I," I'm about to say that I can imagine, but I can't. "I cannot imagine that. No, that sounds impossible."

"And that is why I am the best!" She says triumphantly.

I nod. That is a lot to think about. The episodes of *deja vu* I've been experiencing. It seems that if I am nearby when she does this, I sense it somehow. I am somehow aware of the instants that she's lived over and over again. It explains a lot of them, just maybe not the sense I got when the Rebobs attacked.

Or does it? Circe said something about Morgan being responsible for that.

"Were you the one that sent the Rebobs after Genevieve and I in the cemetery?"

I can hear her muffled laugh through the mask.

"Yeah man, that was me. You're welcome."

"Huh? Why would you say you're welcome?"

"I was like, your, what's the name of that crab in that creepy mermaid movie you old people like?"

"Huh?"

"You know he sings this song to get the prince to kiss the mermaid?"

"Oh. Yeah, I'm not that old, sorry."

"Eh, you old people all look the same to me. But I mean, you got the girl, right? You're welcome."

I am confused. "You had Rebobs attack to get Genevieve and me together? Why did you do that?"

"Nothing like a shared thrill confrontation and terror to get the libido up," she says matter-of-factly.

"No, I got that part. I mean, why would you do that?"

"Oh, right. Mostly to piss Circe off, I think she's got a thing for you for some reason."

"Oh," I say.

"We should go," I say and turn to start walking toward my car.

"Oh shit!" I say, looking up at the hill to where we parked my car on. The hill that is now ablaze "My car. My town!"

I stand there in a dry cow pasture next to Magdalena, and through the hazy smoke, we watch the fire spread out toward the north end of Napa. The wind whips the fire up, and it flows across the landscape like a glowing wave. It is beautiful and mysterious, looking in the foggy smoke, but also ominous and terrifying.

Stopping a fire demon that I can do.

Apparently.

Stopping a fire is a job for firefighters. I hear an explosion and see a brief increase in the intensity of the light from the top of the hill. If I'm not mistaken, that was my car exploding.

"Yeah, that one is on me," Magdalena says, her face lit a mottled red and yellow by the firelight. "Don't worry, I'll pay for the car."

Chapter Thirty-Six

"MILES WARD. If you are enchanted, I'll get it recanted," I say into the phone. I can see on the caller ID that it is Genevieve, but I say it anyway. It's a bad habit.

"You know your phone will tell you who is calling, right?" Genevieve says she sounds agitated.

"Oh, I know. How's it going? You take care of everything?"

"Yeah mostly. I was thinking I'd come back on Tuesday for the election. I still have stuff to deal with here. And I have bad news."

"Bad news? What bad news?"

"Yeah, I was going to share it in person, but. Ugh. The story Emily and I put together on Redbrook? Nobody will touch it. Zero interest. I keep getting told things like 'with as much on the line as there is federally this year, nobody wants to hear about some small town mayoral race.' I'm pursuing alternative online solutions, but I'm not hopeful we are going to be able to make much of an impact with so little time."

"Hmm," I say, "Redbrook has implied that her Dominium Doloris pals are well connected. Maybe there is a conspiracy to cover it all up."

"Maybe. I don't love conspiracy theories, though."

"I mean, with all the chaos and strife and national attention Napa has been getting, you'd think this stuff would get snatched up."

"I, in point of fact, did think that," Genevieve says matter-of-factly.

"Yeah," I say, my mind wanders to the implications of the Dominium Doloris possibly silencing Genevieve and Emily's story.

"Well, now it is my turn for bad news," I say grumpily.

"The fires?"

"Yeah."

"That's national news, I am afraid, but it sounds like it's basically contained."

"It's not threatening the city anymore, but the air quality is shit. Nobody is going out. Stores and restaurants have closed. It's not great."

"It's fine. I'd still like to come out and crash at your place. If that is okay? Then head back on Wednesday?"

"Yeah of course. I'm always happy to have you," I say. That is true. Mostly. I'm not looking forward to the next few days. With the smoke-filled air, it feels like the apocalypse outside. It isn't making the impending election results a more appealing prospect. Having Genevieve here will give me something to look forward to.

"Wonderful. I'll see you on Tuesday! Oh, and if you have an opportunity to let Emily know about the article…"

"That'll be an awkward conversation with a lot of questions I don't have answers to."

"I know! Thanks, Miles, you're the best!" She says and disconnects.

I am going to need more coffee before I call Emily.

Chapter Thirty-Seven

IT'S cozy as I sit reading my book. Genevieve is back. Having her around my apartment is great. But it is also awkward. My apartment is kind of small and not set up for two people.

And then there is Hank.

Ever since he's been rebuilt, he's been chattier and less appropriate than ever. It is hard to have an adult conversation when you're being heckled constantly by a mannequin with an adolescent sense of humor. I think he might be jealous.

Even if we are sitting in the living room reading, he butts in from the other room.

"Miles, we should go down to Grape Reads," Genevieve says.

I look up from the book I am reading.

"Huh? Why?" I ask.

"Says the guy who forgets our birthday regularly," Hank yells from the other room.

"It's election night?" Genevieve says, stabbing a hand for emphasis.

My blank look communicates volumes.

"They are having a little election watch party?"

"Oh," I say. "Right, I don't know. I feel like sitting around and watching votes get tallied is kind of depressing."

"Like standing naked in front of the mirror?"

"Sure, but this is kind of a big deal, especially for Emily. This determines if you have a Lamia for mayor," Genevieve says.

"The Lamia. I think," I respond.

"Yeah, get pedantic. Genevieve's gonna love that."

"Yeah, that doesn't make it any less significant. That's not even mentioning the state or national stuff that you seem so intent on ignoring. I mean, I know it's a midterm election, but c'mon Miles. Get your head out of your ass," Genevieve says with a scolding tone.

"Ugh," I say. "You're right. Of course. I…I don't know. I find this stuff very stressful, and even if things go the way I want, it doesn't make it better."

"Emily and I put in a lot of time campaigning against her."

"Emily and Genevieve are 'campaigning' together? Ooh-la-la."

"That's not what campaigning means," I mutter.

"Huh?" Genevieve asks.

"Okay! I said Okay!" I say. I sound louder and more irritated than I intended.

"No need to bite my head off," Genevieve looks like she's getting cross now too.

"Sorry, I'm feeling a little on edge. Let me get my jacket," I say as I get up and walk into my bedroom.

I'm a little huffy as I pick up my jacket.

"Thanks a lot," I mutter to Hank.

"What are you in a tizzy about?" Hank asks.

I look uncomfortable and close the door.

"You won't stop heckling me. Hank, you have got to back off."

"I'm trying to be funny, you know, lighten the mood."

"Well, it's not working."

"Okay, Miles, I'll be more supportive. I'm here for you, buddy."

"Well. Thank you," I whisper to him. I'm a little suspicious of his sudden change of attitude.

"So, what's up? What's the hot-goz? Spill it, muchacho."

"Nobody says 'hot-goz.' Anyway, Genevieve wants me to go to this election watch party thing at Grape Reads and…I don't want to go," I whisper.

"Why not?"

"Um. Well," I pause it is a good question.

"Is it awkward to be with Emily and your new girlfriend?"

"No."

"Are you worried it is going to be crowded? You don't want to be around people? Agoraphobic? Claustrophobic? Triskaidekaphobic? What are you afraid of, Miles?"

"No, not that, none of that. Wait, why would a fear of the number thirteen have anything to do with this?"

"I'm shrugging helplessly if you can't tell."

"Uh-huh. You're made of rubber. You can't shrug."

"If I'm rubber, you're glue. Everything you say bounces off me and…"

"What is this third grade?"

"The way you are acting?"

"Whatever," I say dismissively.

I pause a moment to collect my thoughts.

"It's…Well. I think Redbrook is going to win, and I don't want to be around people's disappointment, shock, horror, anger, etc. I don't think it is going to end up a happy moment, and I don't have the fortitude to deal with all that. I don't want to see the look of disappointment on Emily's face. You know?"

"Of course, I know. Do you think it is going to be better sitting here hiding in a book? Wouldn't it be better with friends?"

"Well…" I begin.

"Miles! Are you talking to your mannequin again?" Genevieve calls in through the door.

"What? No," I protest. I'm not sure why I'm lying about it. It's pretty obvious I am talking to Hank, and she doesn't seem to care.

"It's fine. It isn't the weirdest habit a guy I've dated has had. But hurry up. We have to go."

"Right, right, sorry, I'll be right there."

"*What the hell kind of guys has she dated? Talking to a mannequin is pretty damn weird if you ask me,*" Hank chimes in.

"Nobody did," I say as I step out the door and close it on Hank before he can say anything else.

The air outside is choked with a grey miasma. It seeps in through the closed car windows during the silent ride to Grape Reads. I'm a little grumpy still, and the smoke isn't helping the tension in the car. When we park, Genevieve gets out and walks across the street without waiting for me. I need to shake off this foul mood I'm in. I sit behind the wheel and take a deep breath. I instantly regret it with a little cough.

A moment later, I am pushing my way through the front door of Grape Reads, trying to look excited, interested, or anything other than grumpy. A handful of people are loitering inside. Employees and some of their friends, family, and a few loyal customers. I quickly count the heads. Unless someone is hiding, there are twelve people here, plus me. That makes thirteen. I briefly wonder if this is a coincidence or is Hank now somehow prophetic.

They have placed a monitor on the counter and have a website up with the vote counts on it. I don't have to glance at the screen to know how it is going. The energy in the room is dour, and everyone is laconic.

I wonder why the people here are so focused on this election. I mean, Redbrook is awful, but there are plenty of other bigger battles going on. I think it is easier for them to focus on the local election; it is a smaller, more personal affair. An event that they can feel an impact on. The national and even state elections feel so large, distant, and out of our control. It's difficult to feel like you actually have an impact.

Everyone is morose except for Ren, who bounces up to Genevieve and me as we walk in. I can tell from their eyes that this is a show trying to keep the mood light.

"So glad you could make it!" Ren says and holds up a tray of canapés.

"We are too!" Genevieve says.

"So happy to be here," I say flatly. Genevieve nudges me with her elbow.

"How is it going?" Genevieve asks.

"Not well. Not on any front, but I assume you are talking about the local election. Redbrook is a couple of thousand votes ahead of Saundersen," Ren offers up with a grimace.

"Saundersen?" I ask. I immediately feel like a pariah as Genevieve and Ren both give me a bug-eyed glare. I can see a handful of others in earshot glowering at me as well.

"Miles," Genevieve scolds, "I don't even live here, and I know that Mayfield Saundersen is the candidate opposing Redbrook."

"Didn't you vote?" Ren asks.

"Yes!" I reply, "Of course I did."

"Did you vote for Mayfield Saundersen?" Genevieve asks incredulously.

"I mean, other than Saundersen and Redbrook, were there any other options?" I ask.

"No." Ren offers up.

"Then yeah, I must have voted for Saundersen. I definitely did not vote for Redbrook. I guess I was focused on not voting for Redbrook."

I didn't vote for Redbrook, right? I always have this fear after elections that I misread the instructions and selected all the wrong boxes. I think this is probably a common fear. I wonder if there is a word for this specific paranoia.

They both look at me, faces flat and placid, arms crossed. I feel judged.

"I mean, it's not like anybody talked about who they wanted to vote for. You all just talked about not wanting Redbrook!"

"Saundersen's gained some!" A voice-over by the screen calls out. Ren moves to see the screen, and I slip back behind some bookshelves and start pretending to look at the spines of books with interest.

Behind a bookshelf, I pull out my phone. I search for a word for the fear of inadvertently voting for the wrong candidate. There is not so far as I can tell such a word. Latin for vote is suffragium. Incorrectly is something like perperam.

"Suffragiumperperamophobia," I say aloud to a book about dog training.

I wander sullenly and blindly; I glower at book after book. My mind drifts over the events of the past few weeks. I lament my inability to slow Redbrook down despite sabotage and unintentional arson. I feel like I have failed my friend.

"You seem a little young," Emily's voice startles me back to the real world.

"Suffragiumperperamophobia!" I exclaim, jumping a little bit as I turn to face Emily. "I'm sorry, young, for what?"

Emily makes a scrunched-up face at me. I'm not sure if she's confused or doesn't like my butchering of Latin. She motions with a little nod of her head at the book I was staring at blindly. I look back and read the title for the first time. *Living with Menopause*.

"Yeah, you caught me. I was taking a moment."

"You don't want to be here?"

"No, I'm pretty sure I know how this goes. And...well, I think everyone is going to be pissed off and looking to point fingers, and I'm worried that those fingers will get pointed at me."

"Miles," Emily says, "I think I know how this goes too, and yeah, some people, especially here, are going to be pretty pissed off. I think we understand what is at stake better than most, and it's infuriating."

"We as in you, Genevieve Russ, and I? Or We as in Sergei?"

"Yes. We. All of us. But my point is that nobody is going to point fingers at you. Everybody here knows you tried. Hell, you even committed felonies to stop her."

"Unintentional felonies. Oh, I guess there were a few intentional ones too..."

Emily interrupts me, "My point is, yeah, it probably didn't work. But it's a much bigger picture than you and your efforts or me and my efforts. It's the effort that counts, and we tried. But the deck was stacked from the get-go."

I ponder that for a moment, nodding absent-mindedly. The deck was stacked. Stacking the deck is what Redbrook does; it's literally her livelihood. Of course, we could never win because she doesn't play a fair game. Ever.

"You know what Emily? You're right. She stacked the deck."

"Yeah."

"No, I mean she would never let a scenario occur where she could lose. She's for sure used magic coercion and any other tactic available to make sure that she doesn't lose. We never figured out most of the people she had in her ledger. She'd for sure have some influential people there, and anyone she can't buy or blackmail she would enthrall. She keeps dozens of them; Fetchs around her house like trophies. Why wouldn't she leverage that more widely?"

"Oh. I meant it more as an expression, but yeah, I mean obviously," Emily says.

I know, have known this to be true, but I can't help but feel like there is more to the picture that I am missing. There is something vital and important that I am not putting together. Is there still something that can be done to stop her?

"I need to think. I need to go for a walk by myself."

"Okay," Emily says. She seems more down in the mouth than she was a minute ago. I guess I have that effect on people.

"I'll be back in a bit."

"Okay, but are you sure you want to go out there?" She asks, glancing out the window at the smokey air.

Nodding, I turn and walk away from Emily. I pass by Genevieve on the way out.

"I'm going for a walk around the block. I need to clear my head," I murmur to Genevieve.

"All right, have fun. You know where I'll be. Don't choke too much," she says in a flat tone. I get the sense she is kind of irritated with me.

"Are you upset at me?" I ask quietly.

"Not really. A little. I think you aren't as invested in this as you should be."

"I think different people have different ways of investing. We focus on different things. I think it makes us a good team."

She smiles at that. "You think we are a good team?"

"Yeah, you know things and read things and write things, and you know you are smart."

"And you are really good at running away!" She says she's smiling, and she's trying to be mirthful, but it doesn't come off well.

"I was going to say I'm good at improvising…" I say. I feel a little hurt, and it must show on my face.

"Sorry, you were trying to be sweet, and I jumped down your throat there."

"It's fine. It's a tense situation. I had a thought, and I need some time to sort it out. I am going to walk around the block. I'll be back in a few."

She nods at me, and I slip out of the bookstore without further comment.

I turn right out the door and walk toward the downtown area. The air is foul. I don't want to be out here any longer than I have to. I slip across the street to Roast! To get a cup of coffee.

"Large black triple americano, please," I say to the counter-staffer.

I order my coffee to fit my mood: dark, bitter and a little nutty. I have a rule: I never order drip coffee after 10 a.m. In the morning, lots of people order drip coffee, so it is usually cycled through pretty rapidly and will still be pretty fresh. By the afternoon, people stop drinking drip coffee, and so it sits in the pot or carafe on a warmer for hours and hours. Some of it evaporates, and then the coffee gets thick and burnt and gross.

But years ago, a friend told me if you want drip coffee, but you don't want the burned dregs, you order americano.

"Hey, I see you in here a lot," the young man behind the counter says. "You from Napa?"

Is it bad that my backup coffee shop recognizes me as being in here 'a lot'?

"Yeah, I mean, I live here. In Napa, not in this coffee shop. I'm not from here again, Napa, not the coffee shop,"

"Mmm," he grunts at me, and his smile becomes a little less genuine. "Nobody's from here anymore."

"You?" I say I am getting the impression he is a localist. Someone who resents outsiders moving into their community and the inevitable change that it creates. On the one hand, I understand; I've seen the changes to this community in the time I've lived here. On the other hand, it irritates me because I don't think anyone would want to live where I grew up. Being a transplant has always seemed the only option. I think there is a touch of localism everywhere, but it feels like it's more strong in Napa than anywhere else I've been.

"Yeah," he says, "third generation born and raised."

"Cool."

He shrugs.

"What do you think about the election?" I ask.

He shrugs again. "Elections are a sham. You get one asshole or the other."

Sadly, I think this is an increasingly common sentiment in elections. You can't influence it, so why bother? Ultimately, this is the disappointing outcome of lesser-of-two-evils politics. I don't know anything about this Saundersen guy. I didn't even know his name until ten minutes ago. But I voted for him because I don't know him to be an antediluvian troll. But I don't know that he isn't. Truth be told, I don't know anything about him.

I get my hot coffee handed to me. I raise it and take a sip.

"Perfect."

"Have a good one," he grunts at me.

I am considering staying inside the coffee shop. You can smell the smoke a bit here, but it's not so bad. Looking out the window, the grey film in the air almost looks like mist. But not quite. There is a yellow tint to the world. Everything looks filthy, old, and somehow denigrated by the sepia haze.

A sensation is spreading through my limbs, frenetic energy. Anxiety. I need to move. Standing still is making me crazy. So I slip outside into the smoggy streets and stroll through the almost abandoned downtown.

I'm too trepidatious now. For myself, for my friends. For all of these people.

What happens if Redbrook gets her way? In a day-to-day sense, honestly, probably nothing. What does it mean for the zeitgeist of the place? The context of the place? Probably everything.

Magic is about context. You can manipulate magic by changing the context. Places have a magic of their own. You can change that magic; you can shape it; you can make it something more or less than it was. Ultimately, that is the threat that Redbrook represents. It's subtle and easily dismissed, but it is significant.

A lone car roars up First Street. A candy-apple red muscle car, it's going entirely too fast and is entirely too loud. I feel like there is one of them every time I come down here. I sigh and lean back and look up at the gray sky. The smoke is so thick it's like a ceiling above me, like I'm trapped under an immense filthy yellow-grey blanket.

The game is rigged. That was what Redbrook did at The Lantern. She did it with impulsiveness curses and stacked decks of cards. It seems like that is how she operates how she has always operated. She doesn't play unless there is no way she can lose. So she's rigged the election. But how?

There are checks; there are balances. Can she have enthralled all of the election staff? Has she enthralled enough influential people to push the odds in her favor? If she had the resources, she would grab as much control as she could.

Maybe if I'd approached it that way sooner, maybe if I had tried to find who she was influencing, we could have stopped her. But it's too late now. The results are being tallied as we speak.

Despite everything, it seems like she won. Despite all the effort, despite everything. Redbrook won. It wasn't that long ago I thought she was dead. Hell, it wasn't that long ago. I didn't even know who she was, and now she won. If I am honest with myself, what bothers me most is that this means: I lost.

I feel tears well up in my eyes. Are they tears of rage? Are they tears of sadness? Frustration? Or are they, as I fear, tears of shame? Is my pride the only victim I care about in this?

Taped to a light pole, I see a colorful poster. Redbrook's smiling face with her phony blonde wig and ostentatious amounts of jewelry is leering at me from the poster. I take it off the light pole and read it. Redbrook has already arranged a reception tomorrow at the Oxbow Commons. She is so sure of her victory that she is already planning to make a speech about it. I roughly fold the flyer and shove it into my pocket. I'm sure Emily will want to see this.

Looking around, I realize that I have walked a giant loop around the downtown, and I am once more standing before Grape Reads. This was why I didn't want to come here today. I've got enough of my own feelings that I am not comfortable sharing with others. I don't want the burden of other people's feelings as well. I don't want to be confronted with my own shame of failure.

This walk was supposed to give me clarity and a plan. Something. But all I found was the crushing weight of hopelessness.

It isn't long before the election is called. The results will be counted for days still, but the results are already so dramatically in Redbrook's favor it's highly improbable that the outcome will change.

There are tears and anger and grumbling. I've all but

checked out, and I am going through the motions of being social, biding my time until we can leave. Genevieve and I drive back to my apartment in grey silence.

Genevieve has to return to Portland in the morning. We spend a terse evening eating takeout and reading. We go to bed early. She is gone by the time I get out of bed. Outside of my bedroom window, the sky seems to be sharing my mood. The normal morning marine layer mixes with the smokey sky to create an unnatural and creeping darkness. A kind of darkness that swallows light and shrouds the world in an ineffable primal fear.

Chapter Thirty-Eight

IN THE OXBOW COMMONS, there is a crowd. Okay, maybe 'crowd' is the wrong word. There are maybe thirty people milling about in the cold smokey haze. There is a stage under the train tracks with an immense PA system. It's entirely too much amplification for the turnout.

There is a table off to one side with free coffee and donuts. They remain untouched. The foul odor in the air has taken away everyone's appetites.

The hazy marine layer has made the air unseasonably chilly and ominous. Nobody here is expecting cold, so nobody is quite dressed for it. People seem cranky and stand huddled, hugging their arms to their chests.

Toward the front, near the small stage, I see Emily standing with Ren. I work my way toward them.

"Hi Emily, Hi Ren," I say as I sidle up next to them.

"Hi, Miles," Emily says, looking dour. She's got a long flowery dress on with a long but thin tan coat over the top. It is made of a loosely knitted material and doesn't look nearly warm enough. But I know it's not just the cold fouling her mood.

"Hey, Miles," Ren says in a wool sweater and long khaki

pants, much more sensible attire for the weather. They look miffed anyway, and I can't say I blame them.

"I'm surprised to see either of you here," I say, coughing slightly as I do. I've slowly been developing a sore throat due to the smoke.

"It's not often you get to see a truly classical fiend's acceptance speech," Ren mutters.

Emily glowers in silent agreement with Ren.

"Where's Genevieve?" Ren asks, "I thought she'd be here."

I am about to answer when Emily cuts me off. "She had to go back to Portland. Her mother got sick, and her sister had some important last-minute business trip. Genevieve went back to help out."

I didn't know all of that.

Actually, I didn't even know that Genevieve had a sister. She only told me she had something 'to deal with back home.' Now I'm feeling kept in the dark. My already dour mood is not improved by this exchange.

I'm about to say something when the crowd suddenly goes ten decibels quieter. I turn and look at the stage to see Lorelei Redbrook walking up to the front of the stage. There are a number of city police standing at points around the stage and in the crowd. On the stage in the back, I can see Hale. He is there in his expensive suit, grinning like he was just acquitted.

Redbrook walks up to a mic in the center of the stage. She taps it twice, and feedback shrieks over the audience. Ren covers their ears. Emily stares Redbrook down like, somehow, if she looks away, all of this will suddenly become real.

"Is this thing on?" Lorelei Redbrook says in a rehearsed tone. She's using a falsetto voice and a folksy-sounding midwestern-ish accent.

"Whoo, so it is. All right! I know you all have places to be and want to get out of this smoke, am I right? So I won't keep you long. I am here to accept the position of mayor, don'tcha know, for this lovely city of ours. It's been a hard race, a trying time for this city. We've had terrorist attacks try to derail democracy. We've had arsonists try to take my life. We have this gosh-darn wildfire burning our vines and hurting our tourism! Napa has been under assault! Because people just don't like all the success we as a community have had."

"Could she lay it on thicker?" Emily hisses to me through clenched teeth.

"Based on my personal experiences, I'd say yes, yes she can."

"But we have travailed, and we have prevailed, isn't that right, Napa?" Redbrook says and pauses for crowd reaction. There is some clapping, but clearly, not the fanfare she was expecting. The cold and smoke are sapping what enthusiasm might exist in this audience.

I turn my head and scan the attendees and see a few faces that look familiar but no one I could put a name to. I notice a couple of cameras on tripods recording the speech.

"I want to thank my husband Roy for all of his support through this election," Redbrook says, motioning to a man who is standing off-stage to her left.

"Did you know she had a husband?" Emily whispers to me.

"No. I've never seen that guy in my life."

Glancing at Roy, I see the glassy look in his eye and the lack of responsiveness I associate with a Fetch.

"I think Roy spends most of his time in a closet," Ren whispers. "That sounded wrong. I mean that, literally. I think she keeps him locked away and only rolls him out for press events."

"Say hi to the voters, honey!" Redbrook says Roy raises his hand and gives a torpid salutation to the crowd.

"My campaign manager, John Hale," Redbrook says, indicating Hale at the back of the stage. Hale waves with professional dignity to the crowd.

I can't help but shout out a quick "Boo!"

This receives some glowers from other audience members.

Redbrook, for her part, gives me a glance with a predatory smile.

"I'd like to thank my constituents for all of their support and for helping me to get here! Thank you, Napa!" She says, pausing once more for crowd fanfare, which comes slightly less lackluster this time.

"And finally, I'd like to thank Miles Ward," she begins motioning toward me. She makes pointed and threatening eye contact with me. My stomach drops, and my heart feels like it stops with surprise.

Emily shoots me a nasty sideways glance. I glance back at her, feeling sheepish, and then turn back toward Redbrook. That sense of *deja vu* washes over me once more. I feel like this moment is so familiar. Emily's nasty glance, the warm feeling of embarrassment in my cheeks. The weird, prickly sensation on the back of my neck. I've done this all before.

I glance around quickly, trying to spot Magdalena in the crowd.

"I couldn't have done it without..." Redbrook begins but then stops and looks puzzled.

Time gets wonky. Redbrook steps back slightly. She's got a little hole in her clothes, and something black and viscous is oozing out. Redbrook looks down at her chest and looks back up, her mouth flapping.

I can hear a sound like a hammer hitting a board behind me and then a low, dull wave closing in on me. It is less a sound moving across the land than a silence rolling like an avalanche through the crowd. Not the silence caused by the mere lack of talking but the silence caused by every man, woman, child, bug, and other living creature on earth suddenly holding its breath.

My brain is still trying to get around what is going on when my arms start to burn. Something is very wrong, and some reflex causes me will some of the blood in my body into my warding tattoos. I can feel my connection to the newly improved Hank more strongly.

"Oh," Emily says. Ren grunts, and then they both suddenly fall to the ground like marionettes with their strings cut. I turn, blinking, and glance at the crowd. Everyone has fallen unconscious, including all of the police and Roy on the side of the stage.

I turn back to the stage, blinking hard with confusion. I can see Hale at the back of the stage, still standing, still grinning. Redbrook's body seems to be swelling. She looks distended like an inflating balloon. Her mouth is flapping open and closed silently like a goldfish on the carpet.

"What the..." I start to say, but I'm interrupted when Redbrook bursts like an overripe blueberry. Spraying everything within twenty feet with an oily black-purple ichor. A fountain of it rains down on me, sticking in my hair to my face and soiling my upper half. The stuff smells of rotting swamps and roadkill. The air already smelled bad. This smells worse. I wretch a bit and work to bite back the need to vomit all over the people passed out around me.

All that's left of Redbrook on the stage is her tattered clothing and piles of gaudy jewelry lying in a pool of that black-purple ichor. I glance past her to Hale. Still smiling. He raises his hand to wave. At first, I think he's waving to me, but then it becomes clear he isn't.

I turn and look in the direction he's looking. He's waving up at the rooftop of the Oxbow building, maybe two hundred yards away. I can barely see through the smoke and fog. An awkward, lanky figure is standing up, rifle in hand.

I can tell even at this distance that it is Magdalena. She slings the rifle over her shoulder and gives a little salute back. I can't tell if she is acknowledging Hale or me or just being melodramatic. Magdalena just assassinated Lorelei Redbrook while everyone was watching.

Then Magdalena puts her arms out to the sides like she's about to be crucified and falls backward off the far side of the building, quickly vanishing from our sight. Apparently, they teach melodrama to everyone at the Hizarin Academy.

And there is the *deja vu* again. That feeling like I've watched Magdalena fall and drop off that building before.

When I turn back around, Hale has made his way to the edge of the stage. He's somehow avoided stepping in the pool that used to be Redbrook.

"Poor Lorelei. A magic bullet. Huh. That is a tragedy," Hale says with a complete lack of sincerity. He crouches down and puts two fingers into the pool that used to be Redbrook and rubs them together. He then sniffs dramatically at his fingers and, puckers his face up into a look of disgust, and shakes the goo off so it spatters on the stage with a dull wet sound.

"What happened?" I ask, stunned. My brain seems to be operating about forty seconds behind reality.

"Magic Bullet. Forged from dragon scale is the only guaranteed way to kill the Lamia," Hale says slowly and loudly.

"Yes…but," I stammer.

"It didn't have to be a bullet, of course. It could have been a sword or an arrow or whatever. It's the dragon scale that's important. That bullet absorbed energy from everyone it passed by and funneled it into an ancient draconic spell. Kudos for you being the last one standing," Hale seems to be enjoying his monologue. I let him, not because it helps me in any way but because I'm still trying to process what just happened.

"I thought you worked for her."

"That is the correct tense," Hale says smugly.

Everything begins to clarify in my mind. Like I am tuning in an old-fashioned television station. The fuzz and static clear away, and an image is starting to form.

"It was you," I say. "It was always you."

Hale gives an indistinct nod. I'm not sure it would constitute an admission of guilt in any binding sense, but I get the message clearly.

"You needed a place in the Dominium Doloris. You needed a vacancy, and you hired the Hizarin to make the vacancy for you. But the Lamia was immortal, unkillable by mortal weapons or magic. Even the Hizarin needed something special. An edge. This was about your advancement."

"Plausible," Hale says, still grinning. He's enjoying this moment too much.

"The Hizarin made other attempts, but they didn't work. You needed someone to keep her distracted and let them get close. You knew your old college pal Miles was in town, so you pointed them to me."

Hale gives another indistinct nod and a circular hand motion, indicating I should continue. "An old fashion reveal, I love it Miles, do go on."

"So they pulled me in. I exposed an opportunity when I signed the blood pact with Redbrook, and Circe leveraged it. But that didn't work for some reason."

"It didn't work on either of you. For some reason," Hale points out.

"So you had Circe send me to plant that gem in her place."

"Now, why would I do that?" Hale says, grinning. He is enjoying this far too much.

"Because it redoubled Redbrook's suspicion of me, kept her even more focused on me, and made you look like an ally when you uncovered the plot."

"I was not expecting to get tasered, but that really helped sell it, I'll admit."

"Meanwhile. Circe and Morgan found something that could kill her," I say, I am not leading with too much information here. I don't know if Hale knows where the dragon scale came from.

"They found a dragon scale. Didn't know those were still out there. But if anyone has the resources, it's the Hizarin. That is why you should always hire talent."

"But why not make it quiet in her home? Why all the pomp and circumstance?" I say, motioning around.

"Listen, Miles. Redbrook had become a liability to my

organization. The Dominium couldn't abide by her sloppiness anymore. She draws too much of the wrong kind of attention. She wasn't willing to stop. Now that she's out, there is an opening for me to move in. If it was quiet behind the scenes, nobody would know who I was. This way is better for my brand."

"Can I ask you a question?" I ask.

"I'm feeling gregarious. What can I do for you, Miles?"

"Why are you sticking around for this? Why are you giving me all this information?"

"Because I think you, and I mean you personally, Miles. You need to understand how inconveniences are taken care of by the Dominium. Redbrook was an inconvenience. Believe it or not, Miles, I like you. I've always liked working with you. I respect you, and I don't respect a lot of people. So please don't be an inconvenience, Miles."

"Oh," I say, still dumbfounded.

"In this world of predator and prey, Miles of eat or be eaten, you and I are still alive. The world has thrown its best at us, and we were better. We are more alike than you think. I know you don't like everything I've done, all of the choices that I have made, but I consider you a peer. I consider you a friend."

There is an earnest quality to his voice. He's either doing a very good job of mocking me, or he is sincere. There is something familiar, a loneliness, in his tone. I'm not sure I can accept that we do have something in common, though deep down, I shamefully know it is true. I stand there with my mouth half open, unsure of what to say.

"Well, I need to go," his tone suddenly flippant. "I've got to go give Mayfield Saundersen the good news. Besides, soon all these people are going to wake up. There are going to be questions that I don't want to answer. Good luck!"

I glance over at the cameras.

"Looks like you admitted to a bunch of stuff on a live feed," I say, glancing back at Hale.

"Oh, don't worry about those. I made sure they never got turned on. Being the campaign manager has its privileges!" Hale gloats.

He takes a few steps and then turns back. "Thank you again, Miles. You were very instrumental in this plan. You always knew just enough to get yourself in trouble but not enough to get yourself out. A perfect distraction. A pleasure doing business with you. Maybe next time we can go out for a drink and catch up."

There is nothing else to say. I stand there beneath the stage, staring up at him. I'm not sure what his intentions are. Is he threatening me? Is he trying to recruit me? Is he gloating to torment me?

He smiles a smug smile and then salutes me. He stands up slowly and dramatically from his crouch. Then he turns and walks off stage, silently vanishing through the curtains at the back. Every motion, every step seems to be rehearsed nonchalance. His exit is as much a part of the show as Redbrook's violent ending.

I kneel down next to Emily and Ren and try to wake them. Less than a minute later, I am helping them both back to their feet. We set out to help everyone else we can find who needs it.

Chapter Thirty-Nine

"HEY, MILES," Jeff says. He looks haggard and worn. He still hasn't slept. Or bathed. He smells like sweat and the musk unwashed human. His usually carefully coiffed locks are a greasy, tangled mess.

"You okay? You look like hell," I say.

"Yeah, I'm fine I've been putting in some overtime at work," he says, and once again, I don't believe him.

"What is going on with you, man? You look like you haven't slept or bathed or eaten in days." I say.

"I said I'm fine. It's been a hard week. What do you want, Miles?" Jeff asks, almost growling with impatience.

"I was wondering if I could look at that favor that Goldsmith gave you."

"No, of course not. I gave it to you last week," Jeff says, his voice sounds stretched thin.

It is exactly as I feared.

"What do you mean? No, you didn't,"

"Yes. I did. You came by and said you needed it for something important I gave it to you. You said thanks and left. You were kind of a dick."

I have a weird sinking feeling in my stomach.

"Jeff. I don't know what is going on, but I didn't do that."

"Have you started huffing paint, Miles? We stood right here in this spot, and I handed that little gold paper dragon to you. I have to be honest; I was happy to be rid of it. It was like a burden lifted."

"Jeff, I'm not saying that didn't happen; I am saying it wasn't me."

"If it wasn't you, then who was it?" He asks skeptically.

"I don't know," I say, and I don't, but I suspect it was Circe. Magdalena said that Circe was a master of shape-changing. My head feels light, and I feel a little disconnected from my body. I'm freaking out. Then I remember something.

"Jeff, did you come by my place last week and ask about the most powerful magic I'd encountered? We talked about Goldsmith's horde. You were acting kind of weird."

"What? No."

"Because I thought at the time you were acting kind of weird, but now that I think about it, you didn't tell me anything. But I did tell you about Goldsmith and the Dragon's Favor."

"What? So someone was impersonating me?"

"What day did I come to get the favor from you?"

"Wednesday afternoon, I think."

"That was the day you came by my place. I think someone impersonated both of us."

"Or you are messing with me."

"Why would I mess with you like that?"

He shrugs.

"I think I should go talk to Goldsmith. Do you want to come?" I begin to say, but he cuts me off.

"No thanks, I've got things to do," he says.

"Oh. You sure?"

"I'm sure."

"I guess I will go then."

"Great. See you later, Miles," he says and closes the door in my face.

"Um. Bye," I say weakly to the closed door.

I get back to my car and call Alistair. It takes a few rings, but he answers.

"Hey, Miles. What's up?" Alistair asks.

"Um. I am worried about Jeff," I say. "Has he been showing up to poker night? I know I missed the last game."

"Nope. You weren't available, and Jeff's been incommunicado, so no game," Alistair says.

"Have you seen him this week?" I ask.

"No. Why?" Alistair says curiously.

"I was just at his place, and he's acting weird. It doesn't look like he's eaten or slept, or bathed in days. He smells bad, and he's acting strange. I don't know what to do when a friend is having an episode like this, I mean unless he was possessed. I don't think that's the case. I thought this might be something you were better equipped for."

"Okay. I'll stop by and check in on him. The last time I talked to him, he seemed pretty pissed at you for some reason. Maybe he'll talk to me," Alistair says.

"Thank you. I am worried about him," I say.

"Yeah, don't worry, I'll swing by when I get off work in a couple of hours," Alistair says. "I mean, you don't think he's going to hurt himself, do you?"

"No, I don't think so. He seems kind of manic. Obsessed? Like he's working until he passes out and not eating enough."

"Not great, but okay, I'll stop by," Alistair says.

"Okay, I'll talk to you soon," I say.

Alistair hangs up.

I sit in my car and stare at the dashboard for a while. I have to go see Goldsmith. To see if he can shed any light on the missing Dragons Favor or the Blethspa Amah or, well, anything.

I drive the long drive up the lost dirt road to Goldsmith's old house. It is an interminable drive with just me and my dark thoughts.

Redbrook is gone. Destroyed. That should feel like a win, but it doesn't. It wasn't the 'good side' that defeated her. It was the 'bad side.' It makes me question what we mean by 'good' and 'bad.' Ultimately, it seems I was Hales' pawn, keeping Redbrook distracted so she didn't see the treachery coming. Looking back, I think I have been manipulated since before I was hired by JMBaptiste.

Does that mean I'm on the bad side? Does that mean everyone who has helped me is too? Is there an absolute morality here? Or is intention enough? Maybe it's a matter of timing and context. The same acts at a different time and in a different context will result in a different outcome.

My philosophical spiraling comes to an end as I lurch and bump my way up to Goldsmith's cluttered home.

Sitting in the smokey drive and wait for Goldsmith to come out is torture. It seems like it's taking longer than usual. I wait. I whistle to myself. I drum my fingers on the dash. I turn the radio on, but for some reason, it won't tune into any stations.

Finally, Goldsmith comes out. He beckons me into his home and turns to go inside without waiting for my response. I get out and follow him through his quagmire of junk. Goldsmith, like all dragons, is an epic hoarder. Inside Goldsmith's house, the only smoke I can smell is what is clinging to my hair and clothing. I find that odd.

When I arrive in his makeshift throne room, he is sitting in a dilapidated old armchair. It is a faded yellow with a pattern embroidered into it. The pattern has long since gone threadbare, and it is impossible to tell what the pattern was. He looks down at me from his raised dais. We are encircled by odds ends and bric-a-brac.

"You return, young warder," Goldsmith said with a tone of mild impatience. The only time he didn't take that tone with me was the one time I brought Jeff with me.

"Yes," I say. "Great one, I have brought you an offering," I say and hand him my usual pint of Goldschlager. I've brought him quite a few in the years I've known him. He always takes them and carefully sets them down in the same spot. However, there is no collection of them that I can see. No empty bottles. I wonder if he drinks them or just hoards them somewhere else.

"You have, as always, a question," he says.

"Yes," I say.

"Then ask your question, warder, and be done."

I am only going to get one question, and he might not answer it. Is asking about the favor my best use of time? I'm not sure, but it does seem important. My plan is to ask about it, but as I start to speak on a gut feeling, I change tactics at the last instant.

"What is the Blethspa Amah exactly?" I ask, perhaps too boldly, as he gives me a distasteful glower.

He stares at me stone-faced. I stare him in the eye for a moment. Staring into his eyes is unsettling. It feels like reflected in his eyes, I can see the creation of the universe. An explosion of light and color flashes deep inside his pupils. A feeling of existential vertigo comes over me, like if I keep staring, I will fall into the infinite cosmos. I sigh and avert my gaze to the floor.

Once he's finally cowed me, Goldsmith says.

"It means 'The Final Change.' or that is the best translation I can make in any tongue you might speak," he says.

"Thank you, but that doesn't mean anything to me," I say.

"I will tell you a story," he says wearily.

"When your kind first loped crawled and scuttled across the land. The nights were cold and dark, and you cowered and huddled together in fear when the sun lay low. Then fire came, and your kind would quest for its warmth and light. First, the brave would go forth into raging wildfires to bring back a single burning brand to their village. In time, wars were waged where one clan would attack another to claim their fire. Your kind has always been brutal and savage.

Finally, one of your kind came to my kind and beseeched us. Begged us to grant them the secret of fire. Thinking this might bring peace, we did.

The secret was passed from master to apprentice, from clan to clan, and thus magic first came to man. We thought that this would end your warring, your violence, your aggression. But it did not. Those with knowledge guarded it, and those without coveted it.

And so The Elder, The One, The Ancient, the greatest among us whose honored name you might not speak. It breathed out and gave a gift to your kind, the Blethspa. Change is the most literal translation, but you might also say 'Bringer of Change' and still be accurate.

The Blethspa struck rock to stone and made fire themselves. They tamed magic and granted it to all mankind. And to each age, new Blethspa have been born. Ones who change magic tame it and deliver it to all mankind."

He finishes, and I nod and take a moment to absorb what he's said before responding.

"So what the Blethspa Amah is the final....bringer of change? The bringer of the final change? I'm not sure I completely understand."

"I have told you what I will," he says with an intensity that hits me like a tidal wave.

"Okay, fine, the favor, the little origami dragon that you gave Jeff, is that a dragon scale?"

"It is time for you to go warder. Return in a year and a day."

"But..." I start, but he looks cross at me. I swear I can see smoke coming out of his nostrils. I'm sure this must be my mind playing tricks on me. But maybe not.

"Go now and do not return for a year and a day."

He sounds more intense and grumpy than usual.

"Fine! Fine! I'm going," I say as I back out of the room with my hands held up like I'm being robbed in an old black-and-white film.

Epilogue

MAGDALENA IS WAITING for me outside my apartment when I return. She's leaning against the wall and tapping her foot impatiently.

"Hi, Magdalena."

"What do we do now?" Magdalena asks me.

"I think I am getting out of town," I speculate. "The election is over, fire demon defeated. I'm not a firefighter. I've got no particular reason to be here for the next couple of days while this resolves and all this smoke clears."

"I'm coming with you."

"No. Why would you do that?"

"Circe is missing. She's not my favorite person, but she's my partner. I need to find her. You know where she is. Even if you don't, she's got some weird fixation with you, so wherever you go, she will probably show up."

"I do know where she is. She's trapped in a sort of prison in the Dreamtime."

"Yeah, you mentioned. How did that happen? How did you do that?"

"Nope. Not me. I didn't do it. I don't know how it happened, but I do know where she is."

"Take me there."

"Are you a Dreamwalker?"

"Nope."

"Don't know what I can do for you then."

"So what do I do?" Magdalena asks. If I didn't know any better, I'd think she sounded a little scared.

I shrug.

"No clue," I say.

"Okay, I'm coming with you," she repeats.

I sigh and shake my head no.

"Miles," she says, "I've been a full Hizarin for like two weeks now. I will be honest with you; I have no idea what to do. I'm way in over my head, which wasn't so bad with Circe there, but she's gone now, and I…I'm lost."

She looks so scared and vulnerable. But I know it's all a front.

"Is it all a front? Or are you letting your experiences with Circe cloud your judgment?" I hear Hank's voice murmuring from my apartment.

"She's Hizarin," I mutter through clenched teeth.

Magdalena raises an eyebrow at me.

"But she's just a kid. Twenty-three right? Do you remember being twenty-three?"

"Well yes…"

"I don't."

"Are you talking to yourself?" Magdalena asks.

"No. Yes. It's complicated, but you can't come with me. I don't even know where I am going."

"The next thing I need to do is find Circe. You know where she is. If I stick with you, it's my best bet."

"Don't you have other Hizarin friends that can help you?"

"There are no friends in the Hizarin," she says dramatically. "Do you know how I joined the Hizarin?"

"Yeah, you killed your teacher and took her place."

"That's how I became a full member. And don't judge me. I hear the judgment in your voice when you say I killed her. You didn't know her."

"You are right. I didn't. You said Morgan adopted you when you were six?"

"Not adopted. Morgan saw potential in me. So she took me from my family when I was a little kid. Bought me. She raised me and trained me. She was cruel and awful to me. A monster. She tried to make me one. But I'm not a monster, Miles. I'm not like Morgan; I'm not like Circe."

"But you didn't have a problem killing Morgan."

"Morgan was…a villain. She used people like toys and threw them away when they got old. Besides, she was basically dead already. You saw to that."

I wince. The truth hurts.

"You didn't hesitate to kill the Lamia."

"That's right, and you won't find me apologizing for that either. I'm doing what I was trained to do. It might not be your ethics, but I can use it to do good, too."

"Assassin with a heart of gold?"

"Not gold, but one that still has a heart. Please, Miles. Let me come with you. No killing unless you say."

"I don't know."

"We make a good team! Did you see how we took out that Fire Demon?" She pleads.

I sigh.

"Let me shower, change, and think about it, okay?"

"Okay," she says, nodding sadly like a child who just found out no one is coming to their birthday party.

"Come over at…" I pause to look at the time. "Four?"

"Okay."

"Okay," I say and go into my apartment to shower.

I shower quickly and get dressed. I want to call Genevieve before I talk to Magdalena again. I dress Hank in my outfit and then sit on the corner of my bed. Genevieve and I didn't really talk when she left, and our last conversation ended on a tense note. I hope that she's not still upset with me. I'm still hurt that she didn't tell me about her family.

I dial Genevieve. She answers after three rings.

"Good morning, Miles!" She says, sounding chipper.

I guess she's not mad at me. I decide that I am going to ride that wave and have a talk about my feelings later.

"With all of this smoke," I say, "I was thinking about taking this opportunity to get out of town and come visit you."

"Yeah, I would love it if you came to visit," she says, though I can't tell from her tone if that's true or she's just saying it.

"There's another thing…" I say awkwardly. Inviting Magdalena seems so weird. Unlike Circe, I actually don't think Magdalena is deceiving me. Manipulating me, yes, but I don't think it's a deception.

"There's the other shoe dropping," Genevieve says.

"Circe's sidekick. Magdalena? She wants to come with."

"You want to come and stay at my place, and you want to bring a teenage assassin with you?"

"I don't want to. She seems lost and overwhelmed, and… I've been there. I don't know. I feel empathy for her situation."

"I don't know Miles."

"I don't know either. She won't stay at your place. She can get a hotel or something. I can't imagine cash flow is a problem in her profession."

"Oh. Well, if she's not staying at my place, what do I care?" Genevieve says very reasonably.

"I don't know. I felt like I should talk to you about it before doing it."

"I appreciate that. If you want to travel with a magical assassin, that's all you, buddy."

"Time-bending magical assassin."

"Time-bending?"

"Yeah, apparently, she bends time. It's like her specialty. I guess everyone in the Hizarin has a specialty that's hers. She says it's why she looks like a teenager; she's frozen in time or something."

"Wow. Stuck as a teenager. That sucks! I feel more sympathy for her already."

"I guess I...We...are going to head up there today. The smoke here is bad. Really bad."

"I'll look forward to having dinner with you. You and your time-bending teenage assassin?"

"Me, for sure. I'll figure out details with Magdalena."

"Sounds good. Keep me in the loop!"

With that, we say goodbye and get off the phone. The timing is perfect because only a few minutes after I hang up, Magdalena knocks at my door.

Magdalena already has a bag packed. I invite her inside, and she leans against my counter and waits while I throw together a travel bag. The smell of smoke is seeping into my apartment already, and I am worried all my clothes will smell that way. A few minutes later, I come huffing into my kitchen.

"Do you have a car?" I ask Magdalena, "Because I just realized that mine was consumed in flames the other day."

"Yeah, I have a car. I'm going to make right on your car, seriously. When we get back," she says earnestly.

"All right, you drive us to the airport."

"Okay!" She says, and we rush through the choking nauseating smoke to her car.

She drives a two-seater sports car that I would best describe as 'cute.' It's red with very rounded lines. Leather interior. It's by some Italian manufacturer I've never heard of. At a glance, it doesn't strike me as particularly ostentatious. It looks familiar, but I can't place it. Once I am sitting in it for a while, my estimation of its cost begins to escalate. It has all the amenities and handles like a roller coaster ride. Maybe that's just how Magdalena drives.

As we pull onto the freeway, Magdalena turns east.

"We will probably have our best bet flying out of Sacramento," I say.

"No, Let's drive the whole way. It won't take much longer, and we won't have to deal with airports or people in airports or planes...." Magdalena says. Do airports make her nervous? Or is it airplanes?

"That's like a nine or ten-hour drive."

"It's not that bad. Besides, that's still faster than waiting until we can get a flight."

I sigh and rub my temples.

"Fine."

Riding with Circe on her motorcycle was terrifying. Riding with Magdalena in her car is…surreal. And terrifying. I cannot help but wonder if failing a road test is a prerequisite for membership in the Hizarin.

The minute we get on the freeway, she becomes far less talkative and starts driving faster. Once we clear Sacramento and the traffic lightens, she drives faster still.

Now, we are passing other cars like they are parked. She weaves in-between cars like a needle passing through the tiny gaps in the weave of a fabric. A constant nauseating sense of deja vu is persistent throughout the drive.

"I keep getting this deja vu thing, I feel. Are you finding a timeline where you don't wreck every time I feel that?"

"Something like that. It's amazing that you are sensitive enough to feel it."

"You mean not everyone gets that sense?"

"No. You are the first person I've known who can tell."

"Really?"

"Yeah. But I guess I shouldn't be surprised."

"What does that mean?"

"Circe told me that there were odd things about you. Fascinating specimen. Her words, not mine."

"How so?" I ask because I am genuinely curious. Finding out there is something different or special about me is a surprise.

"You know how magic doesn't stick to you?"

"I mean, I've got wards and stuff, sure, but anyone could do that."

She laughs as she swerves between two tractor-trailers. I get an intense wave of the deja vu feeling. I'm quite certain that in some other version of events, I just became a red smear across the asphalt. I'm not enjoying this.

"No, Miles, like you should be dead ten times over with everything Circe, Morgan, and Lamia threw at you. But you didn't even notice. Like flies on a horse's ass. You're the horse's ass in this metaphor."

"Yeah, I picked up on that," I say. I don't know what else to say. I know my wards and simulacrum had saved me from a curse or two, but the way she's describing me is like I'm invulnerable to magic. I'm not invulnerable.

"I mean, it's not a bad talent to have if you are going to stop dark magic for a living."

"Yeah, I guess not. But it's not a talent. It just. Is."

"That's kind of the distinction between a talent and a skill, right? You don't work for talent. It just is. A skill you work for."

"Sure, but talent doesn't get you far without skill. You are like the poster girl for that."

"I guess. Hold on!" She says.

I look forward and see two parallel cars in front of us. They are going well under the speed limit. We are closing in on them fast, too fast to slow down in time without colliding with them. I don't think even Magdalena's abilities can avert this.

That sense of deja vu sweeps over me so badly that I have to clutch my head. I feel dizzy, sick, and confused all at once. Our car jumps the curb into the center median. We are bouncing and rocking like the car is about to flip over. We accelerate. I can feel rocks and clumps of grass slamming onto the floorboards below me. Dirt and roadside trash are flying in a plume around us as Magdalena accelerates around the cars and flies back onto the Freeway.

"How many different ways did we die there?" I ask.

"I don't think you can count that high."

"I'm going to pretend to sleep now. Wake me up if we get

there," I say, pulling the hood of my sweatshirt over my eyes. I do my best to go limp.

We arrive outside Genevieve's house a shocking seven hours after our departure. It seems unimaginable that a multi-state army of law enforcement isn't pursuing us, but somehow we aren't. Magdalena slows her driving down to merely reckless speeds as we get into Portland and take to surface streets. I explain to her that I will be staying at Genevieve's house and that she might be happier getting a hotel room. She doesn't seem thrilled by the idea but concedes without argument.

I climb out of Magdalena's car, knees still shaking from the six hours of persistent trauma I have just endured. I hastily get my bag from the rear of Magdalena's car.

I close the door, and before I step away from the car, Magdalena roars off, leaving a gut-wrenching sense of deja vu in her wake.

Genevieve's house is a light-blue cottage with white trim. It is in a nice neighborhood on the north side of Portland. I would best describe it as cute. It's got a little unpainted picket fence and a shrub garden in front.

Bag in hand, I walk up and ring the doorbell.

Join Miles Wards for his next adventure in:

Point Sauvignon Blanc

Blood, Wine, Magic: Book 3

Available soon for pre-order.

http://www.justingodey.com/

Want to stay in touch? Join my newsletter at https://www.justingodey.com/newsletter

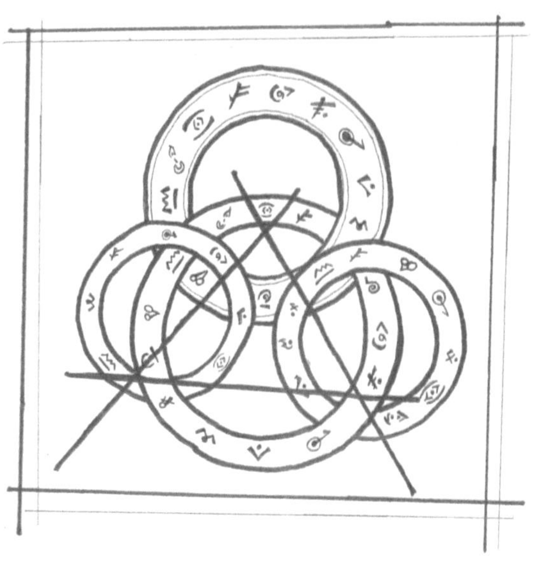

www.ingramcontent.com/pod-product-compliance
Lightning Source LLC
Chambersburg PA
CBHW021240020826
48980CB00026B/697/J
* 9 7 9 8 9 9 9 9 5 3 8 1 0 *